The Small Fortune of Dorothea Q

The Small Fortune of Dorothea Q

Sharon Maas

Bookouture

Published by Bookouture

An imprint of StoryFire Ltd.
23 Sussex Road, Ickenham, UB10 8PN
United Kingdom
www.bookouture.com

ISBN: 978-1-909490-58-1
eBook ISBN: 978-1-909490-59-8

This book is a work of fiction. Names, characters, businesses,
organizations, places and events other than those clearly in
the public domain, are either the product of the author's
imagination or are used fictitiously. Any resemblance
to actual persons, living or dead, events or locales
is entirely coincidental.

'Extract from 'The Book of Mirdad' by Mikhail Naimy,
reproduced by kind permission of Watkins Publishing.

For the women in my family.

My mother,
Eileen Rosaline Cox
96 years old at time of writing.

And my late grandmothers,

Winnifred Albertha Westmaas née Richardson

and

Miriam Ruth Cox née Wight

And my daughter,

Saskia Alisha Westmaas

Chapter One

Inky: The Noughties

I'm Inky; comes from 'Inka', a creative spelling of 'Inca'. Mum's the creative type; she named me in memory of her meeting Dad on a bus from Huancayo to Cusco back in the late sixties, a sixteen-year-old runaway passing through Brazil and Peru on her way to India. She ended up in England. If that seems a roundabout way of doing things, well, that's Mum for you. But I'm getting ahead of myself. The whole story came out when, thirty years later, she and Gran decided to put an end to their cold war. Gran was coming to stay with us in London, which was why we were there that day at Gatwick.

'Here they come!' said Mum, and stiffened visibly in anticipation. She'd been nervous all morning, which with Mum meant she'd been even more silent than usual, responding to my meaningless chatter with the vague *ummms* and head-nods that told me she was hearing without listening. Now even the head-nods stopped and she just stared, fists clenched in anxiety as the glass doors slid open.

A new batch of passengers ambled into the arrivals hall; at first just one or two forerunners, then little clumps of them, pushing loaded trolleys or tugging bulging suitcases. Gran and Aunt Marion had changed planes in Barbados and these were mostly returning tourists, which was obvious at first glance. They radiated laid-back cheer, holiday glee; women with stringy blonde hair in disintegrating cornrows and men in shorts and flapping sandals, faces lobster-red or baked golden, smiling and waving at familiar faces in the waiting crowd. The aura of Caribbean sun and white sand still clung to them; you could almost smell the salty air wafting around them, tingling and cool. I swore I could smell coconuts. You could almost hear that calypso beat, the steel-band pulse, feel that lapping aquamarine sea. They almost danced in, to a reggae-rhythm, waving and cooing to friends and family in the waiting crowd.

Among the holidaymakers, a few naturally brown passengers strolled in. The locals: Bajans and other West Indians. I craned my neck, peering between the tourists for Gran. A hazelnut-brown little old lady in a wheelchair should be easy to spot. We waited.

A few last stragglers came through, and then – nothing. I looked at Mum.

'Do you think they missed the plane?'

'No – Marion would have rung me up. Maybe she had problems at Immigration? I hope her visa's OK. I jumped through all the hoops about sponsoring her, but …'

We continued to wait. And then the doors slid open one last time and there they were.

My grandmother. Spitting nails. A crotchety old bag.

She wasn't even looking out for us; for me, the granddaughter she'd never seen outside a photograph, and for Mum, the daughter she hadn't seen for thirty years. This, I'd imagined, was supposed to be the momentous Grand Reunion, the Big Day when we all fell into each other's arms weeping with joy. But it wasn't to be; Gran was far too busy lambasting the neon-yellow-jacketed airport assistant pushing her wheelchair to look out for us. Her upper body was half-twisted backwards, all the better to look the poor man in the face, her own face distorted with fury. She jabbed the air with an admonishing finger and though we couldn't hear a word, she was obviously bawling out her victim for some unknown transgression. So right from the inauspicious start, I understood that Mum's guarded description of Gran was probably an understatement. Gran was a good deal more than "a bit difficult".

The assistant looked desperate, his relief on seeing us palpable. Just behind them, Aunt Marion came, pushing a baggage-laden trolley, her expression a mixture of embarrassment, anguish, and sheer exhaustion. Mum called out her name and waved wildly. Aunt Marion looked up and waved back, relief flooding her features too, and a moment later she and Mum flung their arms around each other. So at least *they* had a Grand Reunion.

The assistant dropped Gran's wheelchair handles as if scalded, mumbled a few words about a missing suitcase to whomever was listening, and scurried off.

Gran and I looked each other up and down, silently; Gran still frowning as she surveyed me, her unfulfilled rancour still hanging in the air, looking for a place to land. It found me.

'You look just like you mother at you age,' she said. 'Too thin.'

Her frown deepened.

She couldn't pronounce her *th*'s. 'Mudder', she said for 'mother', and 'tin' for 'thin'. I smiled to myself, in spite of the brusque greeting. It wasn't often I got to hear a Guyanese accent. Mum had lost hers over the last thirty years, most of our friends and relatives from back home likewise. And yes, Mum still called Guyana *home*. I didn't.

Mum herself had never returned, never seen her parents again. Her father died a few years ago, leaving the Georgetown family house, and Gran, to Aunt Marion. And now Marion, who had selflessly cared for the two old dears all these years, was also leaving home. Her own daughter, living in Canada, married, pregnant, and about to give birth, had invited her to come and help look after the baby. Who could blame Marion for jumping ship?

Aunt Marion's last daughterly duty was to deliver Gran into Mum's care, and here they were, the two of them. Poor Mum.

Much as I looked forward to Gran coming, I'd been sceptical from the start. Mum couldn't even look after herself; how would she cope with an invalid? But she'd been adamant. It was her *duty*. It was *her* turn now. Marion deserved a life. Mum herself needed to tie up a few loose ends with her mother, sort out some unresolved matters. Make peace. It was the right and honourable thing to do. It would be hard, she'd warned, but together we could do it.

I knew exactly what that *we* meant. I knew Mum. I knew she'd bitten off more than she could chew, and that once more she'd rely on *me* to pull her through. Trouble was, this noble task she'd taken on was open-ended.

I wondered casually how long Gran had to live before she, too, popped off; and then I caught her eye, just for a second. The lines of her frown relaxed, her eyes sparkled, the severity of her lips spread into a smile. Guilt flashed through me. It was as if she'd read my wicked thought. But then, still looking at me, she pointed to the wheels of her chair.

'How you like me round legs?' She cackled at her little joke, and clacked her dentures, the top row hanging loose for a moment. Without waiting for me to respond, she turned away, looked at Mum for the first time, and poked her in the ribs with a long bony finger.

'The child too thin,' she repeated, by way of greeting her long-lost daughter. She stretched out that skeletal finger again, this time to poke *me*. I took a hurried step back.

'Bag o' bones. You don't feed she proper, or what? I know you can't cook but when you got chirren to raise ...'

Mum let go of Aunt Marion and spun around.

'Rich, coming from you! When did you ever cook even *one* meal for us? Talk about pot calling the kettle black!'

Gran ignored the admonition. For my part, I was stunned. I had never, ever, in my whole life, heard Mum speak to anyone in that tone of voice: accusatory, resentful, and rude. It was a revelation. So Mum had an Achilles' heel after all, and it was Gran.

'I hope she ain't a scatterbrain like you!'

'Don't you *dare* tell me how to raise my daughter!'

They glared at each other. Something passed between them. Even I, an innocent observer, could tell that a dark cloud of history hovered over their heads. I willed it to dissolve. *Please, please, don't make a scene. Not here, in public.* This was supposed to be the Big Moment. The Great Reconciliation. They ought to be clasping each other in teary boo-hooing, exclaiming, 'Oh, it's been so long!' and 'Oh, how I've missed you!'

The menacing moment passed, and history fell between them with a thud; an invisible and impenetrable wall. Mum's voice was mild on the outside, cold as ice on the inside.

'Mummy, Inky is eighteen, not a child any more. She feeds herself, believe it or not! Anyway, welcome to England!'

She bent down to formally kiss the old lady. Gran sucked her teeth, pushed her away, and turned back to me instead. She leaned forward and stretched out for me again, this time with both hands, scrawny fingers waggling to beckon me nearer.

'… and she in't got no manners or what? Come child, give you ol' Granny a big hug.' Claw-like fingers closed around my forearms as she pulled me down. What could I do? I let myself be pulled in, leaned down and reluctantly pressed my cheek to her face. It was dry and wrinkled like old leather, yet soft as silk to the touch; dark as mahogany, it smelt of face powder mixed with something biting, lemony, old-lady-ish. She let go of my arms, placed those scraggy hands around my face, and looked into my eyes again. This time for more than a glance. Our gazes locked; hers held mine. I could not look away. These were not the eyes of a life-weary curmudgeon with one foot in the grave. Fire was in those eyes, and life; and, to my astonishment, an amused twinkle, as if she were enjoying a private joke, as if she read me through and through. Condescension fled. But I had no time to think, for Aunt Marion was pulling me away from Gran.

She folded me into her soft and generous body, kissed me on both cheeks. She smelt of stale perfume and perspiration; it had been a long trip, lengthened by the task of looking after a cantankerous old mother. We exchanged words of greeting. I vaguely remembered her; we'd met before, when I was about ten. She'd come to visit us in Streatham, just after Dad died. She'd comforted us and cooked for us; delicious Guyanese meals I'd never in my life tasted before, and won me over.

Gran was quite right; Mum wasn't much of a cook. She was deeply and passionately into health foods and had raised me strong and healthy on a variety of whole grains, organic vegetables and healing herbs. But I hungered for good traditional food, and Aunt Marion had shown me a whole new culinary world: 'good Guyanese cooking', she'd called it. But the memory of Aunt Marion and her luscious menus had faded over time, and today she was practically a stranger.

But not for long. As we walked the long corridors to Short Term Parking, me pushing the luggage trolley, Aunt Marion and I swung into easy conversation; and by the time we reached the lift it was as if I'd known her forever. Behind us, Mum pushed Gran's wheelchair. It was a brand new one, state-of-the art, bought for her by Uncle Norbert, sent to Guyana especially for the trip and her sojourn with us. Mum had told me all these little details over the last few weeks, trying to fill me in on years of family history, yet doing so as vaguely as possible. She'd tried to describe the complicated web of relationships between her, Gran, Aunt Marion, Uncle Norbert and Uncle Neville; who got on with whom, who wasn't speaking to whom, and so on. I'd been intrigued, but I could tell that this was only half the story; that what was left unspoken was the *really* interesting part. Mum was an expert at leaving important things unspoken.

Now, she and Gran were engaged in a boisterous quarrel and it lasted all the way to the car. That is, Gran was doing all the quarrelling; I could hear her tirade from several yards behind. It seemed that one of Gran's cases had indeed gone missing, the one with all her valuables, and that was what she was so cross about, and she blamed everyone, including Mum, for its loss. Mum merely murmured calm rejoinders. She seemed to have regained her equilibrium, and that was a good thing. She'd need it with Gran.

'They'll find it,' I heard her repeat, over and over again. 'They always do. They'll deliver it home in a day or two. You'll see.'

But Gran was beyond calming. It was as if the Crown Jewels were in that case. In a sense, as I was later to find out, they were.

❅ ❅ ❅

We reached home an hour later. The first thing we discovered was that there was no way Gran could use the wheelchair in the house. The doors were too narrow, the hallway too confined. The rooms too small, too cluttered. Later, we learnt the term "turning circle", and that there just wasn't such a thing in our home. Gran would need a rollator to get around. We had to park the wheelchair outside the front door.

We'd rearranged the house so that Gran could live in the former dining room, on the ground floor next to the kitchen. But there was only one bathroom in the house, and that was upstairs, so she'd have to climb the stairs to get to the toilet. Mum thought there might be some help available from Social Services in getting either a stair-lift built in or an extra bathroom added downstairs, but in typical Mum fashion had not actually made any enquiries. There was the question of whether such help was also available for new immigrants; Mum didn't think so, but she was still convinced that everything would work out for the best, somehow, if you just stayed positive and lived in the here-and-now, stress-free.

Mum was brilliant at philosophy and positive attitude, bad at paperwork, bureaucracy, accounting, and other pesky details of mundane daily life. Somehow, we always got by, on a wing and a prayer. As for the huge debt she'd inherited from Dad: if there was anyone in the world who could smile with a noose tightening around their neck, it was Mum.

Dad's ghost still hung over us. It was his liver. In his youth, he'd had hepatitis while travelling in South America, and then the alcoholism of his final years. Liver cirrhosis in your early forties isn't a pleasant way to go. He'd left the chaos of his financial mismanagement for Mum to sort out. She'd been struggling to do so ever since, and it seemed to have no end.

❊ ❊ ❊

Gran was bursting for a wee, and naturally Mum had not yet bought the potty she'd said she would. She seemed to think these things would materialise out of thin air. So our first challenge presented itself: to get Gran up the stairs to the bathroom. She could shuffle slowly on level ground with a stick or an elbow to cling to, but stairs were a major problem. Mum and Marion each took one arm, and with Gran squashed between them, began the slow climb upwards.

I lugged the suitcases into Gran's room. When she was halfway up Gran stopped, called my name. I stepped back into the hall. Gran was looking down. She hooked her eyes into mine again.

'One year,' she said.

'What?' I had no idea what she was talking about.

'One year! At the most. Mebbe six months if you lucky. This ol' body in't got far to go. Just in case you was wondering.' She cackled, turned away and continued up the stairs.

❄ ❄ ❄

Gran lay down on her bed and immediately fell asleep. It was as if sunshine entered the house, dissolving a mist of darkness. Mum and Aunt Marion enjoyed another long embrace, right there outside Gran's door. Mum, half the size of Marion in width and a head shorter, burrowed her face in her younger sister's voluminous breast. A slight tremble rippled through her. Aunt Marion massaged Mum's back with a gentle circular motion, as if rubbing strength into her.

They pulled apart, silently looked each other in the eyes for another eternity, then fled into the kitchen, still holding hands. I followed them.

'I'm sorry to do this to you, Rika,' Aunt Marion said as she poured water into the coffee machine. 'Really, really sorry. But ...'

'Don't apologise! Please don't! I've felt so bad all these years, leaving her to you. Now it's my turn. Inky, see if there's any of that cake left from yesterday.'

It was some kind of whole-grain-nut thing Mum had brought back from her health food shop, and indeed, I found two crumbling pieces in a paper bag in the fridge. I took it out, put it on a tray with some plates, cups, spoons, milk and sugar, and carried the lot of it into the living room, where our dining table now stood. We'd had to rearrange the furniture to make room for it, taking out one of the sofas. That was now crammed into the junk room upstairs, shoved in with all the extra stuff we'd grown out of but never actually thrown out due to lack of time, or, more probably, motivation. The junk room was actually our third bedroom, and would have been useful as such, now that Marion was staying for a week, but then we'd need another room for the junk, which we didn't have. So Marion would be sleeping in Mum's room, Mum with me in mine.

They came in with the steaming coffeepot, still discussing Gran's toilet arrangements.

'If you can get a commode she'll be all right,' Marion was saying as she took her seat at the table. 'You just need to empty it out regularly. But between you and Inky, it won't be a big problem.'

'It's bathing her I'm worried about,' Mum said. She poured three cups of coffee. 'We'll have to get her upstairs for that. And we don't have a stand-up shower, only the bathtub; she can't climb into that.'

'Oh Lord. Mummy's got to have her daily shower. What about this extension you were telling me about?'

'It's only theoretical,' Mum said. 'I was thinking we could add a room. Right there.' She waved vaguely towards the garden. A bathroom extension, if one ever came, would have to go there; it was either that or next to the kitchen, which just wasn't practical. Mum and Marion discussed the possibilities for a while, even getting up to inspect the house. Marion suggested putting up a wall through the middle of the living room, so Gran's room would be right next to this fantasy extension, and the dining room back in its original location. There wasn't much I could add to the conversation. I knew it would never happen. Finally, after all the visionary plans were made, Mum confirmed my assessment.

'It'll never get done,' she sighed. 'How'm I going to pay for it?'

'I thought the Government took care of that kind of thing? That's what Neville said.'

'Not for Gran. She just arrived in the country. She hasn't got permanent residence. I just don't see them investing in her as an immigrant. And,' she added, 'It wouldn't be fair on the

British taxpayers.' After a moment of silence, she added, 'I just can't afford it.'

They both sipped their coffee and ruminated.

'What *I'm* wondering,' Mum said after a while, 'Is what Mummy's going to do all day. Inky and I are both working. Won't she be bored?'

'Mummy, *bored?* Not on your life. You know her saying: 'Only boring people get bored. Interesting people make their own entertainment.' I bet you, in a week she'll own the place.'

That was exactly what I was afraid of. I sipped at my coffee, dipped a piece of the nut cake into it and fished it out with a spoon, hanging on to every word they spoke. This was *my* life they were talking about, *my* world that was about to be shredded by a high-maintenance battle-axe. And nobody had ever once asked *me.*

'But she had that exciting social life back in Georgetown. The politics. The Unions. All her friends, the women's associations, the Old Girls Union...'

'You don't think she'll have that here? Half of Georgetown emigrated to the UK in the last thirty years, the other half to North America. She can't wait to catch up with old friends over here. She's got an address book, so thick.' Marion held up thumb and finger, an inch apart. 'But you know what? Get her a computer. A laptop. Internet. That'll keep her busy.'

'I can't afford a new computer.'

I spoke for the first time.

'She could use *your* laptop, while you're at work, Mum.'

Mum snapped her answer almost angrily, unusual for her. 'No way. Out of the question. I'm not having Mummy poking around on my laptop.'

I realised why, right away. She was afraid Gran might read her private mail, find all those exchanges with her creditors, and discover the terrible secret of her debt. And immediately I knew, vaguely, the way one picks up on things over time without having them actually spelled out, that Gran's incorrigible nosiness, more than her bad temper and bossiness, was the bone of contention between the two of them.

Mum's flight from Guyana so long ago, and her decision never to go back all these years – decades – had something to do with Gran, that much I knew; but not the details. Mum's break-away was a Quint family thing – taboo. I never asked why, Mum never offered an explanation. It was just one of those things, a fact of life. But, meeting Gran, picking up on clues, I now had an inkling. *She* was the reason. She must have done something unforgiveable.

It used to be, when I was small, that I asked to see my Granny. She was the only one I had, and I knew what grannies were like. Everyone else had one; all my friends. They cuddled you on their laps, hand-fed you with cake and spoiled you silly. Dad had been an orphan, growing up with an aunt in Northumberland, so there were no grannies from that side. And so I had clung to my romantic notion, created from those grannies I did know or had read about, and Gran had fed those fantasies. She and I had exchanged such letters! I'd written her one after the other as a child, told her everything, all the things I couldn't tell Mum. And she'd always written back, warm engaging letters that had won my little-girl heart.

I'd made a dream Granny of her, and wanted to make it reality, visit her. But Mum always said no. We couldn't afford it. And then I had grown up, and no longer asked to visit, for I had more ambitious dreams than soft-bosomed cake-baking grannies. The letters had long stopped flowing back and forth.

Now, I hadn't written to her for at least six years. As far as I knew, she and Mum had never corresponded; not once in thirty-odd years. This whole visit had all been mediated and negotiated through Marion.

'But your laptop stuff is password protected!' I protested now.

'You don't know Mummy. She'd hack into my account.'

I thought of Gran and said to myself, *no way*. She's much too old. But Marion seemed to take the notion of Gran as an IT hacker as a serious possibility.

'Yes; I wouldn't trust her with your private files. But you could maybe buy one on instalments,' she suggested, and I laughed to myself. As if any company in the world would ever give Mum credit. But Marion couldn't know that.

'Or better yet, I could get Neville to buy it. Why not?' Mum said.

We all looked at each other then, and laughed in unison. Of course, Uncle Neville would have to buy Gran's new laptop. It was only fair, and he'd do it out of guilt.

Neville was one half of the bundle of trouble (Mum's description) that came after Marion. 'Obnoxious twins, Gran's darling boys,' Mum had said. The other twin was Norbert, who lived in New York City.

I'd met Neville a couple of times, but Norbert only once in my life. I was nine, and we were temporarily rich at the time. Dad, Mum and I had gone to visit friends of Mum's in America – my Uncle Matt, actually, Mum's godfather – and Mum had thought it her duty to visit her brother. It was a mistake; a big one. I don't know what happened, but we didn't stay longer than a day; from my childish point of view it had all been one of those stupid grown-up arguments about money. We hardly ever spoke about him at home, and once when I'd asked about him, all Mum had said was, 'He's just like Neville, only different. Worse.' That told me everything.

Uncle Neville lived in Birmingham. He was a solicitor, stinking rich, and he had actually offered to take Gran in – of *course* he would! – but *unfortunately* his wife Monica was a hard-working solicitor herself and wouldn't have the time to give Gran the care she deserved, and a professional carer was out of the question. The same was true for Norbert's wife in New York; Norbert being just as willing to take Gran in, were it not for his wife's stressful schedule. Norbert was an attorney, also stinking rich. The two of them were in competition to see who could best provide for Gran in other, non-caring ways – i.e. money. Both of them had promised to pay Mum monthly support to cover Gran's expenses, and one of them had paid her travel expenses to London, the other Marion's. Norbert had paid for Gran's new convertible wheelchair, the one she had travelled with. So it was Neville's turn to be generous.

'Why don't we get Neville and Norbert to pay for the bathroom extension?' Marion asked. 'It would be peanuts for them.' But Mum shook her head.

'Never. They'd say it's just a trick of mine to get them to finance my home improvements. And anyway, can you see the two of them collaborating to buy *anything* together?'

That was another family *thing*: that Neville and Norbert weren't on speaking terms, and hadn't been since they were teenagers. A strange situation for twins to be in, but then the Quints – at least, this branch of the family – were all weird, with the shining exception of Marion, and, apparently, Granddad, while he was still alive. But at least Mum's weirdness was somehow cute, whereas Neville and Norbert – well, the least said of *them* the better. Except that now, Gran, with all her own weirdness, was all geared up to occupy a huge chunk of my life, and I'd better develop some survival techniques.

'How ill is she, anyway?' Mum asked then. 'Does she need to see a doctor soon?'

Marion shook her head. 'She's frail, but not *ill*. Nothing's wrong with her except general wear and tear. And as you may have noticed,' – she chuckled wryly – 'her mind's as sharp as a needle. Plenty of life force there. She's got a good ten more years to go.'

Mum squirmed, grabbed the coffeepot and began to top up everyone's cup. Marion placed a hand on Mum's shoulder, and rubbed it.

'I'm sorry,' she whispered. 'I'll take her back when I can.'

But Mum instantly pulled herself together.

'I'll be fine!' She said brightly. 'And I've got Inky as back-up. Inky's a jewel.'

'I was just wondering,' I asked casually, 'Does Gran have – you know – *powers?* Like, knowing the future, or reading people's minds, stuff like that?'

'Ha!' Marion chuckled again. 'Times, I really think she does. She'll say something uncanny, turns out to be true, and you have to ask yourself, how does she *know?* But of course she doesn't. Not really. She's just good at guessing. That's her thing. Trying to impress.'

I nodded in agreement. She'd just been guessing around, trying to make an impression.

'Yes, and she'll stoop to any ...' Before Mum could finish the sentence, Marion broke in.

'And stubborn as a mule. Once she's made up her mind about someone or something she won't give up. She won't give up anything that's hers. Wait till she unpacks her bags. You'll see... And that's just a fraction of it. The rest we had to box and ship over. It'll arrive in about a month.'

'What! More stuff! Where am I to put it!'

'In the junk room, Mum. Where else?'

'But I was about to clear out the junk room, make an office!'

'Ha! You've been saying that for *years!*'

'But I really am going to do it – soon! I can't put any more stuff in there!'

'And even then it's not everything,' Marion continued. 'There's a whole lot we had to leave behind – Daddy's old Berbice chair, other furniture, big things. They're all stored in Lamaha Street, in Aunt Evelyn's old room. And boxes and boxes and boxes of junk. All Daddy's office files. Mummy refused to sell it or give it away or chuck it out. She clings to everything, especially if it belonged to Daddy. It's like she keeps him alive that way. She seems to think she'll be going back home someday. I had to leave her that dream; the house is too big for Evelyn and she wants to move out and rent it out. If only we had the money to renovate it ... Mummy said ...'

Perfectly on cue, a loud banging interrupted her. We all looked up.

Gran stood in the open doorway, walking stick in hand. She banged it against the wooden floor one last time and then, assured that she had our undivided attention, said:

'Where the telephone? I need to call the police about that suitcase. Somebody must be teef it and I need to report it.'

I looked from Marion to Mum. 'Teeth?' I asked.

'"Teef." Thief,' said Mum. 'It's a verb in Guyanese.'

❊ ❊ ❊

That evening Mum called together what she called a Family Council. She had something to tell us, she said. Once we were all seated around the dining table she launched into her spiel. This was a different Mum to the one I was accustomed to. She was authoritative, determined, and very, very serious.

'I just wanted to say,' she said, in this new, stern voice, 'that I want us all to get along, especially you and me, Mummy.'

She looked straight at Gran, who was doing her best to pretend she wasn't listening, flipping through a TV magazine she'd picked up along the way.

'Mummy! I'm talking to *you!*'

Gran looked up then, closed the magazine with some reluctance, and scratched her head.

'Is what?'

'This is an experiment. It can only work under one condition. I'm sorry I snapped at you yesterday but that could happen more often if you don't keep to the rules. Just one rule, really. This is a fresh start; a new beginning. I want a clean slate. The past is past: done with. Whatever happened then has no bearing on now. I want us all to try hard to live in the present, and just get along. Is that understood?'

'Yeah, but...'

'No buts, Mummy. I really want this to work. I really want you to be here. I really want us all to live in peace with each other. That can only happen if we don't rake up the past. It's swept up and thrown away. Gone. This is now.'

Marion fidgeted in her chair.

'That's all very well, Rika, but Mummy...'

'I said no buts, Marion. Please. That's all I have to say, short and simple.'

She pushed back her chair, stood up, and left the room. The three of us were left staring at each other. Then Marion shook her head as if in regret.

'If that's what she wants,' she said. 'Mummy, did you hear? You got to keep your big mouth shut!'

Gran cackled. 'Not possible!' she said.

Chapter Two

Inky: The Noughties

The next morning Gran's missing suitcase arrived, bright and early, just as Mum had predicted. It was immediately obvious what had caused the delay; it was a battered old thing, and it seemed both of the flimsy locks had broken, spilling out the contents. The airport staff had done what they could to fix matters; the case still gaped two inches open, but it was swaddled in several layers of cling-film and bound with security tape. Gran was both furious and ecstatic. Furious because, as she said, 'Somebody coulda teef her tings', and ecstatic because, well, there it was, safe and sound in the hallway, and Mum signing for it. Gran commanded the delivery guy to haul the case into her room. That done, she slammed the door and disappeared.

After an hour she reappeared in the kitchen where I was finishing off the last of my breakfast pancakes.

'Come, Inky. I gotta show you somet'ing.'

No peace for the innocent; I gobbled down the last bit of pancake, shoved the plate into the dishwasher, and followed Gran back into her room.

'Shut the door,' she said, so I did. The open suitcase lay on the carpet, and all around it were various articles; big books of some sort; albums. No wonder the case had not held. Some of the albums were still wrapped in items of clothing; petticoats, blouses, a scarf or two. A couple of knickers and bras, old-lady-grey cotton underwear, were strewn amidst the jumble.

Gran sat down on the edge of her bed, and patted the mattress next to her. I sat down. She took my hand, closing dry, skeletal fingers around it. Again I was reminded of a claw.

'Darlin' why you din't write you old Gran for so long? Ten years, except for Christmas cards. You don't love you old Gran no more?'

The voice was wheedling, cracked. I stuttered some excuse. When you hit your teens you grow out of things to say to an old lady you never met, and the spaces between letters had grown longer, and finally they had stopped altogether.

'I still got all you letters! Right over there!' She pointed to the smaller of her suitcases, the one that had arrived safely with her as hand luggage.

'That one, the black one. Bring it over here, open it for me.'

I got up and lugged the case over. It was an old-fashioned one, without wheels, of battered old leather. I cleared some space, laid it down flat on the carpet in front of the bed and crouched down to open it.

'It's locked,' I said, and looked up at Gran. She was fumbling with a chain around her neck.

'Come, child, take off this ting for me.'

The 'ting' was a bunch of keys. I got up and pried the keyring off the chain, leaving a single golden cross. She rubbed the cross gently between thumb and forefinger before dropping it into her neckline. She took the keys from me, inspected them all. There were at least six, two of which were tiny suitcase keys.

'One of these,' she said. 'Try them out.'

The suitcase lock sprang open at the first try. I opened the lid. Several shoeboxes were packed together in the case, the gaps between them filled by more stray pieces of clothing.

'Good. Now take out everyt'ing for me. Lay them out on the floor.'

I did as I was told; Gran's voice brooked no disobedience or hesitation. She watched in obvious satisfaction as I laid the boxes in a row on the carpet.

'Good,' she said, when I was finished. 'Now put the valise away.'

Again I did as I was told, stepping around the albums and boxes and items of clothing on the carpet, and placing the empty suitcase back in the corner. Gran leaned forward, bending precariously low down from the bed, shuffling the boxes around. She opened one, peered inside, grumbled what must have been some kind of Guyanese curse, and opened another. This time her face lit up in pleasure. She straightened up and again patted the bed beside her.

'Siddown, child. Lemme show you somet'ing.'

She reached into the shoebox and removed what looked like a bundle of letters. This she handed to me with a smile of pure delight.

'Go on, open it!'

I removed the cracked rubber band that held the bundle together. I already recognised the writing on the envelope: Mum's. I knew what was coming. Gran took the top envelope from the bundle and with fumbling fingers, removed its contents. She unfolded the one-page letter, and handed it to me in triumph.

'There! Read!'

My eyes glanced over the first few lines, but Gran spoke again.

'Read it aloud!'

I started again, aloud this time. *'Dear Granny, I hope you are well. Thank you for your letter. I am fine. Mummy is fine. She sends you her love. Yesterday we had the school play; Alice in Wonderland, I was the rabbit. It was fun. Mummy took a photo of me in my rabbit costume, I will send it next time. Here is a photo of me with Daddy, ice-skating. I fell down three times but then I didn't fall down any more. On Saturday I am going to a friend's birthday party. She is going to be seven, I am three months older. Please write soon. Inky.'*

I looked up, and found her beaming at me. I smiled back politely.

'See! I keep all you letters. Every one. You want to read some more?' She reached for the next letter in the bundle. I put my hand on hers to stop her, and shook my head.

'No, it's OK. It's great that you kept them. So those boxes are full of your other grandchildren's letters?'

Her eyes sank, and her smile disappeared. She took the bundle from me, and fumbled the rubber band back around it. She put it back in the shoebox, replaced the lid.

'No. My other grandchildren don't write. Nine grandchildren I got, and only one did ever write me letters, you. The others – nothing. Now Marion's children, they don't count, they grow up in Guyana, they know me. But Neville and Norbert – them children never write me. Just Christmas cards, birthday cards. And photos. Lots of photos.' She sucked her teeth, a long drawn out *choops* sound. Then she chirped up again, grabbed my wrist, and said, 'Hand me that album!'

She pointed to one of the albums on the floor, half-wrapped in a lacy nylon petticoat. I leaned over, picked it up, and tried to hand it to her. She made an impatient flinging motion with her hand.

'No, no, not that. The green one.'

I handed her the green album. She sat back in satisfaction, laid the photo album across her lap, and opened it. She pointed to the first picture on the first page.

'You!'

I knew that photo, and all the other ones in the pages to follow. Gran flipped through the album, showing me the familiar pictures of me growing up, exclaiming over the ones she liked particularly. I knew them all; Mum had them in her own albums.

'One t'ing I got to say for Rika,' Gran said now, 'she never write sheself, but she make sure you write and send photos. What she tell you about me?'

That last was a shot out of left field, in a different tone and a different tempo, stripped of nostalgic chattiness; urgent, probing. I looked up to meet her gaze, and this time there was nothing of the mirth I had seen there before. What I saw this time was – anxiety. I didn't know what to say.

'Why – well, nothing, really.'

'You mother still vex with me, after all these years. She pretend nothing wrong, but she vex bad. She didn't tell you the story?'

I shook my head. 'What story?'

Gran searched my eyes for a while, then seemed satisfied.

'Nothing. It was nothing. Long time ago – over thirty years. She was only sixteen. You mother always take t'ings too serious – she too sensitive. She don't forget or forgive. It was nothing, everyt'ing sorted out. But she don't write and she don't never come back home. Just Christmas cards.'

I was embarrassed. 'Mum always *wanted* to go home,' I explained, 'she always talked about Guyana, she calls it home. But it's a long flight; she never had the money.'

'Don't give me that. Y'all was rich, rich. Y'all did go on big holidays; Kenya, Mauritius, America. But she never bring you home.'

It was true. There had been a few years of wealth and opulence; Dad had even invested in a Docklands penthouse, just before he went bust and his plans to move there dissolved into thin air.

'She said – she said Guyana had gone to the dogs. She said it was no place for a holiday. She said, when things get better, she'd take me.'

But trying to excuse Mum only made things worse.

'Holiday? Since when is going home a *holiday*? She cut you off from you own roots, and that's a crime. You don't know nothing about where you come from. Not true?'

I wanted to say, *I come from London.* There are my roots. That's where I grew up. A London child; a *South* London child, to be precise. Streatham, Norwood, Crystal Palace. Croydon: that's my habitat, my territory. Those are my places, the localities where I prowl. I know the smells and the sounds; I'm sure I could find my way around blindfolded if I had to, and I rarely stray beyond my boundaries, because the sense of home begins to fade, and I start to feel slightly insecure and get fidgety. I will if I have to, of course, and it's fun to take a trip to the West End or Notting Hill or Brighton, or even America. But here is where I feel at home; where I get the sense of belonging. Yes, *this* was home. When people ask me, '*Where do you come from?*' (and they do, because they think I look 'exotic'. Christ. I hate that word!) I say Streatham, and stare them down. Because *that's* where I'm from. Not this foreign place across the ocean, just because my mother grew up there. Not Guyana.

What did I care about some half-baked ex-British colony in South America? A country that can't get its ass off the ground, its act together enough to make itself known, like Jamaica or Barbados? I wouldn't have minded telling people I was from Barbados. Or even Grenada. A lovely Caribbean island, where everyone wanted to go. But *Guyana?* No one had ever heard of it. They all thought it was Ghana. A country at the very Edge of the Known World, and most probably a dump. Mum had hinted as much often enough. Not a place you could be proud of.

But I couldn't tell Gran that. I knew what she meant; something nebulous, subtle; home being where the heart is, that kind of clichéd stuff. I nodded helplessly. She let the silence thicken between us, and then once again cut through it with a different voice, a different mood.

Gran fumbled in the big suitcase again and emerged with a
bottle of some yellow liquid. The label on the bottle said 'Limacol'. She splashed some on her hands and patted her cheeks
and neck with it, then handed it to me. I took it and looked
questioningly at her and at it. 'The Freshness of a Breeze in a
Bottle,' the label stated.

'Go on, go on! Use it!' she said. So I did as she had done. It
was like Eau de Cologne, fresh, tingling but in this case, limey.
I quite liked it, but now I knew where Gran's distinctive smell
came from.

'You mother was always a queer one,' said Gran. 'She was
a Quint, a real Quint. Eccentric, them Quint boys, all a bit
loopy. 'Cept one, me husband Humphrey. And Ma Quint, of
course. Granma Winnie. But she wasn't no Quint.'

I felt something soft, smooth and warm press against my
calves. It was Samba. I bent down and picked her up, placed
her upon my thighs and stroked her shiny black coat. Usually,
Samba would snuggle into my lap, meow gently to ask for affection, and, when it came, show her appreciation by purring.
Today, she simply stood up and padded slowly over to Gran's
lap, where she circled three times and settled into a cosy ball.
She didn't even have to ask; Gran's hand was already there,
sliding over the sleek black fur.

'She *never* goes to strangers!' I exclaimed.

The only response was Samba's smug and steady purr as she
contentedly kneaded Gran's thighs. Gran stroked her absent-
mindedly, and didn't reply. She pointed to a red, much older
album. 'That one.'

I handed it to her, and she opened it at the first page. There
was only one picture on it, a sepia photo of five young women
standing in a row, five beautiful young women in long dark
skirts and white long-sleeved blouses, the buttons up the front
ng into stiff high collars. It could have been a photo of Vic-

torian students from a Ladies Finishing College – except that all the women were ebony-skinned.

'Me mother and she sisters,' Gran said. 'Mother in the middle.' She pointed to her mother, then, one by one, to the four other girls. 'Henrietta, Josephine, Penelope and Elizabeth. The Williamson girls, my Aunties. All dead.'

She turned the page. 'Me and you mother,' she said of herself holding a toddler in a white frilly dress. 'Me eldest child. And look, me and your Grandad, with your mother.'

She and a handsome, fair-skinned young man were sitting next to each other, a baby on her lap. The man wore a dark suit and a bow tie; she wore a white dress just covering her knees. Hemlines had obviously shot up drastically between photos.

Then it was her, Granddad, and Marion, followed by several combinations of those four, occasionally with Mum in between, looking slightly lost. Towards the end, the new babies, the Terrible Twins, joined the group.

The photos stopped abruptly near the middle of the album, the last photo followed by blank pages. Gran picked up and opened yet another album. Here were still more photos, quite different to the first batch. Here, there were all boys. The photos were all black and white or sepia; totally vintage. I loved vintage. I took the album onto my own knees, and slowly turned the pages.

The photo on the last page showed a group of children, ranging in age from about a year to early teens. 'The Quint brothers,' Gran explained. It wasn't obvious that the boys were siblings, as each was entirely different; some had fair skin and light hair, others were as dark as the Williamson girls. The toddler wore a frilly dress not unlike the one my mother wore in the family photos, so I thought it was a girl, but Gran pointed to this child first and said, 'Freddy Quint.' She pointed to the tallest, fair-skinned, boy. 'Humphrey. Me husband.'

So this was my grandfather. Mum had never shown me photos of her family back home. I assumed she had none. I peered closely at the boy who would grow up to be my Grandad. All the boys wore sailor suits, Humphrey included, though he must have been about fourteen, far too old for sailor suits, even then, surely. The boys at the front wore knee-length socks and highly polished shoes or boots. Not one of them smiled. If not for the fact that some were as dark-skinned as Grandma, it could have been any group of English boys from that time, not mixed-blood boys from a distant tropical colony.

One by one, Gran named the rest of the eight Quint boys: 'Fine, fine, boys, but wild. Dead and gone. 'Cept one. Freddy now, the youngest, he was the wildest. Humphrey the studious one, my husband. Them Quint boys ...' She sighed. 'We lived round the corner from them, in Waterloo Street, me and me sister. You could see their house from my room upstairs. Handsome boys, all of them. Every man jack gone off to war. Look.'

She turned the page to show me a photo of the several young men dressed as soldiers, all lined up and smiling into the camera. There were more photos, of young men in uniform. Again, she named them.

'Humphrey, William, Gordon, Charles, Leopold, Rudolph, Percy and Frederick. All a-them run off to fight Hitler. Except Humphrey. Charley, he get killed in Singapore. Freddy, now...'

But instead of telling me about Freddy, she flipped the page. There was a portrait of the man at the other end of the row, presumably the eldest Quint brother.

'Humphrey. Me dear husband. Dead and gone.'

On the last page was a photo of a thin-faced white man with a walrus moustache, staring straight into the camera with pale eyes that, had the photo been in colour, would most certainly be blue.

'Maximilian von Quindt,' said Gran. 'Quindt with a *d*. The first of the British Guiana Quints. A German; a zoologist who came to study turtles. He marry a black woman and drop the *von* and the *d*. All the rest come down from he.'

In spite of the obligation to remain youthfully bored by her old-lady ramblings, I was intrigued. I took the album onto my lap and leaned in, turned back the pages, peered into those faces, those eyes. Who were all these people long dead? They were the ones who went before me; if not for them there would have been no me. They had been living, breathing, moving human beings, filled with life and love, moved by emotions and passions, just as aware of their own lives as I was of mine, and unaware that one day in the distant future a young girl carrying their genes named Inky would be looking at their images and wondering about them; just as one day, perhaps, a hundred years from now, some descendent of mine would look at my image and wonder about me. The ephemeral, fragile nature of life on earth struck me like a hammer-blow – they were once here and now they were gone. And how many other faceless, nameless ancestors had gone before them? People of whom no photos existed; melted into the shadows of history! For the first time ever I felt a connection to the line of ancestry that went before me; my life was simply one little leaf in a huge spreading tree whose roots spread far into the past and branches would reach far into the future. A shudder of excitement went through me ...

Gran snapped the album shut. 'Everybody in that book dead and gone, except me and me chirren and you Greatuncle Rudolph, in Canada. Dead and gone, ashes to ashes. Ah well. We all gotta die one day. Now, child, hand me those albums over there. Those two t'ick ones.'

Something about Gran made you obey. I shook off my sentimental musings and got up, picked up the 'tick' albums she'd pointed to, and handed them both to her. They were each at least two inches thick; one newer and the other older, battered like the suitcase. She opened the newer one. I expected yet more old photos, but I was wrong.

It was filled with stamps, most of them arranged in neat rows, but several of them loose and falling out, some in sheets or groups of four or five, some on envelopes, first day covers, bright, beautiful stamps, from all over the world. She knew the country names by heart, and pointed them out to me: Ethiopia. New Zealand. Iceland. Bolivia. She looked at only one or two pages before shutting it and picking up the old album.

This album seemed not just old but ancient. Its green cardboard covering was cracked and dog-eared, the spine fractured. But she touched it as if it were sacred.

'The family heirloom,' she whispered, and opened it.

I was disappointed. For an heirloom, the album held nothing of beauty, nothing of appeal. No beautiful foreign stamps, no first day covers; the stamps in here were all from British Guiana, and they looked cheap and insignificant, bland and musty in their monotony, primitive in their production. She pointed to one particularly ugly stamp on the last page.

'Theodore Quint's – your great grandfather!' she said. 'Very valuable!' She launched into some convoluted story of its origin; I listened with half an ear.

'A hundred and fifty years old!' Gran whispered. 'Very precious. Worth millions. An heirloom. I holding it for the next generation.'

She closed the album, placed a hand on it as if in blessing, then clasped it to her breast.

'Very, very precious,' she repeated. And in her eyes I recognised a new glint.

I'd seen it before, not too long ago, on the big screen. Gollum's glint.

❋ ❋ ❋

Later that evening I fled the house, leaving Gran to Mum and Marion. I slammed the front door, hurrying out to the pavement before Gran could somehow recall me. There I stopped, rummaged in my shoulder bag, pulled out my pack of pre-rolled fags and a lighter. I lit one, and, sitting on the garden wall, smoked it right down to the filter. That was good.

Mum detested my smoking and had done her level best to stop me from starting; but I had anyway, and now I was hooked, and she had to accept it. But she had her rules: no smoking within the house. Not even in my own room. Never, under her roof, she said. I always protested, 'But actually it's *my* roof!'

Which was true. In a twinkle of good sense Dad had put the house – which he had inherited from his mother – into my name before going berserk with his crazy trading and eventually losing everything else. He'd never re-mortgaged it, which had saved us from ruin; because it was only through re-mortgaging the house that Mum had got rid of a huge chunk of Dad's debt. The Docklands loft, of course, had been repossessed. So it was, indeed, my house, but only in name. Rather, it was the bank's. Mostly.

'Who pays the mortgage?' was all Mum ever said to my homeowner claims. That shut me up.

I crushed the cigarette stub on the wall, chucked it into the wheelie-bin conveniently waiting for next-day collection, and set off on a jog down Cricklade Avenue towards Streatham High Road. I couldn't wait to see Sal.

Salvatore Zoppolo – to use his full name – was my best friend. We'd been part of an inseparable foursome for longer than I could remember – me, Tony, Sal and Cat. Tony'd been my boyfriend, Sal Cat's. And then Cat's parents had moved to

Australia and she'd gone with them, and Tony – well, Tony had got himself a new girlfriend while still officially with me. It was my first dumping by a boyfriend ever. Utterly devastating. Sal, in the throes of getting over Cat's desertion by playing the field, lent me a shoulder to cry on. We became the best of friends.

After a while Sal got tired of drinking himself into a stupor with a different girl each weekend, and I got tired of wallowing in a swamp of self-pity. We both grew up, and so did our friendship. I found there the kind of familiarity I should have had with a girl friend, and I'd had with Cat. But all my former friends had drifted off into their own world, and most of all, they all drank – too much.

I loathed drunkenness. In the year before his death, Dad's alcoholism had sometimes led to violence, and now the very smell of strong liquor made me retch. Friends thought I was a prissy bore for not drinking, I thought they were juvenile. Only Sal had the time and, now, after six months of bingeing, the sobriety, to get to know the real me.

He was waiting for me at Wong's, and had already ordered – he knew me well enough to know what I'd want. I slipped into the seat opposite him and let out a deep sigh of relief.

'Mum's crazy. Stark raving mad!' I said.

Sal pushed away the strand of hair that always fell over his eyes. His father was Italian, his mother English, and his dark good looks turned female heads and kept male predators away from me. I still grieved for Tony, and Sal provided perfect platonic protection.

'I thought it was your Nan who was crazy? That's what you said on the phone …'

'Yeah, but Mum's crazy for setting herself up. Agreeing to take on Gran. Might as well get a job in the lunatic asylum! She'll never manage. She's scatty enough as it is; how's she going to cope?'

'Maybe you underestimate her.'

'Nope. Mum's as scatter-brained as they come. She just about manages to keep the two of us going, and only with my help. How's she going manage Gran as well?'

'With your help!'

'Exactly! That's the trouble. She knew from the start that Gran'll end up *my* responsibility. It's started already.'

'Tell me about it.'

And so I did. Wong's teenage son placed plates of steaming noodles before us, and while we ate I gave Sal a rundown of the day, putting in some catty Gran-mimicry to get a few laughs from him – the way she chewed her cud, the way she clacked her false teeth, her accent, her claws, her myriad boring albums and her Limacol-patting. Then I got to great-great-great-I-don't-know-how-many-greats-grandfather's-or-whoever's stamp album.

'Worth millions!' I said, rolling my eyes in mockery. Sal held up a hand and stopped me.

'Maybe it really is very valuable. If it's that old and rare.'

'Ha! You should see the stamps in it – falling to pieces. And even if they weren't, they're nothing special. Just very primitive everyday stamps, nothing artistic or anything. And from British Guiana, a little backwater country nobody ever heard of. Who cares?'

'Still – you never know. I'd get it valued if I were you. A philatelist might give you a couple of hundred for it.'

'But even if so – she'd never sell it. It's an *heirloom*. A precious heirloom!'

I mimicked Gollum, clasping an imaginary album to my breast and rolling my eyes suspiciously around the restaurant. I couldn't help it. My frustration with Gran, with the whole situation, found an outlet in mockery.

'My preciousss!'

Sal laughed. He reached out and laid a hand on mine. 'She sounds a card, this grandmother of yours. I'd like to meet her.

And I'd like to see this heirloom. One of my uncles collects stamps. He might be interested in seeing them.'

'With any luck she'll leave it to me in her will.'

'You'd better start sucking up to her, then!'

'You bet! I can't wait to get my hands on it – and start a really nice bonfire in the garden. What with Gran's junk, and Mum's, we could heat the whole of London for a year.'

Talking to Sal released some of the frustration I'd gathered over the day, and I calmed down. I felt guilty about the resentment I hoarded for Gran, and told him so. Sal was going to be a doctor, a neurologist – he was in his first year of medical studies – and was already good at dissecting people's minds, if not their bodies. I was in a gap year, working full time before commencing law studies. I had been working hard and saving up to go travelling next year – then Gran burst into our lives. Now, everything was chaos, and I'd probably have to forget Asia. I'd have to stay and help Mum. I moaned on for a while, and then I moaned about my own moaning.

'I'm sorry about all the whingeing,' I said.

'It's normal,' he comforted me. 'You're in your nice comfortable world, just you and your Mum, and your grandmother is threatening to disrupt it. That's all there is to it.'

'I know, I know. But there's more to it. I feel I should – I don't know – feel *love* for her, or something. She's my own grandmother, after all. The only one I ever had. And I used to love her, when I was small. It's all gone. And the way she kept all those letters, and photos. It's quite sweet, actually. I mean, I threw out her letters to me long ago. It means she actually *cares*. I ought to be feeling *something*. Touched, or something. But I don't. All I feel is irritation, and the need to escape. I wish I could love her. But I can't. I don't even *like* her.'

'Love isn't a *duty*, Inky. Technically she's a stranger. She might be your flesh and blood but try persuading your mind that you *have* to love her! You'll have to get to know her properly. Give her a chance, practice patience and tolerance, and …'

'You sound like a preacher or something. Or like Mum. For all Mum's scattiness, she's good with people. If she does feel any resentment towards Gran, she hardly ever shows it.' I remembered their first icy moments, and added, 'Not much, anyway.'

'But you said they were estranged?'

'Well, physically separated, for thirty years or so. I suppose you can call that estrangement. It seems they had a quarrel a long time ago and Mum ran away and never went back, and never even wrote. But I think it's *life* that kept Mum away more than any hard feelings. When my aunt asked her if she could take Gran in she said yes immediately. She never once hesitated, never once doubted it was the right thing to do, she was just one hundred per cent 'yes'. So I guess it's all forgiven and forgotten.

'Mum's strange in that way. She's scatty and negligent on everyday matters, but totally *there* when it comes to people and her responsibilities towards them. It's just amazing, the way she stuck with Dad, through all his troubles.'

I paused, remembering. They had been together a long time, gone through all the highs and lows. They met when she was only sixteen, travelled together, parted, got back together, parted again, married in England. They had gone through miscarriages together, and poverty, and wealth, and his infidelity. Through thick and thin, poverty and wealth, sickness and health; and alcoholism, in her eyes, was just another sickness. She'd never once considered divorce; apparently *stand by your man* was Mum's watchword. Any other woman would have dumped him. But she really thought she could heal him; with love, with Yoga and religion and all her weird Eastern practices. She couldn't, of course. He was too far gone for that. But she tried her best.

'Like I said – don't underestimate your mother. I think she's great, the way she pulled through. And she didn't do too bad a job of raising you, you know. I think she knows what she's doing. I bet she knew exactly what she let herself into with your Nan, and she'll get through it.'

'With my help,' I reminded him.

'Yes. But you always knew that, didn't you?'

'I just wish I wasn't such a beast. To Gran. I wish I could get along with her, stand her presence, at least. I always wanted a Gran.'

'Give yourself time. It'll come.'

'The old sourpuss.'

He said nothing. I played around with my noodles, winding them around my fork. I'd already picked out all the shrimps, saving the best for last. I looked up and said:

'I just feel so mean and nasty.'

'You're not mean and nasty. You're human. And at least you've got a working conscience, if you feel nasty when you *are* nasty!'

I made a face at him, and he made one back at me.

'Time,' he repeated. He reached out and squeezed my hand. 'And patience.'

'She's not exactly paving the way for me.'

'Maybe *you* should pave the way for *her*. I'll help you, if you like.'

'Can you come round sometime this week? Some evening?'

''Fraid it'll have to be Sunday. I've got night shifts all week, and Saturday I'm in Brighton with my parents.'

Sal had taken on a summer job, something in a hospital. My job was waitressing in Croydon. That trip I'd planned to the Far East: I couldn't afford it. I mean it was my money, to do what I wanted, but I couldn't leave Gran with Mum. It wasn't just the money. It was everything. We couldn't afford *any* extras under normal circumstances, and now we had Gran. From the financial standpoint, I had to wonder what Mum was thinking. But I knew. She thought we'd struggle through it. Somehow. *By the seat of her pants,* she always said. It was her watchword.

❀ ❀ ❀

Sal had aroused my curiosity. When I went home I mentioned the stamp to Mum.

'Gran says it's worth millions,' I said. 'Could it be true?'

'I remember that stamp,' Mum said. 'It was Daddy's most precious possession. There's one just like it, in America I think, that's apparently the rarest stamp in the world, so maybe she's right.'

'But if it is, Mum, we could sell it, and then ...'

'For millions I suppose? It's obscene, anyone paying that much for a stamp – for anything, in fact. Think of all the starving children you could feed with those millions! Obscene!'

'But, Mum...'

'Inky, just stop it; right now! It's not your stamp, it's not mine. It's just a scrap of paper. Worth nothing except the value some people attach to it. It's all in the mind. So shut up about it, OK?'

And she wouldn't speak one word more about it.

Chapter Three

Inky: The Noughties

That first week passed quicker than I'd believed possible, but only due to Marion's presence. Marion did all the cooking and all the cleaning, reducing the ever-growing pile of un-ironed laundry in Mum's room to neat little stacks of folded clothes. The kitchen glowed; all the cupboards tidied and the counters clear and gleaming. The house had never shone so brightly; life had never been so easy.

And of course, Marion was there as a buffer between us and Gran. She was there in the morning when we left the house, getting Gran up and bathed and dressed. She fed Gran during the day, kept Gran and her bickering at bay when we both came home from work, exhausted and drained of energy, and cooked up a storm each evening, for Gran's benefit and my delectation. That was the best part of having Marion around: the food. Mum had practically starved me all my life.

I had hoped to find out more about the mystery between Mum and Gran, but the more the week careened towards its inevitable end, the more my hope that I'd be taken into their confidence disappeared. The nearest I got to finding out was the day I walked into the kitchen to hear Marion say to Gran, in a tone of annoyed urgency:

'Tell her, Mummy! You have to tell her! Before I leave! She has to know; Uncle Matt ...'

'Hi!' I said, breezily. 'Tell who what?'

'Oh, nothing, Inky. Nothing important.'

'Look, if it's about Mum, you might as well tell me,' I offered. 'I can act as a go-between. Tell me and I'll tell her.'

At that Gran, who had been untypically silent for the last minute, let out a cascade of cackles.

'Inky, you ears too long! Just like me own.' And at that she grabbed her rollator and trundled out of the room, as dignified as ever. Marion let out a long deep sign and shrugged.

'Why can't you tell me?' I asked. 'I mean it. Why can't you trust me?'

'It's not a matter of *trusting* you, Inky!' said Marion. 'It's just – it's just too much.'

And with that she too walked out. The truth, it seemed, was too bitter for my juvenile ears.

❀ ❀ ❀

On Tuesday, Mum and Gran had a huge flare-up. I suppose it had been simmering beneath the surface for days, and that evening, at supper, it just boiled over. Gran had brought up the subject of the stamp once again. She had been muttering about it ever since she'd shown it to me, bringing it into conversations, hinting at how rare it was, and how valuable, and what a family heirloom. Now she was at it again, and I couldn't help but butt in.

'So how much is that stamp really worth, Gran?' I asked, as casually as possible. To be quite honest, I was a bit ashamed of myself. Ever since my conversation with Sal my thoughts had drifted back again and again to the stamp. What if it was really valuable? I accepted that Gran wouldn't sell it; but once she died? No. I shouldn't be having such thoughts. But if – and when – she died, after all, she *would* die one day, maybe soon, and then – had she made a will? I mean, I was her favourite grandchild, wasn't I? No. Stop it, Inky! I shouldn't be thinking that! That was a really, really nasty thought! What a horrible person I was! I was the kind of person I hated: people who would be ingratiating to old people just to get at their inheritance. But she certainly wouldn't leave it to Mum – what if …? But no.

How can one switch off greedy thoughts? Impossible. They just kept coming.

Anyway, the question just popped out of my lips and Gran, of course, was quick to reply.

'A fortune!' she said. 'A small fortune!' She turned to Mum. 'Enough to pay off your mortgage, Rika!'

How did Gran know about Mum's mortgage? Maybe Mum had told Marion and Marion had told Gran. I knew that Mum didn't discuss her debts and her money problems with anyone, and wouldn't have told Gran herself. She was much too proud.

But if Gran had hoped to get Mum excited about the stamp, fat chance!

'I can't believe,' Mum said, 'I just can't *believe* that an intelligent person could get so covetous about a little scrap of paper, they'd chuck millions at someone else to acquire it. I just don't know what to say.' She went on to sneer about these people who paid millions for such scraps when they could be saving humanity with the same money. At millionaires who had nothing better to do than throw money at scraps of paper. At people who loved scraps of paper.

Gran listened to Mum's rant with a neutral expression, shovelling food into her mouth and chewing slowly, her eyes on Mum, letting her speak her heart.

I myself was astonished; it was unusual for Mum to be so judgmental; unusual, in fact, for her to criticize anyone for anything. 'People are the way they are,' she'd say, when I brought up some human foible or the other. 'Everyone is different. They have their desires and they make their choices, and some choices are more stupid than others. Most people find out when they make stupid choices. They find out the hard way.'

And now, here she was, practically declaring stamp-enthusiasts to be dumbest people on earth.

'So, your father was stupid?' Gran asked, casually.

'My father! He was no father!'

'What! What you saying! You had the best father in the world!'

'I'm saying, he was no father! All that man cared about was those bloody stamps. That one stamp in particular.' She looked at me.

'The man who called himself my father would spend hours and hours holed away in his study peering at stamps under a magnifying glass. It just wasn't normal!'

She turned back to Gran. 'He loved his stamps first, and then you, and then a long space, and then, maybe, his children!'

That's when Gran exploded. 'How dare you! What do you know? He loved us all more than anything in this world! He adored us! He adored you! You don't know him at all! You don't know anyone at all! How you could talk about love! You ran away from home and didn't give a damn what anyone thought! About your own family!'

'You weren't anything of a mother either!' Mum cried back. 'It was Granny who mothered me! She was both mother and father for me!'

'Yes, and even she you didn't care about! She dead and gone and you never even came to see her again!'

And so it went on, accusation and return accusation. And it was all about love. That's the one thing I took from all the talk. Behind it all, behind all the words, on both sides, was a huge gaping hole; a hole where love should have been, but wasn't. It was as if they were both, Mum and Gran, caught in a time-warp, a place they'd been trapped in for thirty years, from which there was no escape. Marion and I just sat there in silence. Finally, Gran said:

'Rika, you don't know what you saying. You just don't know.' Mum did not reply to that, and so Gran had the last word. So in the end, the war of words ended in silence. Nothing resolved, and the wall between mother and daughter as sturdy as ever. The truth was: they were on either side of that wall, and not one of them was capable of passing to the other side.

❄ ❄ ❄

On Wednesday morning, though, Marion made me face a different bitter truth.

'Inky,' she said sternly, 'you know I'm leaving Sunday morning.'

'Yes?'

'Well, who's going to cook for Mummy when I'm gone?'

My voice, when it finally came, was small. A squeak.

'Mum?'

'Ha!' Her chuckle oozed contempt. 'What you think your mother gon' cook? Alfalfa sprouts and wheat-germ burgers? No, darling, sorry. It's you.'

I suppose I should have seen what was coming, should have seen it from the start, but sometimes I'm as much of an ostrich as Mum.

Mum had her own definition of 'delicious'. She was a vegetarian, had been for decades. She didn't, couldn't, *wouldn't* cook meat. If I wanted meat, I had to cook it myself. If Gran wanted meat – and she certainly did: meat cooked in special, mysterious, Guyanese-from-scratch ways – it would be up to me to cook it. Mum had always known this, but never spoken it out loud. She'd left it to Marion to explain, and to teach me. And now the inevitable was imminent: a crash course in Guyanese cuisine.

I was already a tolerable cook, I'd had to be, if I wanted to eat certain things, but this was a whole new world. Every morning

Marion went shopping for the exotic ingredients Gran insisted on having, and since she couldn't get it all in Streatham, she went all the way to Brixton Market, a bus trip away, bringing back a variety of fruit, vegetables and other ingredients I'd never seen in my life, or ever even heard of. Eddoes, yams, calalloo, plantains, cassareep: the names alone made my head spin.

But I was game; I actually liked cooking, and Marion was not only a good cook, she made it fun, interjecting her instructions with funny anecdotes from back home. And the best part, of course, was the eating of it all. Marion looked on with pleasure as I devoured her creations.

'Everything but rope, soap and iron,' she would say, as I tried yet another of her dishes. 'You're a true Guyanese!'

As we cooked she talked, and in those few days I learned more about the place Mum called 'home' from Marion than I had from Mum in all of my eighteen years. Marion brought 'home' to life – made it a colourful, vibrant place filled with quirky and loveable people.

By Saturday I had learned three staple recipes with which, by a system of rotation, I could keep Gran alive and reasonably happy. Marion recommended I teach myself four more dishes, and wrote the recipes down for me. She gave me a list of dishes I could look up on the Internet, and try out myself. And on Saturday she dragged me with her to Brixton Market. Strangely, I had never been there before; Brixton was slightly outside my home territory, and I'm not really a market person. But why not? It would be an adventure.

❋ ❋ ❋

Marion pushed her way through the crowded lane as if she'd done this every day of her life. On her previous forays she'd already found her favourite greengrocer, and that's where she headed, weaving through the shoppers with me following meekly in her wake. The whole place throbbed with life; it was as if, just one corner away from the last Victoria Line station, we'd walked into a Caribbean bazaar, the very air pulsing with tropical colour and energy. Heaped up on the roadside stalls were fruits and vegetables I'd never laid my eyes on, much less eaten. There were butcher shops and fishmongers, long counters reaching deep back from the street and laden with slabs of fresh meat, whole fish, prawns and other sea creatures nestled in ice. Colours and scents and sounds a world away from London; Marion's world, and Gran's, and maybe Mum's, but never mine.

Marion stopped at her favourite shop, greeted the shopkeeper with a hearty 'Mornin' Errol, how yuh doin' today?' and began stuffing handfuls of okra into a brown paper bag. Now okra, I *had* eaten before, so when Marion turned to me to tell me what it was I was able to sound off expertly.

'Actually, I don't like it very much. It's so slimy!' I said.

'Bah! If it was slimy they di'n't cook it properly. Okra only get slimy if you boil it in water. Wait till you try me fry-up okra tonight!'

As she spoke, the woman on my other side, an Indian woman with a plantain in her hand, leaned forward and peered across to get a better look at Marion. Her eyes lit up.

'Eh-eh! Marion, is you? I din' know you was over here!'

Marion looked back and let out a shriek of recognition. 'Jocelyn Ramsingh! Oh Lord, how you doin' gal!'

I stepped back to let them fall into each other's arms, okras and plantains forgotten. Marion turned to me. 'Jocelyn, this is my niece Inky; my sister's daughter. You remember Rika, nah?'

'Rika? Who could forget Rika Quint? Of course! I heard she was in London, her cousin Pamela told me – Pamela and me got children in de same class – but she keep to sheself, like she too good for the likes of we.'

Marion laughed. 'No, is not true, Rika just don't like to mix. She lives in she own world. Inky, this is me old friend Jocelyn, from Guyana.'

Well, I had already gathered that, and as I let myself be scrutinised by Jocelyn I thought yet again that the whole country of Guyana must be like one huge jolly village, where everybody knew everybody else or at least everybody's cousin and everybody's cousin's business, and everybody fully expected that, when everybody else moved to London or New York or wherever, they would keep that village going and feed it with new recruits; people like me, who belonged and yet didn't. We were born here to these villagers, I drew away with as much discretion yet were so far away mentally as to be strangers, except that they didn't realise it. We were Londoners; we'd left the village for the metropolis and our lives were so much larger, so much richer.

So when Jocelyn reached out to draw me into a bear-hug I stiffened, and when she patted my cheeks afterwards – as if I were *her* niece too, not just Marion's – I drew away as with as much discretion as I could. I didn't want to be rude, but *really*, I couldn't let her think of me as a villager.

'Pretty girl!' said Jocelyn, looking me up and down, and immediately corrected that to, 'Beautiful! Her daddy in't no Guyanese, right? I hear Rika married an American. A white man?'

I wanted to butt in right there and declare how rude and irrelevant it was to discuss another person's race, especially in their presence, but they were already off, discussing Jocelyn's own husband's race and how many children she had and how old they were and who they were married to and what race and how many grandchildren she had already, and how dark this one's skin and that one's. I touched Marion's arm.

'Why don't you give me the shopping list and I'll get the other stuff? The two of you can go and have a coffee, if you like!' I would have added, 'Or else we'll be here all day', but I was too well brought up for that.

Marion was delighted at the suggestion, so off I went with the list and the purse. I finished buying the okras, moved to the fruit section and stocked up on mangoes and oranges. I couldn't believe how cheap it all was, compared to the supermarket, but remembered how Marion had complained, the first day, how expensive everything was.

I took my purchases inside the shop to pay for them. The shopkeeper – not Errol, but maybe Errol's son – packed everything into blue plastic bags and told me the price. I opened the purse and gave him a ten pound note, and as he turned to the till to get the change I bent down to pack the goods into my backpack. When I straightened up again the shopkeeper pointed to my purse, which I'd left lying on the countertop.

'You don't belong in Brixton, right?' he said. 'Never leave your purse unattended like that here. Nex' time, you might find it gone!'

The customer behind me, an elderly man, nodded and smiled. 'I was thinking the same thing!' he said. 'Just be careful, Miss! Look after youself!'

I smiled at both in gratitude, feeling stupid. 'Thanks!' I said. 'This is my first time here. I won't do it again.'

'Yeah, I thought you was new, I never seen you face before. Well, then, welcome to Brixton, and I hope I didn't put you off forever! Most of us good honest people!'

Errol's son's warm smile made me feel right at home.

'No, no, of course not. I think you'll see a lot of me in future.'

Yes. Brixton Market had found a new recruit.

'Nice, nice!' He reached across a pile of sick-coloured bottles of fizzy drinks and grabbed a beautiful golden mango, which he handed to me.

'There you go! Have a great weekend! Come back soon!'

As I thanked him and packed the mango into my backpack – this time, my purse clamped under my arm – a new feeling flooded me: gratitude, mingled with shame, and a delicious sense of comfort. Sometimes it's just nice to belong. I suppose that's the advantage of village life.

I met up with Marion and Jocelyn but it seemed they hadn't finished their conversation yet, and had made plans. For me.

'I hear you like Guyanese cooking?' said Jocelyn to me, with a wicked glint in her eyes.

'Love it!' I said.

Jocelyn grabbed my arm, hooked hers into it. 'Well then, you got to come to Brown Betty. Marion and me takin' an early lunch there. Best Caribbean food in town – in the whole country!'

And they marched me off, down a side street where we were accosted by a black preacher with piled up dreadlocks yelling at us to 'Repent! For the day of Retribution is nigh!' Past stalls loaded with cheap bric-a-brac, past a sweet arcade; and then we were at Brown Betty, a narrow little place with one table on the street and a big glass window and an open door. In we went.

The place was crammed. There were only four tables, not counting the one outside, and all of them were crowded with plates piled high with food and surrounded by people eating. There were chairs everywhere, and people standing and talking and coming and going. A buxom black woman screamed when she saw Jocelyn and pushed her way past to enclose her in a tight hug. Her unblemished skin was polished to a deep mahogany, skin so tight and pure it could have belonged to a child. Her hair was arranged in small tight cornrows that started at her brow and rode across her skull to be gathered at the back of her neck on rolls of soft flesh. She and Jocelyn hugged as if they were long-lost sisters, and then they pulled

apart and Jocelyn introduced her to Marion, who was pulled
into a similar embrace, and then it was my turn. Strong arms
closed around me and pressed me against a pillow of a breast;
and all to the tune of 'Welcome, Welcome darling, welcome
my dear, welcome to Brown Betty!'

This was Betty, we learned next, and though the place was
full, Betty found room for us by chasing out the four occupants
of one of the tables who she lambasted for having been sitting
there for four hours and just 'gaffin' de mahnin' away when
other people got wuk to do' and 'keepin' away de custom'.

'Ow, Aunty, leh we stay, nuh?' said a thin black woman,
with big golden hoop earrings and an elaborate corn-row hair
style, grinning up at Betty in supplication.

'You think skinnin' you teeth gon' help yuh? Haul yuh tail!
Every man Jack!'

Reluctantly, the guests got up and left. Marion pushed
Rika into the corner space they had left, and she and Jocelyn
sat down opposite her.

'Just like home!' said Marion in delight, looking around
her at the wooden walls painted in primary colours, posters
pinned to them inviting people to a Jamboree or advertising
hair extensions or 'Cheap Calls to Guyana and the Caribbean'.

'You mean to say, you live here all you life and this is your
first time in Brixton?' Jocelyn couldn't believe it; she looked at
me as if I were some alien.

'Is not she fault,' said Marion, 'is my sister Rika – she always
goin' she own way.'

'No sense of roots!' said Jocelyn. 'My cousin daughter just like
dat. They wouldn't set foot in Brixton – t'ink dey is too good.'

'Brown Betty was a restaurant in centre Georgetown,'
Marion explained. 'Gone now, but oh my! They used to have
the best chicken-in-the-rough in the whole country. Served in
a basket!'

'Ice cream too!' said Jocelyn. 'We used to go every Sunday evening. Then drive to the Sea Wall and eat we chicken.'

'Closed down now,' said Marion, 'But Betty here, she is the granddaughter. And Betty cousin …' She launched into the story of Betty's cousin.

Betty, meanwhile, who had disappeared into the kitchen some time ago, reappeared with several dishes balanced on her arms. She placed them on the red-and-white chequered tablecloth: dhal puri and chicken curry, plus pumpkin bhaji with mango achar, black pudding, metagee and cook-up-rice, channa and chow-mein – all of which I was commanded to heap onto my plate and *eat up, eat up.*

I ate my way through the dishes set before me, each one more delicious than the one before it. I was going to get so fat, but I didn't care. Marion, Jocelyn and Betty looked on with delight.

'A proper Guyanese!' said Jocelyn.

'She eats everything but rope, soap and iron!' Marion informed her.

'That's the way!' said Betty. 'Eat up, darlin', eat up!'

'So when you goin' home?' Jocelyn asked me, in between all the food and drink.

I looked at my watch, and then at Marion. 'Actually, we should leave, in half an hour at the latest,' I said, and Marion and Jocelyn burst into laughter.

'Not that home … *home,* home. Guyana!' said Jocelyn.

'Um – actually, I don't have any plans. Probably never,' I said, and hoped it didn't sound rude. I didn't say that *this* was home. London. South London. And now, Brixton.

Marion patted me on the back.

'You will go. One day you will. Wait and see,' she said.

Later on, I staggered and stumbled home – my present home, that is – with Marion, stuffed full with the most delicious food I'd ever tasted and satiated with enough affection to keep me going until – until I returned to Brixton and Brown Betty, which definitely would have to be soon. For the time being, that would be my Guyana. For it had dawned on me that day: Marion was right. One day, I'd go and find that place she and Mum called home. Meanwhile, I had learned a valuable lesson: Guyana's way to my heart was definitely through the stomach.

❋ ❋ ❋

Marion and I were cooking together one evening when I broached the taboo subject of Mum, Gran, and the Terrible Thing that had torn them apart.

'What really happened?' I asked, as casually as I could. Marion looked at me and shrugged.

'If your mummy never told you, it means she don't want you to know. It doesn't really concern you and it's all in the past.'

'But I just think I should *know*. There's such a tension between them. If I knew I could somehow... mediate. I have the feeling they both *want* to be friends, they both *want* reconciliation but something is holding them back. Maybe it's pride or something. Maybe one of them needs to say sorry and if I knew ...'

Marion sighed. 'So you picked up on that? You're right, Inky. The two of them are just dying to make up but it's like they're caught in a time trap, and they can't escape, both too proud to make the first move. First Mummy rejected Rika and then Rika got her revenge by rejecting Mummy ... it's like a wall of rejection and if only they could just get past that wall – tear it down ...'

'But why, Marion? What happened?'

'Sorry, Inky, you not getting that information from me. It's too personal. Ask your mummy.'

'You know what she's like. She never talks about personal stuff. I asked her a couple of times already and she always manages to change the subject.'

'Then ask Granny.'

'She won't talk either. She just keeps dropping hints. If I knew who had to forgive whom … whose fault it was. Was it really *that* bad?'

Marion didn't answer. She was chopping onions. She rubbed her eyes. But I refused to be ignored.

'Marion – how bad was it really?'

She glanced at me and said beneath her breath:

'It was… *horrendous.*'

Chapter Four

Dorothea: The Thirties

A fly was crawling along the back of her neck. Dorothea flicked her pigtails and it flew away. She turned her mind back to Pa's sermon, both hands, in white lace gloves, decorously folded on her hymn book.

There it was again, the fly, crawling down towards the collar of her dress, tight around her neck. This time she reached behind to chase it away. Her hand dislodged her hat of white lace, matching the gloves. She straightened it unobtrusively. If she fidgeted too much, Pa, up there in the pulpit, would notice and teach her to her pay attention by learning a new psalm out by heart, after the service. So she fixed her gaze on Pa and tried to absorb the sermon, which wasn't too hard as she'd heard it a million times before, if in other words.

It was a most persistent fly. It was back, this time crawling around the side of her neck towards her chin. She slapped at it and the noise fell unfortunately into a potent pause in the sermon. Mums, stiff-backed next to her in the pew, looked down at her and frowned. Dorothea smiled back, scratched her neck as if that was all she had been doing, and focused on Pa. He missed nothing, and up there in the front row she was practically under his nose.

'And so, brethren in the Lord, be alert, for Satan walks among us. Brothers and sisters, let not your eyes be blinded by the illusion of his works, nor your ears be made deaf by his lies! He walks among ye in many a beautiful guise, so let the words of your Lord stand guard over your heart! Let the sign of the cross be written in light above your heads as you go about your daily lives! Let the Holy Book accompany you on your journey through life…'

He held up the enormous black Bible and pumped it as if gauging its weight, which Dorothea knew, was several pounds, for, under Pa's eagle eye, she spent a part of each day strutting about the house with that very same Bible balanced on her head. A young lady must keep a straight back and a high head, Pa said, and the Bible must be her refuge at all times. Only thus could Satan be kept at bay.

But that fly must be Satan, out to tempt her, for there it was again, tickling the nape of her neck, just beneath the hairline. She wrinkled her face and once again swung her pigtails, keeping her hands folded on her lap. The fly was not one bit bothered. There it was again.

The game might have gone on all through the sermon but a smothered giggle and some shuffling behind her made Dorothea glance around. And at once she knew.

It was those dreadful Quint brothers, most specifically, Freddy Quint, the youngest.

There was not a time when Dorothea had not been aware of the Quint boys. They were an integral part of her childhood. Their jungle backyard swarmed with them, a horde of loud, rambunctious boys who claimed it as hunting territory. Dorothea had never stopped to count them; might as well count a cage full of monkeys, and anyway, throughout the years they had been heard rather than seen, their shrill boy-voices yelling blue murder above the backyard treetops or from the alley that linked their homes. Rumour had it there were eight of them.

They lived in a big timber house in Lamaha Street, just a few yards down the alleyway from Dorothea's own house in Waterloo Street. In fact, Dorothea's upper-storey bedroom window at the back of the house overlooked the Quint backyard and, though you could not see what was going on beneath the treetops, you could certainly hear the yelling and the screaming from the wild games they played. True, as they grew older the yard grew quieter, but somehow their reputation as 'mad' and 'wild' remained. All boys. No girls. She'd known them all her life but never spoken a word to any of them, because Pa said they were bad company; but mostly because they were boys, and a van Dam girl never went near boys.

When she *had* seen them, it was in the street, for they had claimed Waterloo Street – *her* street! – as part of their territory, Lamaha Street being far too busy for serious boy-action. Most afternoons the Quint boys came tearing around the corner, still in their St Stanislaus school uniforms, into the calm tree-shaded avenue outside the van Dam house, and converted it into bedlam. They would ride back and forth with no hands or perform circus tricks, swinging their lithe boy bodies over their saddles or handlebars, riding backwards or piling on five to a bike, and of course, racing each other up and down the street. They would weave through traffic as if it did not exist, ramming on the brakes till they squealed and rearing up to ride on one wheel, cowboys on thin iron horses.

Dorothea could not tell one from another, not put names to all the faces, but Freddy, being the wildest of the bunch, had gained Pa's attention when he, Pa, had caught him up the mango tree last year at the height of the season, with a bucket full of the plumpest mangoes. Pa had chased him away and lodged a formal complaint with his mother, that dark-haired Englishwoman, who had accepted it with an apology on behalf of her son, a dismissal along the lines of 'boys will be boys', and a gift; a basket of sweet, ripe, White Lady guavas from the Quints' own backyard.

Freddy Quint was the worst of the lot. He was the only one she could identify by name, him being the youngest and thus the smallest. The rest of them seemed simply an amorphous blob of gangling animal maleness; she had not deigned to separate the whole into its separate fidgeting parts. She only knew they were dreadful, because Pa told her so. All of them were older than her; in fact quite a few years older, but Freddy seemed about her age, thirteen. Normally, they'd have met at primary school but Freddy had gone to the liberal private school in Camp Street whereas she, of course, had attended the Mission School in Croal Street. And now he, like all his brothers, was at the all-boys Saint Stansilaus College. Dorothea had attended the female pendant, the all-girls Catholic St Rose's High School, until, a year ago, Pa had fallen out with the Sister Antony on a small (in his eyes, big) matter of doctrine. Since then Dorothea went to the Government School, Bishops' High. Pa didn't like Catholics anyway, and Bishops' was just as strict. She was safe there, safe from the likes of Freddy Quint.

But all this was mostly in the past. As the boys grew up, so had the neighbourhood gradually returned to its original state of leafy, sun-filtered serenity; one by one the Quint boys approached the more serious pursuits of manhood, and, occasionally, one or the other abandoned home for studies abroad. Only Freddy remained wild, and, to Dorothea, conspicuous. She had never been this close to him, never spoken to him.

❊ ❊ ❊

Now, she glanced behind her again, and frowned. He was up to no good, for sure. He sat immediately behind her, hands tucked demurely under his thighs. It was the broad grin across his face that gave him away, and the smothered giggles of his brothers at either side. All eight of them sat in the pew behind her, book-ended by their parents.

The Quint boys were all tall and lanky, but that was the only resemblance between them. Otherwise, they were as unlike as a random handful of seashells, ranging in skin colour from almost-white through cinnamon to mahogany brown – Freddy being the darkest – and with hair colour and texture ranging between straight blonde to crinkly black. Freddy's hair was a compromise; a mane of dark curls that hung over his forehead and down his neck, almost as long as a girl's, over it a wide-brimmed straw hat which he wore constantly, even in church, even though it was by now worn-out and floppy and quite grimy.

Dorothea wondered why Ma Quint didn't insist on a better turnout for church; but Ma Quint was herself eccentric; 'crazy', was Pa's word for her, as it was for almost anyone who wasn't in his congregation. She was a dark-haired Englishwoman with a 'reputation'; she'd broken all the rules, people whispered, though Dorothea had never quite understood *which* rules she'd broken. Together with her husband, a dark, tall, African man, she added a few more ingredients to the genetic stew that was British Guiana's population. As, of course, had Dorothea's own parents; Pa was white, a first-generation Englishman, and Mums was black, her own parents the children of emancipated slaves.

Dorothea had often wondered what had brought her parents together; she couldn't ask directly, of course, but finally she had got to the truth through Miss Percival, the gossipy best friend of Aunt Jemima, her mother's equally gossipy sister. Giggling, Miss Percival had whispered to her during an unobserved moment at last year's Easter Revival, held at their house.

'Your father was a handsome man, above that dog collar!' Miss Percival had said, 'But most of all, he was white. Your mother was the most ambitious of the Williamson sisters. An unmarried spinster! Getting on in years. And proud. Only the best was good enough for Emily. She wanted a white man, and in the end she caught one.'

Miss Percival giggled wildly at that and poked a finger into Dorothea's chest.

'You!' she said. 'You were on the way, and what would the world have said if Pastor van Dam had made of her a Fallen Woman?'

Another wild flurry of giggles, and she scurried off before Dorothea could ask more. She was confused. What did her being on the way have to do with her mother being a Fallen Woman, or catching a white man? If she, Dorothea, was on the way then of course they were already married. You had to be married to have children. Everyone knew that. And what, exactly, was a Fallen Woman'? Dorothea knew it was something extremely shocking, but nobody ever explained exactly *how* or *why.*

Now, Dorothea frowned, mouthed the words 'Stop it!' to Freddy Quint, straightened her hat once more, and turned back to Pa's sermon; but unfortunately Pa had noticed the little skirmish and now glared down at her with blazing eyes, not missing a beat in the sermon.

'Satan walks in flesh and blood among us!' he boomed. 'He is everywhere! Be ye alert at all times and in all places! Be ye not deceived by the works and the words of the Devil, for they lead you from the Straight and Narrow along the dark winding pathways of Sin!'

After the sermon they all rose for the last hymn, during which the collection was taken. 'Immortal, invisible, God only wise!' sang Dorothea. Behind her, she was aware of the cacophonous croaking emitted by eight adolescent male throats and repressed a smile of amusement. *Boys!* What a strange invention; what a weird, gangling chaos of humanity; almost as if God was having a joke.

The 'fly' alighted once more on her neck, but this time Dorothea was ready. She swung around and grabbed it, and then she held it up: Freddy Quint's wrist, and in his hand, a hen's feather. Dorothea squeezed and twisted the wrist till

Freddy dropped the feather and his face convulsed with pain. Ma Quint, at the end of her pew, leaned forward to see what was going on and the other Quint brothers croaked louder than ever to mask the scrimmage.

Mums had noticed too, and slapped Dorothea's hand. Dorothea immediately let go of Freddy's, not without flashing him a gloating grin of triumph. She turned away and stood once again demurely in the pew. She had not missed a beat of the hymn.

'Most blessed, most glorious, the Ancient of Days!' she sang, 'Almighty, victorious, Thy great name we praise!'

Pa had left the pulpit and now stood at the altar performing some ceremony, his back to the congregation, and hadn't noticed a thing, which was good. But even if he *had* noticed, she didn't care. Causing and witnessing Freddy Quint's comeuppance made her Sunday: for that, she would gladly have committed several psalms, collects and prayers to memory, taking her punishment as a fair price for revenge.

Nobody, just nobody, made a fool of Dorothea van Dam.

❄ ❄ ❄

That very Sunday afternoon, Dorothea was down in the garden cutting roses for the drawing room table when a piercing whistle made her jump. She swung around, but all she could see were the hibiscus bushes growing along the back palings, taller than her, luxuriant with red and yellow flowers. She shrugged and turned back to her roses.

That whistle came again, sharp and loud, and this time it was followed by a call, half whispered, half shouted: 'Dorothea!'

It definitely came from behind the hibiscus hedge. 'Who is it?' Dorothea called back.

'It's me!'

'Me, who?'

'Freddy, Freddy Quint. The boy with the feather?'

'Oh, you.' She tried to put as much disdain as she could into her voice; or perhaps indifference. She wasn't quite sure which was more appropriate. Maybe neither.

'I can see you, can't you see me?'

'No, I can't.'

Instead of an answer, a thump and a crack, followed by the rustling of leaves and branches, and a moment later Freddy Quint stood before her in flesh and blood.

'You broke down the palings! You ...'

'Kicked down a paling, and here I be before you, ma'am, at your service!' He gave her a sweeping bow, removing his hat and circling it wide so it touched the ground. Replacing the hat, he stood grinning before her.

'Pa will kill you! And you better get out before he comes!'

'But he's out. I know he is 'cause I just saw him leave in that old rattletrap of his.'

He meant the Ford, the green Prefect, Pa's pride and joy. Dorothea was offended on Pa's behalf.

'It's not a rattletrap! It's almost new and we've never had a breakdown, and just because ...'

'Just teasin'. But I know he's out, and your Mum too. Like every Sunday.'

He was right, of course, and Dorothea was surprised at how much he knew. Every Sunday Pa took the family up the East Bank of Demerara to Goed Fortuin sugar plantation, which Uncle Hendrik owned. There, Pa had managed to build up a community church to serve the converted Christian East Indian plantation workers and poor families from the surrounding villages. Services were held in the late afternoon, but Dorothea had managed to free herself from attending with the excuse of extra schoolwork; eventually, she had been permanently released from these Sunday afternoon trips; she regarded Sunday as her day off.

Now, Freddy continued. '... and I wanted to say sorry, for this morning. And ask how you got so strong, for a girl. 'Course, if you hadn't taken me by surprise, it would've been different. And anyway I had to let you win, 'cause you're a girl, an' I didn't want to make a scene, 'cause it was in church.'

'Ha! Then beat me now! Come on!' Her eyes bristled with challenge, and she held up her forearm and open palm.

'Well, now, you're a right one! But sure!'

He grabbed her hand and pressed against it. Dorothea pressed back, frowning with intensity. For a full two minutes they wrestled thus in silence; hands clutched and bent arms swollen with muscle. Then Freddy laughed and relaxed, and let her swing his arm down into defeat.

'Whew, you're good, for a girl! 'Course I had to let you win again, 'cause me Mum wouldn't like to hear I was beatin' up the neighbourhood girls. Wouldn't be a gallant thing to do, for a Quint. But really, now, how did you get so strong?'

His eyes seemed to drink her up, brimming with admiration. Dorothea smiled and looked away.

'Tennis!' she replied. She stooped to pick up the secateurs she'd dropped, but Freddy, seeing her intention, bent down and got there before her. Their heads bumped in mid-air.

'Ouch! Sorry! Are you all right?' he rubbed his crown and handed her the secateurs.

She giggled. 'Yes, fine. You?'

'Oh, sure, I got a head as hard as stone. Just hopin' I didn't maim you for life! Now, tell me about that tennis. So you swing a racquet, do you?'

'Every afternoon, after school. I'm in the school team – we beat St Rose's in the under sixteen doubles last week. It was in the *Graphic*!'

It was a good thing that Sports were compulsory at Bishops'; Pa would normally never have allowed her to take it up otherwise. But Dorothea had done well, and he had given his reluctant permission for her to join the team.

'You were in the *Graphic*! With a photo?'

Dorothea nodded.

'Well, now, I missed that. I'll have to look for it, and I'll cut out the photo. I don't usually read the sports pages, but I will now, now I know you're famous.'

'No, I'm not, it was only a school game, but they're considering me for the national tennis team and if I get chosen I get to play in the West Indian Tennis Championships next year, and *then* I'll be famous.'

'Can I come and watch you training, sometimes?'

Those were the words that finally woke Dorothea up. She blushed and looked away, peeling her eyes from the gaze that held hers; black eyes deep and still as rainforest pools and warm as the afternoon sunlight now filtering through the mango tree. She'd talked to this *boy*, this stranger, as if she'd known him all her life, chatted with him right here in the forbidden territory of her own backyard. If Pa saw her, he'd kill them both.

She dropped her voice when she spoke again, this time shy and uncertain.

'Look, I can't talk to you, and you shouldn't be here at all. If my Pa sees me, he'll …'

'I told you, he's out. But we don't have to talk here. Come on over to my place. You've never been inside, have you?'

'No, of course not!'

Like theirs, the Quint house was made of white-painted timber, and stood on high stone columns so that you reached the front door via an outside staircase, but there the similarity ended, for the Quint house was several times bigger, and just as wild as the family that lived within its walls. Probably it had started out as basic as theirs, and as practical: two stories, with a jutting gallery along the front, a drawing room behind the gallery, a kitchen behind the drawing room, a staircase leading up to the bedrooms and bathroom, above it all a roof of corrugated iron, and all around it windows and jalousies and wooden shutters.

The Quint house had a life of its own. As the family that inhabited it had grown so had the house, with extensions upwards and outwards: a high tower topped by a cupola; Bottom House rooms added on willy-nilly; and even an Annex, a separate little cottage joined to the back of the house by a mid-air passage. The house was an architectural monster, yet fascinating; it made you want to enter and explore, figure out how all its parts fit together, or even if they did at all. It fired Dorothea's imagination, already well nourished by the piles of novels she borrowed from the library. She could imagine a wicked witch living there, keeping her prisoners victims in the various rooms, or a miser all alone, counting his fortune, or a community of elves, or a headmistress with a boarding school and a horde of giggling girls her age. But actually, truth was better than fiction and the family that lived there was far more intriguing than any witch or gathering of elves. Pa said they were Satan's brew, and that was enough to whet Dorothea's appetite.

Now, Freddy snapped his fingers to wake her out of her reverie. 'Hey, come down from the clouds! You want to come over, meet my family?'

Dorothea met his eyes again. She smiled, flipped her pigtails over her shoulder.

'Yes.'

'Come on, then.' Freddy held out his left hand. She took it with her right. He pulled her into the hibiscus bush, pushed away the loose board in the palings and held it as she squeezed through the hole. He followed suit. He took her hand again, and the two of them ran through the alley, along the grass verge that edged the gutter.

The moment their hands joined Dorothea knew that her life would never be the same again.

Chapter Five

Dorothea: The Thirties

Freddy and Dorothea reached the Quint backyard a little way along the alley. No need to hold her breath to squeeze between the laths; unlike the narrow gap in the van Dam fence, which Freddy had just this day created, the opening in the Quint palings was wide and permanent, for the Quint boys had long ago claimed the alley as part of their property. They might was well have put in a gate.

This yard, like her own, was a profusion of typical tropical trees and shrubs: hibiscus and oleander adding points of brilliant colour; bougainvillea cascading with red and purple clusters; pawpaw and banana palms and two huge mango trees lending shade and concealment. Freddy led the way down a gravel path between the overgrown, unkempt bushes. Two dogs leapt around them, tails wagging, eager to lick Freddy's face and make her own acquaintance. She laughed, and patted them; she loved animals, but Pa wouldn't even allow a cat, said he was allergic.

'This is Parrot,' said Freddy, fondling the brown one, 'and this is Turtle.'

Dorothea laughed. 'What strange names!'

'I gave them those names when I was about six,' said Freddy. 'Everyone else was suggesting boring names like Frisky and Blacky. I wanted them to have really special names. So Parrot and Turtle they are.'

Everywhere, Dorothea noticed signs of the yard's use and misuse by the Quint boys: a rusting bicycle frame claimed by vines, a weather-beaten, moulding rope-ladder hanging from an overhead branch, and, when she looked up, a broken-down tree-house overhead.

Yards in Georgetown were invariably big, and this was no exception, yet finally they navigated the wilderness and reached the steps leading up to the back door. Freddy turned to her, flashing one of his oversized grins.

'Come on up and meet Ma,' he said, and led the way up.

Dorothea had never seen Mrs Quint close up, but from a safe distance she had always been mainly aware of two things about the woman: she has hair as black as an Indian's pinned up into an unkempt bun, and a huge bosom – a rather terrifying combination. Now, she was confronted with both, and as they entered the kitchen through the Dutch doors, her heart fluttered as she saw the woman's broad back across the room from them.

'Hey Ma, look who I brought!' said Freddy as they crossed the room, and Dorothea's heart skipped a beat. *What on earth am I doing here in the Quint madhouse? Pa will kill me,* she thought, and for a moment she contemplated turning on her heels right there and fleeing, back the way she'd come. *Pa will never know,* came the immediate answer, and a delicious sense of autonomy overcame her.

And anyway, it was too late. Ma Quint swung around, a wooden spoon held aloft like a paddle, as if for attack. But then a smile as broad as Freddy's spread across her face, and she spoke, and Dorothea knew she was safe.

'Why, it's that nice little girl from Church, Pastor van Dam's daughter!' She exclaimed. 'Hello, my dear, and welcome to our home! We don't see many girls around here, so we love them! Is Freddy showing you around? Don't mind him, he might be a bit crazy, and he shouldn't have teased you this morning in Church, but he means well, my Freddy; he's got a good heart, that boy, so I hope you've forgiven him! You can call me Ma – everybody else does.'

She had a strange accent, one Dorothea had never heard before. In her young years, in fact, she had known only two extremes of speech with a hundred graduations between them: her father's clipped, correct English, (which her mother struggled to emulate) and the sing-song dialect of what Pa called the 'hoi polloi': Creolese, the native's talk, the forbidden language. Both her parents kept a strict ear open for any sign of her replacing 'in't' for 'isn't' and 'dis' for 'this'. Ma Quint spoke neither the one nor the other. It seemed to be a melange of the two; the correct words spoken in the warm cadence of Creolese.

'I went 'round to apologise, Mum, and you know what, she plays tennis!'

'Tennis! Really! I used to play tennis as a young girl! Course I had to stop it when I had children. I always encouraged my boys to take it up but none of them did – they preferred football, and cricket and bedlam, strangling each other and tearing off each other's limbs: that's boys for you! Now, sweetheart, what can I offer you? Phulourie', just made today? It's really good. Or something sweet, pine tarts? Let me see what I've got.'

She stepped over to a cupboard in the corner and removed a tin, which she opened and offered Dorothea, who murmured a thank you and took one of the pine tarts; triangles of pastry filled with thick pineapple filling.

'And you must be thirsty, here's some nice lime juice – or shall I make you some tea?'

Already she was reaching for a glass jug, and without waiting for an answer, poured a glass for Dorothea, but only three-quarters full.

'And some ice.'

She moved to the kitchen's Demerara window and unfolded a bundle of terrycloth and several layers of newspaper to reveal a huge block of ice. She chiselled away several chunks, which she then plopped into Dorothea's glass.

'There then, that's you catered for. Go on, have a seat and tell me all about yourself. You're at St Rose's, aren't you?'

Dorothea chewed quickly so she could swallow and speak.

'No, I changed schools,' she said shyly, 'I'm at Bishops' now.' Ma Quint seemed not to hear.

'Those St Rose's nuns are dragons. I heard of one Sister Agnes, that if you cross her, she makes you kneel on grains of uncooked rice in a corner for a whole hour, while learning a Bible passage by heart! Did you ever have to do something like that?'

Dorothea shook her head no so that her pigtails swung back and forth and swallowed, in preparation for speaking, but again, she was too late.

'And another girl we know, Lucy, got suspended for a week, because she was seen in the company of a boy, after school, while wearing her St Rose's uniform, last year! Actually, to be quite honest, it was one of *our* boys, Leo; he was just sixteen, and meant no harm, he was just walking her home, and they were just chatting, but still, rules are rules. It was quite a hullabaloo at the time. Those nuns! Of course, the brothers at Saint Stanislaus are just as bad. That's Catholics for you. Of course I'm not Catholic, but my husband is. That's why my boys all go to Saints. But I like to show them the alternatives. I've been taking them around to other places of worship these last few weeks, so they can get a feeling for the many ways God can be celebrated. I've even taken them to a Mosque and a Hindu temple ... that was interesting. I believe there are as many ways to God as there are humans, and we need to search until we find the shoe that fits, that's why we came to your church this morning. Your father, now, he's quite heavy with the fire and brimstone; I don't think that's for any of us Quints. How old are you, let me guess, thirteen? Fourteen?'

Dorothea swallowed and finally got a word in. 'I was thirteen last month.'

'Ah. Then our Freddy's a bit older than you, he turned thirteen last July. If we'd known, you could have come to the party; it's such a pity, you living that close and not being friends with the boys. We could do with some more girls around here, like I said, too many boys … I would have loved to have a daughter, in fact I did almost have one …'

She stopped, and a great sadness seemed to envelop her, then she continued: 'We lost her. The only girl and we lost her. Not that I would have preferred to lose any of the boys; no, I love them all dearly and equally, but you know how it is … a mother likes to have a little girl to dress up. So I want you to know, Dorothea, that you are very welcome here, and you must come more often and let me feed you and spoil you like if you were my little girl … though I know you're not a little girl any more, but we could be friends, couldn't we?'

Dorothea felt her heart would burst. She didn't know there were mothers like this. Her own mother – well, the less said the better. People called Emily van Dam née Williamson a she-dragon, and for good reason, as Dorothea knew first hand. She was hard and bony and had eyes that only had to glance over you to give you a shiver of guilt, even if you'd done nothing wrong. Dorothea couldn't remember having once been hugged by her mother, whereas just talking to this Ma Quint was like being taken into one long warm embrace. She had to resist running up to her and sinking her head against that soft bosom and feeling those big strong motherly arms close in around her. But it was not to be; not today.

Ma Quint wasn't quite finished. She reached out and ran her fingers along Dorothea's hairline. There the hair was pulled back so tightly it raised her skin at the roots, stretched her forehead, and pulled her eyebrows up into an expression of permanent surprise.

'That looks so painful!' said Ma Quint. 'Doesn't it hurt? Those plaits – they're so tight! Does your Ma do your hair for you?'

Dorothea could only nod. Her crinkly hair was the biggest disappointment of Mums' life. Every morning the two of them sat before Mums' vanity mirror while Mums wrestled with that wayward head of hers, railing at the fate that had passed on her own *bad* crinkly hair to her daughter instead of her husband's *good*, straight hair. Mostly, Dorothea closed her eyes against the pain, and occasionally cried out, but Mums was relentless, not satisfied till every strand was tugged straight against her daughter's scalp, greased with a good coating of coconut oil and braided it into two tight stiff ropes. More than once Dorothea had been tempted to saw them off where they poked down from the top of her neck.

Kathleen, her younger sister, was lucky; she had inherited her father's features, and not a single stroke of the tarbrush. Her hair fell in soft brown waves to her shoulders. *Good* hair, everyone said, to go with her fair skin, straight little nose, and lovely bowed lips. Kathleen, the Williamson aunts agreed, was the pretty one, more likely to get a white husband and move up the social scale. Kathleen was the pampered, favoured one, Dorothea, quite literally, the black sheep.

Now, Ma Quint laid her hands around Dorothea's chin and raised it slightly.

'Such a sweet face!' she said. 'And such lovely big brown eyes! Those lashes! And your skin is a perfect sapodilla brown. She's a pretty girl, isn't she Freddy?'

Freddy only cocked his head at the question, and as if to prevent further comments on Dorothea's looks, grabbed her hand and tugged. 'Come on, let's go,' he said. Dorothea managed only a quick goodbye wave and a last fleeting look at her new idol before he dragged her out of the kitchen and into the house proper.

For the rest of that afternoon Dorothea enjoyed the unique experience of being shown around the higgledy-piggledy Quint house and introduced to its various occupants. The house was huge; downstairs, there was an enormous living area with dark floorboards polished to a high gloss, and giving off a smell of lemony floor-polish. The room was furnished eclectically; cushioned Morris chairs, each patterned differently, alternating with wicker sofas or high backed wooden chairs grouped around tables. A few mats and rugs were scattered around the room. On three sides of the vast living room were windows, with no wall between them: Demerara windows with their slanting shutters alternating with plain glass, and below them, louvred wooden slats. All the windows were open, and the constant Atlantic-cooled breeze wafted across the room, in and out the windows and doors, fresh and stimulating at once. How different from the dark gloom of her own home, similarly windowed yet with the shutters kept closed to keep out the sun and the heat. Here, the combination of light and breeze immediately lifted her spirits. It was like being in heaven.

Freddy dragged her to the gallery, where she met the dour Pa, reclined in a Berbice chair, legs stretched out along the extended armrests, snoring. A book lay open, spine up, on his chest, rising and falling to the rhythm of his breathing. Before Dorothea could stop him, Freddy shook him awake.

'Pa, this is Dorothea van Dam, from round the corner!'

Uncle Henry jumped and the book fell to the floor; Dorothea picked it up and handed it back with a shy hello. Pa only blinked the sleep away and stared, as if to assess the subject of intrusion, before Freddy took her hand again and pulled her away. Upstairs, he led her through a maze of rooms, up and down stairs, and even into the Cupola at the top of the house. Most of the rooms were empty, their occupants out.

'The only time we're all in at the same time is early morning and night and Sunday before church,' Freddy explained. 'But you'll meet them all one day.'

She did meet a fair-skinned one, studying for a Chemistry exam, and a dark-skinned one, who had taken apart a radio and was putting it together again, and though Freddy told her their names she promptly forgot them, because there were so many names to remember, and Freddy was telling her all about all of them simultaneously. She wondered how she'd ever tell the brothers apart.

'Now for Humphrey, the eldest,' Freddy said. 'He'll be with Granpa, in the Annex.'

Freddy led her down the mid-air passageway that connected the Annex to the main house, and there, bent over a large table at the far end, were three men. The first was ancient, obviously Granpa. His thick horn-rimmed spectacles were held together with grubby bits of Elastoplast and wire. He held a magnifying glass in his hand, and seemed not to notice their entry, as he did not look up. The next was a young white man, blond and freckled, age impossible to guess, holding a large open book that looked like a dictionary or other reference book. Next to him, another young man, in his early twenties, perhaps; he too with a magnifying glass in hand. A variety of books, both albums and textbooks, lay open on the table before them, and scattered about the surface were myriad tiny scraps of paper. As Dorothea approached the table she saw that these scraps were postage stamps. The white man and the young both looked up at their approach.

'Granpa!' said Freddy loudly, and now the old man turned dazed eyes on her. 'This is Dorothea van Dam, from round the corner!' Mumbling a greeting, the old man held out a limp hand for Dorothea to shake, withdrawing it immediately.

The white man was introduced to her as Matt, and when he drawled out a friendly 'Nice to meet you,' Dorothea knew he was American.

Then there was the other young man. Like Granpa, this one wore spectacles, wire-framed rather than horn-rimmed.

He stared at her, his gaze fixed on her face and so deep into her eyes he didn't even see the hand she held out. And when he finally did, he dropped the magnifying glass.

Dorothea bent to pick it up, and so did he, but his glasses fell off. Dorothea retrieved both magnifying glass and spectacles, and handed them back with a smile. Today, people seemed to be constantly dropping things and she picking them up. Perhaps it meant something?

'Dorothea; Humphrey, my eldest brother,' was Freddy's introduction.

'P-p-pleased to meet you, D-d-dorothea,' said Humphrey. And continued to stare.

Chapter Six

Dorothea: The Thirties

Two things went wrong on Dorothea's return home that Sunday. Firstly, her parents had returned home before her, much earlier than expected. And then she snagged her dress on a nail when climbing back through the palings. Mums was waiting for her.

'Where on earth have you been all this time?'

'I – I went to visit a friend,' said Dorothea.

'Which friend? Do I know her?'

'Her name is Winnie,' Dorothea said, almost truthfully, and, to stave off more questions, added, 'I haven't known her very long, but she's awfully nice.'

'Winnie? Winnie who?'

Dorothea brain froze; the name, the name! It had completely fled her mind; the name Freddy had briefed her with when he brought her home. As soon as she'd seen her father's car parked in the Bottom House, she'd panicked.

'I'm not allowed to talk to boys!' she'd whispered to Freddy. 'And especially not to *you* lot!'

They stood in the alleyway behind the palings, still at some distance from the house, concealed from it by a towering bougainvillea. 'I can't let them see you! Go away! I'm going to get into trouble anyway!'

'Tell them you were with a school friend,' Freddy had suggested. 'Studying French. Or playing tennis.'

'No, not tennis on a Sunday. I can't lie, Freddy!'

'Then say you were with Winnie Cox. That's my Mum's maiden name. So it won't be a lie.'

'Winnie Cox. That's good. I'll do that. Now please go. I'll manage somehow.' She pushed him away; he grabbed her wrist and pulled her close.

'When can we meet again?'

'I don't know. Next Sunday?'

'I'll whistle. Like this:'

He stuck two fingers in his mouth and let out a piercing whistle. Dorothea blanched.

'Freddy! Don't!'

He only grinned. 'That's the signal. Don't worry, I'm off now. Good luck!'

His face hovered close to hers and for a moment she thought he'd plant a kiss on her cheek, but he didn't; he squeezed her hand once more and vanished behind the bushes, leaving Dorothea to her fate.

And now, in the firing line, the name 'Cox' had completely fled her mind. She scrambled around to remember, but couldn't. What was it? She hadn't really listened to Freddy; she'd been too scared. But there was Mums, waiting for an answer – she had to say something – quickly – something to placate Mums …

'She's a-a-a …*white!*' Dorothea grasped for the surname, but panic had wiped it out; instead, she blurted out the one redemptive word she could think of; the one feature Mums valued above all.

But Mums misheard. Or, expecting a surname, misunderstood. She frowned.

'A White? White? I don't know any Whites or – oh, you mean W-i-g-h-t – one of them?'

Dorothea nodded so as to avoid further intrusive questioning. Her mother's face lit up.

'Edmund Wight – I remember him well. He used to work in the Post Office round the corner – Carmichael and Lamaha

Streets. An Englishman; very dignified, he was, and kind to us children when we were sent to buy stamps. A very respectable family.'

That was a lucky call – the mix up with Wight and white, and Ma Quint being white, and Dorothea telling a white lie that had come about quite by accident. She nodded. At the same time, she knew of her deception and flushed hot with guilt, but Mums didn't notice; she seemed pleased. But any more questions, any more details required, and Dorothea would have to tell more lies, and she wasn't good at that; and lying was a sin. And she might end up in hell, and she wasn't too sure if today's adventures were worth an eternity of fire. *Lying is just a menial sin,* she said to herself. *Surely not!* But still, it was better to be safe.

'Well, that's good company for you. I know it's a large family; Edmund Wight had several children and they all multiplied. This Winnie must be his granddaughter. Where do they live?'

'In Lamaha Street,' Dorothea replied, returning to truth. Her hands were moist with sweat; she was skirting too far along the fringe of honesty, and she was sure her nervousness must show in her averted eyes, in her squeaky voice, in the hunch of her shoulders, which she now straightened.

Mums, satisfied that Dorothea was expanding her social circle upwards, might have continued the questioning but just then, luckily, she saw the hole in Dorothea's dress. She grabbed the skirt of it and raised the hem.

'Dorothea! Just look at that! And it's one of your best dresses! How on earth did that happen?'

'I – I – I don't know,' Dorothea stuttered, and again it wasn't quite the truth. 'Maybe a thorn, from the rose bushes?'

'We'll have to see if Ivy can fix it. Maybe she can take in the skirt. What a nuisance, and an expense. And speaking of roses – where are they?'

'Oh! Oh, I must have left them in the yard! Just let me go…' and she dashed off, back to the yard, back to the spot where her life had turned around for ever.

❆ ❆ ❆

And so began Dorothea van Dam's friendship with Freddy Quint; a secret friendship that, over the following years, would evolve into courtship. With Freddy she could talk or be silent. She could say the things she had never said to any human being. She could speak of the things that troubled her: the domination of the British in the country, for instance. Why were they allowed to dictate everything that went on? Why were white people better than everyone else, looking down on everyone else, afforded all the respect, taking all the good jobs?

'Not all of them, of course,' she acquiesced. 'Your mother is an exception. But everywhere you go, as soon as a white person turns up, everyone just starts mincing and bowing. It's so unfair!'

She and Freddy were sitting up in the tree-house, their special place; his father had built it for the older boys and it was slightly ramshackle by now, but still strong and sturdy enough for the two of them. A rope ladder hung down; brand new, as the old one had rotted over the years.

'For instance,' said Dorothea, 'I was at the library the other day taking out some history books for school. I was standing in line with everyone else. Then a white girl came up and just went to the front of the line and you wouldn't believe it – nobody protested, and the librarian served her first! It's as if she just knew she was superior to everyone else and the worst of it was that everybody else seemed to think so too!'

'Well, why didn't you protest?'

'Freddy! Those were all adult women! How could I, a sixteen-year-old girl, open her mouth in front of them? It would be so rude!'

'I think if something is just wrong, like in that case, you have a duty to speak up, Dorothea. I don't think politeness should count.'

Dorothea gazed at Freddy, her eyes alight with love. 'Freddy! You're right. The thing is, politeness and good manners have been drummed into me since I was a little girl. But you know, I don't think that's how I was meant to be. So often, I want to say things aloud, things that would anger other people, but things that are just right. And it's just a thin veneer of good manners holding me back. It's so hard to overcome your upbringing – in my case, utter and complete deference to the British, drummed into me by Mums. But once I opened my eyes, began reading the newspapers ... I had to educate myself. Mums would kill me if she knew! '

'Break through it, Dorothea. Just break through it. Speak your mind! You're meant to be a tiger, a snarling tiger fighting for her cubs.'

'In my case, my cubs are the people. The underdogs. The poor. It hurts – almost physically! – to seem them mistreated and exploited. And there's nothing I can do about it. Nothing ...'

She launched into a diatribe on colonial politics, and Freddy listened, smiling; and when she was finished he took her in his arms and she felt as if all the anger exploding within her was dissolving into him, and she was at home.

'I love you so much, Freddy!' she murmured. 'You help me to be myself, to find myself. Make me feel – good. Even though I'm not.'

'Oh you are, you are.' Freddy murmured back, his fingers massaging the back of her head. 'You're good in a very special way. Not goody-goody good: but just good, sound, solid good. You're going to go far, Dorothea van Dam!'

It was a sweet, slow courtship that was less passion than a meeting of young souls reaching out for completion; he for solid earth on which to root his roving spirit, she for the adventure and the breaking of the walls that imprisoned her, the cracking of the shell that bound her. Over time, even the Sunday secrecy of their friendship became a cage to break out of. One afternoon, they threw caution to the wind and rode their bicycles to the Promenade, the widened area of the Sea Wall where in the afternoons and at the weekends mothers and nannies took their little charges, or courting couples walked hand in hand; where a military brass band played in the circular bandstand. As they walked up the ramp, their arms almost touching, Dorothea said:

'I feel so exposed, Freddy! So – so *daring!* What if someone sees us and reports back to my parents! And yet – you know, I don't care! I'm so tired of all the hiding, all the secrecy! I almost *want* to be found out.'

They walked down the stairs to the beach and then out along the jetty, the stone wall running out towards the horizon. The tide was out; the dull brown sand baked dry in an undulating expanse stretching out towards the far-off waters of the Atlantic, and even when they reached the end of the jetty the water barely covered the sand. It was hard to believe, out here, that Georgetown itself lay six feet beneath sea level; that the Dutch had built the Wall to protect their capital – Stabroek, as it was then called – from the encroaching sea. All along the coastline, the Wall was interrupted by the sluice gates, the *kokers,* which regulated the flow of water in and out of the country. British Guiana's coastline had been wrested from the ocean; it was the only widely populated land in the colony, for beyond this coastal strip lay dense jungle, and beyond that savannahs, and then more jungle, vast acres of green stretching down to the Amazon river.

They reached the end of the jetty and Freddy took her hand. They stood in silence, gazing out to the horizon. Dorothea's heart was full. Here she was, away from her parents, and with the friend she loved most in the world! What freedom, what bliss! Her fingers reached out and found his; they clasped hands. Eventually, Freddy laid his arm around her shoulder. He chuckled.

'What's the matter?' said Dorothea, wriggling so that she came closer to him.

'Does this count as touching?' Freddy said.

'Why do you ask?'

'Because Mam told me, very sternly, that I wasn't to touch you.'

'And do you always do what your Mam says?'

'Well, when I was a boy I almost never did. Now that I'm grown up – well, nearly – I've figured that she actually does seem to know a thing or two about life.'

Dorothea knew what Freddy meant. Her new-found freedom was not just about Freddy. It was also about his mother, Winnie Cox Quint, and the home whose doors she flung wide open to allow Dorothea, for the first time in her life, to feel the embrace of a strong, warm family with a woman at its core. It was a revelation; and Dorothea felt the cold that enclosed her melting and the barrenness that plagued her bursting into life, budding and flowering. Before long she loved Ma Quint more than her own mother; and the feeling was reciprocated.

'You are the daughter I never had,' Ma Quint told her on many an occasion. 'The daughter I always wanted.'

The daughter that died, Dorothea said to herself. *The one that came before Freddy.*

'I should never have been born,' Freddy had said. 'They'd have stopped long before me otherwise. They only kept having babies because they wanted a girl.'

'How awful!' Dorothea said. 'But, Freddy, can people stop having children just by *wanting* to? I thought children just *came?* That God sent them when people got married?'

Freddy chuckled. 'You don't know a thing, do you? Hasn't your mother ever told you about the birds and the bees?'

Dorothea frowned. 'The birds and the bees? What do you mean?'

'Where babies come from?'

'Pa told me,' said Dorothea. 'From God. God sends babies to the parents, as a blessing. They are His gift to married couples.'

Freddy laughed, and stroked her cheek. 'You're adorable'!' he said 'Naiveté and mettle all mixed up. But I think Ma needs to talk to you.'

And Ma Quint did, and Dorothea listened, and blushed and lowered her eyes, so Ma Quint took her in her arms and told her there was nothing to be ashamed of or afraid of and when the time came she would love someone and one day have his babies.

'I already love someone, Ma!' Dorothea whispered.

'I know, my love, I know,' Ma Quint whispered back. 'You love my Freddy, don't you? And he loves you back. It's such a beautiful thing. You must let it grow, my dear, and God willing, it will become even more beautiful. There is nothing in the world as wonderful as love, especially young love, first love. You must tend and care for it as you would a tender plant, and one day, maybe, it will blossom into an exquisite rose. And then you will be ready.'

Dorothea understood perfectly. She nodded.

Now, standing on the jetty, she said, teasing, smiling into the words: 'And yet you're touching me! Disobeying her!'

'Hmmm – I think she meant something else.' And he pulled her even closer.

'You can touch me any time you like, Mr Freddy Quint!' she murmured, as they separated. 'And any way.'

Freddy's eyes twinkled. 'You honour me, Miss Dorothea van Dam. But you know what? I think Ma's right. I think the best things in life are worth waiting for.'

'I hope you're right.'

They walked back to the Promenade, hand in hand. Dorothea had to get back before dusk, before her parents returned; *although,* she thought to herself, *so what? Let them find out. Who cares? What can they do to me?* Yet still – her time had not yet come. She was still playing by the Rules. And then, suddenly, the Rules came to a rude end.

They had just walked past one of the several benches lining the Promenade, on which sat an elderly couple. Dorothea glanced back at them; she thought she recognised them; weren't they members of her father's congregation? And at that very moment, two middle-aged English women in flowered hats and white gloves walked up to the bench, smiled condescendingly at the black couple, and asked them to move. Immediately the couple rose to their feet. Afterwards, Dorothea marvelled at the recollection; the moment that red-hot rage descended on her, filled her being, and forced her to cry out, so loudly that people all around looked up to see what was going on:

'NO! Just NO! Don't get up!' She physically, forcefully yet at the same time gently, pushed the woman back down on to the bench. The woman, taken by surprise, let herself be pushed.

'You too!' Dorothea commanded the man: 'Sit right back down.' And he, too, obeyed.

She turned to the white ladies, who were so astonished they merely stood there, open-mouthed in shock.

'How dare you! How utterly, revoltingly *rude* of you! Where were you raised, in the gutter? You despicable people! Just go away and leave these decent people in peace! Go back to your gutter!'

The two women gasped. 'Really – I …' began one of them, but the other grasped her elbow and muttered something in her ear. The first woman seemed about to fight, to stand her ground, so the second woman spoke even louder.

'No, Penelope. Let's go. Can't you see? The natives are all watching!'

Indeed, a small crowd had gathered, for Dorothea had not kept her voice down. People were smiling and nodding, nudging each other, tittering. One man clapped. And only then did Dorothea come to her senses and fall with a thud from her cloud of outrage.

'Oh, Freddy! What have I done? Come, let's go!' She grabbed Freddy's arm and they hurried off, to a splatter of more clapping and a call or two of 'Well said!' and 'Bravo!'

Dorothea couldn't walk fast enough; she sprinted to the bicycle stand, Freddy right behind her. And only there did she collapse into his arms, half laughing, half whimpering in mortification.

'What have I done, what have I done?' she repeated through her gulps of half-laughter. 'Oh Freddy, Freddy! I'm terrible! I've made a scene and I bet you it'll be in tomorrow's newspapers!'

'You're wonderful!' said Freddy, and clasped her in his arms. 'You're my bold brave wonderful tiger. You did right. And *so what* if you're in the newspapers? You did right and I'm so proud of you!'

And they rode home, their bicycles wobbling because they were laughing so much.

To Dorothea's great relief – for her time had not yet come – the incident was not in the papers. But she had made a stand and she knew with a clear cold instinct the trajectory her life would take. It was a good knowledge.

❊ ❊ ❊

Sometimes at night Dorothea lay in her bed and listened to Freddy playing his mouth-organ. She hadn't known it was him at first. Even before they'd met she had heard those sweet, poignant strains rising above the tropical night chorus, that raucous croaking of frogs and the whistling and screeching of a thousand night creatures that starts as soon as dark descends. There was something so sad in that music, a longing for something unattainable, a mystery that could never be solved. She had not even known that the music came from the Quint house; it seemed to hover over the roofs of Georgetown, without source, played by an ethereal musician floating through space.

And then one Sunday when they were together, sitting on the Quint kitchen steps eating from bowls of grated green mango spiced with pepper-and-salt, Freddy brought out his mouth-organ and played a few bars, and she knew it had been him all along. Her excitement knew no bounds.

'There's one tune I love especially,' she said. 'Play it for me!'

'Which one? Hum it.'

And she hummed the opening bars of the melody she loved best. Freddy's eyes lit up. "Danny Boy!" he said. He put the mouth-organ to his lips and played it from beginning to end.

'It's so beautiful,' she said. 'It makes me want to cry.'

'I love it, too. When we were small, Mum used to gather us around the piano every evening and play us songs and we all used to sing along, the whole family. I miss those evenings.'

'You mean, there are *words* to it as well? It's a *song?*'

In answer, Freddy sang it for her:

'Oh Danny boy, the pipes, the pipes are calling
From glen to glen, and down the mountain side
The summer's gone, and all the flowers are dying
'Tis you, 'tis you must go and I must bide.

But come ye back when summer's in the meadow
Or when the valley's hushed and white with snow
'Tis I'll be here in sunshine or in shadow
Oh Danny boy, oh Danny boy, I love you so.

And if you come, when all the flowers are dying

And I am dead, as dead I well may be
You'll come and find the place where I am lying
And kneel and say an 'Ave' there for me.

And I shall hear, tho' soft you tread above me
And all my dreams will warm and sweeter be
If you'll not fail to tell me that you love me
I'll simply sleep in peace until you come to me.'

He had a rich, strong voice, a pure tenor that not only hit the notes but filled them with deep fervour and feeling, conjuring vivid pictures in her mind. She listened, rapt, until he'd finished. He looked up.

'Don't cry!' he said, and wiped the tears away with his fingertips.

'But it makes me cry! What does it mean?'

He shrugged. 'There are many interpretations. Ma thinks it's a father singing to his son going off to war.'

'That's so sad!'

'Don't be sad! Here, I'll play you something happy instead!' And he played 'Daisy, Daisy', and she laughed, and sang along, and the sadness blew away.

❊ ❊ ❊

All week long she longed for Sunday; in church her heart beat faster, for escape was nigh. The moment her father's car backed out of the yard she slipped between the palings, ran down the alley and navigated the Quint backyard to run up the kitchen stairs, two at a time. She grew to adore the Quint house and the loud, bumptious life within it, light and joyous, so different from the staid monotony of her own dark home. And she, who had never before questioned Pa's regime or even knew there could be life without it, felt that new thing growing within her, the thing that had shown its fangs that day on the Promenade; a small wild animal coiled in her bowels which she nourished with crumbs of resentment and even anger, so that it grew big and strong; but, caged as it was, she was safe from its gnashing teeth and scratching claws. She knew it was there, and feared it, for once let loose it would tear apart the only life she knew – and then, what next? So Dorothea learnt the secret art of beast-taming, forced her wild creature into docility, and lived by The Rules as laid down by Pa, but only on the surface. She became a skilled actress, playing the part of obedient daughter, walking the giddy tightrope between rebellion and conformity.

On Sundays she attended her father's services and more and more she knew that she was becoming that very person he warned against. The more he spoke of eternal hellfire for those who went against God's Law, the more she knew that either he was wrong, or eternal hellfire was her own destiny, and, if it were the latter, the less she cared. Dorothea knew that her father's God must be an oversized version of himself, frowning down on her with a whip in hand to keep her on the straight and narrow. Ma Quint's God was by far kinder, gentler – a caring Mother rather than a stern disciplinarian, with Ma Quint Her executive and instrument.

But then came the day when her father, God in miniature, really did stand there with whip in hand, or rather, belt. It was a Sunday afternoon and her parents were supposed to be out; didn't they always go up to Guid Fortuin to harangue the natives on a Sunday?

Not this one Sunday. It was the rainy season, and her father had braved the elements to drive up to the village – rain or shine, God's work must be done. She, too, had braved the elements. A little rain would not keep her from Freddy, so she had donned a black raincoat, pulled up the hood, and squeezed through the palings as usual. The central gutter in the alley had long overflowed its banks under the ceaseless downpour, and there was only about a foot of muddy, squishy grass between the fence and the water for Dorothea to manoeuvre, barefoot, shoes in hand. Opposite the Quint fence Freddy had laid down two planks for her to cross the gutter.

She loved the rain! She loved the thunderous downpour on the corrugated iron roof at night, roaring as if an ocean up in heaven had tilted and emptied itself on earth. She loved the sodden sky and cool wetness on her face as she raised it up, opening her mouth and closing her eyes to feel the stinging patter of rainwater on her tongue, on her eyelids and trickling in beneath her hood, through her hair roots, down her neck, under the tight white collar that was her Sunday Best.

Now returning home two hours later, in good time as she thought, it was raining even harder. Through the palings she clambered, not even glancing towards the Bottom House where the car was parked; up the back steps into the kitchen, into the drawing room, peeling off the dripping raincoat as she walked, resolving to dry off the puddles of water she left with a mop. And right into Pa, standing there in the doorway, leather belt drawn tight between his two hands at chest level. Face like thunder. Voice like God's.

'And where have you been, Miss van Dam?'

Later she was to find out that Guid Fortuin Village was so flooded the people could not leave their homes, not even for church; the church itself stood in almost two feet of water. Reluctantly, Pastor van Dam had returned home early, to an empty house and a missing daughter.

Dorothea did not answer. She stood in front of him, jaw clenched tight in defiance, not even blinking. Never once had she looked at him in this way.

'WHERE HAVE YOU BEEN?'

No answer. The livid Pastor grabbed her arm with one hand and with the other slashed at her with the leather belt, thrashing her across her back and her legs, again and again and again, hollering and roaring and calling down the wrath of God, of which he was the living instrument. The wild beast inside Dorothea leaped and snarled and pounced against the bars of its cage but Dorothea would not let it out. She would not scream at the pain, would not cry, and in the end it was Pa who gave up, locking her in her room for the rest of the evening.

There were other punishments over the coming week, too many for her to count, some too silly for her to care, such as no more sugar in her tea and no more jam on her bread. The petty punishments only fed the wild beast.

Pastor van Dam would not let her out of his sight, convinced she was whoring herself, which, in his definition, meant *speaking to boys*. He drove her to school on weekdays, kept her home on Saturdays, and on Sundays, forced her to attend the Guid Fortuin Sunday services once the floods subsided.

Nevertheless, Dorothea found ways and means of meeting Freddy. She grew devious. And she learned to lie without fear of Hellfire.

Chapter Seven

Rika: The Sixties

There it was again; a glint above the treetops, the flare of a diamond. The woman was watching her. Sometimes, the sun glanced off her binoculars and it looked like jewels shining over there, in the top corner window of the house, above the treetops of the backyard. The first time she'd seen it, three years ago, she'd recoiled in shock and fear, but then she'd grown used to it and even enjoyed it. She couldn't see who held the binoculars but she knew it was a woman; she could see the shadowy silhouette in the window. She didn't really care who it was. Much more fun to make up someone, make up a story about her:

The woman was mad, kept locked in that room (which was no longer a room, but a tower) by her husband, a tall dark man who rode a horse. The man was in love with her, Rika, only her name wasn't Rika, of course, it was something far more romantic, like Isabella, and he was desperately in love with her, and Isabella with him, and Isabella wasn't a gawky thirteen-year-old St Rose's High School pupil: she was a very grown up twenty, and she lived in a romantic place like Cornwall or Scotland or even Spain; and she wasn't brown and plain with wiry hair that knotted into thick uncomfortable mats if it wasn't kept plaited: she had long flowing blonde locks, and the man wanted to divorce his mad wife but couldn't, and it was all terribly tragic.

The man's name was … she'd tried several names but they were all far too prosaic. No name seemed good enough for him, but foreign names sounded better. She liked the sound of Jacques, but of course Jacques was merely 'Jack' in French and that wouldn't do. Maybe something Spanish, like Roderigo? Finally, she made him Italian and called him Rafaello, and he was a count, heir to a vast fortune in – in Palermo. She liked the sound of Palermo. And they were planning to run away to Palermo, Rafaello and Isabella, and there Rafaello would pretend he wasn't married, and, consumed with love, they'd live happily ever after. Just one more paragraph …

Rika scribbled away furiously in her exercise book, wrote 'THE END' with a flourish, lifted the loose floorboard in the Cupola, and slid the book into the dark space down there, to join its many mates. The bell for dinner had rung at least ten minutes ago and the last two paragraphs were maybe a bit rushed, and it wasn't as long as *Jane Eyre*, of course, but it gave her a nice warm satisfying feeling to have finished. She got up, pulled herself out of that cosy sense of accomplishment, and made her way down the steep spiral staircase of the Cupola.

They were all around the table, Marion and the twins and Daddy and Granny, and Uncle Matt, and Ol' Meanie.

Today Ol' Meanie was cross because she was late, but she'd expected that. She mumbled an excuse and slipped into her chair.

'I hope you finished all you homework,' Ol' Meanie said, in that grumbling voice of hers. It was the only way Ol' Meanie ever spoke to her. She never spoke to Marion or the boys in that voice. But then, Marion and the boys were Ol' Meanie's darlings, unlike her. Rika mumbled an answer without looking up.

'Was that a "yes" or a "no"? And look at me when you speak!'

Rika looked up and said, clearly, 'Mummy, I finished my English essay but I didn't understand the maths so I left it.'

'And you spent all that time up there struggling with maths? Eh? Two, three hours?'

'Dorothea, darling, leave her,' Daddy said. Daddy turned to her. 'Rika, if you want you can come to my study after supper and I'll h-help you with the maths.'

Rika looked up and smiled at Daddy. 'Thanks, Daddy, I'll come.' That was Daddy; always kind, always helpful, the antidote to Ol' Meanie.

Rika wished and wished that she could be the daughter that Ol' Meanie wanted. A whizz at school, and especially maths; hard-working, sharp-minded, ambitious, just like Ol' Meanie herself – a shining star at school, and, later, a Pillar of Society, the kind of person they wrote about in the papers for all the important things she'd done. Ol' Meanie was not only Founder and President of the GAWU (Rika had no idea what the organisation did, but she knew it was important); she was also Deputy Minister of Women's Progress, an entirely new Ministry created at her own suggestion (initially to be named 'Women's Affairs', which seemed a little too ambiguous) for the day when the PPP came back to power, if ever. She had also founded the Women's Rights organisations WOM, WAV and WAR; her name was constantly in the newspapers for some brilliant speech she had made or some new demand on behalf of oppressed workers or disadvantaged women. Ol' Meanie was famous.

Rika was supposed to follow in Ol' Meanie's footsteps, but she hadn't. All her school reports identified her as a disappointment: *Could do better if she made more effort. Doesn't apply herself. Doesn't pay attention. Intelligent but lazy.* That was how they summed her up at St Rose's; she was headed for Failure, with a capital F. And, knowing that she'd never live up to Ol' Meanie's hopes, expectations and ambitions, she'd found the perfect alternative, up there in the Cupola.

She was the last to finish eating but Daddy didn't wait. He pushed his empty plate away, cleared his throat, and waved a page of paper at them all.

'Children,' he said. 'There's something we need to discuss. I received this letter today, from the solicitors Crosby and Knight.' He waved the letter at them again. 'It concerns you all.'

'Pah!' said Ol' Meanie in disgust and got up. Ol' Meanie made a disappreciating *moue*. There! She'd read that expression in a book recently, looked it up, which wasn't so easy, as *moue,* she discovered, was French, and disappreciating didn't even exist, and had been just waiting to actually *see* someone doing it; and this was it; a disappreciating *moue*. She'd be using it in a story sometime soon.

Isis, who was the only creature Ol' Meanie seemed to love, landed with a thump on the floor. Ol' Meanie bent to pick her up, cuddled her and stroked her shiny ginger fur. Funny, that, how tender Ol' Meanie could be with the cat. Cuddling Isis – who pushed her face into the curve of her mistress' neck – Ol' Meanie walked to the window and looked out, her back to the family. She obviously knew what was coming.

Daddy looked at Uncle Matt. 'Excuse me, Matt, just a bit of family business I need to attend to. It won't take long.'

Uncle Matt grinned his wide American grin and waved his hand generously. 'Sure, go ahead, just pretend I'm not here. Or is it private? Shall I go away?'

'No, s-s-stay,' Daddy said, and continued, looking from one to the other of the children. 'You all know that Mummy is estranged from her own parents, your grandparents. It's a long story and rather sad but there it is; Mummy, being who she is, has always resisted a reconciliation. Over the years they have written her letters requesting some kind of a reunion, especially after Rika's birth. They were very keen to meet you grandchildren but Mummy always refused. I thought it was a pity; children need grandparents. They belong together.'

'They had Ma. Ma's better than ten grandparents rolled into one!' said Ol' Meanie, turning now to face them. Everyone looked at Ma Quint, who smiled somewhat sadly and shook her head gently, as if in disagreement, even though *she* was being complimented.

'The more grandparents, the better!' said the little brat Norbert.

'Yeah, grandparents give presents! Christmas and birthday presents!' That was Neville.

'But only if they're rich,' said Norbert.

'Are they rich?' said Neville.

'Boys! Be quiet and listen to your father!' Granny hammered her fist on the table, and the boys stopped their giggling and scuffling and turned back to Daddy.

'As it so happens, the question of money *has* entered the situation. Unfortunately.'

'Bah! Trying to buy the grandchildren!' Ol' Meanie walked up and down, still stroking Isis. Mildred, the maid, came in from the kitchen with a plate of fresh pineapple slices, which she placed on the table. Six hands reached out simultaneously to grab a slice, leaving the plate empty. Daddy paused with the slice halfway to his mouth, as if realising he couldn't both eat and speak. He put it back on the central plate where it was immediately and simultaneously grabbed by Norbert and Neville. They fought over it for precisely two seconds, whereupon it broke into two more or less equal halves, thus solving the problem. If Rika had been Ol' Meanie she'd have given the boys a slap each but of course she said nothing. Nothing was worse than spoilt eight-year-old twin boys.

'The thing is, the four of you are their only living descendants. A few years ago, your grandfather's elder brother, your Great Uncle Hendrik, passed away without progeny, leaving your Granddad a small sugar estate on the East Bank. He sold it to a neighbouring sugar estate, as he knew nothing about running a sugar cane estate; your grandfather is a pastor. You know that little church on North Road, the Church of the Second Coming? That's his.'

Ol' Meanie, hovering in the background, muttered something which sounded like 'narrow-minded old fart'.

'Be quiet, Dorothea. D-d-don't let your own resentment colour the children's perception or spoil their chances with their grandparents.' Daddy turned back to the children. 'The fact of the matter is, your grandparents only had two children; your Mummy and another girl, your Aunt Kathleen, whom you've never met. Kathleen married several years ago and moved to Canada but unfortunately had no children.'

Ol' Meanie cackled, but there was no mirth in her laughter. 'Darling Kathleen, she of the milky-white skin and soft hair! I bet they found her a nice white husband. What a disappointment; they could have bred out all that dirty black blood!'

'Forgiveness, Dorothea, forgiveness.' Granny sighed and shook her head as if this was an old, old bone Ol' Meanie was picking dry. Which no doubt it was. Ol' Meanie tended to hang on to grievances, never let them go, bring them up again and again at the most inconvenient times. But she'd never spoken of her own parents and this 'Darling Kathleen' before, not in all the thirteen years of Rika's life. Which, of course, made the whole thing intriguing; there was a story behind it, and Rika always loved a good story.

'To make a long story short,' said Daddy, ignoring Ol' Meanie, 'The f-f-four of you are their heirs. Your Aunt Kathleen will inherit half of everything and have the right to live in the house till her death, if she wants to, and the four of you get the other half, and on Kathleen's d-d-death, everything comes to you. But only if they are allowed contact with you. If not, then, it all goes to Kathleen and on her death, to the Church.'

'Buying the children! You should have returned that letter shredded into small pieces!' That was Ol' Meanie, of course.

'Dorothea, as a solicitor I have the d-d-duty to make the children aware of their rights. If you want to, you can talk to them and tell them the whole story of your quarrel with your parents, and see what they think – if it was worth ignoring them for almost twenty years. Otherwise it really is not your d-d-decision to make. You've kept them away this long, but it really is up to them to decide. They're old enough. Even the twins.'

'When they going to die?' asked Neville.

'How much money they going to leave us?' asked Norbert.

'What you going to buy? Me, I want a Rolls Royce!' said Neville.

'Pah! I want a Cessna aeroplane! I going to be a pilot!'

'Children! Let me finish! It so happens, actually, that your grandfather has been diagnosed with cancer, and it's terminal.'

'What terminal mean?'

'It something at an airport!'

'What an airport got to do with cancer?'

Here, Rika spoke up for the first time. '"Terminal" means "fatal". It means he's going to die!'

Rika already knew part of this story. She knew her mother had parents she had quarrelled with and never saw; she knew she had grandparents she wasn't allowed to visit. She even knew they lived just around the corner, in Waterloo Street. Daddy had pointed out the house a few times, and she had wondered about the old people living inside it. But she wasn't really interested in old people, not even her own grandparents. You couldn't really write stories about old people. So those grandparents had never been more that a fleeting thought.

But now, quite suddenly, it clicked. The woman in the window! The Mad Lady! This was it: the Mad Lady was her own grandmother! Her Mad Lady fantasy had been so real, she simply hadn't bothered to work out the actual, physical details of the house and its occupants. Her estranged grandparents had never even occurred to her; she never thought of them.

'I think that's so sad,' said Marion. 'The poor old people, not having any grandchildren. And our own grandfather, going to die! I want to go and visit them, soon, maybe tomorrow. You coming with me, Rika?'

'You're all going,' said Granny firmly. 'The boys, too. It's time we ended this nonsensical standoff. Really, Dorothea – you should have sent them over long ago. Now it really looks as if it's all about the money, and it isn't that at all. It's about compassion, and caring.'

'But money's good too!' said Norbert.

'There's nothing wrong with money,' said Granny, 'work hard at school, get a good job, and earn some yourself.'

'I'm going to be a millionaire when I grow up!' said Neville.

'I'm going to be a *bill*ionaire!' said Norbert.

'Daddy, what's richer; a billionaire or a trillionaire?'

And the discussion turned to jobs and careers and what each of them was going to do. Marion, of course, was going to be a nurse, and the boys would be big businessmen. And Rika? They didn't ask. Rika was the dreamer of dreams.

※　※　※

If they *had* asked Rika what career she wanted, she'd have said 'Novelist' as first choice, and 'Philosopher' as second; but of course she'd also find Romance. She wasn't quite sure how or where she'd ever meet her own special Raffaelo if she spent her time in the Cupola, but she'd cross that bridge when she got to it; she was, after all, still only thirteen.

She was an Introvert, Daddy had said, and she'd looked it up in the dictionary as she did all new words; after which she would try to use them in a story. She understood right away what 'Introvert' meant, and why being one made life so very difficult. And why it would be difficult to use someone like her a story; because Introverts were boring to other people, and so made boring characters. They were quite happy with their own company and could find contentment in things inside themselves, rather than things outside. They never needed to *do* much – just like her – and their entertainment came from quieter sources: in her case, books and films and the stories that blossomed in her own mind.

It meant that she never went to the events others found exciting, and had no friends of her own; not real ones, at least. No girlfriends, and certainly no boyfriends. People thought her odd, and she supposed she was. She was shy and awkward and never knew what to say, and the more she went her own way, the more they left her out and, she was sure, laughed at her behind her back. She really didn't like being an Introvert. She wished she were witty and chatty and vivacious. And tall, fair-skinned and beautiful. Popular, beloved by all; most of all, beloved of Ol' Meanie, who definitely didn't like Introverts. So it seemed indeed that Novelist or Philosopher were suitable professions for her. And if that didn't work out, she could always become a nun.

There were two kinds of nuns, Rika had discovered; the ones who were active, like the teachers at St Rose's, who were quick-witted and sharp-tongued, the ones who wrote those scathing comments in her reports; or like the nurses at the St Joseph's Mercy Hospital, kind and compassionate and self-sacrificing. But there were also Contemplatives; and that was the kind of nun she could aspire to. But then she read somewhere that Contemplative nuns weren't allowed to read novels or go to the pictures. Those were the greatest pleasures in Rika's life and she wasn't about to give them up. Plus, nuns couldn't marry and have children; so how would Romance fit in with being a nun? So nun was off the very short list.

She sighed. Why did one have to *Be Something* in life; why couldn't one just *Be?* She supposed it had to do with earning money. You needed money to live. So really, Novelist was best because then you could sell books and get rich. Surely Enid Blyton – whose books she'd devoured when she was younger – was rich. Very well then, that's what she'd be; but Ol' Meanie didn't seem to appreciate it.

She'd confided this plan to Granny, who was more understanding, but Granny wasn't particularly enthusiastic. 'I know English is your best subject. You can write,' she said, 'But first you must have something to write *about*. Wait until you're older and wiser. You need education, Rika. And life experience. You must try harder.'

Granny said that 'older and wiser' thing about being a Philosopher as well, all of which made Rika feel she was split in two: half of herself seemed far out of reach, sailing up in the firmaments on silver wings, beyond her grasp, beyond her means; the other half down here, trapped in a thirteen-year old body and endowed with all the wisdom of a slug. Trouble is, this earthbound half felt like the wrong half; it was the other that was real and true – but unattainable. And unrealistic. Being realistic meant peeling your mind away from those exalted flights of fancy and attaching it to boring things like household chores and maths. Rika was definitely a Mary not a Martha.

✽ ✽ ✽

Still: she wasn't completely useless. Once a week Granny took her along to St Ann's Orphanage on Thomas Road, and it was there that Rika had found a vocation of sorts. It had started three years ago, when Rika was ten. Granny had several Good Causes she contributed to in various ways. She visited the sick, crocheted doilies and made guava jam to sell at fundraisers for the Blind Society; she collected discarded but wearable clothes among her friends and relatives for the destitute old people at The Palms home, and fed and clothed the Poor and Needy. On that day, she had a bundle of children's clothes for the orphanage.

'Would you like to come with me? Charlie will be there,' Granny had asked Rika, and Rika had slammed her book shut and jumped to her feet. Of course she wanted to see Charlie again.

Rika had broken her arm a month ago, and had lain in the Mercy Hospital for a few days. In the bed next to her was a little Amerindian boy, just seven years old, named Charlie. Charlie had polio, and wore callipers on his legs. And he was an orphan.

Rika had struck up a friendship with him. The only person who came to visit Charlie was a big jolly nun called Sister Maria. Charlie didn't have a Granny to bring him home-made biscuits and fruit, so Rika shared hers with him. He didn't have a Daddy who took him to the cinema most weekends. In fact, he had never even been to the cinema in his whole life.

So Rika asked Daddy if he could take Charlie with them next time, and he had, and it was a Jerry Lewis film at the Metropole, and Charlie had laughed his head off all the way through. Rika thought they should now always invite Charlie to the pictures, but the orphanage nuns had said no – there could be no continuing special favours for just one child. She hadn't seen Charlie again; so this was a wonderful opportunity.

'Why don't you take some of your old books for the children?' Granny asked, and Rika filled her satchel with books she was too old for.

They entered the orphanage gate only to be almost run over by the stampede – if you could call this slow-paced advance a 'stampede'. Children of all ages came shambling up, hobbling on crutches, some of them even crawling, all of them laughing.

They all had callipers on their legs, like Charlie. Suddenly Rika felt shy. She hadn't properly realised what it *meant* to live in an orphanage; she hadn't realised it was an orphanage for children with polio. She felt guilty, somehow, because she had healthy legs, and they didn't.

And yet! They didn't seem to care; they weren't ashamed or unhappy about their plight, it seemed, because the joy simply spilled out of their eyes and into their laughter; they knew Granny already and swarmed around her, letting go of their crutches to grasp the hands she held out, and giggled and shouted in unmitigated glee. And then they all turned to her, Rika; all those shining joyful faces, among them Charlie's. As she reached out to shake one little hand after the other Rika felt at once small and humble yet filled with that same joy, as if *she* were the wounded one and *they* had brought healing.

A moment later a smiling Sister Maria came bustling out, arms spread open in welcome. She ushered them inside and established calm, keeping the children at bay while Granny distributed the clothes one by one. Then it was Rika's turn; she emptied her bag of books on the dining room table. 'Ooooh!' the children sighed, and it was all Sister Maria could do to keep them from rushing forward. Delight swelled in Rika as she placed one book after the other in the eagerly outstretched hands; she smiled and laughed and she longed to bend down and gather those frail little bodies with their callipered legs into her arms.

'Why not read for them?' Granny had suggested, and Rika nodded in excitement. She chose *The Magic Faraway Tree*, by Enid Blyton. Sister Maria arranged a circle of chairs for the children and helped settle them, and Rika read and drew the children into the enchanted world enclosed in those pages. And since then that was how Rika spent her Wednesday afternoons, and to this day it was the highlight of her week.

But Reader for Orphaned Children with Polio wasn't something that impressed Ol' Meanie. It wasn't something you could choose as a career. True, it did momentarily revive her ambition to be a nun, but Granny said an orphanage nun meant more than reading books to children all day; it required a *calling,* the sense of a vocation, the need to *give* one's life to God in service: a need Rika most definitely did not feel. So that was her position today: no ambition, no direction, a dreamer of big dreams and a story expert, but useless at the things that really mattered.

And every day she vowed to revise maths, learn her History dates, and *apply* herself as everyone wanted, but every day she got distracted with some other more exciting task, like developing the love story of Isabella and Rafaello. Her mind was a fickle, fleeting thing; it needed only the tiniest prod to set it flying off in the wrong direction, if not to the Great Questions of God and und the Universe, then to the half-way house of Imagination. Stories fell into her lap at the slightest hint of mystery, such as being watched by a lady with binoculars. She used to think that everyone was like that, making up stories all the time, till Granny said it wasn't so. Other people thought about practical things like sewing up a loose hem or whether the sheets needed changing or whether there was enough rice for the weekend. And maths homework.

Chapter Eight

Rika: The Sixties

Rika was not an outsider by choice, and hadn't been always such a loner, such an outsider. The few girls she'd played with as a child had drifted off over the last few years, formed new bonds and entered a world in which Rika was an alien. Jennifer Goveia, for instance; she and Jen had been thick as thieves when they were children, tumbling around in their respective backyards, collecting caterpillars and tadpoles, racing along the beach with their homemade kites at Easter. Rika was not the kind of child who ran in groups. As a child she was almost normal; shy, yes, and quiet, never speaking unless spoken to; one close friend was enough for her, and Jen was that.

Then they turned thirteen and Jen changed. Or was it *she* who had changed? Rika wasn't sure; maybe they had both changed, but the problem was: Jen was pretty, and she wasn't. Jen seemed to know how to make herself prettier yet, and she, Rika, didn't. Jen had drifted off to form friendships with girls who knew such things. Girls cared about dresses and fashion and went to fêtes; she didn't. Girls hung around in clumps on the corridors of St Rose's until the nuns came and chased them away; they giggled and squealed about arcane matters, and they knew about flirting and wiggling their hips and batting their eyelashes and flicking their hair (if they could). She didn't. The black girls didn't flick their hair, of course, but they were good at wiggling their hips and their tongues were sharp. And the East Indian girls kept to themselves, mostly, and seemed to be all superior and clever and too good for boys, so she didn't fit in with them either.

Rika was lost and tongue-tied in this world of teenage girls blooming into womanhood; a misfit, an outsider. They – at least the ones she admired, like Jen – were charming and elegant and quick-tongued. *She* was awkward and bumbling and never knew what to say; words always came out wrong and stuttering. She knew they laughed at her behind her back, and joked about her.

I'm not normal, she thought, and curled up into an inner ball. *Nobody loves me,* she feared, and the ball grew tighter. *Not even Mummy.* And that was worst of all. Daddy did; she knew that; but Daddy loved his Postage Stamps more than anything or anyone and besides saying a kind word now and then and patting her absent-mindedly on the head, he hardly *ever took notice of* her, or talked to her about things that mattered. It seemed, almost, that Uncle Matt noticed her more than Daddy did.

Uncle Matt was Daddy's friend from way back before Rika was born, and Rika's godfather. His real name was Dr Matthew Surtees and he was an American, from Chicago. Daddy and Uncle Matt were both passionate about stamp collecting, which, in Rika's eyes, was a strange thing to be passionate about because stamps were, actually, just little bits of paper. But, she supposed, you could be passionate about anything you wanted to be passionate about. Apparently the two of them had met at some International Philatelic Congress in London many years ago, before Rika was even born, and they'd been friends ever since; at first they were pen-pals exchanging news and stamps, and then more. Now Uncle Matt came to visit almost every year and sometimes he brought his wife, Aunt Judy, and when he came, he and Daddy pored over stamps the entire time.

Apart from the stamp thing, she liked Uncle Matt. As her godfather, he took a special interest in her. And though she had several real uncles – *real* meaning, brothers of Daddy – Uncle Matt was the only one who seemed to know she was even alive.

Whenever he came from America – which was practically every year – he brought a whole suitcase of books for her, all of which she devoured in a matter of weeks. She had already read almost all the novels in the Public Free Library, and she couldn't afford to buy the new books at Bookers and Fogarty's. So she would write Uncle Matt telling him which books she especially wanted, and he would bring those and some others as well, ones she hadn't even heard of: when she was younger, the Bobbsey Twins, now Nancy Drew and the Hardy Boys. Daddy said it was OK to ask Uncle Matt for books; he was a millionaire and was happy to oblige. Uncle Matt was almost family.

She was close to Marion, but Marion was three years younger, just a child. As for her brothers, the Terrible Twins: how could you be close to little devils who trapped flies under the wire-mesh food-covers, sprayed them with Flit to make them comatose, and then pulled off their wings and laughed their head off at the joke? And taunted you when you tried to rescue the flies?

Of course there was Granny, who had played the mother role all her life; but Granny had a horde of other grandchildren and loved them all equally. And Granny was a close relative; she *had* to love her. It wasn't a choice (though it was strange that her real mother had chosen *not* to love her). And the children at St Ann's, of course, who loved her because she was *there* to love, *theirs* to love – they, too, had no choice, if for a different reason: they would love anyone who came to read to them. Rika yearned most of all to be loved by someone who *did* have a choice – someone who *chose* to love her for herself; someone for whom she was special, unique.

It was hard, being so odd in the midst of such a huge family. Being a BG Quint meant you were just one out of what seemed like millions, and easily overlooked. Apart from her parents and siblings only Granny lived with them, but Granny had had eight sons, of whom two had died, but the others – all except one – had married and produced children. And since Granny was the real hub of the family, and since the Lamaha Street house was the family base, the house often swarmed with Quints, large and small. Granny always had a Quint baby or two to mind, or a few children to keep an eye on; the backyard tumbled with rambunctious boys and girls; there were birthday parties and fêtes for teenage Quints, as well as the usual festivities.

At Christmastime the house bulged and bounced with Quints; uncles, aunts and cousins. Granny would take all the children window shopping, and they'd squeal and point at the wonderful things in the lit-up windows of Bookers and Fogarty's. And after dark Daddy would drive them around town and they'd count the Christmas trees in the windows of houses, all bright and sparkling with fairy lights. On Christmas Day, Granny produced a Christmas Breakfast to die for; Pepperpot and Garlic Pork, washed down with Mauby. On Easter Sunday, Granny and Daddy and a few other aunts and uncles would walk the whole horde – anything up to twenty little Quints – to the Sea Wall, and they'd fly their kites along with every other Georgetowner under the age of fifteen. The sky dazzled with a thousand gaudy home-made kites bobbing and swaying together, each one a symbol of the Risen Christ, and the beach itself was crowded with families; fathers teaching their children the art of kite-flying, mothers comforting children whose kites had plunged and crashed.

And somewhere in the midst of all this festivity was Rika, trying her best to keep up. She went to all the *Beach Party* films with her female cousins, and the James Bond films with the boys. But she was never, really, a *part* of them all.

It was possible to feel alone in the middle of a crowd. Rika had learned that as a very young child. Not lonely, but *alone;* not the same thing. She learned that as she grew older, entering her teens. *Alone:* the times when that sense of awkwardness and bumbling ineptitude dropped from her like an old skin. *Alone* left room for solitude, and solitude she loved. She could be perfectly happy up there in the Cupola with people of her own imagination.

And yet ... someone of her own, someone who knew her, inside out. Was it too much to ask? Just one person.

She dreamed of falling in love, the way heroines did in the books she read. And because there were no heroes around, she fell in love with George Harrison. It was safe to love George, as he would never know what an ugly lumbering loner she was; George would never look down on her. She cut his picture from magazines and hung them on her wall. She went to see *A Hard Day's Night* at the Strand de Luxe, like every other girl in the country. But while they all sat together giggling in the cinema she went alone and sat alone and dreamed alone. So much love to give, but no one to give it to! She gave it to George, who did not know of her existence and could not love her back. But oh, to be loved by a real boy, one of flesh and blood!

Boys! What a strange phenomenon. She didn't know a single one. She knew her Quint cousins of course; a few were around her age, but again, they were family so that didn't count. But the Queen's College boys, who rode past her house on their way to school in the mornings and on the way back in the afternoons, in their khaki pants and yellow striped ties; the Saint Stanislaus boys she'd see in town, in their blue-grey uniform – they were alien beings.

❀ ❀ ❀

Boys didn't like her. She had the proof. Once she'd gone to Book-ers' Store after school and there they were, a little clump of Saints boys just outside the building, and there, right in front of her, was Jen and her friends walking in with a sort of swagger, their skirts hiked up two inches above the knee (if the nuns saw *that* they'd get two weeks of daily detention). The girls ignored the boys and the boys stared at the girls and one of them whistled and Jen and her friends just looked away in disdain. Rika, a few yards behind, followed them in, but nobody stared at her and certainly nobody whistled. So by the time she turned sixteen, Rika knew that her lot in life was to be a spinster. Which was not what she wanted for herself at all, but she just wasn't the kind of girl who could catch a boy, and she forced herself to resign to that fact.

In fact, the only people Rika really felt appreciated her were children: not only the orphans at St Ann's, but her various young cousins. She often helped Granny care for them; she read to the older ones and took them for walks to the Sea Wall, and she cuddled the babies. Babies did not judge you. They did not care if you were not beautiful, or not Top of the Class, or if you would grow up to be a Failure. They felt who you really were. They tuned into your heart, and all you had to do was give them your attention.

Dogs were like that, too. The family dog was Rabbit, about a year older than Rika herself, so they had grown up together. Rabbit, like most dogs in the country, was a mongrel: an affectionate, gentle creature, who wasn't much use as a guard dog. Rika would bring Rabbit into the house and into her room, cuddle her, talk to her of all the things nobody else wanted to hear. In a way, Rabbit was her very best friend.

❊ ❊ ❊

Granny agreed to take the children over to meet their maternal grandparents, and so, the following Saturday, after a flurry of telephone calls and much grumbling from Ol' Meanie, the four of them traipsed over in Granny's wake.

The house in Waterloo Street was big by Georgetown standards, though not nearly as big as the Quint house. It was also well-proportioned and agreeably balanced, unlike their own house, and freshly painted, gleaming white, again unlike their own. Like most Georgetown houses of the area it stood on a huge plot, with a flower garden at the front and a backyard like a small estate at the back, with fruit trees and a vegetable patch. Unlike the Quint backyard, which had always been allowed to run wild, a gardener only coming in occasionally to rid it of the worst excesses, this one seemed well tended.

'This is where your mother grew up,' Granny said, as she let them in the garden gate. That was so strange. They knew nothing of Ol' Meanie's own childhood. And they had forgotten to ask, as children do.

The house had an enclosed staircase to the first floor, and next to the front door, a wooden bench. An East Indian youth in a Queen's College uniform sat on it, reading a book. He glanced up as they gathered at the door and Granny Winnie rang the bell, and when he met her eye Rika smiled, to show him that she, too, liked reading. He returned the smile, then turned back to his book.

The door opened and they entered. 'Hello, Basmati, how are you?' Granny said to the plump woman who stood aside to let them pass.

'Fine, mistress, fine! How you doin'? How Mistress Dorothea?'

'We're all very well, thank you. Is that your son out there? Quite a young man now!'

Basmati frowned, and peeped out the door. When she saw the schoolboy she rushed out, crying, 'Rajan! Is what you doin', reading again! I thought I told you to sweep the yard?'

Basmati popped her head back in the door. 'Just go on up, Master and Mistress waiting for you in the drawing-room. I coming up in a minute. This boy too hard-ears.'

Basmati was every bit as good as Ol' Meanie at long-drawn-out reprimands; the drone of her nagging followed them all the way up the stairs. Rika felt a warm closeness with Rajan. She well understood the draw of a book over the mundane tasks of daily life.

❀ ❀ ❀

They made their way to the drawing room, led by Granny. Master and Mistress were indeed waiting, Master reclined on a Morris chair that had seen better days, and Mistress sat stiff-backed on an equally stiff-backed wooden chair. Rika couldn't help staring. Her grandparents!

She'd had no idea what they would look like, (apart, of course, from the crazed image of Mad Lady she had created) and so was most surprised to find that her grandfather was white – though tanned in the tough, leathery way in which white people grew dark in the tropics – and her grandmother was black, her mahogany-coloured skin hanging like a tired old wrinkled hide on the bones of her face. She seemed so much older than Granny, though of the same generation.

What would it be like, meeting her grandparents for the first time? Rika had lain awake half the night painting her own scenario. They would both come rushing forward, weeping with emotion, and gather all four grandchildren in their arms, and everyone would talk at once, and cry at once. After all, *they* had wanted this meeting, and she knew for a fact that her grandmother watched her secretly. So of course that's how it would be.

But it wasn't. They simply sat there, stiff and silent, not a flicker of feeling on their faces. Rika stopped in her tracks, not knowing what to do. Only Marion knew; Marion, in whom there was not a selfish bone. Marion, who had no subterfuge, who wore no mask. It was Marion who rushed forward, first to her grandmother, with a cry like the mewing of a cat, and threw her arms around the woman. Slow, stiff arms rose to embrace her, and now the ice had been broken the man began to push against the armrests of his chair in the vain effort to stand up, and so Marion rushed to him too and, her arms around his thin frail body, pulled him to his feet.

'Grandad! Grandad!' she cried, 'I'm so happy to meet you! I'm Marion, and look, this is Rika, and Norbert and Neville!'

Rika couldn't move. She was overcome with a sudden shyness; she wished then she could be more like Marion, outgoing and warm and wearing her heart on her sleeve, but she wasn't and never would be. It was only when she saw a tear trickling down the old man's face that she, too, took a hesitant step forward; Marion let go of him and passed him to Rika, who gingerly took him in her arms. The old man mumbled something in her ear and then, to her horror, she felt him trembling, and a moment later she was holding a violently sobbing man in her arms. Over his shoulder she flung a desperate look at Granny, who, with all the expertise of a woman who knew the human heart and how it works, sorted them all out, sat them all down around the coffee table, summoned Basmati to serve them drinks and snacks, and led the way into the obligatory getting-to-know-you conversation, small-talk which covered every subject under the sun except Ol' Meanie.

The woman in the Tower, Rika discovered, was not in the least bit mad. She was just a sad, bitter little old lady hungry for something she, Rika, could give. She promised herself to visit as often as she could.

❊ ❊ ❊

When they left the house it was growing dark and the light was on downstairs. The boy named Rajan was still reading, or rather, reading again, having presumably swept the yard. Rika lingered as the others walked towards the gate. She was not usually the type to speak first, and never started conversations. But there was something about this boy and his absorption in the book …

'What are you reading?' she asked. He held up the book so she could read the title herself.

The Book of Mirdad, she read. It was a slim book, rather tattered. It gave off a sweet, pungent smell which reminded her of the Hindu stalls outside Stabroek Market, decorated with kitschy prints of gods with elephant heads and four arms, sticks of incense giving off long winding tendrils of fragrance.

'What's it about?' she asked. The boy looked at her with dark, soulful eyes; eyes which seemed to scour the last depths of her soul. At first he did not answer; he took his time. Finally he spoke.

'It's about how to find God,' he said.

Rika sat down next to him. 'Really! Is that possible?'

The boy smiled. 'If you know where to look, then maybe, yes,' he said.

'But I'm not sure if I even believe in God. My mother doesn't. I'm not even baptised. But Granny does and I go to St Rose's, so it's all a bit mixed up. I used to want to be a nun but I changed my mind, and I've been having doubts, thinking about the whole thing, God and everything. I mean, what's it all about? What's the point of everything? Why are we here anyway? Mummy's an atheist and I've been wondering if I should become one too. What church do you go to?'

She was amazed at herself. Where did these words come from? How come she was speaking at all, and to a stranger; she, who was so tongue-tied her brain would freeze over when obliged to converse?

'We're Hindu.'

More words came, involuntarily.

'Oh! There are a few Hindu girls in my class. Mummy says the fact that there are so many religions is proof that they're all man-made myths.'

Rajan only chuckled.

'She says the notion of a man up in the sky and heaven and hell and so on is just made-up.'

Rah smiled, and nodded. 'Oh, I agree about that – the man in the sky and all that. I don't believe in him either.'

'What do you believe, then? Hindus have lots of gods, don't they? I've seen all the pictures of them at the market.'

'Hindus don't all believe the same thing,' said Rajan, 'the one thing we all agree on is that there are many paths to God, and they are all valid, and they all lead back to the same source, like all rivers flow to the ocean.'

He stopped speaking then, suddenly. Maybe he wanted her to go, was waiting to get back to his book – she knew the feeling. But she couldn't let him. It was extraordinary; the fact that she had started this conversation, even though she was known to be shy; and that she had continued it, and told him so much about her family, and asked so many questions. But the words and the questions seemed to gush from her; she couldn't stop them.

'That's very – *cryptic,*' she said. She had never used the word 'cryptic' before. It was a new word; she'd read it somewhere that week and looked it up in the dictionary. She'd been looking for a chance to use it, though normally she'd use these new words in writing, not in speech. But trying to get words out of Rajan was like pulling up a tree by its roots. There was something cautious, reticent about him, which made her all the more curious.

'Mummy says nobody can prove the existence of God and so He doesn't exist. She says she only believes things that science can prove.'

This time, Rajan laughed out loud.

'What's so funny?'

'Well, look, Rika: *if* there *is* a God, a final intelligence and power behind all this …' he waved his arms is if to enclose the world, 'don't you think he would have invented science itself? So how could science prove the intelligence that is antecedent to it?'

Antecedent. She would have to look that word up, but for now she could guess its meaning.

'You mean – *before* science? The *source* of science?'

'Yes. I'll make it simple. For instance: an all-powerful creator God would have had to invent the laws of science, so that this universe actually functions. He'd have to figure out all the complications of the human body, and create flesh and blood, hair and nails and everything. He'd have to figure out how to make a couple of planets, and toss them up into a vast sky, and have them rotating and spinning. He'd have to dig the ocean beds and fill them with water. And so on. I mean, what is *our* human intelligence and power compared to that?'

Rika laughed. 'I guess, a bit like an ant compared to a human, right?'

'Exactly! More like an amoeba in relation to a human. Imagine an amoeba trying to figure out the existence of humans! Trying to prove that humans exist! I mean, I'm sure amoeba have their own intelligence, and are smart in their own way, but I think understanding humans would be beyond their reach. So if there *is* a Power behind all this, a higher intelligence we call God, humans trying to prove its existence is just like amoeba trying to prove the existence of humans.'

'And if there *isn't* such a Power? No God?'

'Well, if there isn't, then all this ...' again he spread his arms wide, 'all this is just a fluke. It all happened by accident.'

Rika shuddered; a sense of awe ran through her, an icy chill down her spine, yet the next question was already rising to her lips.

'So, what then? Let's say, there is a God, and he isn't a man in the sky, then what and where is he? If we can't prove his existence – where should we look for him? Does that book tell you?' She pointed to the book he still held, a finger between the pages acting as bookmark. She was interrupting his read-ing – almost a crime, if you loved reading. But she couldn't help herself.

'He's right here in our hearts: the living consciousness in all of nature; humans, animals, plants.' The answer came without hesitation. 'He is the self of our self, the core of our being, the substratum of our consciousness.'

'*Substratum?*' Another new word.

'The foundation. The bedrock. The source.'

'Oh. And that book...' she pointed to it again, '...tells us how to find him? I mean, you said yourself we can't figure him out.'

'Yes.'

'How?'

'Through love. Love with a capital L.'

'Oh.' It was as if she was suddenly struck dumb. No more questions came. Then,

'Can I borrow it, when you've finished?'

'Well ...' He hesitated. 'Well, you can borrow it now. I've read it before. I'm reading it again but I can lend it to you if you really want. But it's a bit hard to understand.'

He handed her the book, and she took it with delight, and smiled at him. 'But I'll have to hide it from Mummy. She'd say it's all nonsense.'

'You have to find your own way,' Rajan said. 'We all have to. It's good to question things and dig deep for answers. It's good to question and keep questioning.'

'I will,' said Rika, and hugged the book to her as if it were precious. She should leave, now, but still felt rooted to the spot, curious about this boy.

'Are you here a lot?'

'I live here,' said Rajan, and pointed to a room at the back of the Bottom House. 'That's my room. My mother lives upstairs and looks after the old people and does all their cleaning and cooking. I look after the garden – after school, of course.'

One question led to another and Rika discovered that he was in his final year at Queen's College and hoped to win the British Guiana Scholarship and go to England and study medicine.

'Really! So you're good at school? I'm terrible, except in English. And French. And Latin. But only maths counts really and I'm terrible at that. You can't get a good job without maths. That's what everyone says. A job in a bank, I mean.'

Her face crumpled. 'That's the main reason my mother hates me. I'm so bad at school, so dreamy, and I'm terrible at maths.'

'I can help you, if you like,' said Rajan. 'It's my best subject.'

Chapter Nine

Rika: The Sixties

And so, at last, Rika had a friend.

He might be a boy, but he was not like at all other boys; more like a girl, in that she didn't need to be pretty for him or wiggle her hips; but then, *not* like a girl, as she didn't have to pretend to be interested in fashion and catching a boy. Rajan shared her great interest in Philosophy. Rajan understood about wondering what it was all about, and he didn't find it boring to discuss vital matters such as *Who am I?* and *Where do Thoughts come from?* And *What is Happiness?* In fact, she and Rajan could talk for hours on such subjects and never grow bored, and Rajan had some interesting views and explanations.

Most practically, Rajan was good at maths, and helped her with her schoolwork, which improved drastically as a result so that Mummy ceased complaining, and lost the title of Ol' Meanie. Almost every afternoon after school, every Saturday and Sunday, every free moment she could wrest from life – except for Wednesdays at St Ann's Orphanage – Rika spent with Rajan. She soon discovered the short cut through the alley – a gap in the palings at the back of the yard, and a corresponding gap in her grandparents' fence - and escaped as often as she could. The hours alone in the Cupola gradually diminished to zero. A best friend, at last; one who knew her inside out. Knew her soul, which was what she'd always yearned for.

* * *

Over the next few years, many dramatic changes took place. Both grandfathers died. Rika moved into her paternal grandfather's room in the Annex, and inherited from her maternal grandfather, along with each of her siblings, a bank book with what seemed to her a fortune in savings, to be administered by Granny until she turned eighteen. The rest of Grandpa's inheritance would come to all four children on Grandma van Dam's death. The latter, meanwhile, withered into a mental decay which kept the grandchildren at bay; visits became more and more seldom and finally dropped off altogether. Only Marion cared enough to keep calling, and then only once a month.

❊ ❊ ❊

But it was the country itself that had gone through the greatest upheavals, and Mummy had played her role throughout. British Guiana's struggle for independence was already legendary. The PPP, led by the Indian Cheddi Jagan and the African Forbes Burnham won the 1953 elections in a landslide. Dorothea, though young, became the Minister of Women's Progress, a new and startling position. Cheddi Jagan began to implement the long-promised social reforms, which would eventually lead to Independence. But his reforms were too radical for Britain: in October 1953, the democratically elected Government of British Guiana was removed from power by the British Government. Claiming that there was a danger of Marxist infiltration; Britain suspended the constitution and sent in the troops to 'restore the peace'.

'What peace?' Dorothea Quint had railed, quite publicly. 'We are already at peace!'

But it was too late. The Ministers of the Government – of which Dorothea was one – as well as the House of Assembly, were dismissed by the British Governor, who proceeded to appoint an interim Government, with Forbes Burnham, Cheddi's one time coalition-partner and soon-to-be arch enemy, at the helm. Many leading members of the

PPP – including Dorothea – were detained without trial. ('Mummy was in jail!' Dorothea's children boasted) and, under a state of emergency declared by the Governor, civil rights were suspended. But the PPP rallied itself, and won the 1957 elections, and again the 1961 elections.

That was too much for Britain. Following the orders of the US Government, the British colonial rulers changed the electoral system from first-past-the-post to proportional representation, and ordered elections for 1964 – reneging on a previous agreement to grant independence before any further elections. Under the new election rules the PNC won in a coalition with the United Force; Forbes Burnham became Premier of British Guiana.

On May 26, 1966, British Guiana became an independent country and was renamed Guyana. The PPP was forced into retreat; as a member of the Opposition Party, Dorothea Quint became the Shadow Minister of Women's Progress. Years of racial unrest, economic mismanagement, and finally chaos followed. Guyanese fled the country in hordes, emigrating to the Promised Lands of the UK, the USA, and Canada in a brain drain that would rob the country of many of its best and brightest. But not Dorothea. She stayed, and fought on.

❊   ❊   ❊

As Shadow Minister Mummy, a Leftist by nature, grew ever more involved with matters of greater import than Rika and her concerns; she fought on a thousand fronts for women, the poor, the downtrodden, and was more outside the house than in it, seen only at mealtimes and then only occasionally.

As ever, Rika and Marion were close, as close as sisters could be who were so radically different: Marion down to earth and practical, outgoing towards others and loved by all; Rika withdrawn, introverted, awkward, impractical. Rika, the

quintessential dreamer, was deemed unfriendly and unap-
proachable by others, whereas it was only that she lacked the
skills of small-talk and feared judgment.

Towards her brothers she felt nothing but alienation. Recently, alienation had turned to rancour. This was because
of Devil. Rabbit, Rika's beloved dog (though he was actually
the family dog, not specifically hers) had died of old age; and
a few days later a new puppy entered the house. Rika was
overjoyed; a puppy all her own, to train and love and cuddle!
But to her shock Mummy insisted the puppy be given to the
twins: it was their birthday after all. Rika had complained to
Daddy. The twins knew nothing about raising a dog! They
did not even *like* dogs!

'Mummy thinks it will help them,' said Daddy. 'She thinks
giving them the responsibility of caring for a puppy will steady
them and make them more conscientious. I think she might be
right. It was our joint decision, Rika. Please accept it. Rabbit
was yours all these years; give the boys a chance.'

But Rika knew the boys would be terrible as dog-owners,
and she was right. For a start, the horrible name they chose for
the puppy. Their first choice was 'Satan', but Granny put her
foot down.

'No Satan is coming into *this* house!' she insisted, and since
Granny always had the last word, the boys grudgingly agreed
on 'Devil'. And Granny grudgingly allowed it. After which the
boys proceeded to train poor Devil to live up to his unfortu-
nate name.

How did they do it? Rika had no idea, as it was done secretly at the back of the yard, behind the highest bushes and
too far away to be heard from the house. The boys would disappear there every afternoon with Devil. Sometimes, they took
household articles with them, like the pointer boom and the
cobweb pole. Once, Granny caught them stealing a chunk of

meat from the kitchen. Rika herself only found out when, on her way to Rajan through the back yard, she heard the angry yells, the excited frustrated yapping emerging from the bushes, eventually turning into nervous barking and then growling, snarling, howling.

She had tried to intervene, though she knew intervention was useless. Years ago she had tried to stop the boys pulling out flies' wings, too:

'How would *you* like it,' she had said, 'if someone pulled out your arms?' The boys had only teased her. This time, she said: 'You're devils yourself! That's wicked, what're you doing to that poor dog? ' But the boys only laughed at her and sneered.

'No more sissy Rabbits in this house!' said Neville.

'You'll see what a *real* dog is like!' said Norbert.

And that was that. She longed to report them to the grown-ups; but the Quint adults did not approve of tale-telling. She tried visiting Devil herself, to counteract the wickedness with love; but all she got for her trouble was snarls and bared teeth, and she backed away quickly.

The final result was a dog so vicious he could not be left to run free in the yard but had to be kept leashed in the Bottom House. There, Devil would greet every person that entered the gate or came down the stairs or went up them or walked past him with the most blood-curdling snarls, his lips drawn back to reveal fangs that looked ready to rip the flesh from any living being, without distinction between friend and foe; the only exceptions to this treatment being Neville and Norbert.

It was the one and only time Rika had ever seen her mother express anger or even mild displeasure at the boys. Mummy loved dogs, and somehow the boys had kept their specific training from her until it was too late to intervene. The result was a tongue-lashing to make the *real* devil, if he existed, smile. Rika smiled too, to herself; she had recently come across the word '*Schadenfreude*' in a novel, and looked it up, and found it described brilliantly her feelings.

They could not get rid of Devil, since no one wanted him; they were stuck with this beast in the Bottom House. The episode, for Rika, had revealed the basic nature of the twins. There could never be any closeness with them, for, it seemed, they lived on a different planet to her – one where kindness and compassion were foreign words, untranslatable.

Finally, it was Rajan who came to the rescue. Rika, complaining to him about the boys in general and their training of Devil in particular, said, in passing, 'I can't even walk through my own yard without that dog barking his head off. If he wasn't tied down I'd be in mortal danger! I wish I could send those boys *and* the dog to the moon!'

'Well, I don't know about the boys, but you could send the dog to the Pomeroon. I know a man there who retrains bad dogs. Gets them as tame as lambs.'

'Really?'

'True. He's famous for it up in Essequibo. No matter how vicious the dog. I've seen it myself. They call him 'the Dog Man' up there; he just has a way with dogs. They all love him and he treats them well and somehow, like magic, they change. He lives just outside Charity; his name's Balram Singh. My grandparents know him well. The retraining takes about six months.'

'You think you could ask him … about Devil?'

'My grandparents could ask him. I'll find out for you.'

And so it was that Devil left the Quint household and went to the Pomeroon to be turned into a lamb. The boys sulked; it was the only time, in Rika's memory, that they had been forcibly denied a thing they wanted, or punished for any misbehaviour. It was good to see the twins howling with rage and nobody taking any notice. Yes: unabashed *Schadenfreude*. But

most of all, she was happy for Devil. When he returned to the
household all sugar and spice, she, Rika, would become his
friend and, maybe, rename him 'Angel'. In a rare moment of
collaboration, Mum had promised her: the rehabilitated Devil
would be hers.

❋   ❋   ❋

Granny Winnie, as always, was the adult pole in Rika's life,
the guiding steady light. Together with Granny she had finally
worked out what she wanted to be: a Librarian. That meant she
could work in the most hallowed building in Georgetown, the
Public Free Library, surrounded by the most precious objects
life had to offer. She could pair people up with books, change
their lives with literature. What could be better?

True, Granny had been sceptical at first.

'The thing is, Rika,' she said, fetching the pestle for the foo-
foo. Rika had joined her in the kitchen; in the background, Pat
Boone crooned on about 'April Love'. 'There's really only one Library to speak of in Georgetown, and only a few librarians; they
are all well-established women who have been there for donkey's
years and I doubt there will be another job available when you're
ready to start work. Librarian jobs are limited in Guyana.'

The cooked and peeled green plantains lay in the stone
mortar on the floor. Granny began pounding them, solidly,
rhythmically. Pat Boone sang of April showers.

'Well, I could – maybe …' Rika thought for a while. 'I could
go to England! There're tons of libraries there! And bookshops!
I could easily find a job there!'

Granny stopped pounding to give Rika a big smile and
some serious attention. She switched off Pat Boone and put
both hands on Rika's shoulders.

'That's a wonderful idea, Rika! But you know, you'll need a
bit more than O Levels to get a librarian job in England. You'd

have so much competition! You'll need a few more qualifications!'

'A Levels?' Rika looked doubtful. It was bad enough having to sit for her O Levels next year; she had hoped that that would be the end of school. Should she continue on to the next stage? Extending the torture of sitting to attention in front of a teacher?

'Definitely. You could do English Language, English Literature, and French. Or even Latin, or Spanish. Why not?'

'Do you really think I could? Could I drop maths?'

'Yes, of course! And then, you know what, Rika? You could maybe even get into University in England! Study English! Nothing but books, all day long!'

'Wow!' Rika was stunned into silence. Then she looked up, and smiled. 'Really?'

'Really! Wouldn't that be wonderful!'

It sounded like paradise. And besides: Rajan would be there.

But, now that she had Granny's attention, there was something more she had to ask; something more important, even, than Rajan.

'Granny?'

'Yes, darling?'

'Why does Mummy hate me so much?'

'Oh, darling!'

Granny carefully leant the pestle against the wall and gathered Rika into her arms. 'Is that what you think? It's not true! Oh, that woman! Lord, have mercy upon her! She doesn't hate you, Rika, I promise! She loves you! Deep down inside she really, really loves you.'

'But then why is she so cold and so horrible to me? She loves the boys much more. Look how they got Devil! I really wanted a puppy of my own, but they got Devil. And she just wants me to be *different*. Bright, and forceful, like she is.'

Granny just kept hugging her, kissing her cheek. It felt so good, to be hugged.

'I don't think she even knew how much that hurt you – giving the boys the puppy – but it's not because she loves the boys more! Don't ever believe that!'

'But then why? Why? Mothers love their children. I don't know any mother as cold as she is.'

'Oh darling! Why d'you … look, she might be a bit harsh sometimes, but it's not deliberate; not personal. She's also been good to you lots of times. You've maybe forgotten. Remember the bicycle?'

Yes. Rika did. Christmas Day, when she was eight years old. Running down the stairs in excitement, and there, next to the tree, completely wrapped in bright red wrapping paper, her very first bicycle – the best present she had ever had. She had whooped with joy, throwing herself on Mum, who had responded with the rarest of smiles – almost a better present than the bike; and then given her a big warm hug. Christmas in general was a time when Mum seemed to soften and relax and be more – well, more like a real Mum. She couldn't deny it.

'Yes,' Rika conceded. 'That was nice. But it was the exception. Mostly …'

'And the Pony Club? You know it was your mother who really supported that expense? Your father is so frugal and he didn't know if it was worth it. Your mother insisted. She said it would be "a wonderful experience for you". Her exact words.'

'Oh!' said Rika. She didn't know that. She had been nine, and, inspired by her favourite book of all time, *My Friend Flicka*, she had developed a burning desire to be among horses and learn to ride. Yes – she recalled now that Mum had been in favour of that hobby. The one thing she and Mum shared was a love of animals; and Mum had even come out with her the first couple of times, walked with her through the stable, stroked the horses' noses. The Pony Club had closed down a few years later for unknown reasons, leaving a vacuum in Rika's life.

'Still,' said Rika now, 'Mostly she's just cold and mean. She really acts as if she hates me.'

'Oh Rika. It's awful that you feel that way. She has her reasons – it's just, well, it might be too hard for you to understand, but I think she's just afraid of love. Afraid of loving too much.'

'But why? Why? Love is beautiful, Granny. There's no such thing as loving too much. It's just impossible!'

'The thing is, once you love – really love, I mean – you're vulnerable. You're susceptible to getting hurt, to losing the one you love. And some people protect themselves by trying not to love. They built a shell around themselves so that the love doesn't get out. But it's there. Deep inside it's still there.'

'Did Mummy lose someone she loved?'

'Yes, darling, she did. And one day I'll tell you the story; it's a long one and I've got to finish the cooking but I'll tell you. Because I want you to know: you should never be afraid of love, or getting hurt. You have to understand that love doesn't come with a guarantee certificate. Once you love you're open to loss. It's only when you're prepared to take the risk of pain along with the joy of love that you truly understand what love is. That's when you really become worthy of love, and truly strong: when you can take the pain and face it bravely, grow through it. Your mother, I'm afraid, has let her pain make her bitter. And withdrawn. And unjust. And it seems you feel it the most of all her children. But now – run along, I have to work. Think about what I said!'

She switched the radio back on. It was Nat King Cole singing 'Mona Lisa'.

Rika ran straight to Rajan. Granny would never have time to tell her the story; she had once promised to tell her own love story, the story of how she met Granddad; but like all other stories it had drifted into the background. Practical matters always took priority with Granny. 'We can't dwell in the past,' Granny always said. Rajan, on the other hand, always had time for her; and Rajan had already dropped hints on this very matter.

❄ ❄ ❄

Rajan had not won the coveted British Guiana Scholarship; but it was still his goal to study Medicine in England. On leaving school with top A Level results he got a desk job at the Bank of Baroda. His plan now was to work at the bank for two or three years, take on gardening jobs, sell as much produce as he could at the Market, save all his money, and apply for a part-scholarship at the University of London. Hopefully, this one he'd win. Rika was certain he would, but, on the other hand, then he'd leave her here, alone. The thought was terrifying. She was still as far from being *normal* as ever; possibly worse, due to this strange friendship with Rajan, and the ideas he put into her head. But what if she, too, went to England, to study Literature and become a Librarian? Then she would still have her best friend.

In his spare time Rajan worked the garden and turned it into a lush paradise, a secret place hidden from the street by gigantic flowering hibiscus hedges lavishly spilling multi-coloured blossoms both within and without. Birds and butterflies made this garden their realm; Rajan, the ubiquitous cutlass as his sceptre, reigned over it with expertise and love. His subjects, the plants, thanked him with bright abundance; almost gaudy, the riot of colours bestowed by bougainvillea, frangipani and oleander. Other flowers – lilies, marigolds, roses, poinsettia – bowed low as if in adulation as he walked the sandy pathways of the front garden, digging up weeds with his cutlass tip or slashing away dead branches, sometimes even whispering to them with love as he bent to raise a bloom to peer into its depths, or to smell its fragrance.

The back yard, on the other hand, he had transformed into a farm. Banana and coconut palms lined the outskirts of the property, while citrus and local apple trees bestowed fruit in season: mammy-apple, golden-apple, custard-apple. There was a sapodilla tree and two mango trees and towering above them all, the genip tree. At the back of the property, Rajan had created his vegetable patch where he grew tomatoes, bora beans, and pumpkins, as well as herbs and spices: coriander, parsley, thyme and wiri-wiri pepper, and healing herbs whose secrets he had learnt from his farmer grandparents: arrowroot, aloe, sweetbroom, noni and more.

Now, Rika slipped through the palings into Rajan's kingdom. She found him digging a hole, a young mango tree with its earthen root-ball lying on the ground beside him.

'Hi,' she said. He looked up and grinned.

'Hi! What's up?'

'Umm – nothing.'

'Liar! You're just bursting with questions. What is it this time?'

'You know me too well.'

'No – it's just that you're so transparent. What is it? But make it quick – when I finish planting this tree I need to go to the market.'

She hesitated, and then jumped in feet first. 'Well – you know I keep asking you to come over to my place and you keep saying no, you wouldn't be welcome. And I asked Gran and she said she wouldn't mind but Mummy would. And Gran says that Mummy had some kind of a tragic love-story. And you know that Mummy won't visit her own parents. And you drop hints now and then about my Mum and your Dad – and – and … well, I just get the feeling there's something there I need to know. A connection between all these things. Some story. Something people keep hiding from me. And I think you know it. And I want you to tell me.'

Rajan looked away, and stabbed the spade into the earth with violence.

'I said make it quick, Rika, and that story would take all afternoon. Another time.'

'Please!'

But Rajan stayed firm. It wasn't often that he denied her anything. This was one of those times.

✳ ✳ ✳

Rajan's garden became a second home for Rika. No matter how hard he worked, he always had a moment's time for her. Sometimes he would take a break; wash his hands and go into the house and return with a perfect golden mango, along with a plate and a knife. He'd cut the mango for her and they would eat it while he talked. Sometimes his mother Basmati prepared chow-chow for her, grated green mango with pepper-and-salt, brought out to her on a plate. Sometimes Rajan would hack a green coconut from the tree, toss it into the air while slashing off the top with three or four swift strokes; with a final flourish he'd cut away the top to create a hole in the nut. He'd stick a straw into the hole, and with a smile and a nod, hand it to Rika.

While she sat on the swing, she'd sip at the sweet clear coconut water while Rajan, sitting on the bare earth before her, would tell her stories of the backlands and the bush and the forest. He had spent his forgotten early years in Georgetown; after his father's death, his mother had taken him and his siblings back to his grandparents' farm on the Pomeroon River. There he had grown up, a happy barefoot boy who went to school by boat, never happier than with his hands in the earth. When he won a place at the prestigious Queen's College, his mother brought him back to Georgetown and since then they had lived at the Waterloo Street house where Basmati had been given the job of carer for the ageing van Dams. A job, as it turned out, which had been found for her by Granny.

❊ ❊ ❊

Rajan brought light into Rika's life. Rajan *knew* her, he *saw* her. For him she was not strange; her being 'different' was not a source of derision for him. Most of all, he nourished her with books; and for the first time in her life, she devoured non-fiction.

She discovered René Guénon, and others of his ilk. Being is divine, she read; Divine Being is the essence of the human soul! That was the essential teaching of all religions, proclaimed openly, as in the Eastern religions, or veiled and secret as in Christianity and Islam. The Kingdom of Heaven is within you! *Within you,* quite literally! To be *experienced*, here and now! All religions are unanimous in their essence, and though incompatible and contradictory in their external applications, doctrine, theology, and rituals, that was their final teaching, their final truth: that God is the Self of our self, waiting for us at the core of our being. Her heart soared. This was IT, the nourishment she had hungered for.

She read books with arcane titles: *The Cloud of Unknowing* and the *Book of Mirdad* and *The Way of a Pilgrim*; scriptures of the old traditions, the *Tao te King* and the *Vedas*. She learnt of the Christian Mystics and the Sufis and the great sages of India, Shankara and Ramakrishna and Ramana Maharshi. She drank it all in, and talked it all through with Rajan. But *The Book of Mirdad* remained the best, her Bible, her source of wisdom and joy; whatever she found hard to understand she discussed with Raj, her friend, her mentor.

But in spite of all the comfort and confidence this friendship and mentoring gave her, still a part of her yearned for normality, yearned to be just one of the others. It seemed an impossible dream. Jen Goveia and her cronies lived in a universe light years away from her own. The sense of rejection – by her mother, by her peers – ran deep, and could not easily be dissolved by the newfound light. It was as if she were split in two: at home with Rajan and the secret kingdom of books, and leaning out, grasping, aching for a foothold in real life, in the real world.

She wanted so much to belong, to be just like other girls her age; to fit in. She tried to keep up with her own generation by a subscription to the American *Teen* Magazine – a birthday present from Uncle Matt – but it was all theory; in practice, she failed at every level. She lived in two worlds, one foot in each: the ethereal world of the spirit, where she felt at home, light-footed and true, and the very physical world of people and things, where she continued to be a misfit, an outsider, bumbling as ever before, and yearning to fit in. How could she ever bridge the gap between these two planes of existence? Was it even possible? And Jen, the lost friend of her childhood, remained the epitome of this longing. Perfect, lovely Jen.

❊ ❊ ❊

And then, all of a sudden Jen had a boyfriend; a real live boyfriend like the ones in *Teen*. His name was Donald deSouza, and he was Portuguese, like Jen (who was half-Portuguese) and he went to Saint Stanislaus but he was *old* – probably in Sixth Form already. He was one of those boys who hung around at Bookers' Snack Bar eyeing up girls in uniform, whistling at them and calling out compliments.

Though she couldn't identify most of the boys by name, she did know Don, because who could miss him? He was the handsomest of the lot – *evil,* the girls all said – with chiselled cheekbones, Elvis sideburns (she couldn't imagine how he was allowed those at Saint; usually they were forbidden, just as girls were forbidden hair decorations and short skirts at St Rose's) and a long lanky frame. He was loud and cocky and very popular; he had a motorbike – the very zenith of coolness – a red Yamaha, and a really *evil* nickname.

All the boys had nicknames, she knew that much, and Don's nickname was 'The Jaguar' – 'Jag' for short. Jen, having snapped up the most popular boy in town, now soared into the upper echelons of teenage society, invited to all the fêtes and courted even by older girls, Sixth Form girls. Jen had *made it*; Jen *belonged*.

Rika had never actually *seen* Jag and Jen together (what an evil combination of names!) – it was strictly forbidden to talk to boys while in school uniform, and Rika and Jen hadn't been anywhere together out of uniform for years – but Rika was had always been a listener; and she picked up all the gossip at school, before classes, in the corridors, at the bicycle stand, during break. She listened in because otherwise how was she ever to learn about real life? You had to learn about life to become a novelist.

Then came the day that everything changed. Rika had gone to the library after school to return some books and borrow new ones, after which she popped over to Bookers to get a new pair of tennis shoes; she'd had a growth spurt recently and everything was too small or too tight or too short; her feet, her blouses, her skirts. School skirts could be let down – this she did herself – and Granny had had her measured for new white blouses – this time with darts! For a growing bust! – but shoes would have to be new. She wheeled her bike across Main Street and parked it outside the eastern entrance to Bookers. She locked it and walked into the store and through to the shoe department. Shoes tried on and bought, she wandered over to the book department to see if they'd brought in any new books since last week – they hadn't – after

which she decided to have a milkshake at the snack bar. She
made her way over there, and stopped.

The bar was full; not only full, but overflowing. Three or
four girls in St Rose's uniforms sat at the bar giggling and sucking at ice cream sodas and milkshakes, their stools swivelled
around to face the gaggle of boys in Saints uniforms fidgeting
in the standing space before them, eating hamburgers and hot
dogs and drinking Cokes and things like that, and flirting. Rika
didn't know these boys, though she had heard their nicknames:
Bonesy, and Rats, Pumpkin and Hotshot and, of course, Jag.
Hobnobbing like this in school uniform was of course strictly
forbidden. Should any of the nuns or lay teachers pass by there
would be deep trouble for all concerned, but school rules were
made to be broken; that much Rika knew. Granted, she had
never had the chance to break them herself in *this* particular
way, because of course no boy would ever speak to her. She was
just too ugly and boring. She shrank into herself.

One of the girls was Jen; one of the boys was Jag. Somebody
made a joke and everyone laughed. Probably they were laughing at *her*. There was no spare seat at the bar, so Rika turned to
walk away; she wasn't all that keen on a milkshake any more.

But a cry brought her up short: 'Hey!' She swung around,
frowning; it was a boy's voice, short and sharp. Not for her,
surely? But Jag was looking her straight in the eye, gesturing to
an empty bar stool; the business-suited woman next to Jen had
left. Jen was frowning, and seemed to be arguing with Jag; the
stool was clearly meant for him but no, he was pointing to it
and motioning to her, Rika, to come and take it. Rika hesitated.
She couldn't do it; couldn't take Jag's stool. Obviously. Everyone
was staring at her. She flushed, and hunched her shoulders, and
turned to go, but Jag reached out and grabbed her elbow and
pulled her to the bar. He turned to Jen and laughed, and bowed
and gestured to the stool, and said, 'You know I'm a gentleman!'

and Rika had no option but to let herself be pulled back and then to slide onto the stool. She flashed a shy half-smile and a mouthed 'thank you' to Jag. She glanced at Jen to see if it was OK with her and to smile and exchange a greeting, but Jen only looked away in annoyance.

This was terrible. It wasn't right to aggravate Jen; clearly she, Rika, had made a grave *faux pas* and needed to vacate the seat and let Jag take it, so she slid off in order to flee but Jag grabbed her arm – again! – and pushed her back.

'Take no notice of Madam here!' he said with a grin. 'Ladies first!'

She looked at him, met his eyes and turned all hot with embarrassment, and looked away again. Jen had turned away from her completely, ignoring her, and everyone was laughing – at her! – and then Jag joined in the laughter and he too was ignoring her. She ordered her milkshake, glad that the attention had shifted away from her, and bent over to fish her purse out of her satchel just as Jen picked up her second ice-cream-soda from the counter. She bumped into Jen's arm and the soda spilled and landed on Jen's school uniform.

'Idiot!' yelled Jen. Everyone stared and laughed and Rika died a little death. 'Sorry! So sorry!' she whispered, and whipped a napkin from the napkin holder on the counter and tried to dab at the glob of ice-cream sliding down Jen's skirt but Jen slapped her hand away. 'Just leave it! Go away!' she snapped, while her friends laughed and Jag himself grabbed a napkin and dabbed at the mess.

'I'm really sorry!' Rika mumbled again.

'Just go away!' cried Jen, so Rika went. She left her milkshake untouched as well as the coins to cover it on the counter, leapt from the stool and ran, not walked, away from the scene. If only the earth would open up and swallow her, she would be the happiest girl in the world. But, of course, she wouldn't be in the world any more, would she; and the world would be a better place without her.

❈ ❈ ❈

That's what she told Rajan later that afternoon. After returning home, changing clothes and doing her homework, she slipped through the paling and down the alley and into her grandparents' yard. Rajan was at the back of the garden, on his knees, pulling up weeds. She sat down on the sandy path beside him. She still smarted all over from the shame of the clash, from the sting of Jen's words and the overwhelming sense of her own futility.

'I'm just a waste of space!' she said to him. 'Clumsy and – and stupid.'

But Rajan only laughed. 'You're clumsy, true,' he said, 'but no way you're stupid.'

'Mummy says I am. And I'm not doing well at school. All my teachers say so. The only thing I'm good at is English, and maybe French. But everything else …'

She shrugged and let out a long-drawn-out sigh of despair. *Maths,* she thought, the bane of her life, and her downfall. It had improved, indeed, under Rajan's tutelage, but would it be enough to pass O Levels? No. She reached over and pulled at a couple of weeds herself.

'You're bored, that's all,' said Rajan. 'But bored isn't stupid. It might even be the opposite of stupid.'

'But everyone hates me. Everyone thinks I'm an idiot. Jen even called me that, in front of everyone. And they all laughed at me. I'm such a bloody fool.'

'*I* don't hate you. I don't think you're a fool. And people call *me* names, too.'

'Really?' She was astonished. Rajan seemed so outstanding in every way, so confident, so established in himself; surely he would walk among people as a king!

'Of course they do! You should hear what the boys at Queens say about me.'

'What could they possibly call you? You're bright; brilliant! You're so ...' She couldn't find the right word. What was it? Rajan was *different*, just as she was, but in a good way, a superior way, and it seemed to her that everyone must acknowledge that.

Rajan chuckled. 'Anti-man, fairy, queer, sissy, namby-pamby, pansy, panty-waist ... to name just a few!'

Rika was shocked. 'No! Really?'

He chuckled, and said, 'What do you think? And that's not all. What about: coolie-boy, yard-boy, jailbird?'

'Jailbird?'

'Because of my father.'

'Your father was in jail?'

Rajan did not speak for a while. Then he said,

'I shouldn't have said that. Forget it.'

'No! No Rajan! I've told you so much about myself. I confide in you so much. You can confide in me! Why was your dad in jail? What for?'

'For manslaughter.'

'Really! Oh, wow! How awful! What did he do? Who did he kill?'

But Rajan was not forthcoming.

'I really can't tell you, Rika. Sorry.'

Rika felt strong. Here, at last, was something she could do for Rajan. He had given her so much; now she could lend him her support. What an awful burden he must be carrying! He had said, once, that his father was dead; now she wanted to hear the whole story. She softened her voice.

'Tell me, Rajan. Just tell me. It's OK.'

'Rika – I can't.'

'You can! You must! Rajan, if you don't tell me now I'll never speak to you again! You can't just tell me a bit of a shocking story like that, and then not tell me the rest! Stop treating me like a baby!'

She put fire into her voice, and into her eyes, and stared him down. Their eyes locked. Finally he looked away.

'Well – all right then. I'll tell you the basics, OK?'

'OK.'

'Well – he killed one of your uncles. Sort of in a fight. It was a huge drama at the time. My mother used to be a maid in your house and – well, it doesn't matter now. But yes, he was in prison, for manslaughter. And then someone else killed him, in prison, some fight they had. So they call *me* jailbird. Even though I was just a baby when it happened.'

Rika took his hand. 'I'm sorry,' she said. 'But you know what my Granny says – don't let's dwell in the past. We have to move on. I'm glad you told me that story. It makes me feel – closer to you. It must be awful – but, Rajan, it's past and you've made a good life for yourself. Never mind what happened back then. And people are so stupid to call you names because of what your dad did. Just idiots.'

Rajan laughed. 'You're right, Miss Socrates! Enough!' he said, and stood up, clapped his hands to rid them of earth, gave her a hand and pulled her to her feet. They walked over to the Bottom House, washed their hands at the tap, and sat down on their bench. They sat together in comfortable silence; Rajan picked up a book – chemistry, Rika saw it was – and she just gazed into space, musing. It was all very well to offer clichéd snippets of wisdom to Rajan. She now felt embarrassed by the homilies she had offered him – after all, Rajan seemed to have coped pretty well without her up to now, just as he seemed to cope with everything, in his own silent way. Her own present day problems still remained, and she couldn't shove them into the past as she had advised Rajan. Nor could he solve them for her.

She watched a kiskadee hopping about on the genip tree in the backyard; a lizard, scuttling up the tree-trunk. At her feet, a group of ants were hard at work, carrying a dead spider to wherever it was they stored such treasures. The spider was so much bigger, and heavier, than all of them put together. It was, Rika thought, as if five or six humans were to carry an elephant, lifting it above their heads and marching along with it to the kitchen. It seemed so effortless, so easy. In fact, everything animals did seemed so effortless, so easy. So – natural.

Why couldn't it be that way with humans too? With her, at least? For Jen and Jag it all seemed so effortless. They were popular and elegant, and popularity and elegance came naturally to them. Whereas she – she had all this internal turmoil, all these thoughts, all these feelings, that made the art of living so terribly hard, so infinitely impossible.

Just thinking about it brought back all the embarrassment, all the shame of today's incident, the sense of wanting to sink into the earth and disappear, the self-loathing that followed. Why? Why did she have such problems, and others didn't? Why was she so bloody *different?* Why couldn't she be like Jen and Jag and all the others? It seemed to her that they were being true to themselves, and she wasn't. She was just different; weird, and it wasn't right to be true to weirdness.

But Rajan was weird too. He admitted it. He wasn't like other boys: even Rika could tell that; but Rajan didn't seem to mind, and that was the difference between her and Rajan. *To thine own self be true,* Rajan had once told her, and she believed it. But who was that self? Should she be true to that shy, cringing being that curled up in agony at each little slight? That couldn't be right, could it? She would have to talk to Rajan more about it. He seemed to have all the answers.

Chapter Ten

Inky: The Noughties

Having done her duty in laying the groundwork for the years of drudgery that lay ahead of us, Marion flew off to Canada, abandoning us to Gran. Early on Sunday morning, Mum drove her to the airport. By the time Mum got back from the airport Gran was on the verge of setting fire to her hair, and I was on the verge of a nervous breakdown.

The moment Mum walked in the door, Gran pounced on her.

'No time, no time, quick march back to de car, we gon' be late!'

'Late for what?'

'Church, man, what you think! It's Sunday!'

'Since when you go to church? And I'm not going anywhere. I haven't had breakfast yet, I'm hungry!' Mum looked at me, puzzled, and shrugged.

'She used to be a militant atheist!' she said. 'What's going on?'

I could only shrug back at her and spread my hands in help-lessness. We'd been at it all morning. Gran had woken me up at 6:30 a.m. She had somehow manoeuvred herself up the stairs all by herself – a first – and into my bedroom.

'Inky! Inky, wake up! We gotta go to church!'

I'd been just as baffled as Mum now was. I sat up in bed, wiping the sleep from my eyes.

'Church? What church?'

'You mean y'all don't go to church? The eight o'clock service! Hurry up, man, we 'gon miss it!'

It took me half an hour to explain to Gran that not only did we not go to eight o'clock Sunday church services; we didn't go to church at all. Though there was a church just a corner away from our house, I had no idea what denomination it was, what went on in there, or if they even had an eight o'clock service. I refrained from mentioning the fact that we were not even Christian. I was not baptised, and when asked, Mum called herself a Vedantist. I was by now extremely adept at navigating difficult issues by omitting certain relevant facts, or rewording others to make them palatable for Gran.

While she was upstairs I got Gran washed and ready for the day – she fretting all the time that we were going to miss the service – and then I helped her down again. After getting her dressed – she insisted on her best Sunday clothes, a navy-blue frock of some artificial silky material, with a white lace collar – I made breakfast for her, and by then it was 7:30. While Gran was eating I made some phone calls to find out if there actually *was* a church service at 8:00. But no one seemed available at this ungodly hour on a Sunday morning; all I got was recorded messages or musak. Gran was by this time quite irritable, shuffling from room to room with her rollator, fretting about how late it was. That's when I spotted Mum's laptop, on the dining table, where she'd been apparently been working the night before.

It's amazing what Google can dig up in just a few seconds: the name of the church, and the times of services. They did indeed have an 8:00 am service. I decided I'd walk Gran over. It couldn't be more than five minutes away. I'd push her wheelchair into the church, find a good position for her at the back, walk home, eat a nice breakfast, and go and pick her up an hour later.

But then Gran began to fret again.

'Is a white pastor, or a black one?'

I stared at her. 'I've no idea! Does it matter?'

'I ain't going to no church with no white pastor. And de congregation – white or black?'

Again I had no idea. And I couldn't believe what I was hearing. I hadn't heard anything so blatantly racist in all my life, and when Gran insisted I call to find out, I refused – it was just too embarrassing. Gran tried to hassle me into obedience but I put up such a fight that she finally capitulated.

'All right – give me the phone.'

'You want to call yourself?'

'Don't bother youself. Just give me the damn t'ing.'

I shrugged. 'Go ahead.'

I tossed her the phone. To my surprise she caught it in mid-air, sucked her teeth, clamped it under her arm, and shuffled off to her room with her rollator. It's hard to imagine any human being shuffling away with a rollator with dignity, but Gran pulled it off. I don't know how she did it. Something about the set of her face, the tilt of her chin. Her bedroom door slammed. I made a face at it and went upstairs, slamming my own door. I'd already called every church in London and nobody, just nobody, was answering. I went back to bed. I was still in my pyjamas; might as well make the most of them.

But just a few minutes later I almost jumped out of my skin. She was yelling my name. I swore aloud and called back:

'What?'

'Come down here right now!'

I got up and stood at the top of the stairs.

'What is it?'

'Get youself dressed and come downstairs.'

'So you decided to go anyway, white pastor or not?' If she'd capitulated, I'd stick to the plan: I'd walk her over, as agreed. We were late – it was long past 8 a.m.by now – but if Gran didn't mind, I didn't either.

'Just do as I say. And hurry up.'

I shrugged. I pulled on a pair of jeans and a T-shirt and went downstairs; I'd shower afterwards. But Gran wasn't having it.

'Is so you goin' to church?'

'I'm not going to church. I'm just walking you over.'

She cackled in triumph.

'You think I goin' to that white-people church? No sirree. We goin' to a nice odder church, pure West Indian. An' you not goin' in that condition. Quick march upstairs and get yourself smart. I not introducin' no scruff to Doreen.'

And, bit by bit, I got the story out of her. All she'd done is call her old friend Doreen. I already knew that all the past week, while Mum and I had been at work, she'd caught up with all her friends and relations in London. According to Marion, there'd been a steady stream of them coming to the house while we were out, and Gran had held court on the living room sofa. I'd not yet had the pleasure of meeting any of them. Now Gran had taken matters into her own hands.

According to Doreen, there was a very nice West Indian church in West Norwood which she, Doreen, attended every Sunday. Lots of singing and dancing, clapping and cheering, just the way Gran liked it. It even had a Guyanese pastor. It was too late for the eight o'clock service, but the ten o'clock one was livelier anyway because that was the one all the families went to, including Doreen's daughter and niece with their children.

'You must be joking.'

'What you mean, I joking?'

'West Norwood. We'd have to take the train, or the bus. I'm not taking you on public transport with that wheelchair. No way.'

That silenced Gran, but only for a moment.

'We'll take a taxi.'

'Ha! You have money for a taxi?'

That silenced her for another moment. Then:

'When you mother getting back?'

I looked at the clock, made some mental calculations.

'It depends on the traffic. Half an hour at the earliest, maybe an hour.'

'We gon' wait for she. Much better. She can drive we over. Then she could get the Lord's blessing after all these years. And meet Doreen, Aunty Doreen to you.'

It turned out to be forty-five minutes. And that was how me, Mum and Gran ended up attending church together that Sunday. There was simply no escape.

❋ ❋ ❋

It wasn't technically a church. It was a large hall with a huge wooden cross just beside the wide open entrance. People were streaming in, all in their Sunday Best. Women all dolled up in last century's formal fashion, boleros and white lace collars and crimplene hats. Men in suits, trousers ending two inches above their ankles, white socks showing. Little girls in frilly white, little boys in sailor suits or bow ties. A trip back in time, or else across the ocean. Or if you wanted to put a positive slant on it, totally retro. Everybody was black.

We were greeted with huge smiles of welcome. You'd think they already knew us, the way they clasped our hands in both of theirs. A tall thin smiling woman in a navy blue dress with white polka-dots and a blue hat decorated with white lace ushered us to a row of chairs near the front; as Gran shuffled forward with her rollator, people smilingly stepped aside to let her pass, like the parting of the Red Sea.

That's when Aunty Doreen found us. Rushing up, she gasped,

'No, no, no, I already got chairs for you, on the other side, come dis way, Dorothea, Rika, follow me!' So Gran turned around and shuffled back the way she'd come and we kind of shuffled behind her and the Red Sea parted again and Aunty Doreen escorted us around the back of the hall to a row of chairs where her entire family was already parked; husband, sons, daughters, aunts, nieces, cousins, grandchildren, even a baby in somebody's arms. All these smiling faces turned to beam at us as we edged our way into the row; first me, then Mum, then Gran, helped by Mum and Aunty Doreen, then Aunty Doreen herself. I found myself sitting next to a teenage girl totally overdressed in a pink crepe creation and white high-heeled shoes, the sort you find in charity shops, and white lace gloves.

She beamed at me. I made my best effort at beaming back, all the while considering my options of escape. Was it too late? The row behind us was still empty. Could I feign a trip to the toilet – I had seen a WC sign in the entrance lobby – scrape back my chair, and make a mad dash for the door? I wanted to do something – anything – to wipe that beam off my neighbour's face. What was a girl her age doing in church anyway? She should be sleeping off a hangover from last night's binge, or turning over in her boyfriend's bed. It just wasn't natural. I was glad nobody I knew would see me here.

The pastor walked up the aisle followed by a children's choir, all of them in white gowns and carrying lit candles, and singing. Arriving at the altar, the pastor held up a hand to bless the congregation, then one by one took the candles from the choir members and placed them in a row of golden candlesticks behind the altar, beneath another enormous cross. The kid's choir traipsed off to stand in a row immediately in front of a line of women, also in white robes. The choir was complete.

Completely without warning, it burst into song. *"Greet somebody in Jesus' name!"* the women and the children cried, and next moment I was swept up in a body of sound, a rousting, reverberating chorus, voices bouncing off the ceiling, rising to the skies. '*Everybody smile! Jesus loves you!"* the congregation belted out, and if they had been smiling before, then now the smiles burst out of them, and all over the hall people turned to each other, left right, and behind them, shook hands with their neighbours, hugged, kissed, and smiled, smiled, smiled to kingdom come. It was a disgusting, saccharine show of fake jollity. Next to me, Miss Pious turned and held out her white-gloved hand for me to shake. I resisted the temptation to slap it away and instead put mine there, limp and listless, hoping she'd get the message. She didn't.

'You must be Inky, Aunt Doreen told me all about you, welcome to Trinity Church!' she gushed. I mumbled something indecipherable and tried to pull away my hand. Nothing doing. She not only grasped it tighter yet; she placed her other hand on the other side of it, so that I stood there trapped in a white lace clasp.

'I'm Lily and I really look forward to getting to know you at lunch afterwards!' she whispered.

'Lunch? What?' I replied in shock, but it was too late, the second verse had started and Lily had turned away to join in, her chin lifted and her eyes glazed in a sort of rapture.

And that was just the beginning. I found out that I had entered some kind of revival tent gathering, the kind you find in places like Alabama or Kentucky or even Harlem. The moment one song ended, the next began, with hardly a breath between. These people seemed overflowing with some kind of inexhaustible vigour that escaped their souls through the medium of voice. Some of them had tambourines or castanets or even drums, and if they didn't, they had their hands and clapped like there was no tomorrow; their bodies twitched and bounced as they sang, as if aching to dance. It was like one huge body of voice, an ocean wave that lifted the lot of us up and merged us into and transported us into some kind of translucent space where nothing existed except a vibrant, rollicking, resonant joy, and try as I might to resist it, I was taken up too, carried up in this surge of sound, that rose and sank and rose again even higher; and in between the waves the pastor cried out *'Praise the Lord!'* and *'Glory to the Lord!'.*

In one song, the choir leader divided us into four groups and we sang a canon which ended up with the whole room resonating to the clarion cry of *'Rejoice! Rejoice! Rejoice!'.* That was followed by a quiet hymn in which they all calmed down and the choir leader sang a solo with the congregation singing the refrain.

To my horror, I felt tears gathering in my eyes, running down my cheeks. I struggled against the tears but yet more came. I sneaked a peek at Mum next to me. Her eyes were closed and down her cheek ran a shiny streak, as if a small snail had crawled down it. And in that fraction of time I knew what it was all about, Life and God and everything, and my body tingled and my breath too was gone and tears rose up in my eyes and I wanted to grab hold of Lily and hug her to death, and everyone else in that hall, all these singing radiant people, and I knew, intimately and with absolute surety the meaning of that word, Glory.

It was too embarrassing for words.

❊ ❊ ❊

Aunty Doreen had prepared a feast for us all, and I tucked in. Church seemed to have opened a yawning cavern inside me that had to be filled with something more substantial than light, and the sight and aroma of so many dishes, the likes of which I'd never seen or heard of or smelt before, except for that small sample at Brown Betty's a few days ago, not even under Marion's crash course in Guyanese cooking, made me almost drool. I ate as if I'd been in jail on a bread-and-water diet. It was a buffet, so everyone grabbed a plate and retired to a sofa or a chair or the garden to eat. Lily had latched on to me permanently, and led me outside, where, with a chicken drumstick, she discreetly pointed out the various individuals she promised to introduce me to later, she said, after the meal. And slowly, slowly as the hours slipped by, I passed from one hearty embrace to the other, and the names of this uncle and that aunt and second cousin so-and-so passed in one ear and out the other. All the women's names seemed to end in 'een'. Doreen, Lurleen, Eileen, Marleen, Charleen, Maybeleen. And everybody was Aunty. It seemed that you had to call women of your mother's generation Aunty So-and-so; everything else was rude.

I grew drowsy. I was tired of it all. These were *Aunty Doreen's* relatives, after all, not mine, though you wouldn't have thought it from the enthusiasm with which they folded me into their midst. If it had been my relatives I might have been more receptive; I'd been hungry for family all my life. But these people seemed to think that, because we'd been in church together, we *were* all now one big happy family, and though I'd felt a bit of that during and immediately after the service, that notion now only made me cranky. I wanted to go home. A girl can only take so much Glory in one day.

Gran, of course, loved it all. She sat throughout the meal in place of honour on the softest armchair, where she graciously held court. People, men, women, children, brought her plates of food and glasses of drink. They sat at her feet as she held forth, wagging her finger and waving her hands to illustrate some point or animate some story. They gathered around her, faces still radiant, and Gran revelled in it. And I realised that this was the thing she must miss the most: back in her own environment she was the Queen Bee, respected and admired, and with us she was not. That's why she made herself into Queen Bee. And that's why I resisted.

Maybe back there in the village a person's age is enough to earn him or her respect; but not for me. It was what you *did* and how you behaved that earned you my respect, and that was the cardinal flaw in the relationship between Gran and me. She'd done nothing yet to earn my respect, and so she didn't have it. She was just an old woman I had to look after. Gran wanted more; I had no more to give. I feared all this fawning would do her no good; it would only go to her head.

I looked around, longing to escape. Where was Mum? I had no idea. I hadn't seen her eating or talking to anyone. Abandoning sweet Lily I got up to look for her. She was nowhere to be seen; but fifteen minutes later she walked in the front door. I realised she had slipped out after the services and now had returned to pick us up.

'Where've you been?' I said in irritation. 'Let's go.'

'Where's Mummy?'

'Where d'you think? Sitting on her throne, surrounded by her attendants.'

Mum threw me a sharp look, smiled ever so subtly and jiggled her head ever so slightly, and I knew we were as one on this. Gran hadn't earned *her* respect either.

❊ ❊ ❊

Sal came around that evening. Gran received him in her room, which by now had been transformed into her official reception area by the addition of a sofa, the smaller one of the living-room suite. The sofa was for guests; Gran sat enthroned upon Mum's best armchair. Sal and Gran took to each other immediately, the only snag being that she entirely misconstrued our relationship. She thought he was my boyfriend.

'Two y'all suit nice together!' she said, approvingly within the first five minutes of meeting him, and later, when she heard his career plans, she almost clapped her hands in glee.

'You catch youself a good white man there, gyal!' she said, loud enough for him to hear. 'You better hold on to he good and tight.' I blushed, Sal chuckled.

'He's just a friend. A good friend.'

'Fren'? Ha! Rain a-fall a-roof, yuh put barrel fuh ketch am.'

Sal and I looked at each other, neither of us understanding, and thank goodness for that. Later, Mum explained the proverb to me: it had to with grasping opportunities as they arose. Now, I steered the subject away from Sal.

'Gran, Sal knows a bit about stamps,' I lied. 'Can he see the albums?'

'Of course. But go outside the room a minute. And shut the door.'

By now I knew better than to ask why: she'd hidden them. Sal and I went outside and shut the door. A minute later she called us back in. The albums were laid out on the bed. She gestured towards them.

Sal was put through the same process as I'd been: first she leafed through the two fat albums with the newer, more colourful stamps. When that was over, she placed the precious heirloom album into his hands.

'Over one hundred and fifty years old!' she proclaimed. 'A real antique. Be careful. It's worth a small fortune.'

Sal gingerly turned the pages. Next to him on the couch, I peered over his shoulder. Though I'd seen it before, Sal's interest had aroused my own, and I wanted to take a closer look; I'd been much too dismissive of Gran and her precious possessions the day she'd arrived. Maybe Sal was right; maybe they *were* worth something.

Some of the older stamps were still on their original envelopes. The addressee's name on the yellowed paper was written in an old-fashioned, spidery handwriting, the ink faded, yet still decipherable. It was always the same addressee: Theodore Quint, 217 Lamaha Street, Georgetown.

'Who was Theodore Quint? An ancestor of yours?'

'My husband grandfather,' was the prompt reply. 'Is he start this album. Is he start collecting stamps. Theodore had a friend, name 'Wight', anodder white man. Spelled W-I-G-H-T. See: Wight name, white colour: funny, eh?' She cackled, and clacked her dentures.

I didn't think the play on words particularly funny, nor did I see the need to mention the man's race. Gran's obsession with white skin, black skin irritated me so much I'd complained to Mum, after church. I told her of the brouhaha we'd had about the white or black pastor: 'That's racism, Mum, pure racism.'

She'd tried to explain it to me: it was a backlash of the extreme racism Gran had known growing up at the tail-end of slavery. It was all she knew. That was the way people thought in her day. More specifically, her own father had been a white pastor and he'd been a disaster.

'So just because of one bad white pastor, she's saying they're all bad? That's rubbish.'

Mum only shrugged. 'Maybe it's the style of service between black and white churches, English and West Indian churches. It's just – different. You saw yourself, at Trinity Hall. Somehow, the descendants of slaves are more willing to let loose, let go of themselves, surrender to God. They had nowhere else to turn. No other support. Nothing to hold on to, so they gave themselves to God and God gave the comfort, their only comfort. The more you give, the more joy you get. That's why the descendants of slaves seem to find devotion so easily. They had nothing, so they gave themselves, and they get everything back. The whole joy. That's the way it works.'

I didn't like the direction the conversation was taking. She was moving away from racism and into religion, and I'd had enough religion for one day. Really, it was totally embarrassing, my behaviour that morning.

'But times have changed! Slavery is over! Black people are equal to white, there's just no difference!'

'Not for her. Those wounds dug deep. It takes more than time to heal them.'

I still didn't get it.

'But her husband was white. I saw the photos!'

Gran's husband Humphrey was as light-skinned as anyone in England, or so it seemed on the photos. They'd been a handsome couple, the two of them on their wedding day; he tall and stiff in a formal black shit and top hat, she in a lacy, high-collared wedding dress. Both unsmiling: dignified and aloof.

'Didn't you see the one with all his brothers?'

I recalled the eight Quint boys. I nodded.

'Very well then: you see, Humphrey was mixed-race. We called it 'a touch of the tar-brush'. And we used to say, if you have only one drop of black blood, you're black. Humphrey's father was dark-skinned, but even he was not pure black. *His* father was dark, mixed race, but mostly African. His mother, my Granny, was English, and white. Black hair, blue eyes. Women – men too – tried to marry up to breed out the black. People spoke openly of it. It takes several generations to get that out of a family's system. I'm glad it's out of yours.'

'You're glad the black blood's out of my system?' I was shocked that Mum could say such a thing.

'No; the acute awareness of variations in skin colour. How much white blood you have, how much black. How many kinks in your hair. How thick the lips, the nose. My generation grew up with that. You're lucky yours didn't.'

'Yeah. You bred it out.'

After all, she'd married a white man as well. It seemed to be the thing to do for the dark-skinned women of my family. And each woman came out a shade lighter; Mum being what she called 'sapodilla brown,' a Guyanese expression referring to a brown local fruit I'd never seen, and me being light olive. Now, Gran was going on about this postal clerk, some Edmund Wight, a friend and colleague of our ancestor Theodore Quint.

'One day, this Edmund Wight sign de stamps heself. And de stamp become famous. De British Guiana Black on Magenta. That's why I tell you, this album precious. Because Theodore sign them stamps too. This one.'

She tapped it with her fingernail. It was one of the most primitive, ugliest, the most insignificant-looking of the lot, slightly smudged and faded, stuck to a wilting torn off corner of paper. Across it was a postmark, stamped *'Georgetown'* and *'April 3rd 1856'*

'See!' she said, pointing to a scrawl in the right bottom corner of the stamp. 'T.A.Q. Theodore Anthony Quint. That's what make it valuable.'

'Really! How much do you think it's worth?'

Gran shrugged. All of a sudden she appeared indifferent, as if she'd retreated into an interior cavern and no longer cared.

'Couple thousand dollars,' she said. 'Thirty thousand?'

Sal looked at me. 'What's the exchange rate, dollars to pounds?'

I'd learnt over the past week to interpret Gran's economics. 'She's talking about Guyana dollars, not US dollars. In fact, she's talking about BG dollars, British Guiana dollars, before the devaluation. Mum told me there used to be two BG dollars to one US dollar.'

'That's even less in pounds,' Sal said. 'But, you know, Mrs Quint ...'

'Call me Gran! Like Inky!'

'May I call you 'Nan'? Like my own grandmother?'

Gran beamed at that, and squeezed his hand.

'I was saying, Nan ...' the word came so easily. I glanced at Gran. Delight shone in her eyes.

'I think it might be worth more,' said Sal.

Gran's eyes gleamed. I thought I saw something crafty in there; an imp, peering through the slits in her wrinkled face. But I could have been mistaken.

'Like, fifty thousand?'

'I've no idea. Do you want us to find out for you? Inky and I could take the album to a dealer and get an estimate. Maybe we can get a good price for you. You could sell it, and …'

'Sell it? Sell it? You jokin'or wha? This is an heirloom, boy. An *heirloom*. You don't know what an *heirloom* is?'

Vexation was written all across her face. Sal had fallen in her estimation. She almost grabbed the album from him and slammed it shut.

'Go away. I got to put dese t'ings away.'

Chapter Eleven

Inky: The Noughties

Sal and I walked down to Wong's. We walked in silence, yet somehow I knew that Sal's thoughts were aligned with mine. When I'd first seen Gran's stamp albums I'd dismissed her talk of precious heirlooms as idle imagination. What she'd said today, however, had made some sort of sense. I didn't know the first thing about philately, but I did know that some stamps were worth fortunes. Not Gran's, necessarily, but hers were old and just maybe there was some truth to her story. They *might* be rare. Might someone want them, and pay good money for them? And Mum had debts; Mum had to turn over every penny three or four times. Surely …?

After all, Gran was living in Mum's house, eating her food. Gran didn't have a pension. She had nothing, beyond the pittance sent by Norbert and Neville to help cover her maintenance costs – and which did not include rent. Surely it wasn't fair for Gran to hang on to that album while Mum gave her room, board and personal care? *If* it was worth anything …

But maybe it wasn't. Maybe the album was just as worthless as it looked. I couldn't imagine anyone paying a thousand for such junk. I wouldn't pay even a *pound* for it. Maybe it was just a far-out fantasy. But then, I'm not a philatelist.

When Sal and I finally spoke, I found out he had the very same fantasy.

'Even if she's not going to sell,' he said, 'She should have it evaluated. See if you can talk her into that.'

I nodded. It was exactly what I was thinking. It had to be done.

❊   ❊   ❊

It wasn't easy, persuading Gran to hand over the album, to take it out of her possession and to a dealer. Not that she didn't want to have it assessed; she was as curious as we were. But there just wasn't a dealer in wheelchair-distance from our home, and Mum and the car wouldn't be available all week. And so, reluctantly, she placed it in my hands, with the admonishment to take good care of it, protect it with my life.

'Of course,' I'd promised, and here we were.

We'd found the dealer on the Internet, and met at Victoria Station to take the Tube. It was a little shop wedged between a clothing store and a record shop. I placed my backpack on the counter and unpacked the album under his bored eyes. I guess he was used to people coming here, amateurs with no inkling about stamps, with their old grandfather's heirloom album.

I felt a bit ridiculous, standing there while he turned the weary pages. The album seemed to have gone through wars; the pages were dissolving round the edges, some of them eaten away by some tropical termite. Originally black, some were partly white with mould. The whole thing smelt of moist, rotting cardboard. It was a wonder that most of the stamps themselves were actually intact, and in much better shape than the paper they were attached to.

The dealer leafed through the whole thing once, then turned back to one of the pages. He took out a magnifying glass and regarded one particular stamp; the *right* one. I held my breath. He stared at it for a long time, after which he looked up.

'Excuse me a minute,' he said, 'I want to make a phone call.'

Without waiting for a response, he slipped into a back room. After about five minutes, he returned. He looked as bored as ever. He gave us a perfunctory nod before pulling the album back over the counter and giving the ugly little stamp an even closer inspection.

'Where did you say you found this album?'

'It's my grandmother's,' I said. 'She arrived from Guyana about a week ago. It belonged to her husband.'

'Ah. I see. Well, it is of some interest and I might be able to sell one or two of the stamps to collectors. I'll give you ten pounds for it.'

'No, sorry. It's not for sale.'

'One hundred pounds.' The new offer shot from him without hesitation.

'It's not for sale,' I repeated, and drew the album to me. I closed it and picked it up to return it to my backpack. The dealer placed a hand on the album. Grasping fingers closed around it, tried to ease it from my hand.

'Why don't you just leave it with me,' he coaxed, 'I know someone who might be interested. He might make a better offer, but he has to see it himself first.'

I shook my head. 'Sorry, no.' I gently pulled the album out of his grip and slid it into my backpack. 'Thank you for your interest,' I said, and turned to leave. But the dealer wasn't letting me go. He lifted the counter flap, hurried through it and planted himself in front of me, blocking the entrance.

'Here's my card!' he told me, thrusting a red embossed business card my way. 'And would you give me your grandmother's telephone number? I'll speak to my contact and perhaps we can make a deal. Maybe I can persuade your Nan to sell.'

Sal and I looked at each other, and we both nodded slightly.

'All right,' I said, and told him our home number. He wrote it down.

Back out in the street, Sal and I both burst out laughing. He opened his arms and I fell into them. We danced a little jig together, in the middle of the pavement.

'I told you so!' he said. 'I had a feeling. I bet you anything he calls with another offer.'

I laughed. 'Bet taken. How much?'

'I say he's going to offer up to five grand. He'll start with a thousand, and go up. I bet you ten quid. And you?'

'You know me – I like to think positive!' I said, 'The top offer'll be over that. Something between five and ten grand.'

'And will she sell, if it's a high enough offer? I bet another ten, that she'll eventually sell.'

I stopped laughing, stopped dancing. Reality pulled me back to earth.

'She won't. It's an heirloom.'

❊ ❊ ❊

When I got home I found Gran already excited; the laptop had arrived, donated by Neville. She had already unpacked it, and, using the simple illustrated first instructions, plugged it in and switched it on. Now she wanted me to show her how to use it. I had already initiated her into some of the wonders of the Internet the week before, and she couldn't wait to go surfing herself.

'Gran, I've no time now,' I said. 'This evening. I've got to go to work.'

'Pah! This evenin' you ain't gon' have no time either.'

'I will. I promise. And don't you want to hear what the stamp dealer said?'

I took the album out of my backpack and handed it to her.

'Just one minute.' She disappeared into her room with it and closed the door. I took off my shoes, hung up my jacket. There was a pile of letters on the floor next to the front door. I picked them up, leafed through them; one was for me, from one of the universities I planned to apply to. Mum's mail was familiar: the usual letters from the bank, Marks and Spencer, British Home Stores. All demanding money. She'd cut up all her credit cards and store cards but the debts were still there, dating back to our time with Dad. One letter had a handwritten address; I'd seen these letters before; they came fairly regularly, all with the same handwriting. The writing looked vaguely familiar, but it was hard to be sure, as Mum's address was neatly printed. I wondered causally who it was she still exchanged personal snail mail letters with, and put the whole lot on the bottom stair for her to take up when she came home.

I knew what she'd do with most of them: throw them unopened into the filing cabinet and lock the door, waiting for her next salary. She paid off the backlog bit by bit each month, but she'd never, ever be on top. And she preferred not to open letters of demand until she had the means to pay. It was her ostrich-head-in-the-sand method. Now, I went into the kitchen to make myself a cup of coffee. Gran reappeared in the doorway.

'So what he say then?'

'He wants to buy it. He offered a hundred pounds. But he's going to call you to offer more. Sal thinks the next offer will be a thousand.'

Gran's eyes lit up. 'How much is that in BG dollar? Le' me think ...' She did some swift calculations, and came up with the answer.

'He got to be joking. What I tell you, fifty thousand, no less. A small fortune!'

I looked at Sal and rolled my eyes. OK, I knew that £1000 was too little, but it was Gran who had to be joking. But then I remembered. Fifty thousand BG dollars. Put that into pounds, and what did you get? About ten grand, the amount of my bet with Sal. Maybe I'd win the bet, if Gran was right. Next to

Mum's debts, though, ten grand was peanuts. But every little helps, as they say.

❊ ❊ ❊

I kept my promise. After dinner – I didn't have to cook yet, as Marion had left some pre-cooked meals in the freezer – I gave Gran a half-hour lesson on Internet surfing and word-processing, but then the phone rang, interrupting us. It was for her. And I could tell by her side of the conversation that Sal had been right.

'A *t'ousand*? A t'ousand pound? You makin' joke or what? My dear young man, dis is a Family Heirloom. You know what *family* mean? You know what *heirloom* mean?'

She listened to him for a moment, and then the words we were to hear so often in the next few weeks:

'Haul yuh tail.' She hung up with a flourish and looked up at us, grinning in wicked satisfaction.

❊ ❊ ❊

After that, Gran was tired. I helped her prepare for bed – Mum was working late tonight – and then returned to the computer. I wanted to do a little research of my own. I entered a few words into Google, waited for the screen to open.

One mouse-click later, I had what I was looking for. I read a few paragraphs. I gasped aloud. At that very moment the phone rang. It was Sal.

'I was just about to call you,' I hollered. 'I've been on the Internet, and …'

'I know,' said Sal. 'I just went there myself.'

❊ ❊ ❊

By the time Mum came home I had turned into a caged wildcat, pacing the house restlessly. The moment she walked in the door,

I pounced on her. 'Read that!' I yelled, shoving some printouts into her hand.

'I'm starving,' she replied. 'Let me at least eat my dinner first!'

'No, no way you're eating. Read it NOW!'

I dragged her into the living room and plonked her down into the couch, just beneath the reading lamp. She rolled her eyes and read a few paragraphs with mild interest. That's when she looked up. I saw the light in her eyes, and knew that she no longer thought of food. I had finally caught her.

'T. A. Q … is that …?'

'Yes. Our great-great-great-many-times-great grandfather, Theodore.'

It was amazing. I still couldn't believe it. I had thrashed out the story with Sal for over an hour, and I still couldn't believe it. I was beside myself with excitement. I wanted to call up everyone I knew and tell them, shout it from the treetops. But I couldn't. How could I? Telling the world, here and now, would spoil everything. What I did know was that our lives had changed forever.

Back in the mid-nineteenth century, 1856 to be exact, the stock of stamps in the colony of British Guiana sold out before the new shipment had arrived from England. The Postmaster, a Mr Dalton, needed stamps in a hurry and so he asked a local printer to produce an emergency issue of one-cent and four-cent stamps. They did so.

Dalton was not at all pleased with the result. The stamps looked so primitive; they were so easy to forge. Dalton devised a solution: before selling each stamp, the postal clerks should sign it with his own initials as a security measure. The clerks signed them 'E.D.W.', 'P.M.D.' and 'T.A.Q.'

Of that signed emergency issue, only one stamp supposedly survived. It bore the initials 'E.D.W.', for E.D. Wight. Its journey to the present day took it from British Guiana through Scotland, London, France to, finally, the USA. It was last sold at auction in 1980 to a John E. DuPont of Philadelphia for $935,000, and had remained in a vault ever since. It was the rarest stamp in the world.

'And now there's a second,' I said. 'Ours. Signed T.A.Q. For Theodore Something beginning-with-A-Quint. Every bit as unique as the DuPont one.'

'If there're two of them, it's not unique.'

'There's one E.D.W. and one T.A.Q. Both are unique. We're rich!'

'It's not ours,' Mum said flatly. 'It's hers.' She got up.

'But ...'

'Don't even think of it,' Mum snapped. 'It's hers. *Hers.* Do you really think she's going to give it to us? To *me*?'

'I know she said she didn't want to sell it,' I said. 'But surely when she finds out ...'

'Ha! You obviously don't know Mummy! If she doesn't want to sell it, she won't. And no force in the world can make her. And the more you or anyone else tries to pester her, the more she'll refuse. Don't even *go* there.'

She got up and strode towards the kitchen. She opened the fridge with a vehement tug, reached inside for rocket salad, mozzarella. From a cupboard, she removed more of her special healthy ingredients. She attacked the salad, ripping the leaves into shreds.

'And, Inky, please don't talk about this to anyone. If I were you, I wouldn't even tell Gran.'

'She's already has an offer,' I said, and gave her a quick run-down of our meeting with the dealer.

'See? There you have it. Everyone's going to want to cash in, starting with that crooked dealer. Ten pounds, indeed! He must have known from the start. And once he starts talking, the shit is going to hit the fan. I hope you didn't leave any contact details?'

I confessed to leaving our number with him. 'But not the address,' I said. 'He can't do much with the number.'

'Don't you believe it. He can hassle us to kingdom come. And once word gets out ...' She shuddered. 'But till then, Inky, not a word to anyone. This should stay in the house. I mean it. Can Sal keep quiet about it?'

'If I tell him to – of course!'

'And don't, whatever you do, tell Uncle Neville.'

'Of course not! And Marion?'

'She's trustworthy,' Mum said. 'But I'll talk to her myself.'

'I don't really understand,' I said to Mum. '*Why* can't people know?'

Mum looked at me, and shook her head as if in pity at my naïveté. 'You don't know Gran,' she said. 'But you'll find out.

'I can't wait to see her reaction!'

'Inky!' The urgency in Mum's voice made me look up. 'What?'

'Don't tell her yourself. Let me do it. Please. Trust me on this.'

'Mum, I don't get it. Why all this secrecy? You don't even get on with her; she talks to me much more. She *likes* me. If you tell her, she'll only quarrel with you.'

Mum sat down at the kitchen table with her salad bowl and started to eat. She avoided my eyes. 'The thing is, I know that stamp, from way back when. There's a lot of family history attached to it, emotional stuff you can't possibly understand. It was Daddy's, his most precious ... Oh, it's a long story. Maybe I'll tell you sometime.'

❋ ❋ ❋

That night, or rather, the next morning, I discovered why Mum seemed always so exhausted. I woke up early to go to the loo. The iridescent hands on my bedside clock said 4:25a.m. Outside the window, a full moon sailed across a clear navy sky, and the room glowed with a gentle white light. On my way out, I noticed Mum's door was open; I peeped in and her bed was empty; the bedclothes heaped against the foot of the bed. I assumed she was in the bathroom, but found it unoccupied. When I returned to my room, the bed was still empty.

I tiptoed downstairs, taking care to avoid the two boards that creaked. I thought Mum'd be in the kitchen, maybe drinking a glass of warm milk, which was what she did when she couldn't sleep. But the kitchen door was wide open, the light switched off. Across the hallway, the living room door was closed, and a crack of light at its base was an obvious clue to Mum's whereabouts. I gingerly opened the door, peeped inside. Mum sat at the dining table, her back to me, so absorbed in whatever she was doing she didn't hear the door handle's click.

'Mum?'

She jumped, and turned around, an expression of clear guilt across her face.

'Oh, Inky! I... I didn't hear you come in! I was just ...'

She turned back to the dining table and a familiar click told me she'd closed her laptop.

'I've got some extra work, and I thought this was the best time to do it ... with Mummy in the house everything's so hectic. No time for anything!' she said, answering a question I hadn't asked.

Sometimes Mum took on freelance assignments, writing articles and even short stories for B-class magazines and journals, as well as editing and proof-reading jobs. Her full-time job as a storyliner for the daily soap *Bed and Breakfast* – a never-ending story centred around a thriving hotel in Blackpool – might have been enough for just the two of us, but not enough to take care of Dad's crushing legacy of debt. And now we were three, with Gran.

'Oh, OK. I saw your empty bed and wondered where you were. Want me to read it when you're finished?'

Sometimes, Mum asked me to read over her freelance stuff and give my opinion. Not this time, though.

'No, it's OK. You'd just be bored by this one. I'll manage.'

'OK, then I'll go back to bed.'

'Good night ... I mean, good morning!' I thought I saw relief cross her features as I turned to go. But I may have been mistaken.

Chapter Twelve

Inky: The Noughties

The phone was ringing. I happened to be in the bathroom, helping Gran to get washed. We still hadn't figured out a solution to the shower problem, and getting her ready for the day took the better part of an hour. First she had to be helped up the stairs, our arms around each other's waists, and then she had to be washed at the sink.

I clattered downstairs to answer the phone. Someone wanted to speak to Gran. He didn't ask for her by name. First he established my identity, and then he asked for 'my grandmother', which pretty much established what the call was about.

'She's busy right now,' I said. 'Could you please call back in about an hour.'

I ran back upstairs.

'Who was that?'

'Someone about the stamp.'

'Eieiei! They must want it real bad! They gon' call back, or what?'

'Yes,' I said. 'But I wanted to tell you something before you speak to anyone. You have to be careful, Gran. People are unscrupulous. They wouldn't be calling if they didn't think it was worth a lot. And I think it is.'

'I told you! Fifty thousand dollars!'

'I think … probably a lot more.'

I could hardly contain myself, but Mum had asked me not to tell – yet. I didn't understand that. What could be the harm in it? I didn't think it was a good idea for Mum to be the one to tell her. There were obvious tensions between her and Mum, whereas my relationship with her was good, under the circumstances. Gran liked me, approved of me. She was trying to win me over. Whereas Gran bickered constantly with Mum, which was why I had ended up taking over most of the Gran's care. I was the one Gran invited into her room every evening, the one she showed the old photos and told the old stories to, again and again. The one she most connected to.

I made up my mind to disregard Mum's plea. Mum harboured a barbed, bulky load of old mental baggage, and whatever it was she feared came from some unresolved childhood conflict. It had nothing to do with our present circumstances. Obviously, I was the best one to break the news to Gran.

And anyway, circumstances had simply taken over. The dealer was going to ring back. He would be calling back within the hour, and now I knew the real value of the stamp I had to prepare Gran to talk to him. Later, we could discuss strategies. Mum had made it clear to me that we had to be extremely careful from now on. No more shady stamp-dealers picked off the Internet. We had to be professional. And so did Gran.

And anyway, my hints had started an interrogation I could no longer stop. My concealed excitement must have been contagious, for she picked at it with the determination of a dog digging for a bone.

'A lot more? Like what? Seventy t'ousand? A hundred t'ousand? How you know? You find out something? Ow!' She snatched her head away from my hands. 'You don't know how to comb black people hair, or what? Give me that comb!'

I gave her the wide-toothed comb and she styled her hair herself, her deft fingers bringing order into the sleep-matted mane in a matter of minutes.

'I read something about it,' I said. 'You can read it when we go downstairs.'

'Tell me now,' she insisted.

So I did.

She took the information as calmly as Mum had done.

'E.D.Wight,' she mused. 'Edward Wight. Pa Theodore's boss. I knew him; an old man. Two a-them used to work at the Post Office down the road – at the corner of Lamaha and Carmichael. Humphrey's father George worked there too. Opposite the train station. Mums used to send we there to buy stamps.'

'The one-cent stamps were used for newspapers,' I said. 'So I guess mostly the wrappers were just thrown away. Nobody keeps newspaper wrappers. So Theodore must have kept the stamp, seeing as it had his own initials on it.'

But Gran wasn't listening.

'Come, child, I finish. Let we go downstairs. I want to read this t'ing you talking about.'

I put away the comb, tidied the bathroom a little, and helped her down the stairs.

A stair-lift. Or better yet, the bathroom extension Mum and Marion had dreamed of. She could afford it now! She could afford a carer, a personal nurse. Mum's troubles were over – we were rich! Jubilant, I thought of all the ways Gran could make her life, and ours, easier. Over the past week she had become quite handy at fixing her own food, but the counters were too high for her. *A new kitchen,* I thought. One with low cupboards and counters. Hell, why aim so low? A whole new house! Why not? In Richmond! One of those lovely villas in Croydon. Why not! We were rich! Then I remembered. She was rich. Not we. And she clung to that little bit of paper like a barnacle to a rock. Damn. She would have to see sense. I would make her see sense. She trusted me. I would talk her into selling it.

Finally established at the table, her breakfast in front of her, Gran asked for the article. She read it as she ate. I watched her face, but it remained expressionless; the only clue to her thoughts was a slight raising of the eyebrows, and a simultaneous slight pause in the chewing. I guessed she had reached the part where DuPont won the stamp at auction; the part where I myself had leapt to my feet with a yelp.

'So?' I said, when she put the page down without even a glance at me. 'What do you think? It's nice, isn't it?' The understatement of the century; but Gran's lack of reaction unnerved me

She sucked her teeth. 'Them people plenty stupidy,' she said. 'What you got a stamp for, if all you gon' do is keep it in a vault?'

She was referring to the present owner of the famous stamp, DuPont, John DuPont, currently serving a prison sentence for murder. The stamp had been in a vault for years, decades.

'What you expect him to do, take it to jail with him?'

She sucked her teeth again. 'If you got something you treasure, you got to be able to look at it, take it out, admire it, thank de Lord, show you friends, show you grandchildren. Just like I show you.'

She obviously had missed the point.

'Gran, that stamp – I mean *your* stamp – is valuable! You have to take better care of it. You can't just keep it in an old stamp album! I mean, it's a miracle it survived this long, and ...'

'All you-all young people do is break you head over worries,' she said. 'In me day, we didn't have these worries. Look how Theodore keep de stamp, pass it to he chirren and chirren chirren. We did know how to take care of good t'ings, heirlooms an' t'ings. We didn't need no vault to keep it safe.'

'Yes, but you didn't *know* how valuable it was. If you had known, if Theodore had known, I'm sure he wouldn't have just left it lying around the house. It's so tiny! It could get lost so easily!'

'Who say anything about it lying around the house? You see it lying around in my room? I know how to keep valuable

things safe. What you frighten? We old people, we got we own
ways. If I got a treasure I does keep good care of it. Safer than
me own teeth!'

She clacked her false teeth at me and cackled at her own
joke.

'You should really give it to Mum to give to the bank.
They'll keep it in a safe, till you can take it to auction, and ...'

Oh dear. I was supposed to persuade her gently, surrepti-
tiously. I'd let my own excitement run away with me. That was
not a smart word. She jumped on it immediately.

'Auction? Who say anything 'bout auction?'

'Well ... of course ... I thought ...'

'All you young people can thing about is money, money,
money. You don't know what an *heirloom* is? Is something of
value a family passes down the generations. You don't sell an
heirloom. You don't put it in no auction. You never heard of
sentimental value? You never heard of *respectin'* you ancestors
and *honourin'* them by taking care of the things they leave you?
If you turn everything into money you don't know you lose the
past? An' if you lose the past you don' know you *lose you soul?*
I never gon' understand you young people. Money, money,
money. What de world comin' to, I don't know. Everything
going down de drain. Is all money, money, money.'

'But ...'

Clutching the wheels of her chair, she gave it a brusque
push so that the chair shot backwards and almost hit the wall.

'But *what?* You eyes get big, or what? You eyes get big an'
you mind get small. You read some stupidy article, an' all you
can think of is money. Before you go to that damn dealer, all
you could think is that Gran holdin' on to some damn stupidy
piece of paper, some raggedy ol' stamp album. You din' place
no value on it. Is I did value it, because is a family heirloom. A
Quint family heirloom. You own family; not even *my* family,

I is a van Dam. One of the famous two van Dam sisters. We got we own heirlooms, jewels and t'ings. The Quint heirloom is that stamp album. Theodore Quint is not *my* ancestor; I only marry into the family. I was keeping' this heirloom to pass down to the next generation, *your* generation. My husband pass it on to me to pass on. Is my holy duty. But all you young people could t'ink, is money, money, money. Auction and money. Auction and money. Money, money, money. What the world comin' to I don't know. Lord have mercy upon us. Save us from the Scribes and Pharisees. Rescue us from those of small heart, from those devoid of morals. Lead us into green pastures, oh Lord.'

As she spoke she eased herself on to her feet, grabbed her rollator, trundled off into the living room, turned right, shuffled down the hall and into her own room, again, with me right behind her, trying to get a word in edgeways. Nothing doing. Gran wouldn't let a thing like a rollator and a slow pace take one spark away from the fire of her anger, and she scorched me well and truly. As she crossed the threshold into her room, she held on to the doorframe and slowly, wincing with pain, turned around to face me. In spite of the wince, her jaw was thrust forward and her eyes burned holes into my guilt.

'You, Inka, you! All these years I was t'inking you is the worthiest of my grandchildren, you the only one who ever bothered to write me. Even Marion's children, small children I helped raise – never a word to the old grandma once they leave the country. Never a thought for their old grandma. You, I thought, you is of the old understanding. You is not of this modern times; you is the one who would value the heirloom. And now? You is just like all the rest. Money, money, money.'

Her very slowness gave her dignity. She turned her back to me and shuffled off. The door slammed shut in my face.

❋ ❋ ❋

'I don't understand it,' I said to Sal on the phone, '*she* was the one who first mentioned money. *She* was the one who named sums, and asked me how much it was worth.'

'Well, obviously, her reasons for wanting to know the market value are different from yours,' Sal said. 'I believe that for her, the higher the market value, the greater the sentimental value as an heirloom. Which doesn't mean it has to be converted into hard cash. Whereas for you, the stamp as heirloom has no value whatsoever. You just don't care. And that's what upset her.'

'But if you think about it, it's really just a scrap of paper. *Her* words, and they're true. Just because some people want to pay thousands and hundreds of thousands for that scrap of paper, doesn't make it actually *worth* that much. Why such a fuss?'

I could feel Sal's shrug through the line. 'Why do we attach a value to anything, for that matter?'

'I can understand a family heirloom if it's, say …' I paused to think of an example. 'A piece of antique furniture. Or an old sapphire brooch. Something beautiful, something that in itself is a relic of the past, a piece of history. You'd never think of throwing away, say, a beautiful old painting. Or a marble statue, or an antique necklace. You'd want to hold on to it for its own sake, for its beauty. But a stamp? A scrap of paper?'

'You think too much. Just accept that it is so, and figure out how you can make it up to Nan.'

'*You* can talk. You don't know her when she's being a bitch,' I grumbled. 'She's only ever been nice to you.'

'Tell you what. I'll come over this evening. I'll see if I can calm the waters.'

'No work?'

'Nope. Two days off.'

'Good. Maybe you can work the miracle. I expect some heavy flirting with her.'

He laughed. 'Done.'

The minute Sal went off the line the phone rang again. It was the same caller as earlier, a dealer, I supposed, but not Mr Martin, the dealer. Maybe Mr Martin's boss. Again, he wanted Gran. I rapped on her door.

'What you want?'

'Telephone for you.'

A moment later, the door opened. Gran stood in the doorway, crouched over her rollator, eyes smoking.

'Gimme that thing.'

I gave the phone to her. She shuffled backwards, the door slammed.

❋ ❋ ❋

When Mum came home I confessed everything. I'd done exactly what she'd told me not to do and Gran still fumed in her room. Mum sighed.

'There's a reason I asked you to let me tell Mummy,' she said. 'She's difficult. I told you she's difficult.'

'Difficult?' I scoffed. 'She's a nightmare. I honestly don't know how you and Marion turned out so nice.'

Mum laughed. 'Maybe we got it from Daddy,' she said. 'He was sweetness incarnate. Or Daddy's mum, Granny. Ma Quint.'

It was the first time she had ever mentioned family connections from back home. We were making progress.

'Yeah, and Neville and Norbert got their crankiness from *her*. Makes sense. Speaking of which, Norbert called earlier. Gran didn't want to speak to him. He was most intrigued to hear that Neville bought her a laptop.'

We both laughed. Neville and Norbert were engaged in a private battle in which each tried to outdo the other in proving they were the better son, Mummy's favourite. Gran loved their oneupmanship game, as it meant they showered her with ever more generous gifts, and she played it for all she was worth. The rollator, a radio, her own TV set, a more comfortable mattress – all provided by them. Now that Neville had given her a laptop, Norbert would have to think of something better, even more useful, even more state-of-the-art, and Gran would sulk until she got it. The trouble was that Gran wanted luxuries; Mum and I wanted the practical stuff. A stair-lift. A bathtub lift. A potty-chair. Boring stuff, but necessary. Stuff Gran would never think to ask for.

'Anyway,' Mum said now, 'I'd better go in and talk to Mummy. About the stamp, I mean.'

'Good luck. And tell her to tell Norbert to get her a stair-lift. Then Neville can donate a potty chair.'

❀ ❀ ❀

After Mum disappeared into Gran's room, the phone rang yet again. It was Marion, from Toronto. We'd kept her informed about the stamp, and from the start she'd been strange about it. Agitated. Asking all sorts of questions, probing questions. Obviously, she was jealous that Gran had the stamp and now Gran was with us and might give it to *us* instead of *her*. I decided to be careful with Marion in future. Really, when money comes into the picture you can't trust *anyone*.

Chapter Thirteen

Dorothea: The Thirties

Freddy had been acting strange all afternoon; distracted, morose, silent, and she knew he had a secret, but the more she probed, the more he clammed up. Something was wrong.

Finally, he turned to her and his eyes were wild and fretful.

'Dorothea, we need to talk. There's something … something big. Would you come out with me tonight?'

'Tonight? You mean, after dark?' The very notion thrilled her. It could only mean one thing: he was going to ask her to marry him. *That's* why he was so nervous. The silly! Did he think she was going to refuse? Yes, that's what it had to be. The moon was full, and it was going to be a romantic proposal. Maybe he'd take her to a candlelight dinner somewhere. Somewhere public. Palm Courts, with its open-air terrace, palms waving in the cool sea breeze. With roses and violins. Champagne. And then she'd say yes. That was a given.

Pa would say no, of course. He railed against the Quints as much as ever; there was no chance he'd let her marry one of them. She was only eighteen; she had three whole years to go before she could officially flout Pa's wishes and marry Freddy. But with a secret engagement, a ring hidden in her top drawer, a promise to marry, she could easily wait out those years. Or … and here her heart began to flutter. Maybe they could elope. Maybe *that's* what he was going to propose tonight.

But elope – where to? In the novels she read, set mostly in England, couples eloped to Gretna Green to marry, but there was no Gretna Green in British Guiana. Here, everyone knew everyone else and really, there was nowhere to go, for just a few miles inland the jungle began, and just down the road, visible from her bedroom window, was the great Atlantic. Trapped between the forest and the ocean, Georgetown really was a world unto itself. No, there could be no elopement. Faced by this stark reality, her heart calmed down.

'Yes,' Freddy said. 'You think you can slip away?'

'Sure I can. But not through the gate, Pa locks it every night.'

'You'll have to come through the alley, as usual. I'll pick you up. At ten?'

She nodded, and they made their plans. Freddy was so solemn. Really, it could only mean one thing.

❊ ❊ ❊

The drawing room was flooded with moonlight as she tiptoed down the stairs. Glancing through the back window, she saw the signal: Freddy was waiting already, flashing his torch.

She unbolted the back door, opened it, and crept down the back stairs, into Freddy's arms. He held her still for a moment and again she knew that this was *it*. It was strange, in a way, the thought of marrying Freddy. They'd been friends for so many years; so close they almost knew each other's thoughts. For her it seemed obvious that they'd spend the rest of their lives together, but at times she feared it was not so for him; maybe she was just a sister to him; not pretty enough, not exciting enough to want as a wife. That was what she feared the most. If not for that tiny doubt, she'd even have proposed marriage herself.

But now, locked in his arms at the bottom of the back stairs, she knew. There was nothing brotherly about that embrace, or about the ache in his eyes as they caught hers in the moonlight. But then he pulled away.

'Come!' he whispered, and shone his torch down the path between the trees. He led her to the loose paling in the fence, and they both slipped through, not speaking. The night was alive with the usual chorus of night creatures; the frogs had ceased their croaking, but a trillion bugs had taken up the shrill peeping and chirping of a tropical night.

Freddy led her not to the right, to the Quint house, but to the left, where the alley emerged into Lamaha Street. There, his bicycle was waiting, leaned against the fence.

He wheeled it onto the road, she edged herself on to the crossbar, he swung his leg over the rear wheel and they rolled away. At Camp Street he turned left, which surprised her; central Georgetown would have been to the right. Now they were heading towards the Sea Wall.

'Where are we going?' she whispered.

'To the end of the world,' was his answer, and as he said that she felt a little flutter of fear. Maybe she had misgauged his mood. There was an element of dread in him that she had not picked up before, so blinded she'd been by her own wishful thinking.

'Freddy, what's the matter?' she asked for the umpteenth time. His arms held her firmly on the crossbar. His face was just inches from hers, his expression grim. Again, fear clutched her heart. What was going on? Surely he wasn't going to end their friendship? That couldn't be. It just couldn't.

The street was empty as the glided up towards the ocean, past Queen's College on the right and the hulking contours of the police barracks on the left. Only a single car passed by them, heading for town, and the only sound of traffic was the clop-clop of a dray-cart horse's hooves. Georgetown was a city that slept early. They were alone.

When they reached the Sea Wall Freddy helped her to the ground and put the bicycle on its stand. He removed a blanket form the carrier and tucked it under his arm. He held out a hand to her.

'Come,' he said.

Silently they walked up the stone steps to the Sea Wall. The moon sailed overhead in a cloudless sky, full and bright. Before them stretched a seemingly endless expanse of hardened, undulating mud, for the tide was out and the ocean far away, glimmering silver against the horizon. A cool ocean breeze swept over them, billowing Freddy's shirt and playing with the hem of Dorothea's dress. They seemed alone in the world.

Near the bandstand the Sea Wall expanded into the wide Promenade where every afternoon families congregated or nannies brought their little charges, and everyone relaxed as the day drew to a close; a place to be light and gay.

Right now, there was no gaiety. There was no escaping it. Something was very wrong. Dorothea almost didn't want to know. She felt a need to hold on to the innocence of the instant, to keep these last moments of hope alive forever, not to allow entry to the dread that gripped her heart.

Freddy unfolded the blanket to half its size, and laid it across one of the wooden benches. He gestured for her to sit, and managed a half grin that only wrenched her heart, so contrived it was. A lump rose in her throat. She tried to swallow it but it was stuck.

Freddy sat down beside her. They sat in silence for a while, holding hands. It was as if he, too, wanted to hold on to the moment, to the expanse of ocean before them and the vastness of the sky above them and the softness of the moonlight.

'It's so beautiful,' he murmured finally.

'Yes.' She whispered back.

'I don't know how to say this.'

Her eyes filled with tears.

'Just say it.'

And then he turned to face her, and looking into her eyes, it all came rushing out.

'England's at war, Dorothea. And we've all signed up. I, and all my brothers. I'm going to have to leave you; I don't know when I'll be back. Maybe never.'

An anguished cry escaped her lips. In all the fears that had crowded her mind these last few minutes, she had not imagined anything as terrible as this. Yes, she had heard the murmurings of war; they were hard to avoid, with the newspaper headlines and radio newsreaders all trumpeting the latest developments. But it had not interested her. That was in Europe, across the ocean, a world away. But now that distant war had reached out its cold hand and wrapped its fingers around her life.

Spontaneously they fell into each other's arms and he held her still as she heaved and sobbed and tried to speak, patting her back as if she were a child needing comfort.

'But … but why? Why fight a war? It's not our war … it's Britain's …'

'We are British citizens,' Freddy replied. 'It's our duty.'

'You don't have to go, do you? You can choose to stay, can't you? Oh Freddy, don't go, please don't go!'

'I'm a volunteer,' said Freddy. 'We all are. No, we don't have to go. But Britain needs every man. I can't shirk this, Dorothea. I'd be the worst cad.'

'Britain … Britain … it's so far away! Don't they have enough men of their own?'

'There are never enough men,' Freddy said, 'when it's a question of war.'

'And your mother … she's letting you go? Just like that?'

'She's as upset as you are. She's sending eight sons off to war. What mother would be happy at that? But she too knows we have to go. I couldn't look myself in the mirror if I didn't.'

For the first time, the reality of the world she lived in came home to Dorothea. But it wasn't really her world. Britain, Germany, Hitler, Winston Churchill ... till now, they had all been just names, from the radio, from the newspapers, like names from a play, not real people. Those places: England, Germany, Austria, France ... they might just have well been on the moon.

Yet they were only across the ocean, this very ocean at her feet. Yes, she'd heard her father discussing the danger of Hitler with the other menfolk who sometimes came to visit. Yes, she'd been aware that war had finally been declared. But it was all so far away. It had nothing to do with her. BG had problems of its own, and she was determined to help solve them. This was across the ocean – it was nothing. Or so she'd thought.

How wrong she'd been. How foolish. Once, her father had said, 'Thank the Lord I only have daughters.' And even then, the reality of war, and the men who must fight it, had not dawned on her. She began to cry now, in earnest. Freddy held her and let her cry, and tried to comfort her.

'I'll come back, my darling, and then we'll marry. I promise you. I'll be fine. I just know it.'

But they were just words, empty and almost mocking in the face of her anguish.

Her tears dried up. Freddy produced a handkerchief and wiped her face dry. He smiled, a funny lopsided smile. 'You're so pretty in the moonlight,' he said. 'So beautiful.'

Just words.

They looked at each other in silence. Then Freddy spoke again, this time hesitantly.

'Dorothea ... would you do something for me, if I asked?'

Not even a pause. 'Anything! Oh, anything!'

'You're so pretty!' he said again, and let his fingers glide down her cheek. 'It's a bit impertinent, I suppose, but ...'

She guessed what it was, and already she was saying yes in her heart. He had not asked her to marry him, but she would be his wife in every other way. That was what he wanted; and so did she.

'... but, would you let down your hair for me? Unplait it? Now?'

The shock must have shown on her face, because he quickly said,

'But of course, not if it's too much trouble. And not if it will get you into trouble with your Mum.'

But already Dorothea had pulled off the ribbon and her fingers worked feverishly at loosening the tight weave of her left pigtail, and when that was loose, the other. And then she ran her fingers through her hair like the teeth of an oversize comb, pulled the strands away from her head. The kinks and crinkles, released from bondage, sprang into their natural coils as if this was the moment of glory they'd waited for all their lives. And the skin of Dorothea's forehead, no longer stretched to its limit, relaxed, and her eyebrows sank into their natural arches, and her eyes lost their taut upward tilt and grew soft; and Dorothea sat before Freddy with her face framed by a glorious spreading mane of strong black tresses fanned out beneath her shoulders; a magnificent mane of wild, wayward hair that, she knew now, would never again be tamed. Freddy reached out and touched her hair, helped fan it out and pat it into shape.

'Beautiful,' he whispered. 'So beautiful.'

'Freddy,' Dorothea said now, 'I want to be your wife, now. Not when you come back. Now, and here. I want you and I want your baby. Right now. Tonight. Right here. Please, Freddy. It's what I want. Give me a baby, Freddy, please. I beg you, please.'

Chapter Fourteen

Dorothea: The Thirties

When Dorothea awoke, the first thing she noticed was the matt of hair against her cheek. Immediately she was wide awake, remembering. She sat up in bed, drew up her knees, and allowed herself five minutes of dreaming. The wildest contentment mingled with abject despair; she buried her face between her knees and sobbed.

But only for a minute. She stood up and walked to the mirror. Her hair was a total mess, tangled and matted beyond salvation. No comb could ever be dragged through it. Not even Mums' brutal attack would ever restore order and obedience to that thatch of knots. Most important of all: Dorothea could not care less. Filled with a new spirit of freedom and courage, she knew exactly what needed to be done. She stood up, walked to the wardrobe, and rummaged in the bottom drawer for her sewing box. She immediately found what she was looking for, and returned to the mirror.

The scissors were rather small for the job; what she needed was secateurs, yet she managed a gross first cut. Her hair lay all around the vanity seat, like the debris from a cut hedge. On the floor it seemed much more than on her head; she was amazed at just how high it piled. And her head itself felt so much lighter, liberated. She regarded herself in the mirror, cocking her head. The cut was bad; uneven, jagged, straight across the top, longer on the right side than on the left, because she was right-handed, and, she was sure, totally ragged at the back. It needed further work, and for that there was just one solution.

It was early dawn yet, her parents still in bed. She got up, left her room, and walked to the bathroom down the corridor. Pa's razor lay on his shaving table next to the sink. She picked it up. That wasn't perfect for the job either, but it was good enough for her purpose.

When she was as bald as could be, under the circumstances, she contemplated herself in the mirror. She liked the look. It made her look just as naked and free as she felt. She found a broom, swept the hair from the floor, and disposed of it in the bin, took off her clothes and stepped into the shower. The cold water on her skin was a further liberation. It signified the new beginning that was this new day. She worked up a fine lather of Palmolive soap, threw back her head so that water gushed into her mouth, and celebrated the morning with a silent scream.

This new sense of freedom brought no joy. Inside, her heart was cracking apart. And yet, there was a tiny spark of hope.

❊ ❊ ❊

She was deliberately late for breakfast; this grand event called for an Entrance. So she waited till they were all seated and about to say Grace when, as she knew, Pa would call her. That's when she walked in to the dining room, head held high. They sat there with their mouths open; Pa, Mums and Kathleen. The latter broke the silence by bursting into giggles.

'Dorothea turn bald-head!' Kathleen cried, in blatant Creole. A sharp slap on her knuckles from Mums followed; it was her parents' cross that Kathleen, otherwise so prim and proper, loved to slip into bad language. Perhaps it was her own attempt at rebellion, one that Dorothea had never tried. Until now.

Pa's jaw began to work as he struggled for words. Dorothea decided to pre-empt him.

'I done with you all!' Dorothea announced with a perfect Creole lilt. 'I'm goin' to get a baby from Freddy Quint. Today I'm moving out.'

✼ ✼ ✼

Once more in her room – she had not stopped to revel in Pa's shock or for Mums to remove the hands covering her face – she threw a few clothes into a pillowcase, took a last long look at her face in the mirror, and saluted herself in farewell. She rather liked the look, though it might still need a barber's hand. A shaved head *meant* something. It meant that she now belonged to Freddy, forever; that wherever he went and whatever he did, her heart belonged to him. Whether he stayed in BG or left for the battlefields of Europe, it did not matter. Here was her bared scalp, a trophy prepared for him and shown off to all the world: *I am his!* Whereas Mums had claimed her with those dreaded pigtails, Freddy now claimed her through this naked skull, so pale against the cocoa brown of her face.

She left the house through the front gate. Ram, the East Indian gardener, on his knees as he worked on the weeds in the front garden, stared as she walked past and placed his palms together, bowing his head as if in deference to some Hindu goddess. Other people stared too; pedestrians on the middle walk of Waterloo Street, and people on bicycles riding past on Lamaha Street, pointing and laughing. She did not care. She opened the gate to the Quint residence. Their gardener, Singh, doffed his straw hat as she walked past, head held high. It was the first time she had ever entered through the front gate.

Up the bifurcated front staircase. Another first; it had always been the back stairs and the kitchen for her. Always secretly, covertly, always in hiding, in shame and fear. All that was at an end. She rapped sharply at the door. A few seconds later, it opened.

'Hello, Humphrey!' she said in greeting. Humphrey's jaw fell open like a gaping fish, and his eyes bulged as she walked past him into the gallery. She threw him a friendly smile in passing; she knew how much Humphrey cared for her, and how shy he was and in need of kindness. She always gave it when she could. Humphrey had only recently returned from Law studies at the University of London, and was currently completing an internship in a Georgetown law firm. If he'd volunteered for the war effort he'd have to give that up.

Most of the others sat at the breakfast table; six or seven brothers, their parents, and Pa. Leo was missing; Leo had recently married and his young wife was pregnant. He'd be with her now. All the brothers were either in their first jobs or finishing off various studies. Young men in the prime of youth, none of them ready for war. It was a travesty. All looked up as she marched into the dining area, bulging pillowcase in hand, followed by a still gaping Humphrey. A collective gasp of shock greeted her. Freddy sprang to his feet.

'Dorothea! Your hair...!' he cried

She glanced at him and resisted the temptation to fly to him and throw her arms around him. Instead, her eyes sought Ma Quint's.

'Ma,' she said, 'I left my parents. I can't live there no more. I'm going to have Freddy's baby. Can I move in here with you?'

A moment of shocked silence followed these words. And for a split second Dorothea feared she had done everything wrong. Her courage and sense of freedom this morning – it was all illusion; she was a bad girl. A fallen woman, a harlot, as Pa would say. Freddy had used her. Ma Quint would hate her. The Quint brothers would mock her. Father Quint would throw her out for intrusion. It was all a huge mistake …

And then Ma Quint stood up, pushed back her chair, walked around the table and placed her arms around Dorothea, who buried her face in her shoulder and smelled the sweetness of her hair and the warmth of her body, and knew she had come home. At last, Ma Quint released her, and, holding her at arm's length, regarded her, squinting.

'My, Dorothea, I always said you were a pretty girl and now we can all see for ourselves – what a noble head you have! But you've got to grow back that hair of yours, right? We'll find a nice flattering wig for you till then. And you know you're welcome here; you know you're my daughter. But it's not as easy as that. You're still a minor – your father must be dealt with, and there are legal ramifications. But we'll talk about *that* afterwards, when we're alone. And now, I'm sure you must be hungry. There's Leo's chair, sit there. And have some coffee.'

❃ ❃ ❃

After breakfast, Ma Quint took Dorothea upstairs to her room, sat her down on the bedside, and took her hand.

'Now, dear. You tell me all about it. Don't be afraid or ashamed. You know me.'

So Dorothea told her.

'So,' said Ma Quint, when she'd finished. 'It was just the one time?'

Dorothea nodded. Tears bulged in her eyes; they'd been rising steadily all morning and pressed urgently for release. Dorothea fought them back.

'Then why do you think you're pregnant?'

'You said, you told me … how to *not* get a baby. We didn't do that. We didn't use anything.'

'So, no protection? None at all? Not even … withdrawal?'

'No. See, Ma, I *want* a baby. Freddy's baby. If he's going off to war I want this from him! And I told him so.'

'Aha. Now tell me dear, when did Aunty Flo last come to visit?'

Dorothea frowned. 'I don't know … can't remember. Does it matter?'

'Yes dear, of course it does. Weren't you paying attention when I explained it all to you? A woman has to keep track of these things, whether she wants a baby at all costs, or it's the last thing she wants. So we need to figure out your chances of being with child.'

Dorothea thought back, and when she had a notion, told Ma Quint, who shook her head, and squeezed Dorothea's hand.

'If that's the case, my dear, then it's very unlikely that you conceived. We should know in a few days.'

The first tears leaked out of Dorothea's eyes. 'You mean … you don't think it worked? But I so want … I want so much … I thought …'

And then she gave up the struggle and the floodgates opened. Ma Quint held her until it was all over, crooning words of comfort, a strong hand held against her back. At last the reservoir of tears dried up and Dorothea drew away.

'I'm sorry, I'm so sorry. I'm such a baby. And you're so strong, I mean, your boys, all of them, not just Freddy … going off to fight. How can you bear it?'

'A woman can learn to cry inside,' was all Ma Quint said. 'I offer my tears to God, and He dries them. And now, dear, let's take care of you; there's more we need to discuss. Come with me.'

Ma Quint led her into the bathroom and poured her a basin of cold water from the jug. Ma Quint washed her face with soap, and handed her a fluffy white towel. They returned to the bedroom and sat down again on the side of the bed.

'What I'm thinking,' Ma Quint said, 'Is that you and Freddy better get married before he leaves. He's got a few weeks left before he sails. I've been thinking that's the best solution, because we do need your father's permission and if you're not pregnant he knows now what you've done and getting married is the only way to make that right; in his eyes, at least. And to get his permission for you to move in here. It's also important for your reputation; you can't live here in a houseful of young men and preserve your good name. People will talk.'

'I don't care about my reputation!' Dorothea said fiercely. 'That's why I did this!' She ran her hand over her bald head. But then her eyes softened. 'But I do want to marry Freddy. Of course. Do you think we could? Really?'

'Technically, of course you could. A lot of boys are going to get married before they go off to war. A couple of mine as well, no doubt, not just Freddy. But you do need your parents' permission. You're only eighteen.'

Dorothea frowned. 'Pa won't give it. I know that. He's like that.'

'Not even to make a respectable woman out of you? After all, if you're living here with Freddy under one roof you'll be living in sin, in his view. Surely he'll want to change that.'

Dorothea shook her head. 'You don't know Pa. He'll say, giving me permission would be tantamount to rewarding me for my sin. He'd rather see me burn in hell.'

'What a strange religion he has!'

'He's like that. But I've heard somewhere, I read in the papers, that an underage girl can get permission from the courts, if the parents refuse?'

'It's true. But, Dorothea, taking the legal route won't be easy. Much better to get this sorted with your father, to get his agreement.'

And that was how Winnie Quint approached the matter. Wearing her Sunday Best she visited the van Dam house and spoke to Pastor van Dam in her best clipped English accent. She presented the case to him, not mentioning the fact that

Dorothea probably *wasn't* pregnant; promised to do all she could to avert a scandal – scandal being the thing that Pastor van Dam most feared – and wheedled his permission out of him; and, with the speed of light, in a simple and quiet civil ceremony, attended only by relatives on the bridegroom's side, Dorothea van Dam married the love of her hitherto short life and became Dorothea Quint.

❀   ❀   ❀

Even before that event, Dorothea had had to accept certain conditions imposed by Ma Quint, to which Freddy, surprisingly, and to her great disappointment, agreed. 'No babies, Dorothea,' said Ma. 'If you happen to be pregnant now, then very well, I'll stand by you. But if not … I can't have you planning one in cold blood, when Freddy's about to leave for an undetermined time. You must protect yourself. I'll take you to my doctor to get you sorted out with a cap.'

'But …'

'No buts about it, Dorothea. We don't know how long this war is going to last or what the outcome will be, God help our souls.' She crossed herself. 'A child needs a father, and not having one around isn't easy – for the child or the mother. You have no idea; you're almost a child yourself. If you were to have a child then guess who'll have to be co-mother, and no, I won't do that deliberately. I've had eight boys and that's enough. No, Dorothea. You must be sensible. I want you to live here with me and wait and pray for Freddy to come back just like I'll wait and pray for all my boys. We'll give each other strength, comfort each other, as women in wartime always do.'

And Dorothea had to acquiesce. She believed with all her heart that she was with child, but reason told her she wasn't. And reason proved correct.

❀ ❀ ❀

And so she and Freddy lived together as man and wife. It was a time simultaneously fraught with despair and filled with light; the very knowledge that soon he would be gone dug deep into their beings and gave them a joy that lovers in safer times can never know, a joy made all the stronger and more magical by the knowledge of looming separation.

Most evenings she and Freddy rode to the Sea Wall, Dorothea on the bar of his bicycle, and they would hold hands and gaze out over the ocean and smell the salty air and feel the cool breeze on their skin. Freddy would play his mouth-organ, and the wind would whip the melodies from him and carry them away. The strains of 'Oh Danny Boy' would fill her with a melancholy so deep she thought she would burst. And her sorrow carved a hollow in her heart, which the very next moment would fill up with joy; and she grasped that joy while it was all hers. She learned the meaning of living in the present, for the future was too dire to consider. There was only the *now*, and the need to fill each moment with love; but that love too carved into her being, making room for yet more sorrow to come. But sorrow was in the future and she pushed it away. For now.

❀ ❀ ❀

Meanwhile, more mundane matters had to be taken care of, things like visits to doctors and the outfitting of the room she would share with Freddy, and, of course, the buying of a wig. There was no way, Ma Quint said, she could allow Dorothea to leave the house with her head shaved.

'But it's important!' Dorothea pleaded. 'A symbol of my love for him!' But Ma Quint was adamant, and that very first afternoon, the wig-outfitter arrived with a selection of styles.

None of the wigs were anything like Dorothea's original hair. It was as if girls of African descent, should they ever be in need of a wig, snatched at the chance to outwit nature and flaunt a head of *good* hair, European hair, straight, curly, long, short, brown or even blonde, it didn't matter as long as it was European. Dorothea chose a wig of black, curly hair that fell heavy to her shoulders and swung as she moved. Mums would have loved it; but there was no Mums to admire her. There was only Ma Quint, mother-in-law and mother of her heart.

❊ ❊ ❊

Dorothea continued in school, where rumours of her immoral situation (it was a shotgun marriage, everyone whispered; Dorothea has *done it!*) soon trickled through and the girls snickered behind her back. The rumours trickled upwards and reached the headmistress, Miss Moody, who summoned her for 'a little talk'.

Dorothea told her story.

Miss Moody nodded. She had had dealings with Pastor Van Dan in the past, unpleasant dealings. She took Dorothea's side.

'Very well, Dorothea,' she said. 'Usually, when a girl marries she leaves school and stays home until she has babies. What a waste of brains, I always say. A girl should finish her education before she even thinks of marriage. And in your case, it would be a crying shame; you know you're among the candidates for the British Guiana Scholarship.'

Tears in her eyes, Dorothea nodded. 'And if I win?'

'Then you can go to England and study whatever you want. Under normal circumstances. But with this war on … The scholarships have been suspended, Dorothea. Who knows how long this war will last? If you win, maybe you can go later. But who knows. Who knows.'

❋ ❋ ❋

The brothers were called in for their medicals and Humphrey failed his. It was his bad eyesight, and the fact that one leg was slightly shorter than the other that let him down. Ma Quint grasped that failure – Humphrey's shame – as her single comfort in this dreadful time. Humphrey would be staying; one of her sons was spared the ordeal of war. Dorothea wished with all her heart that Freddy, too had failed. But it was not to be.

Two weeks later, seven Quint brothers boarded the ship that would take them to the war, and Dorothea's heart broke a final time.

Chapter Fifteen

Dorothea: The Forties

Dorothea tucked her pain into a pocket of her being and returned to work. The day Freddy set sail for the war she plunged into schoolwork with all the passion she could no longer give to him, and passed her final exams with flying colours, top of her year.

She allowed herself not a second's mourning, not a moment's self-pity. The indulgence of missing Freddy was not for Dorothea. She looked for a job, and found one right away at the *Argosy*. She worked for half a year as a cub reporter, specialising in stories on women and children; as the only female reporter it was she they sent out to interview the mothers and the daughters and the wives of the men who made the news. Because, of course, only men made the news. Very soon, Dorothea had her own little column. The first one had been about the lowering of the age of consent for marriage to eighteen.

Encouraged by those articles, women wrote letters to Dorothea. From all over the country, the letters poured in, heartfelt, often desperate letters in which women told of their troubles and confided in her stories of sometimes horrific circumstances. She replied to each one privately, sometimes through the girl's aunt or cousin. Word spread. More letters came.

She kept her column free of controversy; the time had not yet come. Dorothea found she had a wit of her own, and with that wit tackled serious subjects with a light and breezy tone. And yet, for those who had ears to hear, a coded message was there between the lines. Her knife was yet sheathed. She knew she had to tread carefully. After all, there were men's toes all around the office. She avoided stepping on them. For the time being.

After six months of this, the Sunday Editor, Mr Braithwaite, called her into his office. They were starting up a Woman's Page, he told her, and how would she like to be in charge of that page, as Women's Editor?

She would, indeed. He smirked.

And how would she like to sit on his lap? And did she know how pretty she was?

If she was pretty, Dorothea certainly did not care. Her hair had grown back, of course, but she kept it short, like a man's, never longer than an inch, moulded to the finely chiselled contours of her head in a tight black cap. With her high forehead and squared chin it gave her a regal aura, that of an Ethiopian queen. The last thing she was interested was sitting on some man's lap; certainly not her boss's.

Now, Dorothea slapped Mr Braithwaite's cheek, right and left, and walked out. She reported the incident to the newspaper's owner, sent in her resignation, and that very day applied to the *Graphic*. Would they like a Women's Page?

Yes, they would. The editor there had been following Dorothea's stories and liked her style. They'd be delighted to have her.

Of course, she had to wait out her notice at the *Argosy*. She let it be known that her very first article at the *Graphic* would be on the subject of Sexual Harassment of Women in the Workplace. She had a stack of letters, she said, to illustrate her case and now her very own first-hand experience.

Management at the *Argosy* promised to sack Mr Braithwaite if only Dorothea would stay, and offered her a higher salary than the *Graphic*. The sacking of Mr Braithwaite being what she wanted, Dorothea decided to stay on.

The new Sunday Editor had not yet quite *grasped* Dorothea. He wanted her to concentrate on 'Women's Issues': fashion, weddings and children. Dorothea played along, for the time being. The country was in the first throes of its fight for independence, and unless they were directly concerned, readers were more interested in the PPP's attacks against the British Establishment than in some poor women beaten half to death in a village up the East Coast.

But privately, Dorothea got busy. She now had her own rickety old car, a green Ford Prefect, in which she drove all around town and up and down the coast and to the villages along the Demerara River, visiting women in their homes and intervening where she could.

Through her Women's Page she built up her connections. She attended functions and made herself known among the Ladies of High Society. And the men. She found out secrets, for people confided in Dorothea. Behind the scenes, she pulled strings and connected wires. She found advocates for her causes in the highest echelons of society.

And when the background work was done, Dorothea opened her writer's mouth and the truth poured out. Women's Rights, Dorothea wrote, were every bit as important as the struggle for Independence. A country could never be free as long as its women were not; women were the backbone of society and if they were kept down, society could never learn to walk, much less run. And with Dorothea there to champion them publicly, with her literary tongue ready to lash anyone who dared doubt, a host of ready-formed groups crawled out into the light. Women on the Move, for equal pay for equal work. Women Against Violence, seeking justice for the perpetrators of domestic abuse, and help for the victims. Women Against Repression, consisting of East Indian women rebelling against forced marriage. It was a revolution within a revolution, and Dorothea was in the vanguard. She was the patron saint of WOM, WAV and WAR.

❊ ❊ ❊

'Missing in Action, Presumed Killed.' There were the words, in black and white. Ma Quint's fingers crushed the telegram into her palm and an anguished cry escaped her lips as she collapsed … into Dorothea's arms. Dorothea let her gently down to the floor and held the older woman's head in her lap as she, too, cross-legged on the carpet, read the telegram. Just to make sure.

But in a way she had *known* something was wrong. There had been that empty, gnawing feeling in the pit of her stomach. Freddy's letters had always been sporadic, but never more than three months apart. The last came over six months ago. But it was not just that. Dorothea felt a sense of dread. As if she knew, just knew, that Freddie was… but no, she couldn't even think the word. It couldn't be. Even to think it was to lose faith. As she as she had faith, as long as she hoped, as long as she didn't give him up …

These last five years Dorothea had lived from letter to letter and news story to news story. Working as she did for the *Daily Argosy* she got the war reports as they came in, before the general public. She had followed the action and the death toll, the victories and the defeats, as avidly as any man. Her heart, linked to Freddy through the mystery of prayer, had been with him throughout. And then – silence. No word from him, no flutter in her heart to tell her that he was alive and awake and listening for her. Just echoes of her own hopes.

The Quint house had turned eerily silent after the boys had left; it seemed so empty, though there were still five of them: the parents, Pa, Humphrey, and Dorothea. Leo's wife and one other hastily-married daughter-in-law both lived with their own parents, and as none of them had ever been as close to Ma Quint as Dorothea she, in fact, became a de facto daughter, and a sister to Humphrey.

Poor Humphrey. Left behind as unfit for the rigours of war, he was in danger of being the object of pity and even derision, and Dorothea felt protective towards him. And so she showered him with attention and small kindnesses. She learned that it was just as well he had not been called up, for his was a tender and sensitive soul, and as he opened towards her, sharing the poetry and prose he so loved with her, she learned that within him was a different quality of strength, one that was directed inward instead of outward, less obvious to the eye but there nevertheless. It was Humphrey, more so even that Ma Quint, who had taught her how to cling to a tender yet indestructible thread of faith within, when everything she held dear in life was taken from her.

Both she and Ma Quint had taken refuge in their faith. Dorothea had prayed and prayed until her heart seemed to bleed. Had it all been for nothing? Had God not heard her prayers? Had He abandoned Freddy, left him to ... she could not even think the word. She felt deserted, lost. For Ma Quint, of course, it was worse, much worse. She had seven sons over there, seven loves to pray for. For Ma Quint, there would be no reprieve until all her boys returned from war safe and sound. Or not. Now, grief and dread flung a garland around them both and drew them closer to each other.

Ma Quint stirred now, moaned, and sat up. They looked into each other's empty-but-full eyes, laid their arms around each other and, there on the floor, sobbed out their heartbreak.

❊ ❊ ❊

Dorothea was not one for useless self-indulgence. She turned her back on grieving now, just as back then when Freddy had gone off to war. She had to keep her mind off Freddy. She had not cried since the day she'd waved goodbye to him from Georgetown's wharf, watching his ship grow smaller and smaller till it was but a dot on the horizon, and finally gone. Then she had dried her tears, walked away and plunged into her work. But now:

'Missing in Action, Presumed Killed.'

The tears, she found, had not dried up at all. They had gathered in an ocean deep under the surface of her soul. The telegram was a swift arrow, piercing the membrane that held that ocean in. Now it burst open. And yet ... somewhere inside her a voice cried out: *he's not dead! He can't be! I'd know it if he were!*

Dorothea flung herself even deeper into her work. It was her way of forgetting, her way of distraction. No cause was too small for her to champion. Dorothea Quint was a name known even in the deepest pockets of British Guiana's rainforest. It was known in the Savannahs along the Brazilian border, cut away from the capital by a million acres of jungle. It was known in the Amerindian settlements up and down the mangrove-lined creeks where no newspaper, not even a radio signal, ever arrived. The name was carried by word of mouth, whispered among the women as they grated cassava and padded barefoot along soft black paths through the Bush, bent low with their loads of coconuts and plantains strapped to their backs. It was known by the East Indian women in the villages in the flooded rice fields on the East Coast, by the African women in the shantytowns of the capital. 'Dorothea Q', they called her now.

In a society strictly segregated by class and colour, Dorothea Q was not like any other woman of her rank. A British Guianese woman's main goal was to find a husband higher-ranking and lighter-skinned than herself; Dorothea was not looking for a husband. Women's minds revolved around beautifying themselves to make them prey for such eligible bachelors; if they were touched by the tarbrush, by lightening their skin and straightening their hair through the magic of a fledgling beauty industry, and highlighting the curves of their bodies through fashionable clothes. Dorothea cared neither for her face, nor her hair, nor her clothes. She wore a series of simple cotton dresses all of the same cut, faded by the sun and frequent washings, their gathered skirts hanging limp around her hips. For Dorothea, the body was merely a vehicle needing no more than basic upkeep and fuel to keep it going, necessary for her work.

One of the biggest changes from the well-brought up English pastor's daughter was her speech. No more the clipped, enunciated English drummed into her by her father and strictly watched over by her would-be-white mother, such that not a single 'h' slipped through the net and not one syllable was lost; the English that had won her the reputation of being a snob back in the days. Now, Dorothea spoke like the natives, a sing-song Creolese that revelled in the bastardization of suffixes and the misplacement of pronouns and the maltreatment of verbs. 'I'm not going anywhere' became 'Me in't goin' nowhere'; 'What are you thinking?' would be 'Is wha yuh t'inkin'?' She was one of them, 'them' being the low-born, the blighted, the descendants of slaves and indentured servants, the black and the mahogany and the crinkle-haired. Dorothea made a point of it.

In fact, Dorothea could put on any accent she wanted. She could 'talk white' as well as her father, and 'talk pretentious white' like her mother. She could 'talk Coolie' like an East Indian, peppering her speech with 'ow, beti!', and talk 'Indian English', spicing her speech with gerunds. The first time she mimicked an Indian – mocking the pompous Minister of Trade and Industry with whom she had locked horns that morning – Ma Quint and the rest of the family doubled up in laughter. So she continued to mock. 'I am not agreeing with this ridiculous notion of Indian ladies entering the male workplace,' she mimicked, bobbing her head from side to side. 'An Indian lady's place is in the service of her husband. In the kitchen among the pots and pans. The pots and pans are her best friends. Ladies are of a very fragile disposition and their greatest joy is in being Mother. Mother is God.'

'You should go on stage!' Ma Quint laughed, wiping the tears from her eyes, and that is exactly what Dorothea did. She joined an amateur theatre group at the Playhouse and now and then they put on a play; and always Dorothea got the comic roles, whether male or female. Invariably, she brought down the house. She delivered deadpan lines that had her audience roaring with laughter, without so much as a twitching lip. Acting was her only hobby, her only form of relaxation. Everything else was work. She never smiled. Certainly never at her own comic turns.

Women worshipped her; men feared her, for her tongue was as sharp as a razor; yet she wrapped them around her little finger with her caustic charm and disarmed them with feminine wit.

People called her beautiful; but hers was not the soft, graceful beauty of the minx, curling itself around men's hearts and loins in order to melt and seduce. Hers was the beauty of a queen or even a goddess, fearless and indifferent to the affections it might win, or lose. She held her chin high, which combined with a gaze that met its mark straight on, and the swift, confident swing of her stride, made her look arrogant. And arrogant she may have been, but only on the surface. And as life continued after that terrible telegram, arrogance became the mask behind which she hid a crumbling heart; the scaffolding with which she held herself upright in the knowledge that Freddy was gone.

And yet – was he really gone? Without a body ever found, how could anyone be really sure? Certainly, Ma Quint did not believe it.

'He is alive; I know it! A mother knows these things!' she said, from the moment she recovered from the first shock of the telegram, and that was her standard reply to the condolences immediately following the news, and to any reference to Freddy in the past tense thereafter.

As for Dorothea: she took refuge in rationality. It was the only way to keep going. She would believe the worst, and keep going. So she forced herself to believe that Freddy was dead until information to the contrary told her otherwise. That was the only sensible attitude.

Sometimes, though, her heart seemed to cut loose from the earth of reason to swing up to the sky, joining Freddy wherever he might be. Whenever she heard the melancholy strains of a mouth-organ she started, and looked up – was it him? She suffered from insomnia most nights, and on such occasions she took to riding her bicycle to the Sea Wall where she would walk for miles in the moonlight or the starlight, the Atlantic wind whipping at her skirt and moulding it to her legs as she walked; and there she would look up at the vastness of space and the twinkling of stars and he would be there, all around her, a knowledge and a being as strong and as near as God. And she would call to him, and he would answer.

❋ ❋ ❋

Years passed; the war ended. With the exception of Howard, killed in Singapore, the other Quint brothers all returned from war, safe and sound. The surviving Quint brothers were now all married, except Humphrey. They had all moved out of the big higgledy-piggledy house, established their own households and were busy building careers, families, and, in some cases, already emigrating. Each one was different, and each had lived up professionally to the nickname given him in his youth: 'The Businessman', 'The Revolutionary', 'The Mechanic', 'The Artist'.

Humphrey had always been 'The Philosopher', the quiet one, and so he remained; withdrawn, even-tempered, sweet-natured, happiest when buried in his books and his stamp-albums. Many an evening Dorothea sought his company for the solace it gave her. Humphrey helped her wind down after a hard day's work, becoming the brother she'd never had. Humphrey was the only man – apart from Pa Quint – with whom she did not wage war.

She liked to visit Pa with Humphrey. Pa's Annex was like a little mid-air island set among the trees behind the house. It had windows along all four sides so the breeze whipped through, except for the one corner with his desk and the two wooden chairs, one for Pa, one for Humphrey.

Pa kept his best stamps not in albums but in biscuit tins. One stamp, he kept in a tin all of its own. He showed the stamp to Dorothea. It was smudged and faded and not in the least impressive, but Pa let her look at it through a magnifying glass.

'See those letters there?' he said. 'T.A.Q. Theodore Anthony Quint. My father! One day, the Post Office ran out of stamps so the Postmaster General had a batch printed by local printers. But they were badly done, easily forged. So he tell the postal workers to sign them wit' they own initials before selling. Grandpa was one-a them workers. He save this stamp as a souvenir, and give it to me.'

'There's only one other stamp like this left in the world,' Humphrey told her. 'And nobody knows about this one. The other one is considered the rarest; it went to auction recently and achieved a small fortune. We prefer to keep this in the family. The only other person who knows about it is Matt. He wants to buy it, but we won't sell.'

'What makes a stamp so valuable?' Dorothea asked.

'Rarity,' Humphrey answered. 'These were one cent stamps, for newspaper wrappings. People don't save them. They look so cheap, not worth collecting. But this one – I love it!'

Pa replaced the lid on the biscuit tin. 'Pah! You can have it. It's all yours. When I dead and gone the family going to throw out everything in here, all these ol' man tings.' He waved around the room. 'If you want this stamp, you better take it now.'

'Can I have that in writing? That you have given it to me? I can quickly draw up a document.'

Dorothea wrinkled her nose. Humphrey, the lawyer, could get a bit pedantic at times. Why did he want it in writing, that his grandfather was giving him this silly scrap of paper? She asked him later.

'Because,' Humphrey said, 'There are many of us brothers, and human nature is greedy. This stamp is worth a lot of money on the market. Not that I would ever sell it; for me, it's the sentimental value. I just want to own it, to look at it, to imagine my grandfather initialling it with his own hand. It's family history. If you loved stamps, you'd understand. But I need it to be official, that Pa gave it to me. I don't want anyone challenging my ownership.'

'But who would ever do that?'

The answer was immediate. 'Leo. 'The Businessman.' Even as a child he turned everything he could to money. Last year, when William had his first successful exhibition, you know what Leo did? He went to the storeroom and found all of Will's old paintings and sold them. Made a small fortune. And kept the money. That's why Leo and William fell out. So I want it official, that this stamp is mine.'

Humphrey smiled at her. 'And you're my witness.'

Pa died a week later. As he had predicted, all his old-man things were thrown out. Humphrey claimed the stamp collection. No one else wanted it. The rest of what he left was split six ways among the six surviving brothers. And Humphrey moved into the Annex.

❈ ❈ ❈

The greatest changes, though, in the intervening years, had taken place in the colony itself. British Guiana was slowly stumbling towards Independence. From the midst of the most oppressed sector of society, the East Indian sugar labourers, had arisen a saviour: Cheddi Jagan, a man of the people, charismatic, outspoken, and passionate. He had studied dentistry in the USA and returned with an American wife, Janet, a woman of substance and every bit as zealous as Cheddi himself.

Cheddi and Janet let their voices be heard, and people listened; the country, in particular the hordes of downtrodden sugar workers, rose up in protest, demanding human working conditions and the end to imperialism. Cheddi and Janet founded the People's Progressive Party, a multi-party, multi-ethnic, multi-class, party supported by labourers and intellectuals. The PPP joined forces with the country's second party, People's National Congress.

Elections were coming up in a year or two; with Cheddi as the country's leader, Dorothea was sure, British Guiana would win independence from Great Britain. She could hardly contain her excitement. She herself had joined the PPP and risen up the ranks; now, she threw herself into the struggle for Freedom. Independence! That was the dream, and Dorothea dreamt it day and night. Cheddi was a man of the people; his wife a living example and inspiration to her; yes, women could be leaders, could make their voices heard, could put an end to oppression. Dorothea found a political home, and applied herself to *change*. The country would change, and she, Dorothea, would help change it.

❈ ❈ ❈

One evening, when Dorothea was sitting with Humphrey, she noticed that he was unusually nervous. He'd read her a rather good poem by a local poet, published in the *Argosy*, and Dorothea was talking – she regretted the fact that Guianese talent was never promoted in the schools; it was always English poets.

'All the characters in all the books we read are English, white-skinned,' she said. 'And they all eatin' strawberries an' cream and scones. Why not Guianese children, eatin' mango and pineapple? We need more local writers!'

But Humphrey wasn't listening. She could tell. His eyes, usually steady and fixed on her, were jumpy today, and he kept rubbing his nose and sniffing, though he didn't have a cold.

'What's wrong, Humph?'

'Ah … nothing.' He linked his fingers and cracked them.

'Ouch! Don't do that! It makes my skin crawl!'

'Sorry!'

'Humphrey, don't tell me nothing's wrong because is not true. Tell me right now what bothering you.'

Humphrey began to stutter; he always did when emotionally disturbed.

'I-I-I …' he started again. 'I wanted t-t-t-to ask – ask you if, if, if …'

Dorothea had a strong premonition of what was to come. And she was right – the next words came rushing out.

'If you would marry me.'

She said nothing for a while. And then she took his hands in his.

'Oh, Humph. You're so sweet. A darling. And I don't know what I'd a done without you, these last few years. But I'm sorry. I can't marry you. You're a good friend, almost a brother. And anyway …'

She paused. Humphrey finished the sentence for her.

'… you're waiting for Freddy.'

And it was true. Five years had passed since that awful telegram. He had officially been declared dead. No one hoped any longer that he would return, not even Ma Quint. Even Turtle and Parrot had died of old age, taking with them further memories of Freddy. But still …

Dorothea sank her head. She could not look into Humphrey's clear dark eyes, see the love there, and not respond. She couldn't do it. And so she only whispered:

'I'm so sorry.'

Chapter Sixteen

Rika: The Sixties

Granny had asked her to go to Bookers pharmacy after school to get some Benadryl Expectorant; a grandchild she was taking care of this week had a cough. The thought made Rika nervous. She would have to walk right through the whole store to get to the other end.

Just as she had known, a clutch of boys in Saints uniforms was hanging around outside the store, Jag among them. He was sitting on his motorbike, which was parked just in front of the bicycle-stand area, so Rika had to walk right past them wheeling her bicycle. They all turned to watch as she approached, and stopped talking; there was nothing she could do but walk straight past them, her face burning. One of them let out a wolf-whistle as she passed by, and the others chortled heartily. She parked her bike and it took all her effort to walk, not run, into the store.

She walked through the east wing of the store and emerged into the park area, which she had to cross to get to the drug store and supermarket in the west wing, when she heard somebody call her name. She stopped and turned; it was one of the Saints boys who had been with Jag at the entrance. He was sprinting towards her, calling her name:

'Rika! Hold on a moment!'

So she stopped and waited for him to catch up. She had no idea what his name was; he had reddish-brown skin and his hair was cropped very short, like black carpet.

'Hi!' He stopped running and sauntered up. He came with a slight swagger, and his grin was a little too wide, that of someone feigning friendship.

'Hi,' she said, and waited.

'I got a message for you,' said the boy, without introducing himself, as if assuming that Rika would know. 'From Jag.'

'From *Jag*? A message?' Rika frowned.

'Yeah. He said to tell you, you got beautiful eyes and evil lips. And nice curves.'

'What! I …' Rika was lost for words, but she didn't need any because the boy had laughed out loud and then turned around and sprinted back the way he had come. She was left standing, staring after him, her cheeks red-hot, her heart thumping and her thoughts in disarray.

A moment later she shuddered as if to shake off the shock, and turned to walk towards the pharmacy. She bought the Benadryl, paid for it, walked back through the store. As she reached the east exit she hesitated. She had to pick up her bike but it would mean walking past those boys again, walking past *him*, and she didn't know if she could without her legs turning to jelly. So she stopped at the door, eased herself forward and peeked around the corner first, and saw that the boys had gone. She picked up her bike and cycled home as fast as her legs could take her. Later that afternoon, as soon as she could manage, she slipped through the palings and down the alley and into her grandmother's yard.

At first, Rajan was nowhere to be seen; just buckets filled with genips around the tree; a ladder leaned against the trunk. Then Rajan called from above; she looked up and there he was, sitting on a branch high above her.

'Hang on; coming down,' he cried; but before coming himself, he lowered a bucket filled almost to the brim with plump ripe genips.

'Catch it!' he called, and Rika caught hold of the bucket swinging on its rope and lowered it gently to the ground.

Rajan scrambled through the upper branches till he reached the lowest branch; from there he leaped to the ground, landing beside her as nimbly as a cat. He wore torn old khaki shorts and nothing else; his chest was taut and glistening with sweat, and his face, too, gleamed and little bits of tree-bark and a leaf or two clung to his skin. He was barefoot.

'Come on, time for a feast,' he said, grabbing a bucket. He gestured to the wooden bench under the house, and Rika walked over with him.

'What's up?' he asked. She didn't often come mid-week, and when she did it was to tell him of some hurtful incident that had happened in school – Jen Goveia and her gang seemed determined to put her in her rightful place – or for help with an imminent maths problem. Only on Saturdays and Sundays did she come just to chat and talk philosophy. She told him what had happened.

'Beautiful eyes!' he said, and smiled. 'Well, that's true. Nice curves, too. But evil lips? *Evil?* Let me have a look ...' And he leaned forward, as if to inspect her mouth.

'Don't tease! Evil means ...'

'I know, I know ... it's a compliment. So you're flattered? Go on, have some genips.' He grabbed a handful of the little green balls and they rolled from his hand into her open palms.

'I suppose so,' she said. She transferred all the genips to one hand, picked one off its stalk and placed it between her teeth. She pressed down gently so that the soft shell cracked open. The fruit, soft and golden, slid onto her tongue and for a moment she savoured the tart sweet taste of it.

'Ummmmm,' she moaned. 'Heavenly. I think this is my favourite fruit ever.'

'Mine too,' said Rajan, and produced a small cracked enamel bowl for them both to spit the sucked-dry stones into. 'You can take a bucket home if you like. We have plenty. Your grandparents always said we could pick them, sell them, do what we want with them.'

'Thanks,' said Rika. 'But tell me, why did he say that? What does it mean?'

'Who? What? Oh – that boy? What's his name again?'

'Jag. Don deSouza.'

The words had been turning over and over in her mind ever since she'd heard them. *Beautiful eyes, evil lips…* a message from Jag! He had sent his friend expressly to tell her that! Why? What about Jen? She wouldn't like it – definitely not. Why did boys say things like that? Rajan was a boy – maybe he could explain it.

'It got your attention, didn't it?' said Rajan now. 'Just like he got your attention the other day, at the snack bar.'

'But – but why? I'm nothing special. There are so many other girls much better-looking than me. I'm a nobody! And look at Jen, and her friends! I mean why would he say that to *me,* of all people?'

'Why do you let your looks define you, Rika? Why do you see yourself as worthless?'

I stared at him, speechless. I hadn't thought of it like that. 'Worthless? I – I don't know. I just know I'm not a bit like them. Not even close. I don't see why a boy like that – I mean, he's so popular, he could get any girl he wanted in this whole country. Why would he tell *me* things like that?'

Rajan just shrugged. 'He's probably just bored. Looking for a bit of excitement. Looking to get *you* excited. And you are, aren't you?'

'Well, I – I…'

'See? He got your attention and now you're thinking about him. I bet you weren't thinking about him at all last week, before that snack-bar story. And now you are. He was invisible, and now he's not.'

'I still don't understand. He's got Jen.'

'I told you – excitement. Drama. When people get bored with their lives they do something to ease the boredom.'

'But why me? Of all people…'

'You just happened to put in your appearance, right time, right place, and he probably thought you're as good as anyone else. Entertainment.'

'So I'm just – entertainment? Nothing – nothing more?'

'You mean, do I think he's fallen in love with you? No, I don't. I don't think he's really interested in *you*. I think you're a convenient diversion, and he thinks it might be a bit of fun to get a girl who – well, a girl …'

Rajan hesitated.

'Go on, say it. A girl like me. A nobody.'

'Well, in his eyes you are probably a nobody and that's the whole point. The question here is, why are you in your *own* eyes a nobody? Go home now, Rika, and think about that. I've got work to do. Go on, take the bucket.'

And he stood up, as if thoroughly bored with her and the whole subject, and handed her the bucket, in which by now the level of genips had been substantially reduced.

Rika took the bucket and her leave. Lost in thought, she made her way to the hole in the fence and took off for home. Rajan had given her much to think about; but his philosophising was a little too deep for her, too arcane. He seemed not to take Jag's message seriously. He just wasn't interested.

Actually, Rika was a bit disappointed in Rajan. She has thought, hoped, that he'd say something along the lines of 'But you're beautiful too!' or 'You're not a nobody; you're wonderful, unique!' That's why she had turned to Rajan in the first place; for him to offer support, boost her confidence. She knew all too well that she lacked self-esteem. She wallowed in that lack almost every minute of every day, but Jag's interest in her was helping to repair that fault-line of her consciousness.

She'd thought Rajan would see that, and would apply some well-needed compliments to help her on her way. Instead, he had asked questions that practically worsened that crumbling confidence: 'Why are you in your own eyes a nobody?' What sort of a question was *that?* Instead of giving her a hand to help her out of that wallowing pit, he was pushing her back in again! A simple *but you* are *beautiful, and worthy of his attention!* would have worked wonders. Yes, she was disappointed in Rajan – she had thought him more sensitive to her needs, more understanding than that.

❃ ❃ ❃

But he was right about one thing. She couldn't remember when anything as exciting as this had happened to her. *Beautiful eyes, evil lips...* she couldn't wait to look at herself in the mirror. Maybe she wasn't really as plain as she thought. *Nice curves* – but surely she was too fat? She breathed out, pulled in her stomach, regarded her sideways profile in the mirror. Maybe not fat, after all. Maybe she was actually attractive – *Jag* had noticed her! *Don deSouza*! That had to mean something. She wasn't quite sure yet what, but it did mean something. Jag had noticed her. *The* Jag. Maybe she really wasn't as worthless as she thought.

❃ ❃ ❃

Every day after that Rika went to Bookers after school, even if there was nothing she had to buy. Just to see if ... anyone was there. But nobody ever was; at least, nobody of note. There were always a few groups of boys and girls in the various uniforms: Bishops' girls in green with their Panama hats, Queens boys in khaki trousers and yellow striped ties, St Rose's girls in blue tunics, St Joseph's girls in green, Saints boys, Central High School girls and boys. Rika's eyes now invariably roved, looking out for the familiar blue-grey of Saints; and sometimes it was there, but the wearer was never Jag.

As for Jen, as another St Rose's girl she was unavoidable, but as she was in a parallel class they weren't thrown together all that much. The teasing stopped, as if Jen had grown bored with her. Sometimes they passed each other in the corridors, or at break time, but Jen made a point of demonstrably turning away each time, and always with a snort of sheer disdain; and all her minions turned away with her. Rika wondered if Jen had heard. Heard what Jag had said about her: *beautiful eyes, evil lips.* Maybe Jen was jealous? Of *her!*

Rika now looked closer at herself in the mirror every day. Her eyes didn't seem all that special. Big and brown, yes, but her eyelashes were too short and curly; you were supposed to have long black sweeping lashes, like Jen. And her lips were too thick. She'd always known that and it hadn't really bothered her up to now, but now that Jag had said they were *evil* – the absolute ultimate in compliments! – she took a closer look, moved them about, tried smiling and pursing them to see what was so evil about them. Jen's were definitely more evil, thinner for a start, but Jag had said ... Rika's heart sank. *Everything* about Jen was lovely, she thought in despair. *Nice curves* – but definitely too fat, when all was said and done. She'd have to go on a diet. She couldn't imagine why Jag could have said those things about her, a nobody, when he had Jen all to himself. Jen was so very, very beautiful; so sparkly and witty, radiant with confidence, and with the ability to wither lesser girls, like Rika, with a mere glance. That's how superior she was. Like a goddess, and especially since she was Jag's girlfriend. Superior in every way. In comparison she, Rika, felt like something thrown up by the tide. Jen made her feel dirty, inadequate. She had tried to confide in Rajan about this, but all he had said was, 'There's nothing uglier than self-importance,' and changed the subject, as if the very thought of Jen disgusted him.

The incident at the snack-bar still stung Rika to the core. *Idiot.* Jen's face as she spat the word at her. *Idiot!* Yes, exactly. That's what she was. Jen had hit the nail on the head, and it had pierced the very nerve of her being, because it was true. And that look Jen had thrown her. So full of venom! She shuddered just to think of it. The very memory of it made her want to disappear; but oh, to somehow vanquish Jen! If Jen could only find out what Jag had said! *That* would make her sorry …

She stopped at the cosmetics department. Maybe if she wore lipstick it would help. There was the Elizabeth Arden stand with the lipstick samples and a mirror. She tried out a bright red on the back of her hand. But no, that was too obvious. Maybe a pale pink? No, that looked ridiculous. Only white people could wear pink. Maybe a sort of reddish-brown? Yes, that would do. But you couldn't wear lipstick at school, and there was no point wearing it at home. Maybe she could put it on after school, just in case … did she have enough pocket money? If not, she'd buy it next week, when she did. And some perfume. Elizabeth Arden's Blue Grass.

But then Rika caught herself in the mirror and melted into a puddle of anguish. Her *hair!* Never mind about her eyes and her lips. She would never, ever be able to do anything about her hair. The only thing you could do with hair like hers – a mane of black frizzled wire that behaved exactly the way it wanted to – was tie it back in one or two plaits, and that was that. Nothing *evil* about plaits, and there never would be. It was then that Rika, looking into the mirror, saw Jen saunter past with her clique of close friends, giggling together as if at a secret joke. Probably laughing at her. Jen's eyes caught hers in the mirror and she was right; there it was again, that withering, soul-destroying sneer. Rika hurriedly replaced the red-brown lipstick sample in its holder and slunk away. It was all hopeless. Probably she had just dreamt up the thing about beautiful eyes and evil lips. Or else, Jag didn't mean it. He'd just said it to tease her.

❄ ❄ ❄

The latest rumour was that Jag and Jen had broken up. Nobody told Rika specifically, but it floated through the school halls like a wild brush fire, lips to ears, whispered behind upheld hands. Some of the girls looked shell-shocked at the news, others seemed to gloat. Rika was among the latter, but she did it secretly, silently, never saying a word, because, after all, nobody told her, a nobody, directly. It was just something she picked up by the way, being a listener rather than a talker. A thing you couldn't avoid hearing.

Her imagination went into overdrive. Jag had broken up with Jen because of *her*, Rika. Jen was insanely jealous, called her spiteful names, and Jag had stuck up for her. Jag had finally seen Jen's inner ugliness and recognised her, Rika's, inner beauty. Isn't that what Rajan had told her? *Beauty is inside. It's in the soul. Never mind what you look like, Rika; try to find that inner beauty.* Very well; *that* must be it. Jag had seen it, that inner beauty. He appreciated who she really was, the part of her invisible to everyone else. The *real* her. He had stripped away the outer trappings of plainness and seen her *real* self, which was beautiful, as Rajan had said. Because love was beautiful, and Rika could love. Oh yes, she could love. That much she knew. She felt as if love was about to burst open from within, if only someone would prick the thin membrane that enclosed it, and that someone had to be Jag. *How* she would love him! How he would bask in that love!

Dreams carried her away. She saw herself all in floating white, walking up the aisle, and there he waited, so smart in his wedding suit, gazing at her with eyes melting with love – there they were, walking down the aisle together, emerging from the church laughing and hugging, with confetti floating down on them, and there was Jen in the corner, sulking ...

A strident voice slammed into her dream:

'Frederika Quint, let me hear you decline the verb '*cueillir*'?'

Rika started and looked up; Sister Magdalena was staring at her with those fiery eyes that knew everything – everything.

'Umm ... *je* ...' mumbled Rika, and all the girls giggled.

'Let me see what you were writing there,' said Sister Magdalena.

'Oh, but I wasn't, I mean, I didn't ...'

'I know you weren't writing French verbs but you were writing something. Bring it here. No, don't bother.'

Sister Magdalena strode down the aisle; Rika covered her exercise book with her hands but it was no good; Sister Magdalena pulled it away, took one look, and then turned to glare at Rika who was looking up at her with pleading eyes. *Please don't read it aloud. Please don't, please don't.*

She didn't. The Lord be praised, Sister Magdalena placed the book back on her desk and Rika let out an audible sigh of relief; she hadn't even realised she'd been holding her breath.

'If you want to get married, you'd be better off paying attention in class,' was all Sister Magdalena said, a very mild rebuke, for her.

Rika resolved to give up her dreams. They were so silly anyway. Jag would never look at her again. She picked up her fountain-pen and scribbled all over the practice signatures she had made: *Rika deSouza. Frederika deSouza. Mrs Frederika de Souza.*

❄ ❄ ❄

On her was home down Camp Street that afternoon she heard the throb of a motorbike engine as it slowed down behind her, felt its heat as it drew up beside her. She looked up. It was Jag.

He was riding beside her, looking at her and grinning that irresistible lopsided grin of his, his head cocked at a flirtatious angle. Her limbs turned to jelly and the handlebars wobbled.

'Hi,' he said.

'Oh, hi,' she managed to mumble, though the simple words almost stuck in her throat.

'How are you?'

'I… I'm fine,' she managed to stutter.

'Well, I was thinking I'd take you to the D'Aguiar fête next Saturday. OK?'

This time the bicycle wobbled so violently she almost fell off.

'Careful, don't kill yourself! So it's OK, right?'

'Y – yes,' was all Rika managed.

'Good. Better go before a nun catches me with you. I'll pick you up at eight. See you.'

He lowered his wrist, turning the handle so that the motor revved. He had removed the silencer so the exhaust gave out a deep resounding roar, like a giant clearing his throat. He did this three times; he looked behind to check for traffic, lifted a hand in a stiff farewell salute, kicked the gear lever, and zoomed away in a final reverberating crack of thunder.

Chapter Seventeen

Rika: The Sixties

Now, more than ever, Rika longed for a girlfriend. A friend she could exclaim and giggle with over Jag's invitation; a friend who'd hug and congratulate her, jump up and down squealing with excitement, because Rajan certainly wasn't excited. How could he ever understand? He was a boy; worse, he was a young man and whatever else he was good for – talking philosophy, farming, maths and that sort of thing – he didn't know a thing about how a young girl feels when she falls in love for the very first time.

Not having a suitable confidante, Rika began to keep a diary. She no longer wrote her novels in the Cupola; in fact she hardly ever went up there any more – no time! So she kept her diary in her bedroom; it was like speaking to a friend, a friend who listened to all she had to say without judging, a friend in whom she could confide and confess everything. Her life was finally taking off! She had to keep track of it.

Her first date! And with Don, The Jag! And she had to keep it all to herself – what a waste! So it all went in to her diary. She was simply bursting with delight. And it wasn't just delight she longed to share; it was all the peripheral feelings that went along with this most extraordinary situation. She, Rika Quint, the quintessential Plain Jane, had been Chosen! Plucked from obscurity by a Prince in Shining Armour on a Silver Steed! Well, on a Yamaha, really, but he certainly was the equivalent of a Prince in the Georgetown teenage scene. No girl could do better, aim higher.

She swelled with pride at the thought. She must have something extraordinary, some hidden quality to her, just as

Rajan had said; *inner beauty,* he had called it, something that only Jag had seen and nobody else, least of all she herself. He had broken up with Jen. Possibly over her. Possibly he had Known, just as she had, what an immense thing this was. He had seen it in her eyes; *beautiful eyes,* he had said, just as she had seen it in his that moment when they had locked eyes, that first day at Bookers Snack Bar. That was the moment when the whole earth shifted; he must have felt it too; otherwise, why? *Why her?*

Why me? Sometimes the words broke into her euphoria and crackled it into doubt. This couldn't be happening to her. It just couldn't. Why her, of all people, when Jag could have any of the girls at any of the schools, the most beautiful and the most charming, girls with swinging shiny hair and that certain *attitude;* who walked and talked as if they owned the world, girls comfortable in themselves in a way that she, Rika, had never been and, she was sure, never would be. But perhaps there was a chance, now, with Jag at her side?

The D'Aguiar fête! She had heard if it, of course, the last great event before the Christmas Season broke in with all the hundreds of minor get-togethers leading up to the Grand Finale at the Rowing Club on Old Year's Night. At sixteen, you could start going to all these grown-up fêtes. You could leave behind the world of private fêtes held by friends at their homes. There would be a live band and barbecue chicken and rum-and-coke; she knew because she was a listener and that was what the girls all talked about. The D'Aguiar fête in Bel Air Park wasn't just a free friend's party you got invited to because the friend had put you on her list; a boy had to *invite* you, and *pay* for you. And it had happened. To her.

She had been to fêtes before, with unpleasant results. You couldn't really count those fêtes, though, because they had been organised by her older cousins, Quints, part of the extended family. Two of them had been held in her own home, another had been in the home of Cousin Zoe. Possibly Zoe – who was a year older than her and went to Bishops' – had been instructed to invite her, by Granny.

Just thinking of those events made Rika cringe. Like the one at Zoe's. She had worn a dress that was wildly out of date – as she had discovered too late – and much too long. She had sat, silently, along with the other girls, who were all giggling and chatting among themselves and pointedly ignoring her. Why couldn't she giggle and chat, just like them? Why couldn't she be a *normal* girl, who knew what to say and what to wear? So she sat there by herself, not knowing what to do with her hands and wishing she hadn't come. Boys stood around in huddles, glancing at the girls now and then and flexing their arms and slapping each other on the shoulders the way boys do. And then the jukebox had blared out … and the boys had surged forth towards the girls and each boy had chosen a girl and taken her hand and led her to the dance floor and when they had all gone, there she sat, all alone against the wall.

Eventually one of her male cousins – Nicolas Quint – had taken pity on her and asked her to dance, but after that she'd had enough and fled; she'd rang up Daddy and asked her to come and pick her up, and he had.

'Had a good time?' Daddy had asked, and 'Yes,' she had murmured in reply. And that was that.

But this was different. It was an *invitation*. By a Boy. To the D'Aguiar Barbecue. And there was no one to talk to about it. She had tried, with Rajan, but he had not been interested. 'Oh?' was all he had said, and, 'and you said yes?' As if there had been any *doubt* as to whether she'd say yes or not. As if Jag had actually asked her, which he hadn't. He'd simply said he'd take her. Boys like Jag didn't have to ask; they just *stated their intention,* and that was their defining quality. But Rajan could never understand that, and that was disappointing because hitherto Rika had been able to confide all her problems in him; nothing had been too small for him to want to listen attentively and, if she asked for advice, give it, and help her to deal with whatever was bothering her. But not this time. She couldn't ask Rajan for advice on what to wear, and what make-up to buy, and – most of all – what to do with her *hair*.

Her hair was the worst of all. It was an abomination, and just thinking about that hair and those two knobbly plaits made Rika sick to her stomach, and doubt again that it had really happened – that *Jag* had asked her to the *D'Aguiar Barbecue*. Just thinking the words made her knees as wobbly as jelly.

However, it *was* true, because in no time everyone knew it. She hadn't told a soul except Rajan, so it must be Jag who had told some people and they had told others and now the whole world knew. Girls who had never spoken to her in their lives – who had almost looked away when she passed by, humping their school satchels onto their shoulders in clear rebuff – now regarded her with new interest, looking her up and down as if to assess her for some overlooked quality (*but it's hidden! I can't see it myself but it's there!*) and one or two girls actually spoke to her, asking her for confirmation – *Jag asked you? It's true? Really?* – as if they didn't, couldn't, believe the rumours.

And then one or two actually approached her for friendship. Stella and Joanne, in fact, two girls from the parallel form who were not quite popular themselves, but who stood at the outer periphery of popularity. Stella and Joanne smiled at her after class and at the bicycle stand Stella said to her, 'We're going for hamburgers at Esso Joe's, want to come?'

Of course she had said yes.

While eating hamburgers at Esso Joe's, Stella had fingered one of Rika's plaits and said, 'You know, you should really get it straightened.'

Rika blinked.

'You think so?'

'Of course! It would transform you. I can recommend a good hairdresser who will do it for you. You won't believe the difference! I mean, look at my hair!'

Stella twirled one of her black locks and shook her head to show Rika how it swung back and forth.

'You hair is straightened?'

'Yes! Everyone does it these days. I'll give you the phone number – just a sec.'

And Stella scrambled in her satchel, took out a pencil and a notebook, scribbled a few numbers, and handed the note to Rika. 'There! Ring her up – ask for Joyce, and say I sent you!'

❄ ❄ ❄

Later that afternoon Rika rang up the hairdresser and spoke to Joyce, but instead of booking an appointment, she asked the price of a hair-straightening session. She was beginning to worry about money. She usually spent her pocket money on things like snacks and books; now, with this great event looming, she'd have so many first time expenses – a dress, shoes, lipstick etc., and now hairdressing – she was beginning to fear the money wouldn't stretch that far. There were other matters to worry about, but money, for the time being, came first.

When she heard the price of a 'chemical relaxation' – as Joyce insisted on calling the required treatment – her worries trebled. That would be three weeks' pocket money! And she still had to buy a dress, and shoes!

Maybe Granny – who was in charge of doling out her pocket money, as well as most other matters concerning her wellbeing – would give her a month's advance. It would mean no new books for a month, which, considering she had already read most of the readable library books and was already re-reading her favourites, would be a hard sacrifice. Was it worth it?

But then she brought to mind Don DeSouza on his roaring Yamaha beside her, and Jen's sneer at the snack bar; she imagined the look on Jen's face as she watched Rika and Jag on the dance floor, cheek-to-cheek to the romantic crooning of Engelbert Humperdinck, and Rika knew without a shadow of a doubt that yes, it was all worth the greatest sacrifice. No price was too great to pay for this once-in-a-lifetime opportunity. She had to look her best; so, no new books, if need be. Maybe, anyway, she'd be far too busy with Jag to do any reading in the next few months. Who knew what the future held! A *frisson* of excitement, of anticipation shuddered through her: the near future held such delectable secrets, and she'd unfold them one by one! But first, this vexing money problem. How much, exactly, would she need? How much would the material for the dress cost, and the seamstress, and the shoes, and the lipstick and such? Perfume: she'd need that too. It would all add up, and asking for such a huge advance ...

And then she knew the answer. Her grandparents! The bank book! Her inheritance! She *had* the money already; it was hers! She only had to ask for a bit of those savings to be paid out now. She'd ask Granny, who kept the bank books in her special drawer for documents.

But the greatest worry of all, the one that kept her awake at night, was the one of even getting permission to go. Mummy would refuse. Mummy would say something like, 'yes, if you bring home an A in Maths at the end of next term;' and not only was 'the end of next term' too late for anything but the A in Maths was beyond impossible, and that was all Mummy cared about. Mummy didn't approve of parties anyway. Everything except politics and fighting for justice was frivolous nonsense. But surely Mummy had been young once; surely she'd had gone to parties and been courted and knew the terrible, wonderful *frisson* of falling in love? Had Mummy always been so serious, so dour, so funless? So uncaring?

She doesn't care about me, Rika thought; *she only cares about my accomplishments. My achievements, my success. That's all she wants, and otherwise I'm a nobody to her as well.*

But being a nobody to Mummy had its advantages. More and more over the last few years Mummy left the day-to-day decisions concerning Rika to Granny; and so it would be Granny she'd ask for permission.

❊ ❊ ❊

'The D'Aguiar barbecue? Aren't you a bit young for that?' was what Granny said. 'I mean, a private fête, of course; it's time you were out and about with other girls and boys your age. But I'm not too sure about this one. There'll be a lot of rum, and older men …'

'But I'll be with Don!' pleaded Rika. 'Don De Souza!'

'That's the son of Justice DeSouza, isn't it?'

Rika nodded vigorously. Adults were most easily influenced by family names, and placing people in this *good* family or the other.

'They live in Bel Air Gardens,' Rika offered.

'Well, I suppose that's respectable enough. Is he coming to pick you up?'

'Yes, yes of course!' She could hardly tell Granny that it would be on a motorbike; but perhaps it wouldn't. Perhaps he'd come in a taxi. What an honour!

'Very well, then. But be sure to be home by midnight, all right?'

'Oh, Granny, thank you, thank you!'

Rika leapt at Granny and threw her arms around her, making her drop the ball of dough she was about to roll into a puri, but

Granny just laughed and accepted it, in a way that Mummy never did and never would. When last had she been hugged by Mummy? Never, in the last ten years.

'All right, that's enough kisses,' said Granny then, pushing her away. 'And don't worry about your mother – I'll talk to her about it.'

'And – and Granny, there's another problem; a big one!' said Rika. 'I need money! To buy a dress, and to go to the hairdressers, and things like that! I was wondering if – I mean the money is mine, isn't it, the money in the bank? To do what I want with?'

'Well, I think it's intended for more serious things than fêtes, darling. But maybe just this once. You've never asked for any withdrawals yet – unlike the boys! – so why not? Just this once. It's time you went out with people your own age'

They discussed the amount she would need, and Rika proved that she could do some calculations, when necessary, and Granny nodded and took her to the office, where she opened a small drawer in the desk and took out a tiny key, with which she opened the drawer where all the passports and bank books were kept. There was Rika's among all the others. Granny took it out, and the passport, and handed them to her.

'There you are, dear. It's lovely to see you so excited about something!'

Every cell in her body was singing and dancing, and it must have been written all over her face; that soaring, heavenly, utterly exquisite *elation*. It was back, and it filled every atom of her body and every corner of her soul; she could spread her wings and *fly!* Rika twirled away from Granny, arms spread out, laughing out loud with glee.

Chapter Eighteen

Rika: The Sixties

It was time to make concrete plans – time was running short. She needed a dress. What style? What were the other girls wearing when they went to fêtes? She hadn't a clue. So the next afternoon, after school, there she was again at Bookers. She'd try Bookers *and* Fogarty's; and as for style, she'd choose something nice from *Teen* magazine and have it copied by Granny's seamstress.

'Hello, there!' The voice beside her made her look up, startled; she'd been standing there in a quandary, fingering a soft blue fabric and wondering what one could do with it and if it would suit her. Beside her now was a lanky brown girl in a Bishops' uniform with a round soft Afro, grinning at her, as if …

'You're Rika, right? And you're going to the D'Aguiar fête with Don DeSouza? Everyone's talking about it … I'm Trixie by the way, Trixie MacDonald.'

'Oh – hi!' was all Rika could manage.

'You're buying cloth for a dress? This is no good – you can't do anything with it. You know what people are wearing these days? The Granny look! It would look wonderful on you! You want me to help you choose? Hope you don't mind me butting in – I saw you by yourself and I heard you don't have any friends so …'

Rika smiled up at her. 'Would you? Really? I was just thinking …'

And they walked over to the stack of cotton bolts, an array of very small floral prints, and Trixie described the style she thought would work.

'Sometimes the necks are very high but you have such beautiful skin; I would have it scooped low at the neck, with a white lacy edging – this peach would look wonderful on you – and puffed sleeves and an Empire line, and not too long either. Look, let me draw a sketch for you, I have something similar.'

Trixie pulled out the two middle pages of her maths exercise book and drew a sketch of the kind of dress she had in mind. Rika nodded and smiled and agreed with everything, and bought several yards of the fabric; and Trixie recommended her own dressmaker, Hyacinth, who lived near Bourda Market, and promised to take her there herself.

On learning that Rika was going to get her hair straightened, Trixie grimaced. 'Ouch! I did that once. Why not go natural, like me? The Afro look is all the rage in America now.'

Trixie scribbled Hyacinth's telephone number beneath the sketch and handed the note to Rika.

'I couldn't *believe* it when I heard Jag had asked you out; all of us at Bishops' cheered. We can't stand that stuck up bitch Jenny and her friends and she needs a good lesson – but you got to be careful with Jag, OK? He really only likes one thing from girls but he usually doesn't get it anyway. So just be careful. You must tell me everything afterwards, OK? And go and get your hair done. It's time you lost those plaits. They make you look about twelve. And what about make-up? You can't get it at Bookers or Fogarty's; they only have make-up for white skin. It would look terrible on you. Some girls don't seem to even care! I know a little shop where they sell dark-skin make-up – I'll take you there. You want to go to Hyacinth now? We could stop at that make-up place on the way.'

❊ ❊ ❊

The one person – apart from Jen and her gang of bitches – who didn't seem to share her joy was Rajan. Rika was rather hurt about that. In the past couple of weeks – ever since the incident with Jen, in fact – Rajan had clammed up and seemed not as interested in her as before. In fact, he seemed bored at all she had to say about the ongoing situation. He certainly didn't care about her hair or her clothes. Rika understood; it was because he was a boy.

But she couldn't help talking about it. Rajan was really the only person she had to discuss things with, and she was so full of love and excitement and anticipation the words just bubbled out of her – she, who usually stumbled over the spoken word and never knew what to say. If Rajan was bored he never said so; he just didn't react, and that was probably a good thing because all Rika really wanted was a listener, and at least Rajan *listened*.

So she told him everything. She told him all about love. That it was the most wonderful thing in the world. She had read about it in novels, of course, and seen in in films, but that was all second hand, a mere shadow compared to this, the real thing.

The problem with Rajan was that he turned everything into a deep philosophical discussion, which was all very well but could get boring and was beside the point. Now, after a long pause filled with pea-shelling, he said,

'"*We live that we may learn to love. We love that we may learn to live. No other lesson is required of Man.*" Mirdad.'

There he was again, philosophising when she wanted to talk of her feelings for Jag. Rika shrugged. Probably she was just too shallow for Rajan.

She grabbed a handful of peas, laid them on her lap, and began to crack them open, letting the little green balls fall into the bowl between them on the bench.

'I suppose, in the end, love is the answer to all the world's problems,' she added after a while. 'I mean, I feel as if I could love everyone. It's just there. And all the bad feelings I had, they're just gone. And even people like Jen –I could even love her, if only she wasn't so hostile. And my mother. And, you know what? She's much nicer to me now. It's as if love was the answer to all my problems. Oh Rajan! I'm so happy! And I can't wait for the barbecue and to see Jag again and be with him for the whole night! And I can't wait to see what he says about my new hair – it's going to transform me, you wait and see!'

But again Rajan said nothing; he smiled to himself as if at a secret joke and shook his head, almost imperceptibly, but Rika noticed.

'What? Why you're shaking your head? You think I'm talking nonsense!'

He looked up then.

'Oh, Rika! No you're not talking nonsense but I just don't want you to get hurt!'

'But why should I get hurt? Even if Jag doesn't love me the same at first, in loving him this way he's bound to feel it – I just feel so strong, as if I could cure everything and everyone and everyone would have to love me back because – oh, because love is such a happy thing! So don't worry about me getting hurt. It's just so negative. It's not like you to be negative – think of all the things you've told me, about having confidence that comes from within! I have it now, Rajan! I now understand what you were trying to say, and you were right! So don't you go trying to spoil it!'

And Rajan nodded in compliance and said, 'You're right, Rika, and I really hope it works out for you. You deserve it.'

But Rika felt that somehow, there was doubt in Rajan's words; he didn't believe her. But never mind; she would prove to him that this was real; she would prove the transforming power of love. Love had already transformed her. It would go on to transform her whole life. She just knew it.

❊ ❊ ❊

'OoooooWWW!' She clenched her teeth so the scream wouldn't escape her lips; but it was there all the same. Her brain was on fire! It was as if her whole scalp was covered in red-hot coals burning their way through her head, bursting into flames at the core. She squished her face together to bear the pain, gripped the chair so hard her hands trembled. She screamed in agony, but only silently, because this was voluntary, and it was all for a good cause.

And in the end it was worth it. At last, there was the mercifully cooling rinse as Dolly washed out the chemicals, and then some fiddling, and drying and combing, and then – the mirror. The shock was almost too much to bear – Rika gasped in astonished joy. This was really *her*! Her hair! Straight, black and shiny, just as she'd always longed for, hanging down to her shoulders and swinging as she moved her head; soft and feathery to the touch as she ran her fingers through it. Rika grinned at Dolly in delight, and Dolly smiled back.

'See? It make all the difference! Now you'se a real beauty!'

'Yes, yes! Oh, I can't believe it! Thank you so much!'

Dolly shrugged as she removed the shawl from around Rika's shoulders, put away her utensils. 'Just my job, Miss!'

As she cycled home, Rika felt for the first time the breeze in her hair, the coolness on her scalp; she was a new person now and nothing, nothing could ever go wrong again. She was beautiful, really beautiful! The sense of her own beauty filled her with such joy she almost burst open.

❊ ❊ ❊

Granny's jaw quite literally dropped in shock

'Rika! What have you *done* to yourself!'

Mummy took one look at her and just spat 'Pah!' and turned away.

Daddy frowned. 'Is that a wig?' he asked. 'It doesn't suit you.'

The boys laughed and pointed. 'Rika got white-people hair! Rika got white-people hair!' they chanted.

Only Marion approved. 'Oh, Rika, it's lovely!' she said.

Rika, laughing, swung her head back and forth; oh, the sense of freedom that comes with hair that swings and flops and falls!

'Look at it, Gran, just look! It's so beautiful! I love it!'

And she loved herself, for the first time ever; and she knew without a doubt that Jag would love her too.

There was one more person she had to impress, so the next day – Saturday – she was out the back, down the alley and in her grandmother's back yard. Rajan was nowhere to be seen; then she heard the rhythmic swish of a scythe and followed the sound, which led to the front gate.

Rajan was cutting the grass on the parapet outside the gate; it was a twice-a-month job, for the grass grew quickly and it grew tall; and he did it for the whole street. It was done on the first and third Saturday of the month. When he was finished and all the parapets were neatly clipped and the gutters freed of overgrowth, Rajan would harness the donkey – whose name was Sunny – and drive away with the cart piled high with grass, which he would sell to one of the stables. Usually Rika loved to come and chat with Rajan as he worked and pet the little donkey tethered to a lamp post and grazing beside the donkey-cart, and help rake the cut grass and load it on to the cart; but today she had completely forgotten to help.

Rajan didn't see her come; she had to call out. He looked up, pulled out a cloth tucked into his trouser waist, and wiped the sweat from his brow. 'Hi,' he said.

Rika swung her head so that the hair flew back and forth.

'Well? Do you like it?'

'If you like it, that's all that matters,' said Rajan, and returned to his work. Rika was hurt; offended even; she'd expected a compliment. She stood there waiting for a moment, hoping that Rajan would take a break and go into the shade under the house with her, have a drink and a snack. Surely that was the natural thing to do. But Rajan just continued to work as if she wasn't there, so after a while she shrugged and went home, not through the alleyway, but along the street, her head held high and proud.

Chapter Nineteen

Inky: The Noughties

Reluctantly, I reconciled myself to the fact that Gran was not going to sell the stamp. Mum had known it from the start, and that's why she'd curbed my enthusiasm. Gran, she said, clung to relics from the past as if they were limbs from her own body, might as well cut off one of her legs, or her nose. Once I'd accepted the idea, I too became adept at telling callers to 'haul tail'.

And there were callers, and offers. The last offer was for £10,000. And, painful as it was to reject such sums of money, I did so with great pleasure, knowing as I did now that our stamp – pardon, *Gran's* stamp – was worth so much more. The mounting drama in our lives was almost palpable as the third week passed; Gran's stamp the centrepiece of our family life.

'We really should put in a bank safe,' I said to Mum. 'I'm terrified Gran'll lose it.'

'She won't,' Mum assured me. 'You can bet your bottom dollar that the moment we leave that room she hides that album in a place you or me or even the most skilled burglar would never, ever find it. She'll protect it with her life.'

But Gran's life seemed a very precarious protection for a mere scrap of paper – a scrap of paper worth a fortune. I began to seriously worry the following weekend when Sal, a film buff, brought over *Charade* for us all to watch. Cary Grant and Audrey Hepburn helter-skelter through Paris; three murders for the sake of three precious stamps ... was it only fiction?

Watching the stamp-dealer scene in that film, we all shot bolt upright. When one of the stamps in question was declared the rarest in the world because of the postmaster's signature, we all cheered, knowing that the DuPont stamp had been the screenwriter's inspiration.

A few moments later, Gran clapped approval of the film's honest dealer, who returned the precious stamps to their rightful owner, grateful only to have had them in his possession for a while. 'See!' She said in triumph to me, 'That's what I mean! It's the stamps themselves that are precious, not the money you can get for them! That dealer understands it. You get it now? You understand I not crazy?'

I understood. I nodded. Immediately I felt the ice in Gran's voice melt away. 'You young people,' she said in forgiveness, 'You really believe happiness is money. Not true. Not true at all. That stamp dealer – now, he knew happiness. Where it come from? Not from money. You must learn that, Inky.'

She reached out and laid a bony hand on mine, and for the first time ever, I rejoiced at the feel of her shrivelled touch. Our eyes met. I covered her hand with my own. My eyes grew moist.

'Gran, I …'

'Shh!' She withdrew her hand and pointed to the film. I returned to 1950s Paris.

❊ ❊ ❊

Early the following week, a delivery van stopped outside our house just as I was leaving for work; I had lunchtime shifts again. The deliveryman removed a box from the back of the van and set it on the pavement. It was huge; big and square. As I opened the gate to the pavement, he nodded at me.

'Dorothea Quint? Special delivery for you.'

'She's my grandmother. Come inside.'

I led the way to the front door and opened it. The deliveryman followed, wheeling the box on a trolley.

The first thing I saw was Gran, on the stairs, about five steps up. She was clinging to the handrail, but jumped and almost fell backwards when the door opened and I walked in.

'Gran! Where on earth are you going?' I rushed up to grab her elbow. She didn't miss a beat.

'Child! Thank goodness you come back.'

She clutched my hand in hers, and lowered herself to sit on the stairs.

'But where were you going to?'

'I going to the bathroom.'

'But why? What d'you need in the bathroom?'

Whenever Mum and I went out, leaving Gran alone in the house, we placed the potty on a chair so that she could help herself when she needed it.

She ran her tongue over her dentures.

'I need to clean me teeth again. They feelin' furry.'

The deliveryman, standing in the hall, coughed. I looked down at him, remembered.

'Oh, right, sorry to keep you. Gran, you stay right here. I'll be with you in a mo.'

I signed for the delivery and the man left. Gran pointed at the thing he'd left.

'What's that?'

'I don't know! It's for you!'

'For me? Aieeee! Come, child, help me down the steps!'

She had obviously forgotten all about cleaning her dentures. I helped her down to the hall and positioned her over the rollator, which she had abandoned at the foot of the stairs. I really had to go to work and I ought to have left her right there, but I was bursting with curiosity.

'Shall I open in for you? Do you know what it is?' I looked at the label. 'It's from America! From Norbert!'

'Ah, Norbert. Such a good boy! Take good care of his old Mama. Not like some people. Hurry up, child.'

I tore open the outer box. Inside it was yet another box, big and square, but with a picture and writing on the white background.

'*Luxury Commode Chair*', it said. '*Your hygiene needs filled with comfort and dignity.*'

The picture was of a wide, squat wooden chair with a red upholstered seat and back; another, smaller picture showed the same chair with the seat lifted, revealing a potty. I ripped away the cardboard packaging and the polystyrene casing, to reveal that very chair, made of a dark hardwood with velvet upholstery. Nobody could tell from the outside the secret it hid in its bowels; the potty was well concealed within the seat. Gran beamed.

'Ah! Lovely! See, Inky, that's my Norbert! All I got to do is speak the word, and he rush to help me. He send this t'ing all the way from America. Y'all could learn a t'ing or two from him. If y'all don't behave I gon' go live with Norbert in America. Take the t'ing into me room.'

I lifted the chair – which was quite heavy, being of solid wood – and carried it into her room. Gran followed and gave instructions as to how to rearrange the furniture to give the new chair pride of place. After which she dismissed me. I assumed she wanted to try it out.

❋ ❋ ❋

Two weeks following the arrival of The Chair, Neville invited Gran to visit him for a week. Gran didn't even think twice. That very evening she instructed me to pack her suitcase, and the following Saturday Mum drove her up to Birmingham. I breathed a sigh of relief. The house without Gran felt like swimming out into the ocean after escaping a pond full of sharks.

That week, Mum and I did all the mother-daughter things we'd missed lately. We went to the cinema, we went out for a meal, we went for a walk in the park, and, the night before Gran's return, we had a long, cosy talk, both cuddled against a heap of cushions at each end of the sofa; we hadn't done this for years.

Mum was not a talker. She was the most private person I'd ever known, and even to me, her own child, she'd always been more a silent yet solid backdrop, rather than a proactive guardian, assuming I knew what I should know without her having to tell me. A natural ascetic, she was as strict with herself as she was laid-back towards me, and left me to raise myself, trusting somehow in my own wise judgement. Somehow, by a process of trial and error, it had worked. It was as if, without lectures on her part, I'd discovered right from wrong, and even when I failed myself – for instance, in the nasty matter of smoking – I knew that the strength was there to overcome it, and all I was waiting for was the right motivation.

But now we had all this time to talk, and there was something I had to ask her.

Mum had never spoken to me of her own childhood. Not one word. I'd grown up a London child, all family roots buried within her memory and my genes, invisible and unknown to me. I had no relatives, no family to speak of, beyond Mum, and I was very much bound to my home territory. I'd never thought of leaving it more than for a short holiday. Certainly not forever.

And here was Mum; she had left *her* territory at only sixteen! Gone out into the wilds, never to return! How had she done it? How did she feel? Did she miss it? Was the very texture of Guyana merged into her consciousness, as South London was in mine? Did she deny that sense of home; push it away from her awareness; and if so, was she somehow damaged, stunted,

broken? Who was she?   Maybe that was why Mum always
came across as weird. Maybe, deep down inside, she missed
that sense of home. And family. I mean, who were all these
people Gran constantly talked about? Humphrey Quint and
Freddy Quint, Aunty Agnes, Lurleen, Mabel, Uncle Mervyn,
Wolf, Uncle Matt? Gran's arrival into our life stirred all them
all into my awareness. I was curious.

Mum only shrugged when I asked. 'I don't know all of
them. Granny, of course. Ma Quint; She's dead. Humphrey
was my father. I didn't know him that well; he kept to himself. An academic; sweet-natured, mild, kind but distant as
a father. Dutiful. He'd take us to the cinema and kite-flying
and swimming in the sea. But you always felt he was dying to
get back to his stamps. He loved stamps more than people;
and Mum. He *adored* her.   Uncle Matt – he was different.
He was an American, a close friend of Dad's. A philatelist,
and my Godfather. I loved Uncle Matt. He was more of a
father to me than Dad sometimes. Once I went to visit him
in America, when I was a child. We've lost touch. I guess he's
pretty mad at me.'

'Why d'you think that?'

She smiled ruefully.

'Well – it's my fault. I just left, ran away, never contacted
him again. At least, not till you were born.'

This was it. Just the lead I needed, handed to me on a silver
platter.

'Mum … why? Why did you go off like that? I spoke to
Marion and she said I had to ask you and it was pretty awful.
You were only sixteen! I know Gran did something terrible –
but for you to not forgive her for thirty years … what was it?'

Mum clammed up palpably. I could almost feel that wall slamming down, the shutters closing. But I wasn't letting her off the
hook.

'Mum?'

'It's a long story,' she said at last, 'and I'll tell you sometime. I know I have to get over it myself. That's why I wanted her to come here – but it's harder than I thought. She doesn't let me in, never did. Even as a child. She didn't approve of the way I was. We were so different. I was too much a Quint; they were all eccentric, somehow, and I was just another weirdo. We were a big family, you know, several generations living in that big house in Lamaha Street. People were coming and going all the time; aunts, uncles, cousins, friends and relations. I don't even remember them all.'

I grew nostalgic for a family, a home I'd never known.

'It must be wonderful, growing up in such a big family,' I said. 'Don't you get lonely, with only me as family?'

Mum shrugged. 'You can be just as lonely in the middle of a huge family. That house – it was crazy, sometimes.'

'Tell me about it,' I said. 'Tell me about that house.'

And finally, Mum began to talk. I didn't even notice that she'd changed the subject, away from The Thing that kept her and Gran apart.

Chapter Twenty

Inky: The Noughties

It was a higgledy-piggledy house, Mum said, all sash windows and white wood jalousies, standing high above the ground on fat white columns. It had balconies and a glass Cupola at the top and staircases up the front to the main door, and up the back, to the kitchen.

'Marion and I used to sit on the back steps eating genips,' Mum remembered. 'Sucking the flesh off the stones and spitting them as far as we could. We used to have contests to see who could spit the farthest.'

'What are genips?'

'Next time you go to Brixton market, ask the greengrocer, that Errol. Buy a bag of them. Ripe genips are the most addictive fruit in the world. We used to eat them till our teeth turned furry. We didn't have a genip tree ourselves, but our neighbours did and they always shared – we'd get buckets of them delivered in genip season. I had one friend ... anyway. Me and Marion would pounce on the buckets and gobble them up. It used to drive Mummy crazy.'

'I can't imagine Gran being young,' I said. 'What was she like, then?'

'Just like now. Worse. I had a name for her. Not a very nice name.'

'What was it?'

Mum chuckled.

'Ol' Meanie. But I guess that wasn't fair. She wasn't actually *mean* to me, in retrospect. She just didn't seem to know I was there. I was never good enough for her. I thought she hated me.

But I guess she didn't. I guess in her way she cared, but she just didn't want to show it. Or couldn't. And then of course – things happened – and – and – then it was too late.'

Mum stopped and her eyes turned moist and her voice trembled. I tool her hand to encourage her and it was ice cold.

'What happened?'

At last! I was on the cusp of finding out. I'd led her right back to *The Thing,* the knot of discord they both pretended wasn't there. Not so much a knot, in fact, but a wall, a wall of glass: reinforced glass, thin as a membrane but thick and high as the Berlin Wall. It was subtle, mind you. You had to live with them to notice. Mum did her best to be a dutiful daughter to Gran; there was nothing you could pin to her and say, *see, deep inside you're angry, seething with some ancient rage; let it go.* But it was there, a capsule of venom inside her. And Gran: she pecked at Mum and poked her as if trying to lance that abscess, but Mum dodged away as neatly as a Chinese martial artist.

I felt I had a role to play. The role of mediator, a neutral and wise observer who could listen objectively to both sides, hear out both their stories, and bring about a reconciliation. But first I had to know. There'd never be a better time than now.

When Mum said nothing, I prompted her.

'There was some quarrel, right? You and Gran fell out and that's when you ran away and never went back. I know that much. But what happened, exactly? What did Gran *do?'*

But Mum turned agitated and evasive.

'That's all in the past, Inky. No point digging it all up; that's like inspecting the rubbish you've just swept onto the dustpan. What's the point in analysing it? Just throw it out!'

'But you haven't thrown it out, Mum! It's still there, deep inside you!'

I saw myself in the role of therapist. I would listen, calm and relaxed, to whatever Mum had to say, and Mum would find healing just in the telling. I was sure of it. She was keeping it all locked up inside her and that couldn't be healthy.

'Mum, I think it would do you good to *share* whatever pain it is with me. It's festering inside you; why can't you tell me? I'm your daughter! Don't you trust me?'

I watched her face; it was all closed up now. The easy mood between us all swept away. Some awful memory plagued her. Why couldn't she confide in me? But then her tight lips parted, and she spoke, her face turned away from me, gazing at some spot on the opposite wall.

'Ask Gran. It's up to her to tell you what she did.'

❊ ❊ ❊

Very well, if Mum wasn't going to talk, and neither was Gran, I'd try and find out on my own. I sat down at my PC and plunged into the Internet and searched for Quint, Guyana, British Guiana, Dorothea Quint, Fredrika Quint, Rika Quint. Volumes of stuff came up. Dorothea Quint, I discovered, had quite a reputation, and had had quite a career. She had been a Minister of Women's Progress, and the Shadow Minister of Women's Progress; and then, more recently, Adviser to the Minister of Women's Progress. 'Dorothea Q', they called her. It was, in fact, impossible to search Dorothea Quint's activities without discovering things about the country's history and politics, and so I ended up doing a self-taught crash-course on both – it was all terribly fascinating, but, ultimately, useless as far as finding out The Thing. It just wasn't there.

❊ ❊ ❊

A week later, Mum drove back to Birmingham to pick up Gran and our life resumed from where it had left off. Except that Gran had brought back a heightened dissatisfaction with Neville, and an increased regard for Mum. I never learned the whole story, but it seems that Neville's wife, Monica, had not treated Gran with due respect and their three children not only had no regard for family honour, they had been downright rude.

Two weeks passed, and Gran decided she wanted to visit Norbert in America. We talked her out of it. In fact, Norbert talked her out of it. (Not that Norbert didn't want her; of *course* he did, but *his* wife, Melinda couldn't cope. His words, not mine.) And of course the whole logistics of Gran travelling alone to the USA was a nightmare.

In the course of several long conversations between Gran, Mum and Norbert we established that it wasn't so much *Norbert* she wanted to see, but Norbert's two children – a boy and a girl, cousins I'd never met; and that it would make life much easier if instead of Gran going *there* Norbert came *here*, to London, with his brats.

What shall I say? They came, staying in a centrally located hotel that was up to scratch, and the sooner that visit is forgotten, the better. Brats they indeed were, and if anything was ever to convince me that Mum was right to keep a distance from her brothers, that week in hell did it.

But Gran's newly-discovered sense of family did not end there. Next, she wanted to get to know the rest of the next-generation Quints. A whole new house of horrors opened up. According to Mum, two of the original eight Quint brothers had died before they could father children, and one had never married, but the remaining five had reproduced like rabbits.

One night, I came home from work to find Mum sitting at the dining table, drawing up a family tree, a phone beside her. Across the top of the page she had written down the names of these five Quints, next to them the names of their wives with descending lines leading to rows of yet more names, Mum's cousins, and down from them, yet more.

Mum had seventeen Quint first cousins. Though she had known most of these cousins when they were all children, she had lost touch with all but two of them who happened to live in London. Through these two she was making the connections, filling in the blanks. On Gran's orders.

I was baffled.

'But why? Why does she care about these people? I can understand her wanting to know Neville's and Norbert's children, her own grandchildren, but the other Quints?'

It seemed to me a family-sense gone into overdrive. What Mum and I had too little of, Gran had too much of, and if she cared that much, so I told Mum, she should jolly well do the research herself.

Mum sighed.

'No, Inky. There's a reason for all this. And I think you should know.'

'Go on.'

'It's that bloody stamp. I wish I'd never heard of it. Inky: don't be hurt, but she's looking for a worthy Quint to leave it to in her will.'

I must have looked shocked, because Mum placed a hand on mine. 'It seems she'd had you singled out as the best of her grandchildren – you were the only one who ever wrote her letters – but your talk of selling the stamp shocked her. She doesn't want it sold the moment she dies. She doesn't want all four of her children to inherit it together, because we don't all get on and it'll have to be sold; she knows Norbert and Neville well enough. She wants to find a Quint, a third or fourth generation down from these five brothers, who cares about stamps and who will value it and pass it on. It's a Quint heirloom, and has to stay in the family. According to her. She only told me because I've not expressed any interest in it. She thinks I'm neutral.'

I had to pull out a chair and sit down at that. Tears stung my eyes.

'That's so – just so – unfair!' I said.

Mum shrugged. 'It's not,' she said. 'Inky, it's her stamp. She can do whatever she wants with it. If she thinks it's a family heirloom, then that's her business, not ours.'

'OK. But to make you do all this research; you, the only person to really *care* for her – the person who needs money the most – that's just cruel. It's mean.'

Mum scratched her head and looked embarrassed. 'She'd never leave it to me. Not without resolving the – the issues.'

'Why don't you resolve the bloody issues then?'

Mum gave me an accusing look.

'Inky, you're so mercenary! Of course I want to resolve the issues. But it has to be because they *should* be resolved, not because I want the stamp. And don't you see, if I make a step towards resolving them now – and really, it all depends on me – she'll think I'm only doing it for that bloody stamp. I can't let her think that. *She* has to make the first step.'

Mum is so bloody proud. I told her so. 'You're so bloody proud!'

'I don't think it's pride. I just can't stand hearse-chasers. And anyway, Marion has done far more for Gran than I have. If anyone deserves the stamp, it's her.'

I had to accept that truth. But there was another thing.

'Mum, have you told her about your debts?'

Now it was her turn to look shocked.

'Of course not! And don't you go telling her, you hear, Inky? If anything, that would put her off completely! Mummy can't stand debts and she thinks that debtors are weak, despicable people. Not a word about it, OK?'

'But it's not your fault, Mum! It's *Dad's! He* got us into that financial mess!'

Mum chuckled wryly. 'She'd say it's my fault for marrying Dad in the first place. She'd say I should have known his character, seen he was a speculator.'

'That's just so – not *fair!*'

Mum saw how agitated I was and squeezed my hand. 'Don't worry about it, sweetheart. And please, please don't hold it against Mummy. Be as nice to her as you've always been, OK? Things will work themselves out. You'll see.'

'How can I be nice to her, when she's being so mean? I think she should leave it to you. You need it the most.'

'This is a bad discussion, Inky. It's poor taste to talk about her will. Mummy is still very much alive. And remember, she has four children, not just me. And it really is *her* stamp, to do whatever she wants with. We have absolutely no claims to it.'

'Well then, to you and Marion.'

'Neville and Norbert are her sons. She loves them. In fact, she adores then. They were always her favourites.'

'But they're wankers! And they're rich! And they'd never lift a finger for Gran!'

She laughed. 'Oh, I don't know. They're very generous! Think of how Mummy loves her laptop and her potty chair! She couldn't live without them, and they make life much easier for us!'

I just could not believe how Mum could crack jokes at a time like this. Without a further word I left her to her family tree and flounced out to the garden where I smoked three cigarettes in quick, furious succession. After that I stormed upstairs. I tried to call Sal for a good rant, but his mobile was switched off. So I put on my headphones, flung myself on to my bed, and listened to Bob Marley for an hour.

And when the hour was up I came back down and cooked for Gran and was as nice to her as ever. She sat with me in the kitchen, giving instructions on how to make cook-up rice, a dish consisting of rice, coconut milk, black-eye peas and beef. There were moments I longed to slam the saucepan down on her head. But I didn't.

Chapter Twenty-one

Inky: The Noughties

We settled back into our uncomfortable schedule. Life with Gran was never going to be easy, but Mum and I learned to accept that fact and simply get on with it. It was rather like having painful bunions: it's better barefoot, but you know you have to wear shoes and so you simply take the pain as it comes. That was Mum's metaphor; I didn't have bunions but she did, and I have to give her credit for teaching me how to deal with a major pain-in-the-ass. Though Mum never allowed me to call her that, or to speak of her with anything but respect.

'She's your grandmother,' Mum always said, the moment I spoke a word of censure. 'Deal with it!'

The only person with whom I could let off steam was Sal, who came around whenever he could. We met at Wong's, usually, and at those times I cursed Gran to hell and back, and when it was over I felt guilty and mean but clean, and Sal laughed and absolved me of my guilt.

'Rant as much as you like,' he said. 'Think of me as your personal dumping ground.'

And so I survived the summer weeks. Mum and I worked out a schedule of sharing the care for Gran. I washed and prepared her for the day during the week, Mum at the weekends. I did all of the cooking, Mum did all of the washing up, and took care of the laundry in her own Mum way, which meant taking items as needed from a basket overflowing with unironed stuff.

As for Gran, she was as happy as a child in an amusement park. She began to Discover England, and she did this mostly through television. She was at it all day long. She watched everything, channel-hopping at the first touch of boredom. Pretty soon, favourites developed: she loved quiz shows, and, as it turned out, was good at them; I'd never have guessed it but Gran was a walking encyclopaedia. Certain she, too, could win a million, she persuaded Mum to enter her name for all of them.

She couldn't stand soap operas; she'd watch a few minutes until a character threw a hissy fit or broke down weeping, at which point Gran would make some scathing comment about bad dialogue and bad acting, and switch away. Once she did that to Mum's show, *Bed and Breakfast*, and by the way Mum slapped shut her novel, got up and walked out, I knew that scene had been *her* invention.

Gran also loathed reality shows, but watched them all the same. She justified her addiction by claiming them to be educational; these shows, she said, were a window into the contemporary British soul. She clucked her disapproval at society's downward slide into vulgarity, decadence and coarseness. She delivered finger-wagging lectures on 'We in Guyana', who, she claimed, were better behaved than the godless English of nowadays: the colonized more civilised than the colonisers.

Godlessness, in fact, was her number one theme, and I her number one victim for conversion.

On Sundays we all went to church. Gran insisted. I only went for Gran's sake. If it made her happy, then why not; she was the only Gran I had. And again, there was something about Gran's insistence that made you obey. In fact, it was simply survival. It was less exhausting to ignore Gran's lectures, bear her castigations in silence and give in to her demands, than to put up a fight. So Mum and I chose the path of least resistance.

❊ ❊ ❊

From then on, we no longer spoke of the stamp. Certainly, Gran never mentioned it again. In fact, she didn't even bother to uphold the secrecy of her hiding place. I guessed she kept it under the mattress; that's where all old people keep their valuables. Then I caught her at it: when I was in the room putting away her clothes, she reached under the mattress, brought it out, and peered at her precious stamp, as if deliberately to taunt me. She all but stroked it, crooning, 'My precious'. Out of the corner of my eye I saw her watching me for a reaction. I refused to indulge her. I said nothing. To show annoyance would only encourage her.

And so we lived our lives, carefully tiptoeing around the subject.

And yet. Despite all the commotion of the passing weeks, throughout the upheavals and the quarrels and the upsets, it loitered, the spirit of that stamp. Strictly taboo, it nevertheless lurked in silence, waiting in the backdrop of our lives, a constant unspeakable presence behind all the cigarettes smoked and all the doors slammed; an itch I couldn't scratch. And then, one day, it pounced.

❊ ❊ ❊

It happened on a Sunday, while we were at church, which, the police said later, showed that our house had been watched by those wankers all these weeks.

Mum's negligence was partly responsible. She had not trimmed the hedges, nor cut back the bushes in the front garden for years, and the wilderness outside the house provided the perfect hiding place for an intruder. Then, too, Mum never activated our alarm system, no ear-splitting screech alarmed the neighbourhood.

We came home in a jovial mood, after a nice lunch at Aunty Doreen's. The moment I saw the broken living-room window, I knew what had happened.

That same moment Mum yelled, 'My laptop!' She flew into the house and into the living room and up into her room, leaving me to deal with Gran.

The place was ransacked. Not the whole place; just the living room and Gran's bedroom.

Mum's stupid laptop had always been safe. She could have left it in open on the dining room table and it still would have been safe. That wasn't what they were after.

Gran's mattress lay in the middle of her bedroom floor.

The stamp album was gone. The one with our – that is, Gran's – British Guiana Penny Black. The One Cent Black on Magenta, twin brother to the rarest stamp in the world. A tiny scrap of paper worth a fortune.

I screamed at Gran as I punched in the number for the police.

'I told you! I told you! You stubborn, pig-headed old woman! I told you to put it into a safe! Now see what has happened! You'll never get it back! Serves you right!'

Gran, for once, was speechless. She sat there on her Luxury Commode in the middle of her room, looking dazed. After a few minutes of me ranting she found her voice.

'But how they know? How they know to find this house!'

My carefully cultivated deference to old age flew out the window.

'Of course they found it! You think you can hoard a valuable thing like that and not even *try* to hide it, and it's not going to get stolen? What world do you live in?'

'But I hid it good! Under the mattress!'

I rolled my eyes. Gran wailed:

'In broad daylight! In broad daylight they break in here! Oh Lordy! While we was in Church! Why de good Lord didn't strike them down?'

And so it continued: Gran wailing and me yelling and Mum watching, shaking her head as if wearying of the whole drama.

The doorbell rang; it was Sal.

'Thank God!' I said, hugging him. 'All hell's broken loose here.' I led him into Gran's room.

'Ah, Sal, my sweetheart boy! Give you old Nanny a kiss!'

Sal chuckled and bent over, kissing her leathery cheek. She kissed him back; left cheek, right cheek, left cheek.

'So, what's going on?' Sal asked innocently.

I pointed to Mum. 'Go on, tell him. It's your fault anyway.'

Mum just sighed and turned away. It's what she always does when she's in the wrong. I followed her, still ranting; somehow, I could no longer bring myself to scream at Gran, so Mum had to take the brunt of my wrath. Gran slammed the door after I left the room. Mum went into the kitchen, me hot on her heels.

'You're just so *scatty!* You live in a dream world! I could see this happening *weeks* ago! I *told* you! I told you about the alarm! This is not a safe area, and you know it!' Mum only moved about the kitchen in silence, making coffee.

'The stamp's not even *insured!* I just can't *believe* such irresponsibility! It's like I'm the mother and you're the child!'

Mum had a non-policy of contents insurance: we had nothing anyone would want to steal, so why waste the money? Now that had certainly come back to bite her.

'Would you like a cup too?' Mum asked mildly, as she poured water into the machine. I replied with a new rant. Mum didn't reply. The machine began to gurgle. I ranted on. No reaction. I flounced into the garden and smoked a cigarette, a second cigarette. Sal stayed with Mum and Gran. The traitor.

Chapter Twenty-two

Inky: The Noughties

It took the police all of two hours to arrive. Maybe because it was a Sunday, maybe they had other burglaries to deal with. No doubt if it had been our Docklands loft, they'd have been on our doorstep in five minutes, but that's life.

'Don't touch anything! Leave everything just the way it is!' I yelled at Mum and Gran at the start of those two hours. I stormed upstairs, slammed my door, and buried myself in a book till the doorbell rang. The police had arrived.

I sat on the edge of Gran's bed, seething to myself. They first questioned Mum and Gran, who sat next to each other on the sofa. Sal leaned against the mantelpiece. The mattress still lay on the floor. I pointed to the bedsprings. 'That's where she hid her stamp album,' I said. 'It's gone.'

'So that's all they took? The stamp album? No valuables?'

I waited for Mum or Gran to give details of the stamp. But all Gran did was reach into the fireplace, remove the grid, and produce her jewellery case of carved purpleheart. I couldn't believe she'd chosen the fireplace to hide that box in. What if I or Mum had made a fire in it for her? Typical. OK, it was summer and so it was hardly likely, but still.

She opened the box and showed the officer her gold jewellery.

'They din't find this. I hid it good, nah? See, real gold from Guyana!'

The officer made a note in his book.

Impatiently, I said: 'The stamp, Gran. Tell them about the stamp!' I looked at the officer. 'A very valuable stamp was stolen!' I said.

He coughed. 'A valuable stamp? *How* valuable?'

'Well, it's one of the rarest stamps in the world. A similar stamp was sold for almost a million dollars at auction, but that was in the seventies. So I guess, on today's market …'

'*Inka!*'

'Mum, if you won't speak up then I guess I have to. We've got to get that stamp back and if we don't tell them how valuable it is, they aren't going to look for it. It's as simple as that.'

'Can you confirm that, Ma'am?'

Obviously, these officers didn't believe me. I looked from Mum to Gran in frustration. Mum's face was as if carved from stone and Gran just sat there chewing her cud. It was the most frustrating interview in my life. You'd think the burglars had just dropped in for tea.

. But then, Mum was the most secretive person in the world. All this questioning and disclosure must be driving her crazy.

But finally, Gran saved the day. She couldn't keep it in.

'The most valuable stamp in the world! Worth a fortune' she exclaimed, and launched into a rambling speech that not only told the entire history of the stamp but made it clear that it had magical properties and was, possibly, responsible for the establishment of World Peace.

The police finally left. Mum relaxed. Gran, beside herself with laughter, pointed at me.

'Look at you face! Look at you face! Bring out the camera, Rika!'

I was totally nonplussed. Why was she so insouciant about it all? As if it was all one big joke? Something was going on.

'What's going on? Mum?'

But Mum just shook her head and left the room. Gran laughed some more.

'Them thief-man, they stupidy bad. They got the shell but not the nut. I done take out that stamp and hide it.'

My heart leapt. 'You have it? You hid it? Gran, *where?*'

I think, under normal circumstances, she would never have shown me. But pride made her do so; *this* hiding-place was just too good to keep to herself. She shuffled over to the Luxury Commode Chair. She lifted the red velvet seat. She removed the bed-pan. She carelessly handed it to Sal to hold, sloshing around the urine in it for good measure, spilling a few drops on the carpet, and probably onto his jeans. He took it with, to his credit, only the slightest flaring of the nostrils.

Then Gran reached inside the hole left by the potty and, leaning precariously forward over the rollator, felt along the inside walls of the wooden bedpan box, her eyes vacant with concentration. Suddenly, the intensity on her face melted into a smile of triumph. She withdrew her hand and held up her treasure, encased now in a transparent plastic zip lock envelope: the British Guiana One Cent 1856 Black on Magenta, Quint edition.

Gran gave a most wicked cackle. She clacked her dentures at me and declared:

'See? They didn't find him. Nobody don't like to interfere wit' ole-lady piss!'

❄ ❄ ❄

'And you knew all the time! You let me make a fool of myself!'

Who else could I let my anger out on but Mum? But again, she wasn't accepting it.

'I tried to warn you, Inky. But you just rushed ahead. You were just raging and ranting and you didn't let me get a word in edgewise. It's your own fault.'

'So, now what?'

Mum turned on the tap and held a glass jug beneath it. Gran, exhausted by all the drama, had lain herself down for a rest and promptly fallen asleep, and Mum, Sal and I had fled to the kitchen for a much-needed coffee break. Mum said, her back turned to me:

'Well, we can hope that the police think we're just a bunch of kooks making much ado about nothing. That they think Gran's just a silly old goose babbling nonsense. We can hope they think you're an attention-seeking hormonal teenager. Otherwise ...'

'Otherwise what?'

'Well, what do you think? The cat's out of the bag. Gran just made her little secret public. That means ...' I waited, but nothing more came.

'What *does* that mean?' I hated it when Mum spoke in unfinished sentences. Her ellipses drove me crazy, demonstrating, as they did, her laziness of speech. She liked me to second guess her thoughts, finish her sentences for her, which led to me having to pull information slowly out of her nose and contributing to our famously ragged conversations.

'It might mean nothing. But if some over-zealous reporter gets hold of *that* information ...'

She shrugged and spread her hands into a widening circle, telling me to use my imagination and tell *her* what would happen. I decided not to. Instead, I changed the subject.

'I don't get how they found us, anyway. They must have been watching our house for *weeks*, to know that we all go to church every Sunday. And surely they looked through the album before they took it, and saw that the stamp was missing?'

'Well, for one, these were most likely common-and-garden burglars, not experienced antique thieves. They wouldn't have known one stamp from another, and it was full of stamps. All they wanted was the album.'

'I don't believe it, Mum. They must have at least checked to see if that particular stamp was in it? Surely whoever commissioned them must have told them what to look for?'

'Well …' There they were again, those ellipses. They would hang in the air until either Sal or I asked the next obvious question. I kept silent, tired of the game. But Sal continued to play.

'Well, what?'

Mum looked uncertain whether or not to talk, her eyes slightly glazed over as she withdrew into her dream world, but then a little jolt of decision went through her as she opted for full disclosure. She poured us all coffee, and signalled to us to grab our cups and follow her to the dining table. After we had all taken our seats, she spoke again.

'You see, I did anticipate something like this happening. After we kept getting all those phone calls, I began to wonder if that dealer was unscrupulous enough to try and steal the stamp. And I talked to Mummy about that possibility.'

Another long silence.

'And then?' I prompted.

'I got a replica made, a fake we could keep in the album, just in case. As a decoy. We replaced the original with the fake. Gran hid the original in an original place known only to herself. And that's it.'

Sal laughed. 'And you really had us all fooled! The way Inky went ballistic … that was fantastic!'

I didn't think it was that fantastic, and said so.

'You should have told me! You let me make a fool of myself!'

But Sal, again the traitor, was on Mum's side.

'Uh-uh. You *chose* to go ballistic. Your Mum did try to calm you down but you weren't listening. You ran with your temper. You can't blame her for that! If you'd just shut up she might have told you. Nobody wants to confide in a Rambo.'

I couldn't believe what I was hearing. Sal was always supportive of me; that's one of the things I loved most about him. He never put me down in public. And now this, in front of my own mother! She, who was responsible in the first place for *not* keeping the garden tidy and the alarm on!

'If she was that scared about burglary, why didn't she use the alarm system? We've lived in this house for almost three years and she's never once switched it on.'

Mum said mildly, vaguely, 'It's not working. I think it needs new wiring or something.'

'Well, for goodness sakes …' I had no words left, no arguments.

'Anyway,' said Mum with great finality, 'we have to put an end to this nonsense. I'm going to phone the police in a minute and tell them we found the stamp. I'll tell them Mummy is just forgetful and couldn't remember she'd taken it out and hidden it elsewhere. If all is well, maybe we can keep the secret.'

'Nan'll be disappointed,' said Sal, 'but you're right.'

'The thing is, Mummy doesn't really care about the stamp itself. She's not a stamp collector; she doesn't have a passion for it. For her it's just the fact that it's an heirloom she's been entrusted to pass on.'

'So why the big fuss with the police?'

Mum looked even more miserable.

'You don't know Mummy. She's wily and manipulative. She loves the limelight – used to be an actress. She's got an agenda, and if I know her …'

I let Mum and Sal chat for a while. Mum was wondering how they'd traced our address from our telephone number, and Sal explained how easy that was. They discussed burglaries they had known. Mum spoke about the creepy feeling in her guts, now that invaders had entered her house, her panic at first seeing the broken window. I couldn't help it, I had to butt in.

'And all you could think of was your bloody laptop. Which, after all, is insured.'

'There are some things that are irreplaceable,' was all Mum said to that. 'Work, for instance.'

'You can back up work. You do back up your work, don't you?' Mum made a face so I assumed she didn't. I stormed on.

'You can't back up that stamp. That was the first thing I thought of. The Quint!'

'Well, of course she didn't think of the stamp,' said Sal. 'It's a fake, and she knew it!'

'But the original was still in the house. Gran might think the potty chair's a brilliant hiding place but in fact she just got lucky. A more professional thief would have looked there too. If you ask me it was a pretty obvious place.'

But nobody was asking me. Mum and Sal were once again discussing robberies they had known. Mum even went so far as to tell him about some robbery in Guyana way back in the last century. When I started to roll a cigarette nobody even glanced at me, and when I went outside to smoke it, I might as well have been invisible.

Autumn was in the air. The leaves in the hazelnut tree above me were turning yellow and the slight nip in the temperature made me hug my arms as I sat smoking at the garden table. I wished I'd brought a jacket. On the other hand, maybe that coldness didn't come from outside at all. Maybe it came from inside. Maybe it was a part of that vague sense of restlessness and discomfort that nagged deep inside me, an itch I couldn't scratch. An itch I couldn't even name.

A constant irritation, like a colony of ants burrowing nests within my heart. And I had no idea how to stop them.

Chapter Twenty-three

Dorothea: 1950

Dorothea was alone downstairs. It was near midnight; they were all asleep. She sat at the dining-table, typing, enclosed in a circle of light from the overhead lamp. She knew she wouldn't sleep tonight. The moon was swollen; great and white, sailing across an empty night sky. It would be full in a night or two, and she was wide awake. She might go for a walk on the Sea Wall once this report was finished. Her typewriter clacked away, leaving her cocoon of light to echo into the empty space of the drawing room. A cool sea breeze wafted in through the wide-open gallery sash windows, playing with the papers on the table beside her. She weighed them down with a water glass. Occasionally, a mosquito landed on her bare arm, and she slapped at it, usually missing.

Suddenly Kanga, the family dog, broke into furious barking, leaping at the gate and snarling as if an axe murderer had come to visit. Normally, she'd ignore the noise, for Kanga barked readily: at passers-by on the avenue across the street, at the sugar-cane man strolling by with his cane-juice press-machine, or in sympathy with the neighbour's dogs who were every bit as vocal. Since more often than not it was a case of crying wolf, nobody bothered to check the gate when he barked, but the extra rage in his voice tonight, and the rattling of the chain as he flung himself against the gate, made Dorothea walk to the window.

The figure on the bridge was just a black silhouette against the floodlight from the lamp-post behind him; a man's figure: hands, wide apart, resting on the top of the gate, out of reach of the leaping dog. He wore a hat. Something about the casual pose coupled with the jaunty tilt of the hat made Dorothea's heart leap. She raced to the front door and tore down the stairs.

The dog moved away as she came and stopped his snarling and leaping, looking up at her with eager expectancy; but there were no pats for Kanga tonight. Her hands fumbled as she unlocked the padlock and unwound the chain that held the two wings of the gate together. Then it was open, and she was in Freddy's arms, her hands groping his head as if to ascertain that he was real, no ghost, no vision. His own arms were strong around her, and still, and he was whispering her name, over and over, like a mantra. Even Kanga fell silent, in awe of the moment. He paced around the couple on the bridge, his body snaking in step with his wagging tail, sniffing Freddy's legs, whimpering and hanging out his tongue in approval.

'Come up, come in,' said Dorothea breathlessly, and edged him towards the open gate. But Freddy resisted.

'Is Mam home? I want to be alone with you, first. Just for a while. Can we go somewhere?'

'She's gone to bed. But I can wake her! She'd want me to!'

'No. Let's go. Please. Just for a while.'

'She'll hate me for it, if I keep you from her even a second longer than necessary.'

'Please.' Dorothea thought of getting her bicycle, for old time's sake, but the car would save time.

'Just a second.'

She raced back upstairs, grabbed the car key, and flew back down to Freddy. They opened the gates together, then she backed the car into the street and Freddy closed the gate, winding the chain back around it without locking it.

Dorothea found it hard to keep her eyes on the road as she drove. It was as if not seeing him for even a moment would make him disappear again. As if gazing at him would fix him there forever, next to her, looking back, grinning that same old Freddy grin. His hand lay on top of hers on the gear stick, moved with hers as she changed gear. At the Camp Street junction she stopped for traffic and almost forgot to start again. Freddy had to remind her.

She turned left, towards the Sea Wall. They had not discussed where they'd go. They knew. They did not speak. Not until she'd parked the car and they'd walked up the stone steps to the Promenade and walked the little way to *their* bench, his arm holding her close, so that by the time they sat down, she knew for certain that he was real.

There was too much to say, so they said little, and for long stretches, nothing. The moment was just too vast to cram it with words that could never express the fullness in their hearts. Sometimes Dorothea began a sentence. *'We thought you were …' 'It was so…' 'Where were you, why didn't you …' 'I can't believe …'*

But always Freddy broke her off by covering her mouth with his. He held her face up to his and kissed it all over; her lips, her cheeks, her nose, neck and ears, but most of all her eyes, placing his lips in their soft hollows and holding her still. She knew his own eyes were closed.

It was Dorothea who pulled away first.

'What is it, my sweet?'

He pulled her back, began the kissing all over again. She resisted.

'I forgot … There's something …'

He stopped, let go of her completely. Side by side they sat, like strangers.

'You're married,' he said at last. 'I should have known.'

She turned to face him, took his hands in hers.

'Freddy, I'm sorry, I'm so very sorry, I waited so long, I wanted to wait forever. But then …'

'So it's true? It's what I feared the most. I hardly dared hope, when I came home, to find you there. And then you were there, just like you always were, just as if you belonged there. So I assumed you'd waited.'

'I tried so hard. I wanted to. I didn't say yes, at first.'

'Who is it?'

'Humphrey. Your brother. We're engaged; the wedding's next month. But maybe ... I don't know. He's so sweet, so happy ... he tried so hard. He kept asking, and we're so close, and it just seemed the right thing to do. Freddy ... I'm just so tired, so exhausted. Since you've been gone I've been running, running, running; fighting, fighting, fighting. But always it's been like I'm running in one place and I just want to close my eyes and ... be normal. Marry and have children. Especially, have children. I always wanted children. Remember? *Your* children, but if I can't have those then ... well, I began to think about it and then one day I just said yes.'

'Old Humph,' Freddie chuckled. 'Who would have guessed? He always had a crush on you ... since the day he met you. Humph. You could do worse; he'd be a perfect husband. But of course you can't marry him. Not now. You'll break it off.'

He searched her face. She lowered her eyes, but only for a moment.

'Yes. Yes, of course. I feel terrible, but what else can I do? We were going to have you declared dead. But you're not. You're still my husband. He'll understand. Humph's like that.'

'That's the worst of it. On the one hand, Humph's the best. But because he's the best it's the worst, doing it to him.'

'I know. I feel so bad. But he won't make a fuss.'

'That's what makes it so awful. Knowing Humph, he'll just smile and be happy for you. For us.'

'Yes.'

For a while they said nothing, just sat there holding hands. The sea breeze had withdrawn; it was so still she could hear him breathing. Somewhere behind them, from the town, a dog began to bark, and then a second, and then a whole chorus of them. Dorothea examined the tight knot of guilt that had risen in her heart. Humphrey's face appeared before her, on the day she'd said yes; the light in his eyes, the sheer joy of his smile. How could she take that away? How selfish, how mean! But then Humphrey's face melted into Freddy's and the guilt transmuted, became a bliss so perfect she knew there was no question; she was Freddy's, had always been. Saying yes to Humphrey had been the betrayal. Understandable, forgivable, but a betrayal nevertheless.

'Dorothea?'

'Yes?'

'Have you – did you – you and Humphrey …?'

She didn't let him finish.

'No. We're doing it the traditional way, waiting for our wedding night. Humphrey was never one to break the rules.'

'You used the present tense. As if there's still going to be a wedding night.'

She chuckled, and squeezed his hand.

'A slip of the tongue … it means nothing.'

'Nothing means nothing. That's one thing I learned while I was gone.'

'You still haven't told me where you've been, what happened … Freddy, what's the matter?'

Shock, and then puzzlement, passed over his face, distorting it. Just for a moment, then it was gone. Now he looked dazed.

'What was that?'

'Blood just ran over my tongue.'

The way he said it, awe-filled and in a whisper, sent a chill through her; like a cool breeze enfolding her body. But there was no breeze and the chill came from inside.

'What do you mean?'

He smiled, and squeezed her hand, as if to reassure her.

'Nothing, really. It was just weird; a taste on my tongue. Maybe a gum was bleeding.'

'Gums don't just start bleeding, and then stop.'

'Well, mine just did, so they do. Let's get back home. I'm tired.'

'Wait a minute!' Dorothea said, but Freddy was already clambering to his feet. He reached out a hand for her to take. She noticed his movements were slower than they used to be, that he winced when he pulled her up. There was pain there, physical pain, but also something in his eyes, in his expression, something new, deep, alien. She knew then that she was not the only one to have changed in the years since Freddy'd been gone. How could it be otherwise? He'd been through a war, and somehow survived. How? Well, that was the tale he'd have to tell. For the moment, though, it was enough to feel his hand in hers as they walked back to the car.

She held it as if it were a lifeline.

❄ ❄ ❄

Dorothea opened her eyes. Freddy was sitting beside her on the bed, gazing down at her in the half-light of early dawn. She smiled, and reached for him.

'You're so beautiful,' he sighed. 'I can't believe it.'

'I can't believe you're back. Here, in flesh and blood. And last night ...'

His eyes softened at those words, and they gazed at each other, half-smiling, remembering the melting of their bodies that was simply the echo of a union that had already taken place; the union of two souls perfectly joined, two halves that craved each other and, having found that which was missing, dissolved into each other. She reached out and touched his lips.

'And so are you. I love you.'

He sank down to her, buried his face in her neck. She squirmed and laughed, delirious with happiness. But only for a second. She sat up in bed. The falling away of the sheet from her bare breasts, glistening smooth and brown, made Freddy reach for her again, but she brushed his hands away and stood up, grabbing the sheet and wrapping it around her body, and stepped back from the bed.

'Today's a big day! Freddy, you go in the shower now, before they all get up. And at breakfast you make your grand entrance. I can't wait to see Ma's face!'

'And Humph?'

'I'll go to him, as soon as I'm dressed, and tell him. The sooner he knows the better.'

❀ ❀ ❀

Dorothea smuggled Freddy into the shower, tiptoeing with girlish giggles down the corridor. On the way there they bumped into Basmati, the maid, who let out a little cry of shock, as if she'd seen a ghost. Dorothea placed a finger on her lips and her eyes sparkled in mischief. Basmati smiled and nodded, and stepped aside to let them pass.

They showered together, and tiptoed, still giggling, back to her room. They dressed. Freddy had a rucksack of old and faded clothes, and he put those on. Dorothea put on her best dress.

When she was ready she hugged and kissed Freddy and walked slowly, solemnly, to the Annex. Humphrey was an early riser; she knew he'd be up, and when she knocked, his 'Come in' was immediate.

He was sitting in the Morris chair, reading a book. His face broke into a smile of pleasure when she entered. Taking in her expression, it faded.

'What's happened, Dorothea?'

She sank to the floor beside the chair, put both her hands on his knee, and looked up at him.

He covered her hands with one of his own. She swallowed. 'Humphrey, I …'

She stopped.

'What?'

'Freddy's back. He came last night and I'm sorry, I'm so very sorry, but I can't marry you. We spent the night together. I'm so sorry. I never wanted to hurt you. I should never have said yes. I …'

The words gushed out, words that carried all she felt; the joy and guilt, and sorrow on his behalf. Humphrey slipped from the chair and knelt on the floor beside her. When the words stopped coming, he spoke.

'Freddy's my brother. I'm g-g-glad he's back; of course I'm glad. And I'm glad for you, for your happ-p-p-iness. That's what I want most, Dorothea, your happiness.'

'But *your* happiness?'

'Let's just say, it will make me happy to see you happy. Maybe I never deserved you anyway.'

Dorothea began to cry then, tears of gladness and of sadness. 'No, no, it's *me* who doesn't deserve *you*. I wish, I just wish …'

But she didn't know what she wished. She wanted them all happy, but that was impossible.

'Shhh.'

Humphrey placed his arms around her and held her close, rocking her sobs away.

Chapter Twenty-four

Dorothea: The Fifties

Dorothea and Freddy crept down the stairs and hid behind the curtain to the dining room. Ma Quint was walking back and forth between the kitchen and the breakfast table, serving breakfast to Humphrey and Pa, who were arguing about the two political leaders who had recently emerged in the fight for Independence; Forbes Burnham, of African roots and Cheddi Jagan, of Indian. Ma Quint's voice broke into the argument.

'Now you men just be quiet and eat! No politics at the table!'

At once, the men were silent. A chair creaked; Ma Quint was about to sit down herself.

'Now!' whispered Dorothea in Freddy's ear. She pushed him out. Freddy walked up to the table. Dorothea, her hands over her mouth to hold back her excitement, followed him in.

'Yes, Ma, and we all know you'll always have the last word!'

Ma Quint looked up, the spoon in her hand hovering above her egg, ready to strike. She dropped the spoon and sprang to her feet; her chair clattered to the ground.

'Oh my good Lord! Oh my sweet Jesus!' Ma Quint's hands flew to her heart and pressed against her breast, fingers splayed. Freddy took her in his arms, rocked her back and forth.

'Oh Ma. It's good to be back.'

'You're real! You're not a ghost! Flesh and blood! My Freddy! I knew you'd be back! I knew it! I knew you weren't dead!' Ma Quint blabbered on, touching Freddy all over, ruffling his hair, feeling his arms, rubbing his back, sobbing and speaking simultaneously. Freddy continued to rock her.

'Yes, Ma. It's really me.'

Pa and Humphrey were standing now, waiting their turn. Freddy had to forcibly pull himself out of Ma Quint's clasp. He hugged his father, who said nothing more than a muted,

'Well done, boy, well done.' And then Humphrey.

The slight hesitation before the brothers embraced came from Freddy, not Humphrey; and it was Humphrey, not Freddy, who spoke.

'Welcome home, b-b-brother!'

❋ ❋ ❋

'We were in Burma,' Freddy said. 'In the jungle. They call it 'the green hell', and that's the proper name for it. Funny how I had to go halfway across the world to see the jungle, when we've got so much of it right here.'

Breakfast was over, but they all still sat around the table as Basmati cleared away the remains. Even Ma Quint, having rattled on non-stop filling Freddy in on all the news of the last six years, was now silent. It was Freddy's turn to speak.

'War, and jungle; two hells by themselves, but in combination – well, there's nothing worse.' He paused, his eyes glazed over and he shuddered as if to shake off the memories. But then he returned to them, and his glance shifted to Ma Quint and then to Dorothea and back to Ma Quint. He spoke of war. Dorothea heard not a word; she wasn't listening, simply drinking in the sight of him, the sound of his voice, melting in the glances he threw her way between words. But both Humphrey and Pa listened avidly. Pa's shelves were filled with every book on the First World War ever published, and the next several minutes were filled with expressions such as 'our battalion advanced' and 'the Japanese attacked'.

Ma Quint and Dorothea glanced at each other, and each knew what the other was thinking. Finally, Ma Quint butted in.

'But you, Freddy, what happened to you? You can talk the war talk later; just tell us what happened to *you*.'

Freddy grinned, and poured himself another cup of coffee. 'Well, see. There was this chap, a Scotsman, 'Red' we called him. Flaming red hair, he had. From Dundee. Hamish was his real name. Well, Red and me, we were best mates. And when he got wounded, and couldn't walk, I helped him. Our battalion was making its way through the Burmese jungle, single file. There wasn't a path, you see, it was thick jungle, and we were last, so by the time we came through, the others had trampled a way ahead of us. Still, the undergrowth was thick and progress was slow and we fell further and further behind. The last thing I remember was this terrible blast. Then I was out, gone. To this day I can't tell you what happened. I don't know.'

Another long silence. Ma Quint rustled in her chair. 'Go on, Freddy. What happened next?'

Freddy laughed, a wry laugh, lacking mirth.

'They found me, half-conscious. Red was dead by that time. I was dehydrated, dying. I don't know how long I'd lain there, or why I hadn't been eaten by animals by then. At least, nothing worse than insects. Flies and ants were all over me.'

'Who found you?'

'Monks. Buddhist monks, two of them. They had water. They carried me, miles and miles through the jungle, barefoot, to their monastery. Monastery! That's a big word. It was a crumbling building, made of dried mud, with a couple of huts around it where the monks lived. It was a small community, just five of them. They nursed me back to health. They knew all kinds of herbs and things. It took a couple of weeks, but I recovered fully. But I had lost my memory.'

'Amnesia?'

'Yes. Total. I could not recall a thing; not my name, or what I was doing there, or where I came from. Or you, Dorothea.

It was all gone, my mind a blank. That's a strange thing. More so because I couldn't speak a word of their language, or they of mine. But they taught me. I learned Burmese the way a child does and pretty soon I was fluent. And I lived their life. For years. It was a good life. It was as if a whole new person was born, they day they found me. Sometimes I had flashes of my former life; but nothing I could put together coherently.'

'And that's where you spent the last six years?'

Freddy nodded. 'I was happy. Like a child. It was all simple and good. I had no need to know the past; I didn't care. According to their Buddhist teaching, the past was irrelevant anyway; there is only the present. There is only the here and now, and that was perfect. Always perfect. I could have lived that way the rest of my life.'

Another long silence.

'But something happened. Your memory came back?' prompted Ma Quint.

'Yes. Now and then we had visitors, other monks from other monasteries. Some of these monks don't even have a monastery, they are homeless, simply wandering on to the next stop, all their lives. Well, one day, two monks arrived. They'd been to Rangoon some time before. They didn't have much baggage, they never do. But what they did have ...'

He paused. Dorothea's eyes clung to him, to every word. She could hardly breathe. This wasn't the Freddy she'd known, the Freddy she held in her memory and cherished in her heart. This was a new Freddy, a Freddy who had been through hell and survived, a changed man she could not grasp and did not know

Freddy seemed to have drifted away again. He kept doing that, as if his time with the monks had usurped a space in his mind to which he kept returning, forgetting the present moment, and her. Dorothea felt almost jealous; was that space better than the space they shared? What was in it? Was he happier there than he was with her? But no, that could not be. After all, he had returned. He was here, in flesh and blood.

'What did they have, Freddy?'

He seemed to have completely forgotten his own last words. 'Who? What?'

'The wandering monks. You said they had something, something that reminded you. Of who you really are.'

Freddy's eyes locked with hers.

'A mouth-organ,' he said. 'They had a mouth-organ. They had picked it up somewhere. One of them had a talent for music and had taught himself a few tunes. The moment I heard that sound ... well, I asked for it, and he gave it to me. And I played. I could play, Dorothea! Everything I'd ever played, so long ago; suddenly I could play all those melodies again. And with the music came the memories. And I was Freddy again; Freddy Quint of Lamaha Street. And I remembered home, and you, and I wanted to come home. I had to go. I had to come.'

Relief swept through Dorothea. However strong that Burma life had been, finally he had left it. For her.

'So what happened then?'

'Well, I'd have preferred not to have anything to do with the British Army again, but I needed a passport. I went to Rangoon and went through the official channels. I asked them *not* to notify my family. See, I wanted to come back and surprise you; I wanted to find out how things stood. I didn't know if ...' he stopped, looked at Dorothea, and started again. 'So all I wanted was to get to Britain, and a passport. They brought me back, and I went through all the official stages, became a civilian again.

'I needed to go to Scotland first, to Dundee. I wanted to meet Red's people, tell them what had happened, how he'd died. Give them closure. You understand?'

He looked at her, pleading, and she did.

'They were wonderful, practically adopted me as a son. I felt so at home there. I stayed for two weeks. But then I left them. I got on a ship at Liverpool. We docked in Georgetown yesterday. Then I came home. And here I am.'

Freddy did not leave the house that first day, and neither did anyone else. They could not get enough of him. Ma Quint and Dorothea pampered him as if he were a baby, buzzing around him like bees around a fragrant flower. Pa wanted, and got, a detailed report on the War in Asia though the eyes of a soldier, and all through that tale Dorothea sat at Freddy's side, holding his hand. And even Humphrey took his demotion from fiancé to brother-in-law with good grace and even empathy, which made it all the worse for Dorothea.

After lunch, Freddy prised himself away from Dorothea for a man-to-man talk with Humphrey. He never spoke of what was said there in the Annex; but to Dorothea he said,

'Of the two of us, Humph is the better man. Are you sure?'

She squeezed his hand and that was her only answer.

❋ ❋ ❋

And so Dorothea and Freddy were given a second chance at married life. The days passed by in perfect bliss; she took time off from work to be with Freddy every minute of every day. All Freddy's old friends came to visit; those of his brothers who had moved out, moved back in to be near him and hear his story. Humphrey, empathetic as always, withdrew to allow the couple the space they needed; he turned to his stamps with all the more dedication. Dorothea, in her ecstasy, hardly noticed.

Only one incident marred the honeymoon: Kanga, somehow, found his way out into the road, was hit by a car, and killed. Kanga had been Dorothea's dog in particular; she was the main dog-lover in the house, and she wept at the death.

But the next day, Humphrey brought home a puppy, an adorable little ball of golden fluff, and placed it in her arms.

'For you, Dorothea!' he said, and his eyes shone at her pleasure. She leapt from the Morris chair in the gallery and flung her arms around Humphrey.

'Oh, Humph! You're a *darling!* I love you!' she said, and Humphrey blushed in pleasure; being the lightest skinned of the brothers, he *could* visibly blush.

'Is it a boy or a girl?' Dorothea turned the puppy upside down to check, and said, 'A girl! A girl dog – how wonderful!'

'What will you call her?' asked Humphrey, still flushed in the glow of Dorothea's gratitude. But Dorothea turned to Freddy.

'*You* name her, Freddy! You're so good at dog names! Go on, Freddy, find a girl name for her! Something soft and cuddly!'

Freddy stroked the puppy and thought for a moment. Then he said,

'What about Rabbit?'

'Rabbit! Perfect! You're Rabbit, little puppy!' said Dorothea, burying her nose in puppy-fluff, and then she placed the puppy in Freddy's arms. She grinned wickedly, and said to Freddy:

'You know that tigers eat rabbits for breakfast?'

'I don't think you'll eat this one. This little rabbit is going to melt your heart – it's getting a little tough.'

'Not since you're back!' said Dorothea, kissing the puppy. She placed Rabbit on her lap and turned her over to scratch her tummy. Plainly enjoying it, the puppy licked her hands. 'Oh, she's so cute! I love her!' cried Dorothea. 'Thank you, thank you, Humph! You always know exactly what will make me happy!'

'Thanks a lot, brother. This is a fine present!' said Freddy, bending over to fondle the puppy's head.

'My pleasure,' said Humphrey. Something in his voice – a crack, a hesitation that was not his characteristic stutter, made her look up at her brother-in-law, so that she was able, for just an instant, to catch the expression in his face as he turned away.

'OK, I-I'll be off then!' said Humphrey, and walked off.

'What's the matter with him?' said Freddy, but Dorothea knew. She reclaimed the puppy from Freddy and cuddled her for a few minutes, and then she said,

'Wait here, Freddy. I have to go to Humphrey.'

She walked to his room with Rabbit in her arms. She knocked on his door and entered without waiting for a come-in. Humphrey lay on his bed, face buried in his pillow, and his body heaved as he wept.

'Oh!' said Dorothea, and rushed to the bed. She sat down and placed a hand on his back as if to steady him, but all that did was instigate a volley of the most desperate, heart-broken sobs.

'Humphrey, I —'

Humphrey lifted his face from the pillow and turned it away from her, so that she could not see it but only hear.

'Go away! Just go away, please! Your pity only makes is worse!' the voice was shattered. The words, however, were vehement, filled with a passion as she had never known in him. And she knew then of the vastness and strength of his love, and of the pain she had gouged into his being. She returned to Freddy, and for the first time since his reappearance, doubt clouded her mind.

'How can we ever be happy, causing him such grief? How can we live under the same roof?'

'We can't,' said Freddy. 'We won't. We'll find our own place, build our own family. Humph will surely find someone else.'

'He won't,' said Dorothea. 'I know him.'

'Then he'll marry his stamps. He'll find happiness there.'

Dorothea frowned at Freddy's flippancy, and said nothing. Freddy met her eyes, saw the critique in them.

'Aw, come on; I'm only joking. Let's go into the yard and show Rabbit around.'

And so, with a click of their fingers, they put Humphrey behind them.

❊ ❊ ❊

One other person in the household did not share in the general celebration of Freddy's resurrection, and that was Basmati. Normally she was a cheerful woman who chattered away with her employer family as if she too was a member, but she had changed. She shuffled around the house, clearing and setting tables, sweeping the rooms, wiping dust-bunnies from the stairs, peeling plantains, grating coconut, taking down the baskets of dirty laundry for Doris, the washerwoman, in a bubble of glumness which made it hard to even look at her. Preoccupied as they were with Freddy, no one noticed. Today, the third day after Freddy's return, her misery seemed worse than ever. Only Dorothea noticed that today Basmati was wearing a pair of cheap sunglasses. To Dorothea's experienced eye that could only mean one thing. She said nothing, that first day. She'd noticed a gradual deterioration in the maid's disposition over the last few weeks and had been quietly watching. She knew the signs. She also knew the husband.

The next day, Basmati was again wearing the sunglasses, and she walked with a limp and moved with such stiffness that Dorothea followed her into the kitchen after breakfast. Basmati stood with her back to the room, washing the wares, her back heaving as she worked.

'Basmati!' said Dorothea.

'Yes, Mistress?' Basmati's voice was small, a squeak, really, and she did not turn around.

Dorothea walked up to her and placed a hand on her back. Basmati flinched. She was a short woman who once must have been pretty, one of those sweet-faced East Indian girls with long plaits down their backs and perfect middle-partings, who walked to school in groups of twos or threes, book-bags over their shoulders; invariably, they were good students who worked hard and got top marks. Almost as invariably, they left school early to get married.

Now, Basmati must be in her late twenties, Dorothea calculated, like her. Her mother, Sita, had also worked for the Quints and Dorothea could remember the daughter was near her own age (for she was in the Form beneath her) and would come to the house after school in her Bishops' High School uniform, sitting quietly on the back steps doing her homework, waiting for her mother. Then suddenly she'd disappeared, only to reappear a few years later when Sita took ill and offered her daughter as replacement maid. The mother never returned to work; a few months later, Basmati had reported Sita's death and asked for a permanent job.

The first few years she had brought babies and toddlers with her, worked with them around her feet or strapped to her back; quiet, well-behaved children. Though no older than Dorothea, Basmati's body was now that of a forty-year-old woman, thick-set and lumbering, her face puffy and lined, her dark skin splotched with shadows. She wore a sari, the *palu* tightly wrapped around her upper body, covering both arms and riding up her neck to her hairline.

Dorothea gently turned her around but she kept her face lowered, pushing back the sunglasses as they slid down her nose. Dorothea removed the sunshades and tilted up her chin. Basmati's left eye nestled in a patch of violent purple.

Dorothea, not saying a word, drew back the *palu*. The skin on Basmati's arms was a geography map of purple bruises.

'Who did this to you?' Dorothea said quietly, but in answer Basmati burst into tears.

'Mistress, Mistress, please don't say nothin', he only gon' beat me worse!'

Dorothea said nothing, but unbuttoned the woman's sari blouse and removed it. Basmati's heavy breasts hung in a limp red hammock of a brassiere; she crossed her arms bashfully over her chest, but Dorothea's attention was elsewhere; on the back, on the veritable continent of purple and black whose tip reached up into Basmati's hair and whose nether regions disappeared into the waistband of her skirt.

'Excuse me!' Dorothea said, and lifted the hem, torn and tattered around Basmati's swollen ankles. Under the sari she wore a red underskirt, ragged and frayed, which Dorothea lifted as far as she could, bunching up the extra yards of the sari. Basmati's thighs were a puffed, swollen mass of bruises.

Basmati moved her hands from her breast to her face and started to sob.

'Mistress, please don't say nothin', please don't write nothin'. Is all right. It don't happen too often, only when he drunk.'

'So, so, *only when he drunk*. And how often is that?'

'Mistress, it use to be only weekends, Saturday night. But last month he lost he job at the dock and he done use up all the money on rum, and every night he cuffing an kicking me. But mistress, I don't mind, so long he leave the chirren alone.'

'And you think I'm going to send you home like this?'

Basmati fell to her knees.

'Mistress, I begging you, leave me be! Oh Lord, have mercy! If he hear I done tell you, he tell me not to say a word, I don't want no trouble!'

'No, Basmati. That's not the way to do it. The more you say nothing, the more you make yourself complicit in the violence. It has to stop, do you hear me? It has to stop! First of all, you're going with me to a doctor. And then you're coming home with me. You'll stay here for a while. We'll sort this out together.'

Usually, Dorothea spoke in comfortable Creolese with Basmati. Not today. Today the seriousness of Basmati's plight dispelled the bantering lilting casualness of dialect with its implicit sense of parity; it called for the sternness of disciplined syntax, as if only authoritative language could translate into authoritative action.

'We're going to Doctor Singh,' said Dorothea, 'and then you're coming back here for a rest. No work today.'

'No, mistress, no! Me chirren, what about me chirren? If I not there he going to beat them!'

Dorothea, dressing Basmati again, said, 'Don't worry about your children. I'm going to pick them up after school, bring them all here. They can all stay 'til we find a suitable permanent home. You'll be safe here. Just don't worry. Everything's going to be all right.'

'But, mistress, I got one child at home, the baby. My Aunty does look after he; he name Rajan. I can't leave Rajan home.'

Dorothea draped the sari over Basmati's shoulders. 'I'm going to get him for you. How many children do you have altogether?'

'Five, mistress, the eldest, a girl, ten years old, going to Bishops'. Two in primary school. A boy in Central.'

Basmati had stopped crying. She was quiet now, and acquiescent, trusting in Dorothea; Dorothea had that effect on troubled people. She now took Basmati's hand.

'Then after we get the older children here we'll go to your place and get Rajan.'

Chapter Twenty-five

Dorothea: The Fifties

Dorothea reversed the Ford Prefect out of the yard, over the bridge and on to the street. Freddy closed the gates and got in. It was the first time he had left the house since his arrival. He sat in the back seat, next to Basmati; he had insisted in coming, just in case there was any 'trouble', 'trouble' being resistance from Basmati's husband. The presence of a man, he thought, might be helpful.

Dorothea only laughed at that. 'I've done this before,' she said, 'and one thing I've learned: these husbands are basically cowards. Especially the Indian ones. They bully their wives because they can't bully anyone else. They're social failures. When they come face to face with someone who isn't afraid of them they sag like vines. But come along. You can see me in action. I've changed a bit from the shy eighteen-year-old girl you left behind!'

The first outing today had been to collect Basmati's older children from their various schools: the two youngest girls from primary school in Kitty, one boy from Central High School and the eldest girl from Bishops', both in Georgetown. Now, the four of them, still in their uniforms, were safely at the dining table being fed afternoon tea by Ma Quint.

Getting the baby – actually, a three-year-old, but they called him 'Baby' – was going to be trickier. Basmati and her family lived in the same compound as the Aunty who took care of him during the day. With any luck, her husband would be in a drunken stupor in the back cottage and not notice a thing, but, Basmati said, maybe he wasn't. She trembled in fear.

Dorothea drove along the length of Lamaha Street and turned left when she got to Vlissingen Road towards the Sea Wall. Basmati lived in Kitty, the first village outside Georgetown up the East Coast. As they entered Kitty, Dorothea lifted her eyes to the rear view mirror.

'You have to direct me to the house,' she said, but, not meeting Basmati's eyes, she half turned to locate her on the back seat. Basmati had hunkered down, her head below window level.

'Don't be afraid,' Dorothea said, 'We're with you.'

'Mistress, we just pass de rum-shop where he does drink. I didn't want he see me in the car.'

'Well, better he should be there than at home. Come on, sit up and tell me where to go.'

Basmati cautiously raised her head to peek through the window, pulling it down again immediately, like a turtle.

'Turn left at Lacy Street, two blocks down. Next to the corner shop.'

It was a narrow street, the grass verges untended and overgrown with weeds and bushes, the bridges over the gutters precariously ramshackle, the gutters themselves brim-full with stinking black water, torpid with weeds and refuse. On Basmati's instructions, Dorothea pulled up outside a one-story wooden house on thin high stilts. The wood of its walls had once been painted white, but now the paint was grey, cracked and peeling. Several of the window panes were missing completely, the window shutters awry on rusty hinges. Behind the house, beyond a tangle of shoulder-high bushes and brambles, a second, smaller wooden house peeped through, on low stilts, one of those two-bedroom back-house cottages that housed entire families.

The front garden was tiny, completely overgrown with a flowerless bougainvillea hedge strangled by a creeper and several other nameless plants. A few rusty garden tools lay neglected among the weeds: a pitchfork, a spade, a rake, a battered metal bucket as if someone, years ago, had attempted work on the garden and then abandoned it in despair. A mangy brown mongrel tied with a piece of frayed rope to one of the stilts broke into a frenzy of barking as they entered the gate and headed for the stairs, which were perilously tilted to one side. The banister lacked several lathes, and wobbled as she walked up, following Basmati, followed by Freddy.

Basmati rapped and entered the front door without waiting for an answer. A bulky woman emerged from the depths of the house, carrying a little boy who stretched out plump arms to Basmati, crying out 'Mama!' Basmati gathered him into her arms. The woman looked from her to Dorothea to Freddy, frowning. 'What happening?' she asked.

'Is all right, Aunty,' Basmati said. Her voice was a nervous squeak, as if she expected her husband to come rushing from a back room. 'We come to get Baby. Mistress here, she helping.'

Dorothea smiled at Aunty. 'Dorothea Quint,' she said, holding out her hand. The woman barely touched her hand with her own limp fingers. She turned back to Basmati and whispered:

'You better go quick time, I think he at home in the back cottage!'

'Yes, let's go,' said Dorothea. 'We'll send for clothes and things later.' She headed for the door. 'Bye-bye, Aunty!'

Dorothea led the way out the door into the sunlight, down the rickety stairs. Their coming had already attracted attention. A few neighbours stood on the road next to the car, staring unabashedly. Word must have got out that Dorothea Q had arrived. A young boy wearing nothing but a pair of ragged knee-length shorts shot out from the huddle and raced to the back cottage, zig-zagging between them.

'Me husband nephew! Quick, quick, get to the car!' Basmati's voice squeaked with panic, and her fright was contagious. They reached the gate; the boy had closed it behind him, pushed in the rusty bolt, and Dorothea, the first to reach it, had to struggle to open it again. A man's shout rang out from the back cottage.

'Oh Lord, oh good Lord, is he! Hurry, hurry!'

Dorothea took a deep breath and her fear fled. 'Why should we run away with this child?' she said to Basmati. 'You're his mother. You are leaving that man; he has no right to you. Your body is enough evidence. Let's have this out right here with him. I'm not afraid.'

'Oh, mistress, mistress, you don't know that man, come let we go!'

But Dorothea stood her ground. Arms folded across her chest, she turned to face the man bounding towards them shouting abuse.

He wore a dirty singlet and a frayed pair of limp trousers open at the fly. His hair was long, greasy, hanging over a forehead shiny with sweat. His face was distorted with rage. He flew at Basmati with an animal roar. Basmati cried out and turned her back to him, clasping the child to her bosom. He kicked her, sending her and the boy flying. She managed to hold on to Baby, twisting to protect him from the fall with her own body. Still roaring, the man lunged towards Dorothea. The stench of stale rum encircled him in a putrefying aura. Rage, feral and deadly, burned in his eyes and she yelled out as she too, turned her back to him.

Freddy pounced forward, and with a mighty right-hand blow caught the man on the side of his head. The man staggered backwards, tripped on the metal bucket, and fell to the ground. Stunned, he stared at Freddy, but only for a moment. He glanced to the side, where the garden tools lay rotting, grabbed one of them and leaped to his feet.

Dorothea too leapt forward, aiming for his waist, her arms reaching out to grab him, hold him back. But she was too late. With a brutish bellow he lunged at Freddy, brandishing a pitchfork. Freddy parried, dodged, ducked; there was no way he could get closer. And then he tripped. His foot caught in the battered old bucket, it was Freddy's turn to plummet to the ground. With a roar of rage the man raised the pitchfork high and slammed it down on Freddy. It plunged into his abdomen. Basmati's husband let go of the pitchfork handle and sprung away; he flung open the gate and pounded down the road. The neighbourly spectators stared, some at him, some at the commotion within the yard.

Dorothea's scream was a single frenzied howl. She lurched towards Freddy, fell to the ground beside him. Blood spurted from his belly. She tugged at the pitchfork, trying to remove it, but then thought better of it and ripped off her blouse and shoved it up against the pitchfork prongs; in a matter of seconds it was soaked red.

Everyone screamed: Basmati, Aunty, Dorothea, the child. The little dog strained against its rope in a volley of hysterical barking. Only Freddy, his head now cradled in Dorothea's arms, did not scream; he barely croaked. His eyes groped through pain to catch Dorothea's, questioning, puzzled eyes. His lips mouthed words he could not speak, like a dying fish.

Attracted by all the screaming, more neighbours came to watch. Domestic upsets always made good theatre. Hysterical sobs wracked Dorothea's body, but she managed to look up and scream at the gapers: 'What you-all staring at! *Call an ambulance! He's going to bleed to death!*'

She turned back to Freddy. Blood continued to leak from his abdomen. She mopped at it helplessly with her skirt. 'Freddy! Hold on! Please stay with me! Don't go! Oh my love, my darling, stay with me! Oh God, oh my Lord! Help him! Help him, please! Don't take him away!'

Chapter Twenty-six

Rika: The Sixties

Everything was ready and prepared. The Granny dress lay ironed and waiting in her room. She had bought some white patent-leather go-go boots to go with it, on the sage advice of Trixie, who said they were 'all the rage in America'. Jag had phoned her up earlier that week to say he would pick her up at seven forty-five. Rika had a shower (wearing a plastic cap to protect her hair) and put on her new make-up the way Trixie had explained to her (and as it was described in *Teen* magazine which was now her Bible), and was ready and waiting at seven-thirty, sitting beside the front window.

She was worried. The Granny dress was six inches above the knee, on Trixie's recommendation, and the skirt, gathered in an Empire-line at the bust, was not too wide. She had never been on the back of a motorbike before. She would have to hike up the dress and that might be an awkward moment. Would her panties show? What if she slipped and fell in the effort to raise the hem almost up to her crotch *and* get one leg over the motorbike seat?

Waiting was agony. She tried reading a book – she hadn't read much in the last three weeks and the due date at the library was looming – she'd have to renew next week or else return the books unread, which she had never done before. But that's what being in love does to you, she thought. It changes your life completely. She couldn't get into the story at all. She forgot what the character had done and said in the previous page and had to keep going back, because half of her mind, or more, was channelled to the street outside, listening for the chug of a motorcycle. Every time one approached, she strained to hear if it would slow down and stop; but none did, and seven forty-five came and went. Her chest tightened as the clock ticked.

The drawing room radio played in the background: Dion and the Belmonts, crooning away. Why must she be a teenager in love? It brought tears to her eyes, and fear to her heart. Was this what it was like? A roller-coaster of emotions, elation and agony, up and down.

He was late. It was already eight o'clock – past eight, actually, as the dining-room clock she kept glancing at was five minutes behind – and still no sign of him. Perhaps he had forgotten – but no. If he had called to actually set a time he couldn't have forgotten. But something else could have happened. An accident! Maybe he had gone back to Jen, who Rika knew was very angry (she knew this because several girls had been only too anxious to tell her; girls these days were extraordinarily friendly to her, and just wait till they saw her *hair*, on Monday at the latest; though one or two of them would be at the fête tonight, the lucky ones with boyfriends).

Little Anthony sang 'Tears on my Pillow'. What was this, Heartbreak Hour on Radio Demerara? By the time the Platters came on with 'Smoke gets in your Eyes', the tears had left Rika's eyes and were trickling down her cheeks. Those who love are blind, said the song. Yes. She had been blind. Jag didn't love her and he wasn't coming. She had been stood up. But no; she had to keep faith.

She looked at the clock again: eight twenty-two (eight twenty-seven, actually)! Something must have happened. She wished she could ring him up, but that would be inappropriate. She already knew his family's phone number by heart; she had looked it up in the phone book. She knew his address, too, and had longed to ride up to Bel Air Gardens and find the house and look at where he lived, but what if he came out and saw her? And Bel Air Gardens was right on the edge of town, past Kitty on the East Coast Demerara. Not exactly a place where you could just happen to casually ride past. And it was a private, gated community. And it was essential to appear casual at all times. That's what *Teen* magazine said.

Eight forty-five. She had been stood up, definitely, Dumped. Or else – maybe – something bad had happened, because surely he would have called to say he was going to be late. He's had an accident! That motorbike! Granny had raised her to be punctual at all times. Of course, she knew of the concept of 'Local Time' which meant that everyone was always late as a matter of course, but surely not Don DeSouza, the son of a High Court Judge?

Ben E. King, with 'Stand by Me'. That was the last straw. She couldn't take it. Would there never by *anyone* to stand by her? Someone to fill her heart and never leave it? The tears flowed freely now; her insides had turned to stew, and her dress had two wet patches under the arms. Never mind her face; it must be a mess, tear-streaked and smudged. She didn't want to leave her seat by the gallery; what if he came when she was gone? But she couldn't possibly let him see her this way, eyes red and cheeks tear-smudged. She ran to the bathroom, washed her face, scrubbed it clean. He wasn't coming. What was the point?

'Rika! There's someone at the door!'

❊ ❊ ❊

She needn't have worried; Jag came in a car. He didn't apologise for being late, and he didn't notice her new hair. In fact, he didn't even seem to notice her at all. He stood in the open doorway as she rushed into the gallery, not having had time even to apply lipstick. He wore tight black pants and a red open-necked shirt, and a glower which Rika understood to be vexation at her not being ready and waiting; he even looked at his watch, so it was *she* who ended up apologizing for tardiness. He said nothing to that, so probably he *was* cross. Probably because she wasn't wearing any make-up. Jen's make-up when she went out with him was probably always perfect. Boys noticed things like that; they wanted their girlfriends to look beautiful. She'd have to do something about that the moment they arrived; she had managed to stuff her compact and mascara and lipstick into her handbag before leaving.

The car, a rather battered white Vauxhall Victor, was parked in the driveway.

'Oh!' said Rika, pleased, 'I didn't know you had a car!'

'It's my brother Paul's,' said Jag, and there was annoyance in his voice as if he didn't like having to explain. He didn't speak at all for a while after that, and didn't look at Rika. He was obviously still vexed with her. She decided to apologize again, and clarify.

'I'm really sorry I left you waiting. I had to go to the toilet... and ...' she stopped. Wasn't it a bit uncouth to talk about going to the toilet? But if she said she was putting on make-up he'd think her vain, especially since she *hadn't* put on any. When he still didn't respond, she just mumbled 'I'm sorry,' again.

'Oh, stop saying you're sorry,' said Jag, and fell back into his morose silence.

What else had she done wrong? Rika tried to think back to any other mistakes she might have made. Maybe her dress was too short after all; not decorous enough for his taste. Really, she shouldn't have listened to that Trixie MacDonald. She tugged at the hemline, wishing the dress was just two inches longer. It surely couldn't be her hair. She was dying for him to comment on it, but he just ignored it, the way Rajan had done. Did boys really not notice girls' hair? There was so much Rika had to learn about them. This silence of his, for instance; what did it mean?

And why was he driving into town, instead of towards Bel Air, where the fête was being held?

'Where are you going?' she asked, and tried to add a friendly tone to her voice so he wouldn't think it was a complaint.

'I need to go and see this guy – he has a garage – my motorbike broke down today and they couldn't fix it – need a baffle – this guy Bruce might have one, otherwise I got to wait till they import it. Damn!' He cuffed the driving wheel. 'Sorry for swearing.'

Relief flooded through Rika. So, he wasn't angry with her at all! Everything was fine.

However, everything wasn't fine. The guy Bruce didn't have the baffle, whatever that was, and neither did another guy, Poker, and by the time they got to the D'Aguiar's it was almost ten, and Jag was in a very bad mood. Rika hurried off to the bathroom immediately, hastily applied her make-up, and hurried back to their table. Jag sat there, glowering.

It was, of course, an outdoors fête, held in the extensive grounds of the D'Aguiar property.

The garden was ringed by various trees, some of which were in flower: a red frangipani just behind them released a delicious fragrance brought to them by a cool Atlantic breeze. The band, a popular one called 'The Young Ones', played various slow-dancing hits from America and England, and the floor was full of couples dancing cheek-to-cheek. Not really dancing even; just shuffling around in each other's arms, in time to the music. It was so very romantic; Rika longed for Jag to ask her to dance. She imagined him holding her up there on the dance floor, swaying with him to Otis Redding's 'Sitting on the Dock of the Bay'; but he didn't ask her. In fact, soon after he had seated her, he shot off to speak to a fellow sitting a few tables away; it seemed that the baffling baffle was still on his mind because the glower had not once left his face; if anything, his scowl had grown darker. Rika felt it was up to her to change his mood, so when he returned she threw him a line to help him get into the spirit:

'I just love this song, do you?'

'What? Oh … no, I don't really like the BeeGees.'

So much for starting a conversation. However, for the first time Jag seemed to take note of her.

'You want a drink?'

'Yes, please. A Lime Rickey.'

So Jag shot off again, but when he returned it wasn't with a Lime Rickey but with a rum and Coke. Rika looked at it doubtfully. She had sipped at drinks laced with rum now and again – Dad often invited her to try his Planter's Punch of an evening – but never had a whole one to herself. However, she couldn't give the impression of being too young for alcohol, so she stirred it with the straw so that the ice cubes clunked together, and then she drained the glass.

By this time, Jag had taken his seat at the table and his expression had cleared a little. It seemed he had finally resigned himself to not finding the baffle. With some luck he might actually ask her to dance, and then everything would be fine. The band had changed direction and now they were playing calypsos, and the couples on the dance floor had all separated and were doing a jump-up, laughing and bouncing and wiggling their hips at each other. It wasn't exactly what Rika had in mind but it was better than sitting here with Jag not knowing what to say or do. She wished she hadn't finished her drink so quickly; at least she would have had something to hold.

And then they were there; a boisterous group of people who all knew Jag; a couple of Sixth Form girls she recognised from school, but the boys were nothing but vague faces she may or may not have seen at Bookers or hanging out here and there in Town, Pumpkin and the rest of them. Jag perked up immediately; it was embarrassing, how easily he swung into conversation with them, how much he enjoyed their company. He and the boys were immediately deep in conversation. Rika tried to listen in but she could make neither head nor tail of the conversation, which was all about motorbike parts, motorbike brands, and motorbike racing.

So Rika turned her attention to the girls, who, now and then glancing at her, seemed to be discussing the new collection of dresses at Fogarty's. It seemed they all bought, and wore, ready-made. Rika felt half-dressed in her Granny dress, and tugged at the hemline again. One of the girls noticed her go-go boots and snickered; at least, Rika thought that was what she was snickering at, but she couldn't be quite sure. She felt as if the whole world was snickering at her. She wished she could just crawl into a hole and disappear.

Jag didn't dance with her, not once. After the barbecue chicken was served – Rika wasn't able to do more than nibble at it, so heartsick she was – Jag seemed to have had enough and he proposed that they go.

'Already?' said Rika in surprise. It was hardly eleven, and she had 'til twelve. She told him so, but he was already standing up and holding out his hand to her, so she took it and they left the fête, which was now rollicking with raucous calypso, the dance floor creaking with the strain of a hundred men and women jumping up and down. They left hand in hand, and at last Rika felt she was making headway with him.

Jag drove back via the Sea Wall. At a lonely spot between Kitty and Kingston he stopped and parked the car. Rika's heart began to thump; it was true! Now they could finally get to know one another.

But Jag didn't seem to want to talk. After switching off the ignition he turned to her and reached out, catching hold of her arm and pulling her closer. Rika suppressed a cry of pain.

The next thing she knew he was kissing her, his mouth crushing down on hers, his tongue forcing her lips apart. His breath was hot on her cheek. She struggled, pulled away.

'What's the matter?'

'No! I – I didn't want – '

'Why not? You like me, don't you?'

'Yes, of course! But— '

'Don't play around with me, OK? I can tell by the way you been looking at me all night that you want this. Don't worry, I got protection.'

He opened the glove compartment and pulled out a packet of Durex.

'Let's go in the back seat – more space!' He actually opened his car door, and before she knew it he was at her door, and it was open, and he was reaching in to help her out. She did not take the proffered hand.

'No, Jag! I didn't want – I don't want – I didn't mean— '

The door banged shut. In a trice, Jag was back in the driver's seat. He switched on the ignition, flung back the gear stick and the car shot forward.

'Jag, no! Stop!' she yelled.

The car squealed to a sudden halt. Her body slammed forward, crashing against the front panel. Jag looked at her, disdain in his eyes. She picked herself up, settled back into her seat. Her arm was hurting; tomorrow, she was sure, it would be bruised. But other parts of her, invisible parts, were hurting far more.

'So?' said Jag. 'Yes or no?'

'No,' said Rika, and she was weeping now.

The car sped forward once more; sped all the way back into town, around corners with squealing brakes, never stopping at red traffic lights. Luckily there was little traffic, and they arrived at her house unscathed. Jag pulled up with another screech of brakes.

Without a word, Rika got out of the car and slammed the door, her only way of protest. Through the gate, up the stairs to the front door. Granny had given her a key; she turned it in the lock, the door opened. A minute later she flung herself on to her bed and sobbed as if her very soul had turned to water, and tonight was the very last deluge.

Chapter Twenty-seven

Rika: The Sixties

She had read all about heartbreak. She'd imagined it, a hundred times. Heartbreak was a lovely word, a beautiful metaphor, a cliché, because of course the heart didn't really *break*. It continued to beat as steadily and reliably as ever before. That was the irony of it all: that there was no actual physical reflection; that the utter devastation inside her did not somehow blow up her body, the way it did the soul. A heart was not just a physical organ. It was the centre of the soul, its very core, and nothing could describe hers better than the word *shattered*. She wept into her pillow all night long and the next morning even Daddy noticed the redness of her eyes and the blankness of her gaze.

Thank goodness for the twins. They'd been their usual rambunctious selves all weekend, and today, at breakfast, they were still up to it. The latest thing was that new ditty that was making the rounds at all the school:

Ting-a-ling-a-ling!
School-call-in!
Teacher-panty-tie-with-string!

The twins, of course, took the sing-song chant to one more level, feeling, if they could, for the panties-band though the dresses of girls and snapping them to see if they were 'tied with string', and getting slapped for their trouble, and running away giggling. Rika, who wore jeans outside of school, they thankfully left alone. Now, she was grateful for the twins' attention-seeking gambits, however annoying. What with Granny telling them off and Daddy hiding behind the Sunday *Graphic* and

Mummy in her study typing up a report – you could hear the furious rattle of her typewriter all over the house – she could wallow in her heartbreak as much as she wanted.

The only one who noticed her utter desolation now was Marion, who, sitting next to her, squeezed her hand under the table and gave her a quizzical look. 'What's the matter?' Marion mouthed, but Rika only shrugged. Marion would never be a true confidante. At thirteen, Marion could hardly be expected to understand; her empathy was of a more general kind, in keeping with Marion's fundamental character. Marion had the rare gift of being truly *good* without being *goody-goody*, a huge difference. *Good* came from within; it was an inherent disposition, perhaps the way all people were *supposed* to be, and that's why such people were so attractive, whereas *goody-goody* was imposed form without; an adhering to arbitrary rules, together with the smugness of superiority and priggishness towards those less virtuous. Marion was the former. She quite simply empathised automatically; she was like a radio whose receiver picked up and tuned in to the feelings and moods of those around her, and her response was always one of support.

'Are you having a bad day?' she'd say in genuine sympathy to the glum-faced cashier at the shop counter, and the girl would immediately look up and meet Marion's eyes and see the caring there and smile gratefully, and the two of them would exchange a few friendly words and that would be it. Marion just loved everyone, and everyone loved Marion, and Rika wished she had just a fraction of such sheer *lovability.*

Instead, she was what she was: a tongue-tied alien who never knew what to say, a foot-in-mouth outsider who fell hook, line and sinker for the little lures of flattery thrown out carelessly by the likes of Don DeSouza, the classic cliché playboy; the worst of it being that she had been warned, and she'd fallen anyway.

She could see it all so clearly now, having howled into her pillow all night long. And the trouble was, weeping didn't make it go away. The heartbreak was still there, a real, visceral, physical pain. It hurt as much as if Don had taken a knife and ripped into her; a searing agony.

Marion's solicitude was too much for her; another bout of despair swelled up within her so she scraped back her chair to flee; which finally drew attention to herself. Daddy, looking up from his newspaper, noticed the redness of her eyes and the general desolation painted all over her face.

'What's the matter, pet?' he asked. 'Had a bad night's sleep?'

'*Ting-a-ling-a-ling!   School-call-in!   Rika-panty-tie-with-string!*' sang the twins.

'Shut *up*, you two!' exclaimed Marion, who could be firm when it came to defending others; all part of her niceness.

'Are you all right, dear?' said Granny. 'You look tired – but you came home early – I waited up for you.'

'No, I didn't sleep well,' Rika muttered. 'Think I'll go back to bed,' and escaped.

Rika had recently moved into the Annex, the room that had once been her grandfather's, and then her father's before he married. Wood ants had hollowed several of the boards on the north wall of her own upstairs bedroom, and the entire wall of that side of the house was being replaced. The good thing was that she had her own little bathroom, and some privacy; it had become her own private realm, separate and special. Now, it was a place to mope and mourn. Back in her sanctuary, she placed a pile of the most sentimental records she could find on the gramophone, closed all the shutters, flung herself on to the bed, pulled the sheet up so that she was entirely covered, and curled herself up into a foetus to cry herself to sleep. Oh, the agony of it all! Oh, the chagrin!

She slept until after lunch. Mildred had left some food for her – cold chicken and cook-up rice – but her appetite had left her completely. Feeling somewhat better after her rest, the acute pain now reduced to a dull ache, she decided to see if Rajan was around. He was the only one she could bear right now. Rajan would understand. Or would he? Rika remembered now Rajan's utter indifference to her excitement about Jag. He had shrugged the whole thing off and even pooh-poohed her excitement. But then: *'I don't want you to get hurt,'* he'd said, and now she *was* hurt. So Rajan was the shoulder to cry on. He would forgive her for having snubbed him somewhat the past week.

Yes, he was there, and as it was a Sunday, he wasn't working, but reading; a book on chemistry, Rika noticed. Rajan was studying hard for that scholarship. He looked up when she appeared, and, unlike the day before, smiled in acknowledgment. He closed his book and put it aside.

'You look glum!' he said, as she drew nearer. 'Date didn't go well?'

'Oh Rajan! It was a disaster! A complete catastrophe!'

Rajan patted the bench and she sat down beside him. The kindness in his eyes was an open invitation and so the whole story poured out; the lateness and the rudeness and the neglect and the baffle and the Sea Wall and the kiss and the groping and the Durex and the *finality* of it all.

'It's over before it ever began,' she wept, 'and I love him so much. I still love him and it's all over!'

'So you going to spend the rest of your life feeling sorry for yourself?'

'Don't! Just don't be all superior and judgmental about it! You could at least *feel* my pain and share it and feel sorry for me!'

'No,' said Rajan. 'I don't feel sorry for you. Not at all!'

'Well, I came here because I thought you *cared* and because I thought you'd help me but if that's the way you feel …'

She got up to go, but Rajan grabbed her wrist and pulled her back.

'Stop being silly! It wouldn't help you if I did because all you'd do is keep on wallowing in your misery. How would that help you?'

'Let me go!' Rika shook her wrist but Rajan held fast. 'You never took me seriously. You never even *cared* that I'm in love – you don't even know what love is! You're just into your philosophy and your maths and your bloody scholarship and you don't care!'

She stamped and glared at him, no longer crying. He gazed back at her, then patted the bench beside him once more.

'Sit down, Rika. I want to tell you something.'

She looked at him, dry-eyed now, for a moment, before obeying.

'Well, what is it?' The words were challenging, defiant. He was silent, as if willing himself to speak. Then he said:

'I *do* know love. I *have* loved. Just as strongly as you … think you do.'

'Really?'

'Really. A few years ago. A girl from my village, near Charity in the Essequibo. We knew each other since we were kids, went to the same primary school. After my father died, my mother took me and my brothers and sister back to the country to live with her parents. So this girl and I – her name's Fatima – we were really close friends until we were ten and then my mother brought me back to town to attend Queen's College – I won a scholarship – and I lost touch with Fatima. My mum was working here and we didn't go back up-country for years, because she had to be here all the time, to look after your grandparents.

'And then we went back to visit *my* grandparents. We were both sixteen, Fatima and I, and – well, we fell in love. Of course, being from a Muslim family, she wasn't allowed out much at all but somehow we managed to sneak out once or twice. Then her parents caught us and that was that. As a Muslim, marriage to me was out of the question – my mother wouldn't have minded but the Husain's were strict – no way they would let her marry a Hindu. Instead, they arranged a marriage for her with some rice farmer from the Corentyne and next thing I knew she was married and gone. I never saw her again. Never will.'

Their eyes met; his glistened with unshed tears and in them was such depth of feeling, such exposed pain, that Rika could not bear it for long; she looked away.

'I'm sorry,' she murmured. But Rajan was not finished.

'Love doesn't always find fulfilment,' he said after a while. 'And what I learned …what I discovered … is that even if it doesn't, it's worth it.'

She reached out, took his hand in silent sympathy. But he wasn't finished.

'I was only sixteen when I lost Fatima. Sixteen-year-olds can know love just as much as an adult. Better, because you're pure and innocent and not yet wary of love and all the pain it can bring. That's when we can love the truest. That's what I think, anyway. And then you get hurt and you put a scab over the wound and start accumulating scabs and you end up as an adult with one huge hard scab over your heart. Don't let that happen to you, Rika!'

She shrugged. 'Well, at least now I know not to make a fool of myself again. I'll be so careful now!'

'See!' said Rajan, grinning, 'That's exactly what I meant! The first scab!'

'Thanks anyway … I do feel a bit better. Thanks for telling me your story.'

'Hope it helps,' said Rajan, and looked at his watch. 'I've got to go now, help Mum get the old lady upstairs.

'I'll come too – say hello,' said Rika.

'You should visit her more often,' said Rajan. 'Even if she doesn't recognise you.'

'Yes. I know,' said Rika now. 'I'll try. Don't make me feel guilty!'

Rajan chuckled. 'So you *do* feel guilty, do you?'

'Of course I do!'

'That's a good sign,' said Rajan. 'Come on up.'

❊ ❊ ❊

Gran van Dam – as the four of them called their maternal grandmother – was sitting in her usual place at the gallery window. This was where she'd spent her days for the last two years, ever since her husband died. She had aged considerably since that day when Rika had met her for the very first time. Possibly the death of her dear Albert had speeded up not only the ageing process, but the collapse of her mental faculties.

Rika had last visited her six months ago, with Marion and, at Granny's insistence, the boys. It had been an awkward encounter; what can you say to an old woman who doesn't know who you are, who simply looks right through you? Gran van Dam's eyes saw nothing of real substance but reached out for that invisible never-to-return Albert. Once again, Rika had been put to shame by Marion, to whom the problem, real or imagined, of being totally transparent simply did not exist. Marion was just her usual caring self, conversing with Gran as if she understood every word and would reply in kind; even if she didn't.

'What's the point? Why do we have to come? She doesn't even know it's us!' the boys had complained, and Rika had not said, but thought the same. Marion had had the kindest reaction; Marion hoped she would soon be able to join him in heaven.

'In other words, you want her to die soon!' taunted one of the twins.

'And that's *mean*!' jeered the other.

Put like that it did not seem so kind.

'I want her to go heaven so she can be *happy* again with her husband!' explained Marion with puckered brow. She was not used to being accused of meanness.

'It's still wanting her dead!'

Now, Rika walked up to her grandmother, stooped down and planted a kiss on the withered cheek. Gran van Dam grabbed her wrist and stared at her with unseeing eyes. 'Albert! Albert! Albert!' she croaked.

In alarm, Rika looked up at Rajan.

'Does she think I'm him?'

Rajan shrugged. 'She does that to everyone who comes near. Not to us any more – it seems we are too familiar. But everyone else.'

'She didn't do it last time.'

'No. It's getting worse. That's why I said you should come more often.'

He stepped forward, bent down.

'It's Rika, Granny, your granddaughter! Come to visit! Let go of Rika now, Gran.'

He drew up a chair for Rika to sit on, and carefully pulled away the fingers, one by one. Rika stepped back gratefully, rubbing her wrist where the hand had gripped it like a tight bird's claw. At last the old woman allowed it, and her hand dropped limp to her lap.

'Just talk to her for a while. It'll do her good.'

'But she won't understand a thing!'

'At some level, I think she will. Just talk.'

'But what shall I say?'

'It doesn't matter. Just talk. Speak to her as if she's all there. There's a part of her that will hear. I'm sure of it.' Rajan turned and left her alone with Gran van Dam.

So Rika spoke. Speaking had never come easy to her; it all depended on the person she was speaking to. To her surprise, being with Gran van Dam loosened her tongue. She spoke to her of matters she told few people; most of all, she spoke of Jag and the error of his ways, and hers. Up to now she had only confided in Rajan. She took Gran's hand – frail, soft and weightless – in hers, and stroked it as she spoke. Somehow, this gave her comfort. Almost from the moment she started to speak, Gran van Dam stopped calling for Albert. Was she really hearing? Listening, even? What went on behind those unseeing eyes? Rika talked on.

Rajan returned after a while, and smiled to see them deep in one-sided conversation.

'Come Granny, it's time to go upstairs!' He enunciated each word clearly, separately and loudly. 'It's time for bed.'

Rajan swept Gran up into his arms; by the looks of it she weighed no more than a bird. 'Off we go!' he said, and walked off with her towards the stairs, Rika following behind. Upstairs, he took her into her room and laid her on the bed. Basmati walked in, bearing a basin of water.

'Bedtime, Granny!' said Basmati, setting the basin down on a stand on wheels which she proceeded to roll towards the bed. 'Hello, Rika! How things?'

Rika exchanged a few words with Basmati and then she and Rajan returned to the yard.

'Marion said last time she hopes she goes to heaven soon to join Albert!' said Rika. 'Do you think that's what really happens? That we go to heaven and meet our loved ones that have died? I don't even know if I believe in heaven. Do you?'

Rajan laughed. 'That's three questions!' he said.

'Well just generally, then. Do you believe we go to heaven when we die, and we all meet up again over there?'

Rajan took time with his reply. 'I don't think heaven is a real *place* where people walk around in, well, in heavenly bodies,' he said slowly after a while. 'I think it's simply a state of consciousness. You don't actually *go* there when you die, in a body. But what you are, who you are, everything you've put into your mind all your life – you *become* that. I do believe we live on because consciousness cannot die. It just *is*. So I believe we return to an original state of consciousness – an ocean, if you like – where we are all one, and free of our bodies. And if we have filled our consciousness with ugliness then we live in hell. And if we have filled it with kindness, we are in heaven.'

'So you think she *will* join Albert, but not in the same form he was in here, but in a sort of – of universal soup? So she won't even know it's him?'

'That's putting it – roughly. "Universal soup" – no, not really. Because that would mean we take all our ego-junk with us there and mix it all up together. No, I believe we each have our individual journey, and the ultimate goal is happiness. I think if we have lived well, that happiness, pure happiness, bliss, is what comes after.'

He stopped speaking, as if carefully considering his next words.

'There's a certain philosophy that compares life to a sparrow flying through the night and into a lit room – which is our life on earth – and then back out into the night. I think it's the other way around. I think that *life on earth* is the night, and the real daytime is elsewhere. That we long for daytime because we have known it once; the memory is slumbering deep inside us; and everything we do, all seeking for happiness, is really only a longing for the day. Because we have to return, sooner or later: We have to. Maybe at the end of this life or the next or the next.'

'So you believe in Reincarnation? Returning again and again?'

Rajan looked at her and laughed again. 'What's this, the Inquisition? But, well, I'm a Hindu; it's in my blood, I guess, the belief that we do return – not as the same person, of course – to pay our debts; to learn and grow until we are ready to never return. To learn to live, to learn to love, that's what I believe. Yes. To never return. To be in the daylight forever, and free. That's what it's all about. That's heaven.'

Rika smiled. 'That sounds good! Better than heaven and everlasting hellfire, anyway. But, Rajan, I have to go. Granny is taking us all to Brown Betty's this evening for Chicken in the Rough. I don't want to be late. But we can talk some more next weekend, OK?'

'Seems you recovered already from last night's disaster!'

'Ha! Jag?' she grimaced. 'He can go to hell for all I care!'

❋ ❋ ❋

The next day all her resolutions – to be strong and confident and not-caring-about-Jag – flew out the window, because Jag rang after school. Rika had spent a strange day. Girls were eager to hear what had happened on the one hand; on the other, the grapevine had delivered some conflicting Chinese whispers. Some had heard she and Jag had quarrelled and had left the fête early for that reason; others had let their imaginations free and sidled up to her with nudges and lascivious winks. Rika decided not to confide in anyone; let them guess as much as they wanted.

'Hi,' Jag said now. 'I just wanted to apologise for what happened Saturday night. I was a bit drunk and a bit worried about the baffle and I behaved badly. I'm very sorry.'

The moment Rika heard his voice, and more than his voice, his apology, she melted, forgot all her good resolutions as well her conversation with Rajan, and forgave him everything. The forgiveness was immediate and complete.

'Oh, it's quite all right!'

She smiled into the telephone, wanted to kiss it. Is this how people felt when they smoked a joint? 'High', they called it; she'd overheard some of the girls talking about it between classes. High, like floating. Jag only had to speak and there she was, up in the clouds, and a little giddy.

'No hard feelings!' she added.

'Good. Then I'd like to take you out again.' He sounded relieved, and quite humble. 'If you'll let me? Give me a second chance?'

Wow. He was actually *doubting* she'd say yes! So she had to reassure him.

'Oh yes, of course! I'd love to!'

'Fantastic!' said Jag. 'I'll come and pick you up tomorrow at four, OK? Better if you wear pants; I'm coming with the bike. I'll take you for a spin.'

'You got the bike fixed?'

'Yes, I found someone with the same model that had been in an accident. He was selling off the spare parts so I was able to get an old baffle. I've got my baby back! So I'll be in a good mood this time and we can really connect. You up for it?'

'Yes! Yes, of course!'

'OK; see you tomorrow!'

❊ ❊ ❊

Tomorrow came. At school Rika was confident and less mysteriously silent than the previous day. She held her head high and now and then whipped it so that her hair swung, the way she'd always envied in other girls. A few of the girls came up and touched it; they asked where she'd had it done, and she told them. They asked what she'd worn at the fête and she told them. They asked about Jag and this time Rika let casually drop that she was going out with him again. This evoked sighs and big eyes and admiring remarks. Rika was on top of the world; she remembered Rajan's words about feeling good about oneself being the natural state, the state we were all meant to be in. Yes, it was true! Confidence and happiness were natural feelings; she felt true and whole and just *good*. This time, everything would work out the way she wanted. It had to.

She didn't really have any fashionable pants so she decided to wear her newest jeans, which, she discovered, were just a bit tight. She hadn't worn them for several weeks and she must have grown in the meantime, filled out. She nevertheless squeezed into them and found a decent blouse to go with them. She decided not to wear make-up this time; her first attempt had been such a disaster she felt embarrassed just thinking of it.

Jag arrived on time; obviously, his contrition was genuine. She skipped down the outside steps to meet him and clambered up behind him on the Yamaha. They roared off. Jag headed north to the Sea Wall and for a moment Rika feared he was thinking of a repeat of last Saturday – though of course, things would be a little less convenient on a bike – but he didn't. Once there, he headed east and they sped along the East Coast road, past Kitty and the Carib Hotel and up towards Ogle. The wind lashed her hair against her face; she had to hold it back and wished she'd thought to put it in a ponytail. But! It actually *whipped!* Just like white-girls' hair! It was a miracle! She finally had the hair she'd always wanted, and she'd be grateful for that.

They passed Goedverwagting; Rika wondered how far up the coast he'd take her. But at Le Ressouvenir he slowed down and turned left, into a side street, and then he stopped.

'There's a nice little restaurant here,' he said. 'I thought we could have a drink.'

Rika nodded and followed him upstairs. A sign above an open doorway said 'Elmo's Corner'. Jag led the way in and right through to the balcony, which overlooked the Atlantic, brown-and-white and lashing against the Sea Wall just beneath them.

Jag ordered a Coke for himself and a Lime Rickey for her. As they sipped their drinks, he chatted with her about everyday things. He asked her about school and her family and she gave clipped answers because the shyness was back in full force. This was exactly the time to act confident and regal so it was a shame that her newly acquired aplomb could desert her just when she needed it most …

Jag made no attempt at seduction. He took her home before dark, and promised to call again, which he did. He didn't even try to kiss her. He was a paragon of good manners and chivalry. Rika felt proud enough to introduce him to Granny and the rest of the family; but, no, perhaps it was a bit too early.

The next day, and the day after that, Jag took her for motorbike rides, always to a different destination; sometimes up the East Bank, as far as Houston, sometimes the East Coast. 'We can go to swimming at Beterwerwagting one day soon,' he promised. 'If your parents let you? My family has a beach hut there. Or to Red Water Creek. Whatever you prefer.'

Always he was polite and respectable and respecting. Never did he put a foot wrong. Rika's popularity at school climbed to new heights. She had a boyfriend; and *what* a boyfriend! She glowed. *This is* me, she thought. *The real me! I am strong, beautiful and confident. Just like Rajan said.*

❋ ❋ ❋

On Thursday afternoon, while sipping drinks at Esso Joe's after a thrilling ride up the East Coast Road, Jag said,

'I'd like to take you somewhere nice Saturday night. What about Palm Court?'

Rika was so startled she almost choked on her Lime Rickey. She coughed so much Jag had to get up and slap her back.

'Thanks – sorry! I – I just – really? P-palm Court? Really?'

'Yes really! Why not?'

'I just thought I'm, well, I'm a bit young?'

Palm Court was by no stretch of the imagination a teenage hangout; it was in the top echelon of Georgetown's restaurants. Businessmen took their guests there for lunch, and well-heeled couples dined there on their anniversaries.

'Don't worry about your age – just say yes or no!'

Did she even have the sort of formal dress that would be required? She couldn't wear that Granny thing, after all; not again, and not there. And yet …

'Well – yes, of course! Oh Jag! I'd love to! Thank you!'

'OK; it's a date, then. I'll pick you up at six – I'm borrowing the car again.'

He dropped her off at her gate and Rika made her way up to the Cupola in a daze.

I'll buy a new dress. Ready-made! An evening dress! Oh! I can't believe it! Palm Court! Where will I get the money for the dress? And I'll need new shoes, again! I spent all that money I took out from the bank last week – I can't possibly ask Granny for more … But, it's my money after all. I'll just take it. Get my bankbook and passport from the office. It's MY money! She'll never know.

The thoughts swirled in Rika's head for the rest of that evening and kept her awake that night. She scribbled it all down in her diary, the writing hardly legible, the emotions gushing out on to the page, rambling, agitated. But the diary wasn't enough; the words welling up, the questions, the fears and the ecstasy needed an oral escape. She longed to talk to someone, preferably Rajan, pour out the thrill of it all into willing ears.

Instinct told her Rajan wouldn't approve. He had warned her off Jag, after all – and how wrong he had been! Really, she should go over to Rajan tomorrow to let him know he'd been wrong; that Jag was, now, almost her boyfriend, to judge by his behaviour these last few days. So attentive! But even though he'd been proven wrong he, Rajan, probably wouldn't approve. And why should she care about his approval, anyway! He wouldn't understand. She needed a *girl* for that.

Rika hurried down from the Cupola as fast as the spiral staircase would take her, then took the proper stairs two at a time. She grabbed the telephone receiver, dialled Trixie's number.

Chapter Twenty-eight

Rika: The Sixties

'That's a lovely dress!' Granny said when Rika emerged on Saturday evening, all dolled up. 'Who made it?'

'Oh – ahmm – I – um ...' Rika scrambled to think up a good lie, and she found it quite easy to create a half-truth, which wasn't quite the same as an out-and-out fib.

'It's actually ready-made!' she said. 'I borrowed it from my friend Trixie.'

Granny accepted this story, and Rika continued to the Morris chair beside the window, which had become her regular waiting-post for Jag.

'I'm glad you have a nice friend at last,' said Granny conversationally. 'You must invite her home one day – I'd like to meet her. Are you going to a party?'

'Actually, Jag's taking me to dinner at Palm Court!' Rika said.

Granny knew by now that Jag was her boyfriend, and thoroughly approved. Jag was from a good family, and that, really, was all that mattered. Respectability was a guarantee for good behaviour.

'Palm Court? My, that's posh! He must be really serious!'

That's exactly what Rika thought. She was delighted to hear Granny confirm it.

❀ ❀ ❀

Jag didn't come late this Saturday. In fact, he was a minute early, and Rika was at the door and down the front stairs even before the car had turned into the driveway. Jag met her at the gate, looked her up and down, and whistled under his breath.

'Eeev-illl!' he breathed, and his blatant admiration swung Rika up to the top of the world. He took her hand and led her to the car, opened the passenger door for her. Rika couldn't stop smiling; her cheeks almost hurt. She had to stop staring at him! He was so handsome! He wore a crisp royal blue short-sleeved open-necked shirt, not tucked into the waistband but hanging down to his hips, in the new formal men's style called shirt-jak – a cross between a shirt and a jacket, not requiring a tie. It had been decided on high that the wearing of jackets and ties for men in this tropical climate was pandering to the ex-colonial masters; thus the shirt-jak. The PM and all the Ministers and businessmen and important people all wore shirt-jaks now. Jag looked wonderful in his.

He'd had a haircut, too, which she wasn't sure about – she had loved that stray lock of almost-black that hung roguishly over his forehead, loved the way he swept it away now and then, and missed it. But that rascally smile of his seemed warmer than ever, those charcoal eyes more approving as they wandered up and down her length. She pulled at the hem of her dress as she eased into the passenger seat. She should have gone to Hyacinth this morning to let down the hem.

Jag drove around the corner into Waterloo Street. They whizzed past her grandmother's house; there was Rajan, harnessing the donkey to a cart laden full with cut grass. He hadn't seen her, or so she hoped; she still hadn't told him about all the exciting developments of the past week. She'd talk to him tomorrow. Or maybe she wouldn't. Rajan couldn't, or wouldn't, understand. Rajan with his strict work ethic and self-discipline and ascetic philosophy. Rajan didn't live in the real world. She felt a pang of regret for Rajan, which, she realised, was a sense of pity. Rajan, saving up for university by cutting grass verges. Poor Rajan. She hoped he'd make it, and become a really good and famous lawyer or doctor … she'd have to explain to him …

'Rika?'

'Oh – sorry. What did you say?' She shook herself out of her reverie and turned, smiling, to Jag.

'A penny for your thoughts. You were sitting there smiling to yourself and shaking your head – like if you were talking to someone.'

'Oh – well, nothing really. I can't even remember.'

Jag punched a button on the dashboard radio and Petula Clark burst into 'Downtown'. Rika's heart sang along; this was the life! She imagined she was in New York City instead of boring little Georgetown, painting New York red, with Jag. Jag tapped the steering wheel in time.

'What's your favourite music?' Jag said, turning to Rika. 'Mine's the Rolling Stones.' So Rika told him about the Beatles and realised she was no longer in love with George Harrison.

❈ ❈ ❈

At Palm Court a live band, the Rock'n'rollers, was playing. Jag ordered a meal for her and she ate without knowing what she was eating. She sipped at the rum and Coke Jag bought for her and gazed as if hypnotised into his eyes. It was unbelievable. He was saying the words she longed to hear – or almost.

'I really like you,' Jag said. 'You're – different. So sweet and simple; I love the way your eyes shine.'

'I like you too, Jag!' Rika whispered. And she whispered even more softly: 'I think I – I love you!'

She was shocked at her own bravado. You shouldn't tell a boy you loved him – not before he had said it to you. That much she had learned from eavesdropping at schoolgirl conversations and reading *Teen* Magazine. You had to wait and be coy and coax the longed-for words from his lips, and then, only then, you could say 'I love you too,' *too* being the operative word. He had to love you first; but he had only said *like!*

The word *love* had slipped out before she could think, and it couldn't be unsaid. Rika broke into a sweat at her *faux pas.* Thank goodness for the sequined bodice – it wouldn't show dark circles under the arms.

'You know what?' Jag said. 'I was reading the *Reader's Digest* the other day and there was a quiz called 'Test how lovable your girlfriend is' and I did it for you, and it turned out you are one hundred per cent lovable! How about that!'

'Really!' Rika glowed. Those were surely the most wonderful words she had ever heard in her life. And he had called her his *girlfriend!* She really was his *girlfriend!* Unbelievable!

Jag walked up to the band and whispered something to the leader, who nodded. The next song was 'Angel of the Morning'. Jag asked her to dance, and led her to the dance floor, where a few other couples were swaying. He held her close as they moved; surely he could hear the thumping of her heart! His hand on her back burned into her, pressed her closer. What was that cologne he was wearing? Was it Old Spice? Boys these days wore Brut, but Rika, inexperienced as she was, could not tell the difference. She only hoped she had not sprayed too much Blue Grass on to her neck, because his face was close, so close …

She was by far the youngest person on the dance floor. The women around her, they were, well, *women.* Grown up. One of them even had grey hair, and Rika was sure that she was looking at her, Rika, disapprovingly. Jag must have noticed too, because he whispered into her ear: 'that old hag is just jealous – all she can get is an old goat to dance with!' And Rika felt skittish and girlish; she giggled and buried her face in his shirt-jak. Inside, she was all bubbly, like champagne, and then she felt Jag's lips on her forehead. She was young, in the prime of life, and *lovable.* It was hard to believe, but it was true. She had nabbed the best man in the whole of Georgetown – here she was with him; that was the proof.

They danced to a few more slow love songs – 'The Way You Look Tonight', 'The Twelfth of Never', 'Love me Tender', 'Love is a Many-Splendoured Thing' – and then the band had a break, so Jag led her back to their table, and she had another drink.

They spoke again about music. It turned out that their tastes were completely different. Apart from the Rolling Stones Jag liked female singers like Petula Clark and Nancy Sinatra. Rika was more eclectic in her tastes. Apart from the Beatles, she liked soul music – Otis Redding was a favourite – traditional Latin American music, Indian music and, her latest discovery, Bob Dylan.

'It's just so hard to get his records over here – I must be the only Guyanese who likes him,' she said. But Trixie had an LP, *Greatest Hits,* and she had fallen in love.

'I never heard anything by him,' said Jag, 'but I think my sister is a fan. She went to America last August and brought back a lot of LPs. I'm pretty sure Bob Dylan was among them.'

'*Blonde on Blonde*, that's his latest – oh, I'd love to hear that! It's got songs I never heard, and this one I heard the other day on Radio Demerara: 'Sad Eyed Lady of the Lowlands'. It was so sad it made me cry! I just wish we could get those records here!'

She and Trixie had gone to the Sandbach Parker record store, leafed through all the LPs and confirmed it: no Bob Dylan.

Jag was silent for a while and then he leaned forward over the table and said:

'I have an idea. Let's go over to my place and look at my sister's record collection. I'm pretty sure she has that LP. In fact, I'm certain. We could listen to it if you like.'

'Really? You don't mind? Bob Dylan is a bit strange – I don't know if you'd like him!'

'Anything for you, my love!'

Jag winked at her and raised his hand to click for a waiter.

A frisson of excitement shuddered through her. She was going to Jag's home! She might meet his sister – a much older girl who had left St Rose's last year and was now, she believed, working at the Royal Bank! She couldn't wait to tell Trixie. In fact, she couldn't wait to tell Rajan, since she'd now definitely proven him wrong. He'd been so sceptical, cutting even, about Jag. There was a running commentary going on in her head, as if she was standing outside herself and watching from a distance, telling Rajan what was going on, like a cricket commentator. She'd tell him tomorrow. About Palm Court – Rajan had certainly never been here – the music, her feelings for Jag. Jag was so *nice!* So kind and attentive towards her! *See, he took me to Palm Court,* she would say to Rajan, *and he was nothing but a gentleman!* I was right to fall in love. Love is never wrong – it can't be! It makes everything right! He's not as bad as you thought! Perhaps Jag would kiss her afterwards – her first kiss! – and she could tell Rajan about *that.* Rajan would be as sceptical as ever, but that was because he had once loved and lost. That made you mistrust love. She would tell Rajan everything. She was proud of herself, and confident; she would never again be that shy social outcast, Rika Quint.

❊ ❊ ❊

Jag lived in Bel Air Gardens just outside of Kitty, so he headed back towards the Sea Wall and eastwards up the coastal road. There was a cattle-grid at the entrance to Bel Air Gardens and a watchman in a little sentry box, who smirked when she met his eye in passing, which made her cross. This was the entrance to an exclusive gathering of mansions circling a central park.

Jag drove around the circular road to the south side of the park and stopped outside a large concrete house lit by security floodlights. The house was built on high stilts in the traditional style, but with a large modern balcony enclosed by an ornate wrought-iron balustrade all along the front. A watchman in a khaki uniform sat on a chair just inside the Bottom House, and sprang to his feet as the car turned into the drive. He opened the gate for them and Jag drove past and stopped under the house.

'Here we are!' he said. 'I have my own room down here. My parents are in Barbados this weekend so you don't have to worry about anything.' Part of the Bottom House area was built up, and Jag pointed to the wall. 'That's my own little kingdom.'

'Oh!' was all Rika managed to say, as Jag opened the passenger door for her. She wanted to say she was feeling a little dizzy and even slightly sick, but held back the words. She'd had one rum and Coke too many, which, combined with her nervous excitement, caused an occasional tummy rumble. She got out of the car, stumbled. Rajan caught her and led her to the door of his kingdom.

He took a key out of his pocket and shoved it into the lock, swung the door open and gestured for her to enter. She stepped in ahead of him. He closed the door.

'Jag, I …' she started to say, but the next words were smothered because Jag's lips were on hers, pressing down, and her arms were clamped tight to her sides by his embrace.

Jag pulled away. 'What's the matter? Don't you want to kiss me?'

She wiped her lips with the back of her hand. His mouth had been so slimy!

'I – I … I thought we were going to your sister, to listen to that record?'

'Oh, that. You really want to listen to some singer? I thought – oh, never mind. If you insist. Let's go up and see.'

He unlocked a door, which, Rika found, led into a stairwell that took them up to the main floor. Jag led her through the gallery and sitting room to a passage leading apparently to the sleeping quarters and opened a door which, it turned out, was his sister's bedroom.

'She's not in,' said Jag, opening a door, 'but you could look through her records. Just go ahead.'

By now Rika had lost all enthusiasm for Bob Dylan. She didn't like being in his sister's room without her permission, didn't like leafing through her record collection in her absence. Most of all, she didn't like being alone with Jag in his parents' home, with his parents absent, the house completely empty. The spectre of last week churned in her. Not again. Surely not! But that kiss, downstairs ... it was the same. Exactly the same.

She stopped rifling through the records.

'What's the matter?'

'I don't think she's a Bob Dylan fan,' said Rika hesitantly. *And I think you know that. I think you lied to me.*

It was all a ruse, to get her here with him, alone. What if he tried to *rape* her? Her heart by now was racing madly. She was entirely in his hands! His face, downstairs, after the kiss – it was exactly the same as last week: hungry, leering. And this time she was alone with him in a big house, and no one nearby except the watchman. But the watchman wouldn't be on her side. The watchman belonged to Jag's family. He would never protect her, if she screamed.

'Can I get you a drink?' said Jag.

'Yes, please.' Well, thank goodness for that. If he was going to get her a drink he couldn't be thinking of rape. Silly me! Rika's heart slowed down and she began to breathe again. Panicking for nothing. Of course he's not going to rape you. This is love. He was just a bit – overeager. Boys are like that. She knew it from eavesdropping and *Teen* Magazine. They can't control themselves. But he was going to get her a drink, so everything was all right. 'Just a Coke, or a Lime Rickey,' she called after him. 'No more alcohol.'

'As you wish,' Jag called back.

She followed him out of the door and sat down in a chair to wait. Her legs felt like jelly – the aftermath of her panic. That's what came of being such a weed. People were right to reject her. And if she wasn't careful Jag would reject her too. She wished she'd talked more to Trixie about what to do when a boy tried to kiss you, because that was horrible, and as far as she knew it wasn't supposed to be horrible. She was doing it wrong. It was all her fault. She was so childish – Jag must be laughing at her and already planning to dump her.

'Come, let's go back downstairs,' said Jag as he reappeared, two Coke bottles steaming icy mist in his hands. 'You go first.'

So Rika reluctantly led the way back down to Jag's room. She had been hoping they'd sit on the balcony and enjoy the night air and the sea breeze, and just chat about – things. She'd wanted to suggest it but for some reason she couldn't get out a single word – it was as if her brain was frozen. She needed distance – she needed him to prove his good intentions. She needed him to be *ordinary* – not somebody who kissed her by force. She needed time to find her bearings. But maybe it was all right. After all, he had taken her up to find the LP and he had gone to get the drinks, so it had to be all right. *Calm down, Rika!* She told herself sternly.

Back in Jag's room she looked around; there was a faux-leather red couch and two matching armchairs in the area nearest to the door, as well as a sideboard on top of which stood an oversized radio and a gramophone, a pile of LPs next to it. The back of the couch divided off this sitting area from the sleeping area; a large bed took up the other half of the room. There was a wardrobe as well, and a door, which, presumably, led into a bathroom. The walls were covered with posters of tanned female film stars in bikinis, and motorcycles. Behind the posters the walls were painted black.

Jag gestured to the couch; she sat down. He put his Coke down on the sideboard and looked through his records; he chose several, removed them from their jackets and piled them on to the gramophone. The arm moved forward and back and the first record dropped on to the revolving disk. The arm moved forward again, the needle touched the record, and a second later the Rolling Stones were getting no satisfaction.

❋ ❋ ❋

Jag picked up his Coke bottle and stepped across to the couch. He dropped down next to her, and placed his right arm along the back of the couch.

'I really like you,' he said again. His voice was slow, low and conciliatory; there was a rasp to it. She looked at him, into his eyes, hoping, longing to see reflected there the love she longed for. Love with a capital L. But his eyes seemed cold, opaque, unreadable; and this time around she did not say *I like you too*, and certainly not *I love you*. She said nothing, for doubt and anxiety had seeped into her soul again and that spoiled and diminished the clarity of spirit she had once known. *Love* was missing; that glorious, pure sense of unity and rightness – gone. She was sure it must show in her eyes.

'You look scared,' said Jag, and his hand dropped to her neck where his fingers played with the neckline of her dress. 'Are you scared?'

She tried to speak but only a croak came out. The words she wanted to say stuck in her throat. She nodded. She longed to turn back the clock, turn it back to Palm Court and that wonderful sense of unity. She was sure that if he knew, if he felt, how much she had to give he would love her too and he wouldn't behave like this: grabbing at kisses and lying to her about Bob Dylan. What did he *want?*

'It's all right,' Jag said, and his fingers crept up to play with her ear. 'It won't hurt. I'll be gentle. I keep forgetting you're so innocent. I really like that, you know. Your innocence.'

His voice was crooning, suggestive; he told her of his longing for her, his care for her, his experience, how he would do it slowly and gently so she wouldn't feel any pain, and how much she would enjoy it because, he said, he was by far the best lover in Georgetown. How lucky she was, he said, that her first time would be with him, such a good lover, and how much he respected her purity. But now was the time to grow up, he said.

'I'll make a real woman of you.'

He moved nearer, and at the same time, his hand on the back of her head drew her closer too. Her body stiffened; *stop, stop!* She wanted to cry out, but no words came. She was paralysed with trepidation; not exactly fear, for surely he wasn't dangerous, but nervous energy that filled every cell of her body. Trembling slightly, she sipped the dregs of her Coke through the straw and then Jag took the bottle from her and placed it on the floor and moved in. All of a sudden his mouth was crushing down on hers, his tongue pushing her lips apart and probing to get past her clenched teeth.

With all the force she could muster, she jerked her head back, but Jag tried to follow with his face.

'No, no!' she cried, as if at last the words, the only words available to her, had broken out of her body.

Jag drew back with an expletive.

'What's the matter?' he said, his forehead creased with annoyance. 'You know you want it!'

'No! I don't! I can't!'

'You're just scared. I know it's the first time. Look – I'll be gentle. Just relax. You're so stiff. Relax and you'll see how sweet it is. Real sweet. Come on now, don't be a little prude. You'll like it. All girls do.'

He placed his hand on her right breasts, cupping it, and kneaded it with his thumb. Rika grabbed his wrist and pushed the hand away. There was a slight scuffle as he tried to resist. Their eyes were locked in a silent battle; in his flashed anger, and then something else as he gave in, removed his hand, and put it on her cheek, a sort of managed, calculated capitulation.

'It's all right, baby,' he crooned. 'I know it's all new for you. Just trust me. I know what I'm doing. I just want you to taste the sweetness. Come on now. Be good to me. You love me. You know you do. This is what big girls do with the men they love. You don't want to stay a little girl forever, do you? A tight little virgin? Let me help you. Let me. You don't have to do anything. Just relax. Relax, baby. Relax.'

But she only stiffened all the more in his arms, and pushed against him. His rasping voice sounded not sweet but poisonous, treacherous, lying. She could almost hear the falsehood in his words. Hear the deceit. And when he moved in again for another kiss she lashed out; involuntarily her right hand flew to his face. She slapped it, hard. He flinched as her nails caught and scratched him across the cheek. He drew away and touched his cheek, now marked by three red welts.

'You little bitch!' he looked at her, venom in his eyes.

'Take me home, Jag! Please take me home!'

She was crying, blubbering like a baby, and she didn't care what he thought of her, didn't care about the horrible name he had just called her.

And then all the fear and disgust and disappointment that had been churning in her since the moment she had entered this building rose up in her body and erupted through her mouth in a stinking gush of vomit, all over Jag's crisp new shirt-jak.

'Aaargh!' He sprang to his feet, vomit-coated arms held up, and threw her a look loaded with such malevolence she could have sunk through the floorboards. He dashed to the bathroom at the back of the room.

All the way home – racing through Kitty, squealing around corners, honking at bicycles – he regaled her with expletives and diatribes.

Cock-teaser. Frigid little prude. Tied-up pussy. Fucking virgin. Leading him on. Playing stupid games. Deliberately flirting only to lock the gates. He should have known better after last week. He gave her a second chance and she threw it away. Idiot girl.

It didn't matter. Inside she had turned to stone. She could not even cry. She didn't care what he said. It didn't matter. It just didn't matter. All she wanted was to run to Rajan and tell him everything and beg his forgiveness.

Chapter Twenty-nine

Inky: The Noughties

The night after the burglary we were all at home when the doorbell rang. I opened the door a crack as far as the chain would let me. My heart skipped a beat. George Clooney stood on the threshold; that is, a twenty-something version of George Clooney, all dark brooding eyes and charm. 'Yes?' I said, opening the door wide and trying hard not to stare, or appear anything other than thoroughly bored.

We exchanged a few words and I returned to the dining room, leaving the front door ajar. They had finished eating and Gran was on her feet, already shuffling towards the door.

'It's a *Daily Mail* reporter. For you, Gran. He wants to interview you. Is it OK?'

'No!' cried Mum.

'Yes!' cried Gran. Gran was louder. And quicker. She shoved her rollator forward, right into Mum's path as she raced to the door, blocking her path. She blocked the hallway, too, and so it was Gran who first got to the front door. She flung the door wide open.

'Come in,' she said, ignoring Mum's protest. She and I exchanged a glance; she rolled her eyes, shrugged in resignation, and submitted to what seemed our destiny. Gran led the reporter into her room, Mum hard on his heels. I followed them into the room and, like the day before, sat down on the edge of the bed, still trying not to stare at George. Mum shrugged again and sighed and sat down on the sofa next to Gran. George sat on the Luxury Commode Chair, seat down. He switched on a tape recorder, laid it on the table next to Gran's laptop.

'My name's Ted,' said George. 'Ted Fisher. And as I understand it, a very valuable stamp belonging to you was stolen. Would you like to tell me more?'

Mum piped up, some kind of protest or denial, but Gran simply ignored her and launched into the same spiel as the day before.

'An original British Guiana One Cent 1856 Black on Magenta! My husband's grandfather Theodore Quint make that stamp famous, he sign it 'T.A.Q.' Passed down from father to son, a family heirloom, priceless. Millions of pounds worth.'

The stamp had made a huge leap in estimated value from yesterday; Gran had obviously thought this out carefully. Not only was she not (yet) admitting that the stamp had *not*, in fact, been stolen; she was actually hyping it, jacking up its value. And slowly it dawned on me: *Gran was creating buzz.* Nobody apart from us yet knew about her precious stamp, and it was valuable only because of the *other* British Guiana Black on Magenta, the DuPont stamp. *This* stamp, Gran's, was at the moment just what it was at face value: an ordinary scrap of paper, worthless in itself. It would only become valuable *when the world knew about it.* When the philatelic world, and the general public, discovered its existence. When as many people as possible wanted it, coveted it. Until then it remained a worthless scrap of paper.

Throughout all this George's expression hardly changed. He kept his eyes on Gran and nodded every now and then as if deeply intrigued. But his eyes kept wondering over to me, and then he would start and yank them away and back to Gran. It was as if there was a magnetic pull between our eyes. I know I felt it, and I was reasonably sure he felt the same. In fact, I was certain. This was the first time since Tony that a man had had such an effect on me; I had to force myself to stay calm and be aware of what was going on.

And I knew exactly what was going on. This was media manipulation and product promotion at its finest, and Gran seemed born to the art. On and on she rambled, telling the story of the stamp, her family history, the inestimable value of this wonderful heirloom.

I noticed how she'd dropped her dialect for the reporter's sake. Her speech had been grammatically flawless, no mutilated *th*'s or false pronouns. But the more she spoke, the more her language began to degenerate.

'I am inconsolable! To think that I, a poor old lady with not a penny to me name, should be the one to lose this precious heirloom that been in my husband family for over a century!'

George interrupted now for the first time. 'Mrs Quint, where did you keep the stamp album?'

'Under the mattress!' she wailed. 'I know, I know, is a stupid place. My granddaughter done tell me is stupid. But what do I know, an octogenarian just come to dis country from me homeland. I just a poor disabled lady, see me Zimmer ting? And that chair you sitting on, is me potty. I can't even walk up de stairs to go to the toilet.'

George jumped as if he'd been pinched in his bottom, and turned bright red. He looked around the room as if for an alternative seat to the Luxury Commode Chair, but finding none, stayed put.

'How old are you?' he managed to ask.

Gran told him, adding several years to make herself pushing ninety. Once again I recognised her plot. She was now playing up the *human interest* side of the story. She knew how the media thrived on maudlin sensation. She hadn't devoured those reality shows for nothing.

'See, I can't walk a step on me own. I totally dependent on daughter and granddaughter, bless their hearts. I come all the way from Guyana, only last month. I ain't got nobody left in the world to look after me. And me daughter here, struggling to make two ends meet. We is just a poor immigrant family. We was in de church praising the Lord when the attack came.'

George's eyes glowed with the wonder of it all. I could almost read his swirling thoughts, the headlines forming in his head: '*Rare Stamp Stolen from Wheelchair Immigrant Grandmother*'. All the stuff about her keeping it under the mattress, saving it for her granddaughter; the fact that this stamp, unlike the DuPont one, had remained in the Quint family for over a hundred years; the heirloom stuff, the 'sentimental value' stuff. The stuff of tabloid middle-spreads.

And then Gran dropped her bombshell. In the middle of the interview, she remembered. Oh, what a silly old goose she was! *Of course* the stamp hadn't been stolen! She was so absent-minded! She had taken it out of the album and hidden it, and then forgotten she had done so. It all came back to her She had it! She actually had the stamp! She pointed to the Luxury Commode Chair. 'It's in there!'

George's eyes glowed brighter yet. He had found it: the perfect scoop. Promotion and an overnight breakthrough as a front-page journalist would be his. '*Wheelchair Grandmother finds Million-pound Stamp in POTTY CHAIR!*'

He stood up and removed his camera from around his neck, waved it and smiled at Gran, all charm and sweetness.

'May I?'

George took several photos of Gran, and then one or two of me with her, of her with the potty chair, her lifting the potty seat to triumphantly remove the stamp and wave it at him. And then he said:

'Thank you so much, Mrs Quint. This is a wonderful story. May I have your telephone number, just in case?'

That was my chance. I gave him our number, and I gave him my mobile number as well, just in case, and gave him my most charming smile. And George smiled back at me knowingly, and I knew for sure I'd be hearing from him again, and it wouldn't be about the stamp.

❀ ❀ ❀

We were at the breakfast table, on the third morning after George's article, which had been published in the *Femail* section of the paper; we'd read it online. Even though it had, as I'd predicted, been embellished and slanted to make it predominantly a women's human interest article, the central fact was big news.

The legendary DuPont stamp, the rarest stamp in the world, had a challenger! Since they were not identical – one being signed 'E.D.W.' and the other 'T.A.Q.' – they were truly rivals for that title. But unlike the DuPont stamp, *this* one was not buried in a vault; this one was *out there*, floating around in the real world. It could be seen, admired, inspected, discussed – and, perhaps, acquired. At least, that's what they thought.

In the following days, the media took up the chase. Mainstream newspapers, magazines and TV news reporters all hounded her, and she basked in the attention. Gran loved it. You'd think that she had been discovered herself, rather than the stamp.

She now fancied herself as a minor celebrity. She agreed to one interview after the other, including an appearance on a breakfast TV show. Our little household, already in a state of disarray, descended into chaos as Gran's schedules took precedence over our own and her demands grew ever more rarefied. It was awful.

'I got to go to the hairdressers! And I need a new dress!' she fretted, and when Mum tried to talk her out of that – 'I just can't afford these extras!' – Gran flipped.

She flung her spoonful of porridge across the table.

'Is who raise you up since you was a baby?' she bawled at Mum. 'Is who buy you story-books and bicycle and Pony Club and them Beatles records and Schoolgirls' Picture Library and t'ing? And now when you old mother want a little something extra, such a fuss. Such a fuss. I don't know what the world coming to! You young people so selfish!'

So saying she stood up, grabbed her rollator, and trundled off to her room, there to sulk for an hour or two. Mum was almost in tears.

'I can't take it! I can't take it anymore!' She sprang to her feet, her own breakfast unfinished. 'Inky, listen. I need to scream. I really need to scream. I'm going up to my room to scream. Just don't worry, OK? It'll be over in a few seconds. Just ignore it and if any passers-by come knocking at the door tell them it's OK; nobody's being murdered. OK?'

She rushed from the room and up the stairs. I heard her door slam. I was not just worried, I was scared. This wasn't Mum. Mum *never* lost her cool. The last time she'd raised her voice was way back when I was fourteen and I'd done something truly terrible, but not so terrible that I could even remember what it was. Mum was so laid-back, she was supine. Mum *never* screamed! Maybe she was cracking? *Could* Mum crack? I'd always believed not. Now I wasn't so sure.

I wondered for a moment whether I should follow her, try to calm her down. I decided against it. Maybe she *needed* that scream. Everybody needs a good scream now and then, or else a good cigarette, even Mum. It was a sign that she was human, a healthy sign. I took a deep breath and continued with my breakfast, ears pricked for Mum's scream from up above.

It never came.

I waited and listened. Nothing. Five minutes. Nothing. I finished my coffee. I needed to go out for my hit of nicotine, but by now I was beginning to worry. Mum wouldn't *do* anything to herself, would she? Slit her wrists or something? I knew *I* would if I had Gran on my hands and no cigarettes. Well, maybe; I'd certainly want to.

But, I thought, maybe Mum was having a good cry instead. That would be just as good as a scream. I decided to put off my nicotine hit. I needed to check on her. What if she'd already slit her wrists and was lying on the bedroom floor right now, bleeding to death? I had to go up. It was my duty.

✿ ✿ ✿

Halfway up the stairs I smelt it. That sweet, almost sickly scent that sometimes pervaded the house, creeping under doors and embedding itself into clothes and hair and upholstery and carpets and curtains so that the whole house was subtly suffused with it, like babyskin fragrance. And I knew what Mum was up to. She wasn't human after all.

I rapped on the door.

'Come in!'

I entered.

She was sitting cross-legged on a folded blanket on the floor, in her meditation corner. A single candle glowed on a makeshift altar. Two thin, white strands of smoke rose from a stick of incense.

'Oh, excuse me. I didn't hear you scream, so I came to make sure you're OK.' Automatically my voice lowered to almost a whisper. It was a reflex, a response to the muted atmosphere. Mum smiled, stood up and opened the curtains. Sunlight flooded the room. 'I'm fine. I dissolved the scream.'

I nodded, uncomfortable with such talk. 'OK, then.' I paused respectfully before changing the subject. 'Mum, I wanted to tell you something.'

I took hold of her hand and sat down on the edge of her bed, pulling her down beside me.

'I just wanted you to know, I'll pay for Gran's hairdo and her new dress. It's OK. I've got a bit of savings and I'd love to help.'

She leaned forward and hugged me. 'You're a sweety,' she murmured into my hair. And I knew everything was all right. But then she yelped, sprang to her feet.

'Look at the time!' she cried. 'I've got to go to work!'

'Work? But today's Saturday!'

'An emergency. Two of the storyliners were ill this week. I've got to go in and finish writing the script. I'll be back by one. If you could get Mummy's hair done by then …'

I nodded. 'I'll take care of it.'

She dashed off, leaving me in the room. The bed was still unmade. I decided to make it for her. I tugged away the rumpled duvet.

That's when I found the letter. It was buried among the rumpled bedclothes, both the open letter and the envelope. The letter was slightly crumpled, as if it had been crushed and then smoothed out again.

It was one of those familiar ones, the ones with the hand-written envelopes. I remembered seeing it among this morning's post, which Mum had taken upstairs before breakfast. A pile of unopened letters lay on her desk; bills most likely. This one, she'd opened and read …

Now, I swear I'm not a snoop. I don't go around reading people's letters for fun. But there was just something about *these* letters in particular. Perhaps a pattern I'd unconsciously seen in Mum's behaviour when they arrived, a pattern of slight, almost imperceptible dismay, a slight blanching of the skin. I was only vaguely aware of such reactions, but over time – for I had seen many of them arrive, and many of them taken upstairs – that was the general impression. So yes, I might as well admit it. I was bursting with curiosity.

Downstairs, the front door slammed. She was gone. All was quiet. I couldn't help it. My fingers operated on their own volition, unfolding the letter, and so did my eyes, reading it.

It was a letter from a literary agent. Now, I know nothing of the world of literary agents but I do love novels and I read articles about my favourite authors and even I had heard of this agent, a really big time guy.

It was a letter of rejection. Not even a personal one. Her name had been added in handwriting to a form letter that even I could tell was a duplicate, sent out to hundreds, if not thousands, of hopeful aspiring novelists.

'Dear Author,

Thank you very much for sending us the manuscript of The Six O'Clock Bee. *Though we enjoyed reading it very much we are sorry to inform you that ...*'

And then I knew. Mum was writing a novel. Or had written one. Or both. That's what she did when she got up early in the morning to work. The realisation came to me in a flash of both great admiration and deep compassion. Oh, the poor thing. The poor, poor thing.

Mum was a good writer, but not *that* good. No one knew this as well as I did. I was her first reader, after all. Oh, she was successful in her own way, and many of her love stories for women's magazines got published. But a whole novel? She couldn't do it. No way. Not that I hadn't encouraged her:

'You should write the next Harry Potter!' I'd told her a couple of times, but she'd laughed me off. Not my genre, she'd said; but that's the kind of thing that made fortunes, and not love stories.

'Or, at least, something like Bridget Jones,' I conceded. 'That made a couple of millions too. Something light and funny.' We'd both laughed our heads off at Bridget Jones. Now, if Mum could duplicate *that* ... But she hadn't wanted to talk about it. She shook her head and refused to say a single word more on the subject. Secretive, evasive, private: in every subject that was in any way important to Mum, she kept her silence. It was so aggravating.

Now, my heart sank for her. In fact, I teared up in compassion. Poor Mum! Poor scatty, mediocre Mum, born to lose. No wonder she'd cracked this morning, if only for a short while. I wished she *had* screamed instead of doing whatever mysterious thing she did with incense and candlelight. Maybe a good scream would get this thing out of her system, once and for all.

I decided not to make the bed after all; because then she'd know I knew and would be embarrassed.

All those rejections, all that effort; it was enough to make anyone depressed.

As I turned to go I saw her filing cabinet. One of the doors was open. I glanced at the shelves: a row of upright arch lever files, all in different, bright colours, as if to brighten her day, whereas I knew for a fact that their contents did just the opposite.

Poor Mum. Poor, poor Mum. I wished I could help; I wished I was rich and could pour my benevolence down on her. How happy she'd be, how grateful! I had savings, it was true; I had worked since I was sixteen; squirreled away a bit of my wages whenever I could, a little nest-egg for my gap year in Asia. Apart from that, I could just afford a small rent for Mum and my own food, and what remained was enough for Gran's new dress and hairdo, but not enough to pay all Mum's bills.

My glance fell on the back of a bright red file. Written on the spine were the letters 'REJ.'

I'd seen this one before and always thought 'REJ.' was simply a sloppily spelled 'REG.', short for 'Registration' or 'Register' or something official like that. But with my newfound intelligence I instinctively knew: 'REJ.' was for 'Rejections'. I reached out, removed the file, and opened it. I was right.

It was more than an inch thick; chock full of rejection letters.

I leafed through them, and looked at the first. It was from ten years back. Mum had been at this for over ten years, and this was the only result: a humiliating, devastating file of rejections. A quick check told me that they were for three different novels. *Three!* Whatever else you could say about Mum, lack of perseverance wasn't one of her flaws. I sighed and replaced the file.

Lowering my glance to the floor of the cabinet I saw Mum's other shame, in a pretty Ikea storage basket: a collection of unopened letters: demands for payment she could not pay. I shouldn't have done it, but I did: I pulled it out.

And then I frowned. On the top of the pile was an envelope that shouldn't be there. A personal letter, covered in stamps, unopened. I couldn't resist; I picked it up and inspected it, turning it over in my hands. It was a long white envelope with a smattering of Guyanese stamps, and a Royal Mail sticker on it saying 'Signed For'. It was addressed to Mum and the handwriting – I recognised it now, that flourish, from the letters I'd received as a child – was Gran's. Yes – written on the back, as a return address, was Gran's name and address in Guyana. There were some words written beneath the return address:

'Rika: you said in your letter that I am not to write you. But you MUST read this. Please!'

* * *

So Gran had written to Mum and she had never opened it, never read the letter. In spite of that urgent appeal to do so! Typical! I tried to figure out the date, the stamp was smudged, but the 'Signed For' notice had the date: 1984! The year of my birth! Eighteen years ago, and Mum had never read it!

And yet, why was it on top of the other letters? Surely that meant she had been looking at it recently? What was going on? Oh, the will power it took me to resist opening that letter, reading it! Here, I knew, would be the answer to all my questions, the solving of the mystery. But I lacked just that last little bit of brazenness. And the will power it must have taken *her*, to keep it for eighteen years, never reading it, yet holding on to it! Why? Why hadn't she thrown it away, if she couldn't bear to read it? Why? What did it say? Reluctantly, I laid the letter back in the box, shoved the box back into the cabinet. But one day, I swore to myself, Mum would read that letter. She had to. I would force her to.

❀ ❀ ❀

Our old friend the stamp dealer rang to say that his contact had made a final offer of £15,000. Gran could take it or leave it. 'For all we know,' he said, 'the stamp is a fake. It hasn't been validated, has it?'

Once again, Gran told him to haul his tail.

But when a Mr Peterson from Stanley Gibbons – the authority on stamps, apparently – called, she took the phone into her room and closed the door. When she came out again fifteen minutes later she was subdued but serious.

'That man,' she told us, 'say the experts saying it might not be a real genuine British Guiana One Cent. He saying, the only way to prove it is to let them examine it. If is a fake is worth nothing. But if is authentic, original from 1856, it going to be famous. But first I got to let them analyse it. Otherwise them experts going to always doubt.'

Her brow puckered at the dilemma: obviously, Gran wanted her stamp to be granted full recognition by the philatelic world. On the other hand, in order to do that she'd have to let them get their hot little hands on it. She couldn't have it both ways, and she couldn't boss them into recognising the stamp.

'Rika,' she said, after a moment of rare reflection, 'I think I going to do it. Otherwise people going say I is a liar. Yes, I going to let them prove is real.'

* * *

Television began to bore Gran. She turned to Internet surfing instead. Mum took the huge step of installing Broadband – which I'd always nagged for anyway – and Gran now sat from mornings to evenings with her Neville-donated laptop, checking out God knows what websites. Gran joined online discussion forums, dropping in to leave an anonymous caustic opinion, and dropping out again. She chased up old schoolmates. She wrote articles for Wikipedia – articles on obscure points of Guyana's history, such as the Enmore Massacre, which nobody was going to read anyway. She made sure I read them, though; she was horrified by my lack of background knowledge on Guyana.

'You is a woman without roots,' she told me; 'if you don't know where you come from how you going know where you going?' I could have told her I come from *England;* I didn't need some irrelevant dump of an ex-colony sitting on the edge of nowhere as my roots. I kept that opinion to myself.

What worried me the most was Gran's new emailing tic. For not only did she look up old friends, she followed the footsteps of long-lost Quints, digging them out of their cubby-holes all over the globe, from New Zealand to Ireland, from Finland to Chile. That's how wide our family had spread. Gran drew an enormous family tree which she blue-tacked to her wall, and as soon as she knew the names of third, fourth and fifth generation Quints, she filled them in. And, if she could get hold of their address, and if they were old enough to read and write, she emailed them to introduce herself.

It worried me. For, as Mum had told me, I knew what she was looking for: a suitable heir for the Quint.

Which was betrayal of us, her next of kin, her own flesh and blood. I seethed in jealousy, but to speak up would be to worsen matters. In agony, I watched the family tree grow.

❊　❊　❊

Already, flesh and blood was getting far too close for comfort. Soon after Gran's flirtation with fame the calls from Neville and Norbert increased to daily. I never knew the content of those long conversations, for Gran retreated to her room with the phone, shutting the door on Mum and me. All I know is that around that time came the talk of putting in a stair-lift and a bathtub device that would lift Gran into the tub. Those suggestions never came to anything.

But then, one day, the delivery van arrived once more.

Gran had mentioned a couple of times that she wanted a new wheelchair, a motorised one, with which she could go out on her own. This was it; a present from Neville: a luxury scooter, with all the bells and whistles.

Already, Gran had been venturing ever further afield with her wheelchair. She had taken to going off, all on her own, to the Post Office and the Bank, to the grocery and the newsagent on Streatham High Road, and, especially, the charity shops where she hunted for bargains, sniffing the armpits of cardigans and blouses for tell-tale traces of perspiration, but seldom buying anything. And in all those places everyone rushed around the counters to serve her; she never had to stand up, although she could. I know because the first two times I accompanied her, not believing her capable of buying a stamp or a mango for herself. Once again, she proved me wrong.

Now, with her new scooter, she went everywhere. Armed with a map of London, she disappeared into the concrete wilderness. When this first happened Mum panicked and together we scoured the streets, looking for her. When we returned home there she was, laughing at us. Locked out of the house.

With this new freedom came a new sense of entitlement. It was her right, Gran said, to own a dog.

'A dog!' Mum cried.

'Not a big one. Jus' one a them lil' tiny t'ings. I saw a lady in the park today; she had one, just like a toy. I thought it was a puppy but no, it was a real grown up dog. I want one like that.'

'But I don't want a dog! I already have a cat. What about Samba? I thought you liked Samba?'

'Samba is for inside the house, my little dog is to take for walks. I done choose a name for it, Elephant.'

'Why out of the blue do you want a *dog?*'

'It's not out of the blue. I always wanted a dog, ever since I was a little girl. A dog of my own. My parents didn't let me. They said dogs is for boys not girls. Them Quints always had a dog, sometimes two. Turtle. Parrot. Kanga. Rabbit. And remember, Rika? Rabbit? Rabbit was your dog.'

'Not really. Rabbit was the family dog. I wanted the new puppy to be mine alone, but you gave him to the twins. Remember Devil?'

'Ah, Devil, Devil. Yeh, I remember Devil. And I remember Devil get tame. But that was after you left. You never get to see the new Devil.'

I had to laugh. Girls wanting dogs and not getting them seemed to run in our family. I remembered the fights Mum and I used to have, the tears, the tantrums. But Mum had been adamant. Just as she was now.

'No dog, and no Elephant!' said Mum emphatically. 'And I'm late for work.'

'Mum!' I called, as she rushed to the door.

'What?'

'Your shirt's on inside out.'

She looked down.

'Oh. Oh, thanks, Inky. Where's my head today'

'Where it always is. Up in the clouds.'

She made a face, left the room. Her footsteps pounded on the stairs as she dashed up to change.

What would Mum do without me?

'You're a good daughter,' Gran said. 'Take good care of you mother, like that boy in the poem.'

'What poem?'

'James Morrison Weatherby George Dupree – the little boy who took care of his mother, A. A. Milne. You mother didn't read those poems to you?'

I shook my head. Mum hadn't read anything to me when I was little; she'd made up stories on the spot. She didn't like reading aloud, she told me later, but it didn't matter as I'd loved those made-up stories. Stories of a faraway land she called Back-of-Beyond-Land, the land she'd grown up in. Back then, she'd made it sound like paradise. As a child I'd longed to go there, see for myself the sakiwinki monkeys and hear the six-o'clock bee and the kiskadee. She told stories of crazy, funny people who walked the streets and children who climbed mango trees and caught fish and frogs in alleyways; it was a happy place, the country of her childhood. But that happy place was a figment of her imagination, because later, once I'd grown up, she told me the truth. Real stories. Stories of murder and betrayal and poverty, political mayhem and economic downfall. She convinced me the place was a shambles, not worth even a thought. The paradise she'd created for me as a child came all from her imagination. She'd created a homeland flowing with milk and honey, and the child-me had taken it for real. That was the power of her writing. Back then.

I'd told her to write more stories and get them published, but she always shook her head.

'Children's stories don't come to me any more,' she'd explained, as if stories landed on her head from outer space.

'Rika was always a dreamer,' Gran said now. 'Never you know what she got in she mind. People like that, you got to watch out for them. Mind what they doing behind you back. Is for they own good, otherwise they ruin they own life. You mother now, Rika, she don't talk much but she does write. Is *what* she write you got to watch.'

Chapter Thirty

Inky: The Noughties

Gran, we found out, was engaged in a vigorous email correspondence with several Quint great-grand nieces and nephews. She told us all about them. All of them, not surprisingly, were enthusiastic stamp collectors. It's amazing how many passionate philatelists come crawling out of the family woodwork when a priceless stamp turns up. Two lived in the USA, one in Canada. One lived in Guyana, and seemed her favourite. This girl's name was Charlotte; she was fifteen, the granddaughter of one of Gran's myriad Quint brothers-in-law, he himself long dead. Charlotte wrote Gran saccherine-sweet emails on an almost daily basis, several of which Gran read out at the breakfast table for our delectation.

Worse yet, Gran wanted me to connect up with all these dear far-flung second and third cousins of mine. It was high time, she said, that the family closed ranks; that we all got to know and love each other. There was talk of a grand Quint Family Reunion in Miami the following year. Gran bemoaned the fact that the Quints, once such a close-knit family unit, should now be scattered like loose grain all around the globe, knowing nothing of each other, our connections, our roots. And in a way she was right, and no doubt her plan for reunion would have worked, had it not been for the Quint.

It is a well-known fact that nothing so easily destroys family unity like a fat inheritance to be shared or withheld, depending on the whims and moods of one person.

❀ ❀ ❀

And I felt it, gnawing at my insides like a virus, the little rodent of greed. Under other circumstances I'd have loved to connect with this huge family Gran was digging out for me. Dad had been an only child with no connections to the one or two uncles and aunts he had. I had grown up without extended family; Mum's choice, in part, but also a result of the wave of emigration that had swept her home country in the sixties and seventies. She had virtually cut herself off from everyone, and only resumed contact with her original family after I was born.

Gran calculated that now there were over a hundred second, third and even fourth generation Quints in the world. One of them would get the Quint, as our stamp had come to be called by the media. And it wasn't going to be me. There was a name for the virus eating at my substance.

It was jealousy.

And it wasn't even about the Quint, or who would get it in the end. It was about her, Gran.

The thing is: I was learning to love her. And she didn't even know it. I only just found out myself. But all she cared about was the Quint; cared so much that she wasn't even aware of the false love offered by these long-lost cousins of mine.

The Quint was slowly tearing our family apart. It was if a poison leaked from it, infecting us all with rancour and greed and jealousy.

❀ ❀ ❀

Marion called in great agitation. I was suspicious from the start. I didn't tell her about Gran's plan to find a suitable heir, of course, but she seemed to know already; probably through the Canadian Quints. Then she said something that clinched it for me.

'Inky,' she said, 'You have to restrain Mummy. She can't go on like this. Maybe the stamp doesn't even belong to her.'

I knew it; I was right. Even Marion, sweet, kind Marion, was not immune to the destructive power of the Quint. The only person in the family who did seem immune, in fact, was Mum.

I hoped Marion could feel the coldness in my voice as I answered:

'Of course it belongs to her. Her husband Humphrey left it to her.'

'But ...'

'Marion, sorry, I have to go, Gran's calling,' I lied. I could not stomach a word more of this conversation. It was betrayal. In my heart I whispered: *Et tu, Marion.* I cut her off.

*   *   *

Two weeks after sending it off for validation, we received the news that the Stamp – or the Quint, as it now could officially be named – was indeed genuine. Not only *we* received that news; the whole philatelic world did, as well as the British tabloids. Another flurry of attention came Gran's way, and she played it for all she was worth:

No, she was not selling it, and no, she was not going to keep it in a vault or a safe.

What was she going to do with it, then?

Keep it at home and when she died, leave it to a worthy heir, with strict instructions that it should not be sold.

Was the rumour true, that she kept it on her person, in her purse?

Gran burst into whoops of laughter at that.

'Y'all think I born yesterday?'

Where, then, was the Quint?

'Big secret. Only two people in the world know. Me, and one other person.'

I knew who that was; her solicitor. For yes; Gran had engaged a solicitor, one Mr Wainwright, who came around occasionally and locked himself into her room with her and sent her Important-Looking Letters. All Top Secret from us.

The weird thing was, Mum didn't even care, and it drove me crazy. I really believe that the only thing in her head was that damn novel she was writing – and which I still hadn't summoned the courage to talk her out of – and her soap-opera dramas. Which were, after all, her daily bread.

Whenever I reminded her to take action – to have a serious talk with Gran about the future of the Quint – she only rolled her eyes and shrugged, or waved her hands in that dismissive butterfly-wing thing.

'When you think about it, Inky,' she said to me, 'All it is, is a scrap of paper. A little tiny scrap of paper any normal person would chuck in the rubbish. Isn't it crazy, that people run around like headless chickens over a *scrap of paper*? Isn't it fascinating, the way we fixate on a thing and out of our own minds, out of desire, instil it with value? I mean, isn't that where all these problems come from in the first place? Desire?'

'But, Mum …'

'Inky, there's something you don't understand. This whole drama is not about the stamp at all. It's about something else. That stamp is only a catalyst. It's a stand-in. There's something more going on, something beneath the surface. Relationships. Mummy is playing a game. She's trying to draw me in, lure me into playing. And I refuse to play.'

It was my turn to roll my eyes. When Mum waxed philosophical and psychological like that it made me want to puke. Thank goodness it didn't happen too often, for it made communication, a realistic conversation, impossible.

In this case, it meant I had to deal with Gran on my own. Make her see that these sycophantic nieces and nephews of hers were unworthy of the Quint. I had to do it for Mum's sake. Mum was drowning under a sea of debt, and Gran could save her with a finger-click. It just wasn't fair.

Chapter Thirty-one

Rika: The Sixties

It was an extremely subdued, red-eyed Rika who knocked on Rajan's door early the next morning. She had not slept a wink, escaped the family breakfast. All she wanted was to see Rajan. He opened his door and, seeing her, stepped out. She fell against him, a sobbing bundle of wretchedness. He held her, silent, rubbing her back. After a while she calmed down. Rajan still held her. It was good to be held like that, restorative, calming.

After a while Rajan said,

'It was Jag, right?'

She nodded. He nodded too.

'I saw you drive past last night and I hoped you'd be OK. You want to talk about it?'

She did. They sat down on the bench outside his room and there she told him everything. There was no shame, no embarrassment, no indignity in telling Rajan because he did not condemn, did not judge, did not sneer. Did not say *I told you so*, though he had every right to do so. He was so – so big. And strong. She poured out the whole miserable story, holding back nothing, and spared no insults in castigating herself for her stupidity.

Rajan only said, 'You're not stupid, Rika. Just young and inexperienced. You don't know what boys are like. Now you know.'

'I'll never get over this. Never.'

'Yes you will. You will right here and now. Come with me.'

He got up and held out his hand; she took it and let him lead her out to the back, through the garden to the vegetable patch right at the very back, where he grew tomatoes and beans and pumpkins. He knelt down on the ground and beckoned for her to do the same, and she did. With his hands he scraped away at the loose black earth until he had made a shallow cavity, and then he turned to Rika.

'Lay your hands in there,' he said, and she did, and he covered them with earth.

'Now, I'm going to leave you for a while. Just stay like this. Try to let all your misery run down into your hands and ask the earth to take it. That's all. Whenever you feel a new wave of misery, just send it into the earth. The earth will heal you. I promise.'

And he got up and walked away, leaving her there, kneeling on the ground with her hands buried in the earth. The soil was slightly sun-warmed and moist. As Rajan had instructed, she gathered all her misery and sent it down through her arms and into her hands and fingers and down into the earth. After a while she realised it was happening all by itself. As if the earth was a sponge and sucking her anguish, all those tormented emotions, all the regret and shame and self-incrimination, out of her. Warm, and moist and absorbent. Yes: absorbent. Soaking it all up. Mopping up all the turmoil, all the sheer *horribleness* of the past night and the illusion – delusion – of the time before. And then another thing happened; mopped dry, *she* became the sponge, she the absorbent one, and what she absorbed and drew into herself was peace and trust and strength, rising up from the earth though hands and arms and into her very being.

And then something else happened. It happened in a split second, an instant of recognition, like a click inside her brain in which she saw, she knew, she understood. An image of Jag rose up within her, like a bubble. And she realised: *he was never worthy of my love, for he did not love too. Love must meet love in equal portions.* And in that moment of recognition the bubble of Jag popped. Just like that. He simply vanished. And in that moment she knew with all the power of the earth and the sky and the universe *her own worth*, and it was almighty, overwhelming, and true. In that instant she became a woman.

Later, she discussed it with Rajan.

'… and yet, you know, when I was in love with him, at first, it felt so real, so true, so everlasting. How could it just disappear like that? Poof!' She clicked her fingers to demonstrate the popping of the bubble.

'The *love* was real, Rika; but Jag wasn't. I think you were more in love with the *idea* of him. Being in love isn't the same as love. Being in love is like the fizz in soda: just bubbles. So you felt all these bubbles rising up and you mistook them for the real thing. The real thing was the love, not the bubbles.'

She laughed. 'Yes! A bubble! That's all Jag really was. A bubble that popped.'

'Exactly. Yet the love itself was real.'

'You said boys are like that. But you aren't, Rajan. How come?'

'I should say *most* boys are like that, but really, who knows? Maybe some of them are only like that because they want to belong, because if they don't follow the horde they'll get laughed at and mocked.'

'Like they laughed at and mocked you?'

'Yes. See, I didn't want to follow the horde and that's always a dangerous thing. I didn't want to talk about women in that degrading way, use that language, talk about scoring and busting cherry and all that. It was so much bluster. So I held back and that made me an outsider, less of a man in their eyes.'

'I'm an outsider too. Jag said all the girls are doing it now. They all want it. How come I don't? How come, Rajan? Maybe I *am* just frigid and abnormal like Jag said?'

'You're just you,' said Rajan. 'Everyone is different. If you don't want it, then be strong in that. You don't have to do what everyone else is doing. Be yourself. Even if all the girls are doing it, it doesn't mean *you* have to if it's not what you really want. People tend to follow the horde. Some people just want what everybody else tells them they should want. Not following takes strength.'

'The earth gave me strength, Rajan. It did. It just kind of flowed into me. It was amazing!' She looked at her hands as if in wonder; she had washed them at the stand-pipe in the garden, but there was still black earth beneath her fingernails. 'My hands – they were like sensors, picking up all kinds of messages from the earth.'

'Right,' said Jag. 'But really, you didn't pick up anything. You simply let go of the things that weren't right in you and then you became yourself again. That goodness you felt – it was in you all the time. You just had to let go of the things that blocked you from knowing your own goodness. You gave it to the earth. And then your own strength was revealed.'

'It's amazing. Just amazing,' said Rika in wonder. 'It's as if that whole disaster never happened.'

'But it did, and now you're a bit wiser about the ways of men,' said Rajan with a smile. 'Most men, I should say. You'll be wary in future; you'll see. Be picky! And now – why not go upstairs and say hello to your grandma?' He got up to go. She grabbed his wrist.

'Wait,' she said.

'What is it?'

'Tell me. Tell me now. I need to know. I need to know who it was my mother loved, and how she lost him.'

Rajan looked at her for what seemed an age, his face as still as stone; and then he softened, and said, 'All right. I'll tell you in a nutshell.'

He paused, and then continued:

'Remember I told you once that my father killed one of your uncles? It was your uncle Fred, the youngest. He was the great love of your mother's life.'

'Uncle Fred!' Rika exclaimed. 'Wow! It's funny – I thought somehow that maybe it was your dad who was this great love.'

Freddy only shrugged, and continued.

'She waited for him for years after he went to war. Then out of the blue, he came back. And she was overjoyed. They had been married just a few weeks but there was a fight and my father killed him and went to prison for it. She went berserk – turned against my mother and against life itself.'

'Why would she turn against your mother and you? You were innocent!'

Rajan shrugged again. 'I suppose we reminded her of him? It was because of my mother that Fred got into the fight in the first place. Maybe that's why … '

Silence fell between them. Raj looked at his watch again but he made no move to leave.

Almost under his breath, he added one last sentence: 'I was three at the time.'

Rika sat there as if paralysed. Maths might be her weakest subject, but she was capable of simple arithmetic.

'Seventeen years ago,' she whispered after a while. 'And I'm sixteen. And my name – my name is Frederika.'

❊ ❊ ❊

Rika's newfound strength stayed with her all week. It stayed with her when, at school, she found she was no longer the rising star but the butt of whispered jokes and tittering verbal jabs. It stayed with her when Jen placed herself in front of her, arms akimbo, and declared her a weak, wet and watery weed.

'You might like to know,' sneered Jen, 'that Jag never cared for you. He bet the boys he could bust your cherry in a week. He boasted he could do it, and if there was even a grain of personality in your little bird-brain you would have known what a chance you had, to have someone like him notice you. Now he's mine – he was only trying to make me jealous and you can be sure I'm not a weakling like you!'

Jen's words pearled off Rika like the proverbial water off a duck's back – it amazed her to see she truly *didn't care*. The only thing she cared about, right now, was the horrible mess of her hair, which now was as stiff as wire and stuck straight down without the slightest swing or curl. At the roots it was beginning to grow back. It would grow back. It had all been a dreadful error; she had been blind but now she saw and she had learned a valuable lesson. That stiff hair was a reminder, the price she had to pay, but one day it would be gone.

❄ ❄ ❄

That week she spent every afternoon in Rajan's back yard, but she no longer watched him at work. She worked *with* him; she pulled out weeds, set baby tomato plants into the earth, and, on Saturday, helped him mow the parapets along Waterloo Street, raking the cut grass and loading it on to the donkey cart. She had never felt happier.

To make things even better, Uncle Matt had come to stay for his annual holiday, bringing a suitcase full of books for her, and her three most coveted LPs: The Beatles' *Sgt. Pepper's Lonely Hearts Club Band*, Bob Dylan's *Blonde on Blonde* and his *Greatest Hits*. Rika had written to him the previous month to tell him of her new musical discovery, and now with the little record player – also a present from Uncle Matt – in her room she played the new discs over and over and over again.

'So,' said Uncle Matt one afternoon, 'you don't have a boy-friend yet?'

'Not really,' said Rika. 'I mean, I do have a boy *friend*, but he's not a *boyfriend*, if you know what I mean!' And she told Uncle Matt about Rajan, and took him over to Waterloo Street to introduce them. Uncle Matt, as a neurologist, was duly impressed with Rajan and his plans to win a scholarship and study medicine.

'That's a jewel of a boy,' he said to Rika. 'I'd hold on to him if I were you.'

'Oh, but …' Rika began. She wanted to say it wasn't that kind of a relationship. But then again, what *was* that kind of a relationship?

Uncle Matt grinned. 'I think you're a bit blind, Rika. The way that boy looks at you … there's something special there.'

Rika's heart skipped a beat. 'Oh!' was all she managed to say.

'I think I'd like to play Cupid for a while,' said Uncle Matt. 'How about I take you two to the Pegasus on Saturday night?'

The Pegasus, Georgetown's newly built luxury hotel, stood round and gleaming at the estuary of the Demerara River; with its kidney-shaped swimming pool, its top-class discotheque and its poolside dining, it was a step up from Palm Court. Rika's eyes shone as she nodded approval.

They picked Rajan up in a taxi. He was wearing clothes Rika had never seen before: a white shirt, black trousers, and for the first time ever, laced-up shoes; she had only ever seen him barefoot or in scuffed old boots. Simple, but smart and, she suspected, brand new. She guessed that, just as she had done for Jag, he had gone on a shopping spree and spent some of his hard-earned university fund. For her! Again, her heart skipped a beat. They looked at each other; their eyes met and Rika this time searched his for the signs Uncle Matt had seen.

An instant later he dropped her gaze in complete confusion. It couldn't be. Could it?

Uncle Matt led them both through the lobby and out to the poolside terrace. The water glimmered, reflecting the string of lights strung around it. They were early; the band had not yet arrived, but a jukebox in the corner played soft instrumental music. The Shadows, Rika noted, 'Apache'. A waiter pulled out a chair for her at their reserved table. Ever since that exchanged glance in the taxi, Rika's heart had tied itself up in knots, and she wasn't sure if she was capable of speaking a word. All the ease she normally felt in Rajan's company had fled – that look in his eyes, a look that, perhaps, had always been there but she had never noticed before, had in one moment pulled away the scales from her own eyes, her own heart and left her breathless, speechless.

She need not have worried. Once they were settled and their drinks placed before them Rajan reached into his trouser pocket and produced an envelope, slightly crumpled. His face was one huge smile.

'I got it!' he said. 'The scholarship!'

Uncle Matt ordered champagne and they all drank a toast. Uncle Matt got up to feed the jukebox. He returned. The stirring opening bars to Herb Alpert and The Tijuana Brass' 'The Lonely Bull' flooded the terrace.

Rajan looked at her. 'Want to dance?'

Surprised, she nodded. She'd never thought of Rajan as a dancer.

'I can't really dance,' Rajan confirmed, as he led her to the dance floor, 'but I guess there's nothing to it. I just have to hold you.'

And as he held her gently close and they moved to the music, Rika felt it again, more strongly than before, a stirring, a swelling in her heart. She looked up Rajan in surprise, and this time his eyes held hers. His shone in a new and wonderful way. Or maybe it wasn't all that new. Maybe they had always shone this way. She just had never noticed. She had taken that glow for granted. It was the glow of love. Unmistakeable. A lump rose in her throat. She found her voice.

'I'm glad you won the scholarship,' she said. 'But I don't want you to go.' Her voice faltered. 'What'll I do without you?'

'You could come too.' Rajan's hand on her back felt warm and comforting. 'Not yet, of course. But in two or three years? When you're eighteen? Didn't you say that's what you planned?'

'Really? You mean …'

She hardly dared say it, think it. It was too big a thing; too easy, too soon. But then, what else was there for her to do?

'You said you wanted to be a librarian. You could be that over there. Better than working in a bank, don't you think?'

The lump in her throat grew so big she couldn't get a word past it, so she only nodded.

'You're the best friend I ever had,' said Rajan, and his hand on her back pressed her closer. 'More than a friend. Rika, I – I'll miss you too. I'll wait. Please come! You've got O Levels coming up – next month, right?'

She nodded. She tried to swallow the lump in her throat, but it wouldn't budge.

'OK. Do your best. Your maths is quite good now – you'll pass. You should get six or seven subjects. Get those, and then maybe work a year or two; maybe you can even take A Levels. And then come and join me.' He stopped, and then said, again, 'I'll wait.'

Those last words: not explicit, but she knew what they meant, and he knew that she knew. It was a pact, a promise, a proposal. A declaration of abiding love, even though the word *love* had not been uttered. But it hung between them, unspoken, quivering in Rika's heart. Sure and true. Why had she not known it before? Why had she gone chasing after the shadow of Jag, when the real thing was so very near? She sighed in contentment, buried her face in his shoulder, and in reply Rajan pressed the small of her back.

When they returned to the table at a break in the music Uncle Matt teased them.

'So what's the difference between a boy friend and a boy-friend?' he asked Rika, who found the question incredibly embarrassing. She had never once been embarrassed with Rajan, not even when she'd told him the most distressing things about herself; but this question of Uncle Matt's discomfited her, made her feel shy and set off a swarm of butterflies in her tummy. Rajan only chuckled, as if he knew the answer.

❀ ❀ ❀

The next day, Sunday, Rajan phoned her. He had never done so in his life before; there seemed no need. He sounded different; a little shy.

'Would you go to the cinema with me tonight?' he asked.

She didn't hesitate for a second. 'Yes! What's on?'

'There's *My Fair Lady* back at the Astor,' said Rajan. 'Have you seen it?'

'No!' said Rika. 'When it came two years ago a lot of my cousins went with Granny but I had flu at the time and so I missed it. I'd love to see it!'

'Ok, then. I'll pick you up.'

She wondered briefly if he'd pick her up in the donkey cart. And she realised she didn't care an ass's hoof.

Chapter Thirty-two

Inky: The Noughties

One day, when the doorbell rang, I opened it to find a tall thin black woman about Mum's age standing on the threshold.

'Myrtle Patterson,' she said, beaming. 'You must be Dorothea's granddaughter?'

Yes; but Gran was out, I said warily. Another reporter? I thought the Quint was stale news.

'I'm the head of the Bishops' High School Old Girls' Union in London,' said Myrtle Patterson. That changed things. I opened the door wide.

'Gran went to the shops,' I told her. She'll be back in about half an hour. But come in and wait for her.' I let her in anyway, sat her down in the dining room and served her coffee and biscuits, and sat with her to wait for Gran's return, and while waiting we chatted.

It was actually called 'Old Students' Union' these days, she said, as Bishops' had gone co-ed about ten years ago, much to the consternation of the Old Guard; the addition of boys into the hallowed halls of Bishops' was tantamount to sacrilege. Boys spoilt everything. For her generation it would always be the Old Girls' Union. She'd come to invite Gran to an Old Students' Reunion of Bishops' High, right here in London.

'I've been getting so many calls,' she said. 'Over the last few weeks. Ever since your Gran became famous, and all the Old Girls found out she's here. But even before that, through the grapevine. I made some enquiries and found Doreen, who had the phone number. You know we have hundreds of Old Girls here in London?'

No, I didn't. I'd never heard of Bishops' High School, much less their Old Girls/Students Union.

'Small world, eh? Anyway, they're all clamouring for me to invite her to our next Reunion. That's in two weeks' time. Everybody wants to see Dorothea van Dam again.'

'van Dam?'

'Yes. Your Granny's maiden name. You don't know your Granny's maiden name?'

No, I didn't.

'Well, it's about time. Your Granny was famous in her day, you know. A legend, even while she was at school. Back home, back in the days. She was Head Girl in her last year of school, in Upper Sixth. By then she'd changed her name to Quint; she married young, while still at school, as an exception, considering the circumstances – war, and everything. After she left school she became known as Dorothea Q. Such a pity about … Well, never mind.'

'About what?'

'Ask her. I'm sure she'll tell you. I didn't know her myself at the time, of course. I wasn't even born yet, but these things become legends. Growing up in BG we had certain *names*, everybody knew them. Dorothea van Dam is one of those names – later, Dorothea Q. Now everybody wants to see Dorothea Q. All the old Bishops' girls. All old ladies now, of course, and middle-aged women like me. Between your mother's generation and Dorothea's, that's a whole lot of women. If she comes it's going to be packed. We might even have to look for a new venue. How's your Mum? How's she coping with the hullabaloo?'

It turned out that Mum, too, had made a splash, but a different kind to Gran's. Mum had first made a small splash by going out with some boy who all the girls were crazy about; and then she made a big splash, and headlines, by disappearing.

'She ran away,' said Myrtle. 'Just vanished. I remember the hullabaloo well; they couldn't find a trace of her on any of the airlines' passenger lists so everyone thought she was hiding out with a boy. Then a month later we heard she had run off to Peru. A bit of an anti-climax. Anyway ...'

A key turned in the front door. Myrtle stood up as Mum entered the room, still peeling off her jacket.

'Inky, there you are. Have you ...' She stopped in her tracks.

'Hello, Rika, remember me?'

Mum obviously didn't. She frowned, trying to place our visitor. I calculated that almost forty years had passed since Mum's schooldays; unless they had been best buddies she could hardly be expected to fall into Myrtle's arms. But remembering her manners, she smiled and held out her hand.

'Can't say I do,' she said. 'Remind me.'

'Myrtle. Myrtle Patterson.'

'Ah. Myrtle.' Mum's forehead relaxed and her smile broadened. 'Excuse me. It's been a long time. I didn't know you were in London too.'

'Hundreds of us Old Girls ended up here,' Myrtle said. 'I happen to be head of the London Chapter of the Old Girls' Union, so I've kept in touch with many of them.'

Right then, Granny's scooter whirred up the garden path and came to a stop. I helped her get down and took her arm to lead her into the house, setting her rollator down in front of her.

Gran waddled forward and stood in the doorway to the living room, me right behind her.

'Ah. You mus' be Myrtle Patterson.'

Obviously, Gran was expecting Myrtle. No doubt one of her myriad friends and relations had warned her of the imminent visit. She turned around and with an impatient gesture shooed me and Mum away. After which she closed the door,

sequestering herself away with Myrtle. Once again I had to
suppress my curiosity; I shrugged and turned away.

❉ ❉ ❉

One thing about Gran: she certainly knew how to make a
grand entrance, rollator or not. She wanted me, not Mum, to
push her into the hall for the BHS Reunion. We were the last
to arrive, and a trio of women, including Myrtle Patterson,
stood waiting for us in the cold outside the building. We bustled Gran into her wheelchair and, me pushing, off we went.

Up a short flight of stairs via a wheelchair ramp, across a
hallway; then Myrtle and another women flung open a pair of
double doors and Gran rolled in. She made me stop just as we
crossed the threshold. The animated buzz of conversation came
to an abrupt halt. In that silence, a sea of faces, of every shade
from white to black, turned our way. A moment passed, then
a thundering crash of applause burst out and a rush of bodies
lunged towards us. Faces, lit with joy, converged upon her. And
she just sat there smugly, basking in the adulation.

It was only then that I really, truly understood that my
grandmother had been a legend in her own time, an icon in her
own country. I should have known. Mum, of course, had never
told me a thing, but that was to be expected. But those Sunday
after-church meetings at Doreen's house. Why, they had practically told me. I remembered now, all the comments: 'Your
grandmother is such a wonderful woman!' 'What a remarkable
person she is!' 'She was quite amazing in her day, you know.'

Yes, they'd told me. But I hadn't taken it seriously. 'Wonderful!', 'Amazing!', 'Fantastic!' – all words that have lost their
meaning in the hyperbole of modern language.

But with these women, the words were real. When they said
Gran was great, they meant it. It was not just a word. I knew this
with an instinct as sure as a baby's discernment between its own

mother and a stranger. It was as if I'd played with glass beads all my life, throwing around superlatives like confetti and receiving the same in like manner. And now, diamonds. The difference was stupendous.

As the granddaughter, I was engulfed in the sea of goodwill. The women, having claimed Gran as their own, nudged me away into a huddle, where they plied me with food and drink and mollycoddled me like a long-lost relative.

'How *proud* you must be of your grandmother!' I kept hearing those words. I'd heard them before, at Doreen's, after church. Back then, my first reaction had been 'Hello? Proud? Me? Why?'

I was accustomed to people saying those words to Mum. *'How* proud *you must be of your* marvellous *daughter! How* brilliant *Inky is! What* amazing *GCSE results! What* brilliant *A Levels! She'll be Top Lawyer in no time!'* In our crowd it was generally accepted that Mum was a loser and I was the surprise trump she'd somehow pulled out of a hat. But since Gran had come into her life it was *she* who was reaping all the praise. And today, for the first time, I realised that somehow, that praise must have been deserved. And I had no idea how.

I could not, of course, let on how little I knew of my own grandmother and whatever grand things she had accomplished in her heyday. They assumed I knew. So I smiled and nodded and agreed about her amazingness. I played the game as well I could, while all the time I longed to ask, *but why?*

But then again, I reasoned, all this was only in Guyana. It's easy to make a mark in a small insignificant country. They make mountains out of molehills there. Gran would have been a big fish in a small pond. Still, I was curious to know what had given her this marvellous reputation. I'd have to ask Mum. Later.

Mum, meanwhile, had disappeared into her own little bevy of middle-aged ladies, contemporaries, apparently, from her schooldays. People mentioned her, too, to me, but more with a twinkle in their eye and an amused shake of the head, rather like parents recalling past antics of their children that were frightening when they happened but now, in retrospect, could be safely laughed at.

A twinge of compassion for Mum went through me, immediately followed by a wave of protectiveness. Poor Mum. It can't be easy, living in the shadow of such a mother, and then having a daughter so much more successful than herself. I vowed to be nicer to her, kind and loving and more understanding in future. I'd never mention her silly novel writing. Let her do it, if it made her happy. Now that I knew about it I could maybe cushion the disappointment of her rejections, make it easier for her. Yes, I realised, that was my role in Mum's life. I loved her to bits, and in future I'd show it more. And I'd make her even more proud of me. Mothers identify with their children. I would make up for her own lack of achievement.

All of this occurred to me while I stuffed myself with a delicious dish of 'curry and roti'. By now I was sitting at one of several long tables, still surrounded by chattering women, all peppering me with questions. I told them what I was studying and other details of my life, and reaped their 'ah's' and 'oh's'. I realised that as Dorothea van Dam's granddaughter they expected great things of me; in our case, as so often, success had skipped one generation. I looked around for Mum, and saw her further down the table. She seemed happy enough, chatting with a skinny middle-aged woman. Mum looked up at that moment and caught my eye; she whispered a word to her companion who looked up too, smiled and waved at me, then blew me a kiss. I smiled back. Mum signed to me that she wanted to speak to me and that I should not run off; to come to her after the meal, which I did.

❊ ❊ ❊

'Inky, I'd like you to meet Trixie MacDonald. She used to be a good friend of mine, back in the day, though we went to different schools.'

Trixie and I smiled at each other again and shook hands. I noticed two perfect rows of teeth, huge, dark limpid eyes.

'We lost sight of each other way back in – when was it, Rika, when you ran off to Brazil? 1969?'

''67,' Mum corrected.

I looked at Mum.

'You ran off to Brazil?'

I always thought it was Peru. That was the legend; that's how I got my name. Mum and Dad on a bus to Huancayo, climbing Machu Picchu, back-packing along the Inca Trail.

Mum nodded. Trixie laughed. 'And how! It was a case of now-you-see-her-now-you-don't. Poof. She just disappeared. Not a word of goodbye. We didn't even know where she'd gone until …'

'Rika, Rika! How wonderful to see you again! Remember me?'

A rather corpulent woman, light skinned and with plainly dyed blonde hair, butted in, all smiles; she grabbed Mum in a huge hug. Mum seemed somewhat disoriented.

'Um … yes well … Inky, this is …' She stopped, it was plain that she either didn't remember the lady in question, didn't recognise her, or had forgotten her name.

'Jen! Jennifer Goveia! From St Rose's – though I'm now Jenny Baker. I heard you were coming so I had to be here to say hello … and this is your daughter?'

She turned, gushing, to me, and was obviously about to sweep me, too, into a generous embrace when, thank goodness, a hush descended on the hall, and we all turned to the front. Somebody was tapping a fork to a glass. The buzz of conversation dwindled into silence. Myrtle Patterson stood at the edge of the crowd on a podium. Most people sat down so we could all see her.

'Ladies,' she said, 'we have the great pleasure and honour of having among us today a legend in her own time. Let's give another round of applause to the unforgettable ... Dorothea Quint!'

Applause, cheers, knives drumming on tables.

Myrtle launched into a never-ending homily, a homage to Gran, and after Myrtle a woman called a Darleen spoke and then a Kathleen and then a Maureen, grey-haired women, creaking up to the podium with the help of walking sticks and daughters' arms. Each one had stories to tell of my grandmother. Each delivered anecdotes and accolades, honeyed words in honour of my dragon of a grandmother, interspersed by outbreaks of chuckling or clapping or open laughter. Sometimes, a single keyword was enough to propel the audience into a roar of laughter. There were groans and there were sighs, and none of it I understood. I was an outsider in a secret society.

Finally, Gran herself rolled up to the podium. A chair was pushed up for her to sit on; and then she gave her own little speech. She was unrecognisable. Gracious and humble, she thanked them for their kind words and pronounced that the praise was undeserved.

Another crash of applause brought the day to an end.

Through it all, not one person had mentioned the Quint.

❊ ❊ ❊

As for Mum: she had obviously been well-loved, if not as triumphantly victorious as Gran. And she needed to be well-loved again. Deep inside she must be lonely, and drastically lacking in self-esteem. I could help her. I could encourage her and strengthen her. I positively soaked in all these kind and loving thoughts, lolling around in them like in a warm bubbly bath. It made me feel so good.

We were on our way home when her mobile rang.

In typical Mum fashion she answered it. While driving.

❊ ❊ ❊

In my upside-down relationship with Mum, she was the child most often and I the parent. I'd strictly forbidden her from answering the phone while driving. But Mum considered herself a multi-tasker and repeatedly disobeyed; she thought nothing of holding the phone to her ear with one hand and the steering wheel with the other. She'd been doing it for years.

When the law confirmed my authority and made it illegal I'd been jubilant with smug, 'I told you so's'.

Since then, she'd been slightly more compliant. She never got used to using the hands-free – even though she, of all people, should know about the risk of electro smog – but she did allow me to answer the phone for her when we were in the car together. Usually she kept her phone in her handbag, either on the floor in front of the passenger's seat, or on the back seat.

Today it lay in the console under the handbrake, between herself and Gran. When the happy little ringtone sounded we reached for it at the same time – me from the back seat, she from the driver's seat. Her hand got there first; I was too far away, and restrained by the belt.

'Mum, let me,' I said, holding out my hand for it.

She ignored me. She flipped it open with one hand and put it to her ear.

'Hello?'

'Mum, I'll take it. Give it here!' I insisted. I unlocked my belt and slid to the edge of the back seat so as to be flush against the driver's seat. With my left hand I grasped her wrist and tried to wrest the phone from her fingers. She gently pulled it away by leaning to the right, her ear glued to the handset. She listened for a few seconds, then said,

'Yes, that's me ... listen, I'm on the road right now, could you call back in ...'

'MUM! WATCH OUT!'

Too late. Even as the words left my lips the car slammed into the vehicle in front and the world exploded in the deafening clank of metal crunching against metal, a grating clatter that went on forever. *Make it stop*, I cried into myself, *make it stop, make it stop.* The impact tossed me against the back seat like a lifeless rag doll and then it did stop, and the silence was more deafening than the noise that went before; the world had come to an end. My body felt broken into bits. I groaned and turned slightly to free a trapped arm. The fact that I could move, that I felt pain, reminded me that I was alive. Vaguely I registered a yelling voice as Mum's. Then I passed out.

When I opened my eyes, I was lying on the roadside on a woollen blanket, covered with another blanket. A man in a green fluorescent jacket was bent over me. It was dark; lights flashing above me, somewhere a siren whining. People everywhere, milling around, aimlessly, it seemed to me; shrill voices. And pain. My body a single bundle of pain.

'How are you?' the paramedic asked. I ignored him as memory came rushing in.

'Mum? Mum!' I cried. I moved my legs, and all was pain. I didn't care. I struggled to sit up. The paramedic put out a restraining hand.

'Try to keep still, Miss. Your Mum's all right. She's fine.'

'Where is she? I have to get to her. And ... and Gran. Where's Gran?'

'Your Granny's being looked after by the ambulance crew,' said the paramedic. 'She's in good hands. Don't worry, just keep quiet.' But I had no intention of keeping quiet. Something in his voice told me that something was terribly, awfully wrong. Immediately my pain vanished. I scrambled into a sitting position, and attempted to rise. My knee buckled with an excruciating pain; I couldn't help crying out, yet finished the action. The moment I was on my feet I limped off. There were people everywhere; onlookers behind a police barrier, policemen and women striding around in fluorescent jackets with notepads and walkie-talkies in their hands, and, outside a looming ambulance, a cluster of paramedics. That's where I headed.

Mum was standing outside the ambulance, talking to one of the paramedics.

'Mum!' I cried and folded her into my arms. She was as stiff as a statue, her arms refusing to return the embrace.

'Inky! Oh Inky! Thank God you're all right! I … I had to leave you lying there because, because …'

I broke in.

'Where's Gran? How is she?'

Mum's face crunched up. She raised a hand and pointed to the interior of the ambulance. I could see nothing beyond the backs of two paramedics.

'In there. They're still trying to save her. She wasn't wearing a seat belt. Her head … her head crashed against the windscreen. I … I tried to help her, but, but …'

She held up her hands; they were both covered in blood. Her sleeves were bloody right up to the elbow, and beyond. Mum's face filled with agony, and tears spilled from her eyes.

'Inky … she might not make it! And it's all my fault!'

Chapter Thirty-three

Rika: The Sixties

Rajan came with his bicycle, and she wheeled hers out to meet him. They rode in silence to the Astor, and he helped her park hers in the crowded stand and lock it.

'I've got tickets for the balcony,' he said, smiling at her, and led the way up the stairs at the front of the building. Rika felt guilty; Rajan was saving up for England; he didn't earn much. Could he really afford this? And then she felt grateful. Obviously he thought he could; obviously, he thought her worth the expense; and a swelling of contentment made her take a deep, audible breath.

'You OK?' asked Rajan, as he gestured for her to sidle down the row of threadbare velvet seats.

'I'm fine,' she said, and she was. She had never been finer. This was just so – right. No fizz, no bubbles, just a deep sense of the perfection of the moment.

The film began and very soon Rika was swept up in the magic of Eliza Doolittle and her struggle to become a '*lie-dy*'; wasn't she, Rika, just like Eliza, in a way? Looking at life from the sidelines, lost in a sense of unworthiness, deeply aware of being beneath value? But no longer. Somehow, all that had changed, practically overnight.

When Freddy sang 'On the Street Where you Live' Rajan reached over and took her hand, and held it firmly all the way through to the end, slowly stroking the back of it with his thumb. And it was just the way it was when her hands were in the earth; from those clasped hands came a solid sense of unity, of being an entity, strong and real and secure. Tears gathered in her eyes and she turned to look at him, and he must have felt her movement for he turned too and they gazed at each other in the dark. All she could see of him was the faint outline of his head and his eyes, bright and shining and overflowing with tenderness. Rajan changed hands so that now his right hand held hers; his left arm he stretched out behind her and laid on her shoulder. She leaned in towards him and laid her head on his shoulder and all was well with the world. Rika let out a sigh of deep contentment. At last, she was at home. All else would follow on from this moment.

'How did you like the film?' Rajan asked, as they unlocked their bicycles.

'Wonderful! Magical!' said Rika. 'But I didn't like the end. She should have married Freddy.'

'Freddy was the nice one ... they say the nice ones always get left behind. That women like bad men.'

'Stupid women, maybe. That Henry Higgins isn't going to change. Once a selfish bastard, always a selfish bastard. She'll live to regret that choice. She should have married Freddy.'

❊ ❊ ❊

They cycled home in silence and Rajan took her in his arms outside her gate.

'It was a wonderful night,' he said. 'Thank you for coming with me.' He held her close and kissed her forehead. She shuddered in contentment.

'Oh Rajan,' she sighed, because she had no words.

Weightless with bliss, she floated up the stairs and in through the front door. And into bedlam. Her mother was waiting for her; and so, it seemed, was the whole family – Granny and Daddy and Uncle Matt and Marion, eyes wide open in trepidation, and Norbert and Neville, enjoying the show.

Her mother, in vintage Ol' Meanie style, flew at her the moment she walked in the door, grabbing her by the arm and dragging her into the middle of the gallery.

'Who you think you gallivanting around with, eh? Who? Who?' she screamed.

'I – I just went to the pictures, with Rajan. He lives at Granma's!'

'The servant's son? The gardener? Basmati's son?'

'Mummy, I ...'

Rika couldn't believe her ears. Why was Mummy so upset? Mummy did not look down on the poor. Mummy's whole fight, her whole philosophy, her whole *raison d'être,* was that the underclass should have the same opportunities, the same rights, as the middle class in which they themselves were so solidly placed. Equality was Mummy's watchword. Was it all hot air? Did equality come to a stop when it touched her own family?

'Mummy, we're *friends!* We've been good friends for years, and ...'

'... and what in the name of all that's wrong with the world is *this!'*

Mum dumped a cardboard box at Rika's feet. Rika gasped, and sank to her knees. There in the box was her whole life, the secret life she'd hidden beneath the floorboards of the Cupola. Pale blue exercise books, some of them swollen from moisture and age, some still new and slim, all of them filled from front to back with Rika's spidery, almost illegible writing. Her whole life was in those books. Her many attempted and later abandoned novels.

But worst of all: her diary. The diary that sometimes had been the only friend she'd had through the years. She emptied her soul into that diary. It was completely, utterly secret. Not even Rajan had ever so much as glanced at a page. But Rajan was in there. In the newest editions over the past year, every encounter with Rajan, every discussion on matters of the soul, and the meaning of it all, and God, she had captured in words and written into her diary. The confessions she made to herself alone. Most of all, her newfound discovery that Rajan was the love of her life, added only this morning. Heat rushed to her cheeks as she remembered what she'd last written, just last night:

'He is the other half of my soul. I feel myself swept up as if on wings of rapture, and he is there with me, at my side; our souls are joined in a bliss sublime, a bliss that passes all understanding.'

'Who encouraged this? Ma, did you know about this?'

Mum turned to Granny with such venom Rika trembled. Granny, all this time, had been trying to get a word in, trying to intervene, but Mum's wrath was like a wild writhing dragon, filling the room; all the others, Uncle Matt and the rest, stood around wringing their hands or furrowing their brows or enjoying the show according to their disposition. But Mum was beside herself with hysterics.

'Mum, I …' but Mum wasn't listening.

'Never again, you hear me, never again! You never go near that boy again! Never, never, never! I gave you far too much freedom; far too much! That boy! Never! Never! Never!'

'I love him, Mummy, I do! Please!' Rika, confused and despairing, began to blubber, to plead, to beg.

'Dorothea, he's a good boy. He's a good steady student, works hard, and …'

That was Granny. At the same time, Uncle Matt was speaking:

'I met him. A very fine young man, Dorothea. Rika's in good hands and …'

But Mum wasn't listening. She had worked herself into a blind rage by now: blind and deaf and spitting expletives.

Rika had never, in all her life, seen her like this. It was as if a volcano that had lain dormant for centuries suddenly erupted, red hot lava spitting and pouring from its crater. Such was Mum's wrath. Rika's knees gave way and she sank to the floor in a hopeless helpless heap, sobbing Rajan's name. Still Mum raged on.

'Ruined my life! Ruined everything! Destroyed everything! Never again! And you!' she swung around and pointed an accusing finger at Granny. 'You! You knew! You knew everything and still you installed them in that house! You put them there! I could overlook that but now we have *this!*'

'Dorothea! Snap out of it! Be sensible! You're talking nonsense! Basmati was innocent and Rajan was little more than a baby!'

Granny managed to brave Mum's wrath and took hold of her. She grabbed her waving arms and brought them down, shaking her, as if to banish the fury. And indeed, Mum stopped shouting and only seethed. She touched Rika's head with her foot and said, in a commanding voice that brooked no disobedience:

'You will never see him again. I forbid you from going to that house. And you will go to your room and stay there until tomorrow. Go on now. Go on!'

Rika sprang to her feet, the heat boiling over so that the words spouted red with rage.

'Yes I know all about you! You're just a horrible, bitter old woman blaming a tiny child for something that is all *your* doing. Rajan told me everything. I know the whole story. I know all about you and I can't believe you're still so full of poison for a thing that happened so long ago and I hate you, I hate you, *I hate you!*'

She flew at her mother. Dorothea struggled against Rika's wild fury, holding back her wrists as her fingers clawed at her face. Rika was younger, stronger, pulsing with a might she never knew she had, and wrestled Dorothea to the floor; but Daddy came from behind and, stronger yet, pulled her, still kicking and screaming, off her mother, while Uncle Matt helped Dorothea to her feet. Daddy wrapped his arms around Rika, clamping them to her body, but Rika's eyes still clawed at Dorothea from afar.

Granny saw what was coming, and tried to prevent it by lurching at Dorothea. But she was too late. Dorothea swung back her right hand and with a mighty sweep, hit Rika across her cheek. Rika cried out in pain and anger, and Daddy swung her around, out of harm's way. Uncle Matt pulled Dorothea away before she could attack again.

Daddy manoeuvred Rika out of the drawing room and there in the stairwell managed to calm her. He led her into the Annex and to her room. Dorothea yelled after her:

'One thing you can be sure of, you'll never see *that boy* in your life again!'

By the time she and Daddy reached her room, Rika's rebellion had broken. She broke into abject tears, and, convulsed with desperate sobs, sank on to the bed. Daddy sat down beside her, laid an arm around her, and tried to comfort her. After a while she was still.

Then they talked. For the first time in their lives, Rika and her father talked into the night, breaching subjects that were taboo, digging up the darkness between them and laying it all bare.

'Is it true, Daddy, that …'

She stopped. She didn't want to say the words, didn't want to hurt Daddy; but she had to know.

'That I am Freddy's daughter, not yours?'

Daddy, for a moment, looked flummoxed, distraught even.

'How did you – who told you?' he asked.

'Am I?'

His voice trembled as he spoke. He took her hand.

'You are my daughter, Rika; I was your father long before you were born. But yes; Freddy is your biological father. That's why we named you Frederika; in memory of him. You c-c-cannot imagine the horror she lived through – Freddy b-b-bleeding to death in her arms, so soon after his reappearance. It broke her. And then she discovered that she was pregnant. Of course I m-m-married her; and of course I loved you as my own. B-b-but your mother was never the same again. A festering bitterness stole into her heart and ate it up from the inside. She could not even turn to you for comfort, be a mother to you … it was too much. It was like a madness – an irrational, unfair madness, and the only way she could deal with it, I think, was to direct it at those two innocents; Basmati and Rajan. They were victims too, but she didn't care: they became the lightning rods for her fury. She forced Basmati out of the house. They went back to the Pomeroon, but returned when Rajan won his scholarship and Ma found Basmati that job with your other grandparents.

'All she had was her work, and she poured herself into that. You can't even begin to understand her t-t-torment. She turned away from God, from family, from everything and everyone that might cause her hurt. She knew that to love means to open yourself up to p-p-pain; she had reached the zenith of that pain and so she could no longer love. Certainly not me. But not even her own child, her own children.

'Yet I think, somewhere deep inside, she can, and does love you, Rika, but in her own way. Her rage is a symptom of that love. It will blow over. It must blow over. Perhaps this crisis is a good thing. It will force her to confront her illogical rejection of Basmati and Rajan. It makes no sense, I agree; but maybe it's the only way she had of deal with that tragedy, to come to terms with Freddy's death. She had to blame someone. She blamed God; but she also needed a target.'

'Well, she *had* a target! What about the man who actually killed him? Rajan's father? He was to blame, not Rajan or Basmati! What about *him?*'

'She was out of her mind with grief, Rika. In that state you don't think logically. She needed someone to blame and hate and he was quickly caught and put behind bars. He wasn't someone she *knew*. For her, they were all one: the three of them, the reason for Freddy's death. She made no distinctions. It was a madness, a blindness. But, maybe, maybe it's a good thing this all blew up. Maybe it will force her to face that blind spot. I hope and pray that she will find healing. Somehow. You must forgive her, Rika. You must. Understand and forgive.'

'I'll try,' sniffled Rika. But one thing she knew: she would not give up Rajan.

❄ ❄ ❄

Later that night, when all was silent in the house, Rika crept out of her room. She made her way to the telephone and dialled her grandmother's number. After a while, Basmati answered the phone.

'Basmati!' Rika whispered. 'Sorry to wake you up, but can you get Rajan, please? It's urgent – an emergency!'

It seemed to take an aeon until Rajan came to the phone. At first all she could do was cry, and then she managed to say,

'Rajan – I need to see you. Tonight! The gate is locked. I need you to come. Come in the back and come to my room. You know the latticework just beneath it? You can climb up there. My window is open. I'm waiting for you. Please come, please!'

'Why? What happened?'

'I can't talk now!' whispered Rika. 'I need to talk to you – I need to! In person! Now! Please, please come!'

'OK,' said Rajan. 'I'm coming.'

Chapter Thirty-four

Inky: The Noughties

It would be 'touch and go', they said. Not only because of the injury itself – Gran's head had crashed against the windshield and split open – but her age reduced the chances of survival. Even if the operation itself was successful, there was no guarantee.

To put it euphemistically.

In translation, there was a good chance that Gran would come out of this a vegetable.

Mum and I sat together in the hospital waiting room while they operated on her. We clasped hands, holding on to each other as if to life itself; Gran's life.

Gran as vegetable? Unthinkable.

Alone in the waiting room, as the dark night hours ticked away, the silence grew heavy and oppressive. It weighed down on me in a shroud of foreboding and fear. I had to break it, I had to talk, push it away, keep it far from me lest it choke me; talk-talk-talk, no matter about what. I snatched at every passing thought and delivered a running commentary on trivia.

But Mum didn't respond. At first she let out a few 'umms' and 'uh-uhs' but after a while gave that up too and let me jabber on. I glanced at her; she wasn't even listening. She sat beside me with her eyes closed, locked in a world to which I had no access; I might break the outer silence but she'd just created her own. I hated her for it. It was so *rude*, so *uncaring!* How could she leave me alone like that, alone with my empty nonsensical words! Why couldn't she fight the silence with me! I wanted to shake her, scream at her, slap her.

'How can you just sit there like a zombie like that, like a block of wood, like a stone, don't you *see*, don't you *realise*, don't you *care* ... '

And then the tears came, great fountains of tears. I pushed them down just as I pushed away the silence, but they burst their boundaries and they gushed as profusely as had the meaningless words, reducing me to a sobbing, blubbering ball of nothing, bent forward on my chair and almost slipping to the floor.

Then, and only then, did Mum break her silence. She put her arms around me and drew me close to her and held me in her arms.

'She's going to be all right,' Mum whispered. 'She'll be all right, I know it. She can't go. It can't end like this.'

'I'm sorry! I'm so sorry!' I bawled. 'I treated her like shit. I-I didn't know how much I loved her! That I cared! I didn't know!'

Mum only held me closer. 'It's going to be all right,' she murmured, again and again, as if saying the words would make them come true; as if she really believed they were true. I was not so convinced. She could say the words a million times and not convince me. I had seen Gran. I'd seen her head, seen the blood, seen the emergency crew racing with her on a gurney away into the depths of the hospital, taking away my only link with my past, the last tenuous thread I had to my own roots.

But no. Not my only link. Not my last thread. There was still Mum. Talk, Mum! Just talk! Please *talk* to me!

'Mum,' I said, 'Tell me about where you came from. Tell me about Gran when she was younger. Tell me what happened. Why you left. Why you ran away.'

Those were the magic words. The key to break open Mum's silence. She talked. Mum, always good with words, released them now not on to paper, but to my ears. Her words flowed like water, sweeping away my tears in their stream. She painted a picture with her words, creating for me a living image of a charmed childhood. She took me on a trip to a city of white wooden houses and wide green avenues, where girls in green school uniforms tore around on bicycles, giggling in glee as they wove through the traffic; of jungle creeks far from that city where the water was cool and black; of a marketplace bustling with life, where fat black women sold succulent yellow mangoes and Hindu shopkeepers burned incense before gaudy images of four-armed gods.

She told me of the great white rambling house she'd called home, with its magical garden, wild with tumbling bougainvillea, fragrant with oleander and rose, a kaleidoscope of colour, shape and perfume. She spoke of wide avenues where elegant horses ridden by straight-backed straight-faced Mounted Police clopped along in convoys, heads nodding and snorting, shaded by glorious flame-red treetops. Birdsong. Sunshine. Rain thundering on thin iron roofs, waterfalls from heaven.

And people. A big warm woman with black hair that was turning grey, a woman whose very presence warmed the soul and calmed the mind, and a small wiry woman who did just the opposite: the quirky, irritable but much-adored mother she could never please. An absent-minded but kind-hearted father with his head in a stamp album; a wonderful sister as close as a twin; rambunctious brothers as mischievous as monkeys; a beloved American uncle she saw once a year, who came like Santa Claus bearing gifts; nameless children, cousins and friends-of-cousins, tumbling in an abundance of nature. A brown endless ocean and a teenage girl sitting on a wall gazing out at it, dreaming of far-off lands, and swarthy turbaned men who knew all the mysteries of the universe.

'And then', Mum said, 'and then I met Rajan.'

I clung to her words as they echoed through the midnight silence, holding me as in a trance, a bubble of enthralment.

Instinctively, I knew we had reached the climax of the story; the Thing they were so keen to keep from me.

'Mrs Temple?'

I snapped out of Mum's dream-world. The bubble burst

I was so immersed in Mum's story I hadn't heard his approach, and even after he'd spoken it took me a few seconds to return to earth and the bleak emptiness of the hospital waiting room. Mum was quicker on the ball: almost at the first word, she was on her feet.

'How is she?'

I blinked and looked up; a man in a white coat was standing above us. I followed Mum's lead and climbed to my feet.

Only then did I realise that my body ached all over, in nooks and crannies I hadn't known existed. My left knee buckled as my feet found the floor, and I stumbled; my knees were numb. The man caught me, steadied me with a kind smile, and then spoke:

'Mrs Temple … I'm Doctor Stone. I'm in the surgical team that operated on your mother.'

Mum nodded eagerly, urging him to skip the preliminaries. At last he got to the point.

'The operation was successful … she'll pull through …'

Mum's outbreath was audible, and a smile spread across her face. For me, a cloud lifted and I too smiled. I wanted to pounce on Dr Stone and hug him in gratitude, but instead grabbed Mum's hand; she squeezed it. Her eyes were wet with tears, luminous with pleading, probing hope. At Dr Stone's next words a curtain fell over them.

'… but we have to wait to find out the extent of the damage. She's still under anaesthetic, and we won't know till she wakes up whether there'll be any permanent – ah – impairment to her mental functions.'

'You mean …? That she could be …' Mum paused, searching for the right word, but could do no better than repeat the one we were all thinking: 'brain-damaged?' There was no handy euphemism, no softening of the truth.

A mask of exhaustion fell across his face, not so much physical as emotional. He looked as if he wanted to flee. It couldn't be easy, giving such devastating news to anxious relatives.

'We just can't predict anything, Mrs Temple. There's something called shear injury – sort of like breaking the wiring in the brain – that can occur in this sort of damage. Its extent is wildly unpredictable – sometimes a lot, sometimes none. When it's severe, it leaves lasting disability. I've had many, many patients who have had what, according to their head scans, should be modest injuries, just not wake up. Subsequent MRI scans show extensive shear injury. Other patients fly from the back of a pick-up truck at sixty miles per hour and land on their head and end up just fine because they had no brain swelling or shear. The brain's pretty mysterious. At this point we don't know; only time will tell. She's an old woman, and it's been a lot to take; first the accident, then the operation. It's a miracle she survived at all, another miracle that no bones were broken. We've done our best; now it's up to her. All we can do is hope.'

'And pray.'

'Can we see her?' My own voice startled me; it seemed not to come from my throat, but from somewhere far outside me, to bounce off the bare walls and echo down the corridors. I felt drained, my body an empty shell containing nothing but a dislocated tangle of aches and pains.

He flicked his chin towards the corridor that led into the bowels of the hospital.

'Follow me,' he said. 'But as I said, she's still out cold. It'll be several hours till she comes to.'

He led the way. Our footsteps echoed in the empty hallway, beating a lonely tattoo into the night's stark silence. I glanced at the hallway clock: 2:47a.m. We passed a nurse, an orderly pushing an empty gurney, an open door from which disembodied voices echoed into the emptiness. Hospitals at night are vaults where fears fester and hopes are bolstered, human emotion swelling in the still sterility as sludge rises in a stagnant pond. I longed to flee, for all three of us to flee, to sit somewhere in the noisy bustle of broad daylight where all would be fine and we could laugh and chat and be normal. Anything but this.

Gran lying stretched out, still on a gurney, awaiting a further journey and a free orderly, stashed away against the wall of a hospital. Her head was wrapped in white, her eyes closed in the sanctuary of sleep. She looked so peaceful, so utterly innocent, so frail. As if a puff of breath could blow her away. So un-granlike.

Mum picked up one of her hands. It lay lifeless in her own, as limp as a cast-off rag. She bent over and kissed Gran's cheek. Her fingertips touched the head bandage gingerly as if trying to gauge what lay beneath, and she looked up, her eyes searching Dr Stone's for a word of hope and comfort.

He had none to give. 'We'll know more tomorrow,' he said. I felt sorry for him. His duty was over, and he too needed sleep. The rings under his eyes had surely grown darker in the fifteen minutes we'd been together, the stubble on his chin more prickly.

An orderly bustled up with a no-nonsense air. He grabbed the handles of Gran's gurney, released the brake and pulled it away from the wall. He hardly glanced at us. We were not his duty.

'She'll be going to intensive care now,' said Dr Stone. 'You can go with her, but there's not much you or anyone can do. You'd better go home and get some sleep. It's been a long night.'

'I'm staying!' said Mum, before he'd spoken his last words. 'Inky, you go home. I'm staying till she wakes up.'

'Mrs Temple, there's no point. It'll be several hours. Go and get some sleep.'

I suppressed a yawn; his words reminded me of my own tiredness.

'Mum, he's right. We can come back in the morning. You're exhausted. Let's go. Please.' I yawned again, and this time I let it out. It was contagious, Mum's hand rose to her lips as she, too tried to veil a tell-tale sigh of exhaustion.

'All right,' she conceded. 'But please ring me if she wakes up and I'm not here. I'll be back as soon as possible tomorrow.'

I'd been holding my breath; I could never have left Mum here on her own with Gran, but I was by now desperate for bed. Mum can be stubborn when she wants to be, but sometimes she sees sense. I breathed out, audibly. Dr Stone must have heard it, as he patted me on the back, and smiled in sympathy. I resisted the urge to hug him.

'Bed,' he said. 'That's what you both need. Come back tomorrow; we'll all know more by then.' He pointed to the strip of guidance tape on the corridor floor. 'Follow the yellow lines to Reception; you can call a taxi there.'

And so we all parted company: Gran rolled off deeper into the hospital, Dr Stone waved goodbye and turned to walk away. I waited for Mum, who stood watching the back of the orderly pushing Gran away. The orderly and his gurney turned a corner. Only then did Mum turn back to me. She took my hand, in hers, caressed it for a moment and gave me a trembling half-smile.

'Come on, Inky' she said, 'Let's go home.'

Chapter Thirty-five

Rika: The Sixties

She knew he would come, and waited for his whistle. And there it was. He must have entered the yard through the alley. It was like a scene in a novel she might have written. She walked to the window and looked down. He stood just below, his face invisible in the darkness and only perceptible when he shone the torch he held in his hand upwards, to her. Behind him the white staves of the metal palings stood out against the blackness. Rajan himself wore dark clothes, which, considering the clandestine nature of their meeting, made sense. The front door was locked, as always. A good thing Devil was in the Pomeroon; he'd have barked the house down.

She had to talk to him, and it had to be here, in her room. She had to hold him, be held by him, feel his arms around her, his breath on her cheeks, his lips on hers.

'Rajan!' she whispered, and he whispered back.

'I'm here!'

'You have to climb up the lattice. I'll shine the torch for you. Can you do it?'

Rajan was a good climber. She'd seen him in the mango tree, and scaling the coconut palm in her grandmother's yard. This lattice, between the pillars of the Bottom House, was nothing for him. She shone the torch down on him and, catching him in the spotlight, signalled for him to climb up.

He switched off his own torch and tucked it into a pocket. She shone hers on to the lattice, lighting the way up for him. Gingerly, Rajan managed to place one foot in a diamond of the trellis; from there, he pulled himself up and searched for another hole with his other foot. Rika guided him with her light. He reached the top of the lattice and stretched his arm towards the windowsill.

At that very moment, Rika's bedroom door flew open and the light flashed on. Rika cried out and whipped around, to face Dorothea. The torch clattered to her feet. In the darkness Rajan's fingers groped for the window sill and missed; he lost his balance.

With a yell of terror, he fell backwards.

Rika swung around, picked up the torch and shone it downwards. Her hand shook as she searched the bushes down below for Rajan.

❀ ❀ ❀

Later, people said that her scream of horror woke the neighbours four houses away, and set off the dogs of the whole city in a re-layed volley of barking that bounced back and forth and never stopped until morning.

Rajan lay prostrate on the fence between the two proper-ties. In the circle of light given by Rika's torch he lay still and silent amidst the bougainvillea that had otherwise broken his fall, covered in blood, half-turned towards her, the crown of his head impaled by the pointed stave of a fence pole, like an arrow shot through from behind.

❀ ❀ ❀

Rika's screams woke not only the house but the neighbour-hood. But after that nobody heard her. The street was in uproar, for rumours of the horror downstairs whipped from house to house and people came like flies to a feast. The house and yard spilled with people on the phone, shouting. Several sirens wailed in the distance and drew louder; a fire engine, po-lice cars, emergency vehicles with lights flashing. People came rushing on foot; cars stopped, blocking the street. Everyone wanted a piece of the action.

Rika, alone in her room, could only surrender to her screams. Wave after wave of naked agony pummelled her to her bed where she banged her head again and again against the pillow, as if she could simply whack it out, knock it from her life, and scrape what she had seen from her soul. Make it unseen. Great guttural howls emerged from her throat, groans she didn't make herself, animal sounds of a prey hunted down and dying on the jungle floor. Wave after wave of utmost unmitigated anguish, each surge containing the whole of herself, each one a tidal wave sweeping her away in its wake.

And then, suddenly, as if every last emotion, every last drop of torment had been spent in the tempest, there was nothing. Just cold empty reason. A chilling vacuum, a place where noise and inner pandemonium had been and now was cold and empty and chillingly rational.

She had to go.

She couldn't stay in this house; in a matter of seconds home had become a house of horror. Her room was filled with the blood of Rajan. She had seen the worst sight a human being could see: the death of a beloved.

And she couldn't stay under the same roof as her mother. She couldn't even *look* at her mother again, not ever. *Not ever not ever not ever. Not ever.* She couldn't even stay in this country. She just had to – *go*. With that insight she sprang to her feet, overcome by a fervent need for action; to do something, anything. To get away. Forget. Forever.

Rika grabbed her school bag and emptied it on the floor. She threw some clothes into it: underwear, jeans, T-shirts. She looked around: she possessed so little! She hesitated at the three new LP's given to her by Uncle Matt: *Sgt. Pepper's Lonely Hearts Club Band, Blonde on Blonde,* and *Bob Dylan's Greatest Hits.* How could she ever listen to music again in her life? A life that was over. She turned away and opened her sideboard drawer, because there were her true valuables: her passport and bank book, which she still had not returned to Granny's desk – the only stroke of luck in the cataclysm of this night. She stuffed them into a small leather shoulder-bag, along with her purse and her few dollars of left-over cash.

Before leaving she gave a cursory glance around the room, and there it was, *The Book of Mirdad*. Rajan's book; she had borrowed it so many years ago and never returned it, and he had never asked for it. That book: the beginning of everything. The only thing she had of his. Should she leave it or take it? If she took it, how could she forget? And yet – if there was anything that would help her make sense of this horror, anything that could begin to bring healing, it was that book. She walked back into the room, picked it up, and stuffed it into her bag.

She couldn't leave by the front gate; there was too much action there, too many people. She slipped out of the gap in the fence for the very last time and went down the alleyway, into the street. Only once did she look back, and a sickening feeling engulfed her. An ambulance stood on the pavement outside the house. She had heard the wail of its siren, it now stood silent, its lights still flashing. What was the point? She had seen him; seen the stave bursting out of his skull, the blood. She shuddered. Could she ever wipe that last picture of Rajan from her mind? She pushed it away. She would never think of it again. This night had to go. Forever. *She* had to go, forever. How could she even breathe in this place, ever again?

She ran. Ran and ran and ran. North, towards the Sea Wall. Once there, she stood gazing out over the ocean, her body heaving under great deep sobbing, gasping breaths. It was as if there was no air, yet air was all around; the night sky vast and endless and the sea miles away. She thought for a moment of rushing into the sea and never returning, plunging into its waves as it crashed against the Wall, but the tide was out and the seashore was but an endless expanse of dried out hard undulating mud.

Where would she go? The great Utopias of Great Britain, America and Canada were closed to her: she did not have a visa for any of these countries. There was Trinidad, Barbados, one of the smaller islands. Would *they* find her there, bring her back? She'd have to take the risk; her options were limited.

Right now her only option was to run. Along the Sea Wall, she ran, eastwards. She would run as far as it would take her. Run to Suriname. Brazil. Just run and run.

Trixie! She could go to Trixie. Trixie lived in Subyranville, just past Kitty, along this very wall. If she kept running she'd get to Trixie's house. She'd take this one step a time. One day at a time. One destination at a time. The first destination, the only one she could think of, was Trixie. Trixie would help her escape.

She ran and ran, along the Wall.

The hollow growl of a motorbike seeped into her consciousness, growing ever louder. Then it was right beside her, and not passing. She looked down, still running. Beside her, keeping pace with her on his Yamaha, was Jag. He was yelling something at her. Her name. She kept on running.

'Rika! Rika, stop!'

She wouldn't listen, wouldn't stop. She kept on running, along the Wall, faster, faster. The motorbike roared beside her.

Then silence. She realised he had switched off the motor, was doing something with the bike, but that was all behind her. She kept on running; running and crying, sobbing and running. Run, run, run to the end of the world.

Footsteps behind her, on the Wall. She didn't glance back, but she knew he was there, behind her, catching up. Then his arms were around her. And only then she stopped running, and collapsed in a twitching, heaving, sobbing heap into his arms.

'What's the matter, Rika? Why are you here this time of night? It's so dangerous! Where are you going?'

The words were like a switch, unleashing all her agony, all her rage. She screamed at him.

'Let me go, let me go, I want to *die!* I hate you, go away! I hate you, I hate you, I hate you!'

She pummelled his chest with all her might, flinging her head back and forth as the words of loathing and wrath poured out of her. The more she pummelled the tighter he held her, all the while steading her movement before they both fell off the Wall.

And then she was spent, every last atom of her fury used up, and she fell against him in a sobbing, blubbering heap. In Jag's arms she sobbed and bawled and howled.

'I'm sorry,' said Jag. 'But I'm not all bad. Come.'

And then she let him lead her back to his Yamaha and climbed on behind him and let him take her home; to his home, not hers, for now she was homeless.

❀ ❀ ❀

The next morning she crept out of Jag's room while it was still dark. The watchman unlocked the gate for her and she slipped out into the cool pre-dawn. She walked along the Sea Wall back to town; once there she sat gazing out to sea until the sun had risen. The town would be stirring by now. She was hungry but she couldn't eat. Maybe she could get a coffee somewhere. The bank would open at nine.

She withdrew all her money, changed it into US dollars. Then Rika got on a bus that would take her back the way she had come, but further, up to Ogle airport. At ten-thirty she was able to board a small interior plane to Lethem, in the Rupununi savannah bordering Brazil.

From there it was easy. She crossed the river into Brazil, and got a bus along the dusty road through the Amazon jungle to Boa Vista; from Boa Vista, a small plane to Manaus. From Manaus, the world lay open.

Nobody would ever track her down.

✤ ✤ ✤

A month later Rika, having travelled up the Amazon River into Peru, and from the Peruvian rainforest over the Andes into Lima, wrote three postcards: one to Marion, one to Daddy, and one to Uncle Matt. The message in all three cards was the same: she was safe; they should not worry; and she was never coming home. She did not leave a return address. They would not hear from her again for two decades.

Chapter Thirty-six

Inky: The Noughties

The jolly tinkle of my ringtone wiggled its way through a deep and dreamless sleep. Automatically my hand reached for the mobile beside my bed and flicked it open. I opened my eyes a slit. 'Neville,' said the backlit screen. I groaned and contemplated rejecting the call but duty conquered sleep. I grunted something unintelligible.

'Why can't you people answer the house phone? And Rika's bloody mobile is turned off. Do you know how much trouble I had to go to find out your number? I had to call Marion.'

Propped up on my elbow, still lost in a fog of forgetfulness, I only yawned in response to Neville's fury. A moment later, though, all the horror, despair and final relief of last night rushed into my consciousness, a torn and tangled bundle of emotion. I struggled to think, to focus, to remember. Mum had rung Neville from the hospital phone with the bad news, told him to tell Norbert and Marion. On the way home at almost four a.m. she'd sent him a short text message: *'Mum out of danger.'*

Neville must have called the landline first thing in the morning. The mobile screen said seven a.m.

'Didn't hear it.'

'Well, go on. How is she? Is she going to survive?' Groggy from barely three hours of sleep, I updated him on the situation.

'Well, I'm coming down. I'm just leaving home. I'll be there in a couple of hours. Norbert is coming too. He's booked a ten a.m. flight. Please wait for me at home.'

'Wait, wait … I don't know when we'll be home …'

'Well, just be there, that's all.'

'Why don't you go straight to the hospital? We'll be going there later …'

'Why should both of you go? What's the point of going to hospital if she's not conscious? Give me a bell if there's any change … But really Inky, this is so *typical* of Rika. Why didn't you make sure Mummy had her seat belt on? You know very well that your mother …'

'I did. I always do. Gran has the habit of secretly unlocking it. Says the strap bites her. Literally. Listen, Neville, Mum and I didn't get much sleep last night. Can you not call again till …'

'Yes, yes, I know. But listen Inky … what about the stamp? Have you secured it?'

'The stamp? Oh, the Stamp. What do you mean?'

'I mean exactly what I said. Have you made sure it's safe?'

'Not the slightest idea. I haven't thought about the stamp in twenty-four hours.'

'Well, you should! Really, Inky. You of all people should be watching out for things like this. You know Rika doesn't. Has Mummy hidden it again or is it in her purse? Did she have a handbag with her when she had the accident? Did you check?'

'The hospital gave us her handbag. It's probably downstairs.'

'Well, go and check it immediately.'

'I most certainly will not! I'm going back to sleep. Look, Neville, we'll talk about this later. I'm dead tired.'

'Inky, no, wait…'

'We'll talk later. I have to go. Bye, Neville.'

'Inky! Inky, wait!'

'We'll talk later. I have to go. Bye, Neville.'

I switched off the phone and wrapped the duvet around me, longing for more delicious sleep. But Neville had planted a bug in my brain, and there it crawled around. Yes, Gran was out of immediate danger but there was the worry about brain damage. What if that was indeed the case? What if she woke up out of anaesthesia and was a completely different person?

Last night that notion had made me weep for Gran. This morning it made me worry. For the stamp. Where was it? Only Gran knew. But what if Gran woke up today and *didn't* know?

Finally I got out of bed. Mum's bedroom door was open and I peeked in – still fast asleep. Obviously, she'd missed her four a.m. date with the laptop. I tiptoed downstairs. Gran's handbag lay on the hallway sideboard.

I took it into the living room and sat down on the carpet. It was the same voluminous bag of green imitation leather she'd brought from Guyana, with a brass clasp at the top and two rope-like straps, already cracking apart, that fit over Gran's shoulder so that she could hug the cushiony bulk of the bag under her armpit.

First I removed a stack of papers: grocery receipts, letters, a folded map of the area, several pamphlets from various organisations and a stack of ads for a variety of items ranging from hearing aids to car rentals, and a half-completed Sudoku torn from a newspaper. Delving deeper into the bag I removed a tiny *London A-Z*, a photograph wallet, a small bottle of Limacol (Gran had found a shop in Brixton that sold it), a box of throat lozenges, a beer coaster from a local pub, a couple of biros, a bottle-opener key-chain with no keys on it, another key-chain in the shape of a boxing glove in Guyana's colours with several keys on it, a powder compact and a myriad other items. I tipped the bag upside-down so that the rest of its contents fell onto the carpet, tiny things like a book of matches, a hair-pin and a few stray pills of dubious identity.

I searched in an organised manner. First I went through the photo wallet and the purse, searching every secret flap for the stamp. No luck. I returned to the now mostly empty handbag and looked in its side pockets, zipped open a side compartment. No stamp. Satisfied, I replaced all the items into the bag, stood up and replaced the bag on the sideboard.

By now I was quite wide awake, and totally immersed in my quest. Where would Gran have hidden the stamp? I decided the only way to find it would be to go through the whole room with a fine-tooth comb: start at one corner, and work my way through. I looked at the clock on her bedside table; ten past nine. How long would it take Neville to get here? It would be good if I could find the stamp before he arrived. Before he – and Norbert – began turning the place upside down themselves. I couldn't let that happen. I was doing this for Mum's sake, I told myself. To protect her from Neville and Norbert who, once they got their hot little hands on the stamp, would bully Mum into backing off which, knowing Mum and her total indifference to it, she would.

I started with Gran's wardrobe. I removed all the clothes from it and laid them on the bed. I removed the stacks of clothing from the shelves: Gran's neatly folded underwear, her blouses and nylon petticoats and the cotton dresses she'd brought from Guyana. The whole wardrobe smelt of Gran. Her scent, a melange of Limacol and face-powder, hair-oil and coconut and rose oils, and old-lady skin, enfolded me in an atmosphere redolent of her presence.

I didn't hear Mum enter the room, so engrossed was I in my work. I only heard her voice.

'What in the name of twenty million suns are you up to?'

I didn't answer. I just stood there, staring back.

'You sneaky little … little …' Mum was lost for words, for an epithet terrible enough to describe my iniquity. I tried to calm her, reached out for her hand.

'Mum, I …'

She snatched her hand away. I replaced the pile of clothes in my arms to its shelf and took a step away from the wardrobe, sinking on to Gran's commode.

'We have to be sensible, Mum,' I said. 'And practical. The stamp …'

'The stamp. The stamp! Is that all you can think about at a time like this? Mummy isn't in her grave yet, you know!'

Mum's eyes blazed with wrath.

'I know, I know, Mum, but it's not about that. She's probably got this brain damage, Dr Stone said so, and Neville's coming in a few hours and I thought …'

'Neville's coming?'

'Yes, and Norbert too!'

'Oh.' Mum was silent for a moment. The news of her brothers' imminent arrival seemed to have driven out her anger. She stood in the doorway frowning, scratching her head, biting her bottom lip. Her hair was a mess, a mane of partly matted frizz. She was barefoot, her pyjamas mismatched; a plain washed-out purple striped top on faded floral bottoms.

'I suppose they have the right,' she said at last. 'She's their Mum too. And Marion? I told Neville to tell her too. Is she on her way as well?'

'I don't know. He didn't mention Marion. I suppose she'll want to come too if everyone else is here.'

'A family reunion. How nice.'

I smiled at her sarcasm; that was more like Mum. Encouraged by the dissolution of her anger I continued the interrupted explanation of why I was here, in Gran's room, going through her stuff.

'You see, they're worried about the stamp. They're afraid Gran may have hidden it somewhere and might not remember where, after the accident. Neville said he's coming to look for it. He …'

'So you thought *you'd* find it first?'

I nodded. 'Mum, I'm not the mercenary beast you think. I do care about Gran and I was so relieved the operation went well. I do love her … you saw that last night! But we have to be practical as well. Do you really want Neville and Norbert snooping around in her room? She wouldn't want that.'

'She wouldn't want *you* snooping around in here either. Now you just put everything back exactly the way it was. I don't know what devil gets into you people's heads.'

'Mum, I …' I jumped to my feet to explain some more; I didn't appreciate being reduced to Neville and Norbert's level. But Mum had turned away and was already stomping upstairs. I followed her up, leaving Gran's room the way it was.

'I'm going to have a shower, then I'm going to hospital. If you want to come with me you'd better hurry.'

'But Neville … what if he comes?'

'I'm not waiting at home for Neville. If he wants to come he should come to the hospital. That's where Mum is.'

'Does he know which hospital?'

'I didn't tell him. Didn't he ask?'

'No. He said he was coming to our place.'

'Well, serve him right. He'll just have to wait.' She disappeared into the bathroom.

✤ ✤ ✤

Mum was in such a hurry to get back to hospital I didn't have time to fix Gran's room. I promised her to do it the moment we returned. I didn't want to be left at home in case Neville turned up, and Mum didn't want to wait.

The hospital was quite a different place during the day. People bustling everywhere, patients in wheelchairs smoking outside, others rolling around the corridors pushed by white-clad orderlies. Nurses rushed past, grasping papers or bending over gurneys. All the waiting rooms were full. Accident and Emergency patients sat with glazed eyes, sipping coffee in paper cups or leafing through last year's *House Beautiful*, waiting their turn.

No waiting for us, this time. We went straight to Gran's ward. There she lay. Frail and lifeless and so alone among all the hospital gadgetry, a little brown doll enclosed in bedsheet white. Only her face showed, smaller than ever beneath its turban of white bandage, its expression of peace so absolute that for a moment I thought she was dead.

We took seats on either side of her. There were three more beds in the room, separated from each other by curtains. The one opposite her was occupied by a man who seemed as lifeless as Gran; it was mutual oblivion.

Mum had brought fruit and juice for Gran, and magazines. All of it went unnoticed. Gran wasn't moving. We whispered comforting words to each other across the bed, and then a nurse popped in. Gran could wake up at any moment, she said cheerfully, and was doing as well as could be under the circumstances. She popped out again.

❊ ❊ ❊

At around eleven I went outside for a cigarette. I switched on my mobile. Thirteen missed calls, eight from Neville, five unknowns. I called Sal; he had come to the hospital last night to get the door-key, and gone back to feed Samba. We chatted for a while, and then I returned Neville's call.

'Where the hell are you people?' Neville's voice was a veritable snarl.

'At the hospital, of course.'

'And here's me sitting in the bloody car outside your house for the last half-hour twiddling my thumbs! You could at least have told me which hospital.'

'You didn't ask!'

'Well, tell me now! How's Mummy by the way?'

I told him.

'You mean she hasn't come out of it yet?'

I shook my head unhappily, forgetting he couldn't see. 'The doctors aren't happy. They say she's fallen into a coma.'

'Wonderful. Just wonderful.'

'Do you want to come over? I'll give you the address.'

'Well, there's not much point, is there, if she's in a fucking coma.'

'But she might wake up any time. Mum refuses to leave her side.'

'Well, that's good. So that's taken care of. But what concerns me is …'

'The stamp.'

'You said it. Did you search her handbag?'

'Yes.'

The weight of my betrayal sat heavy on my shoulders. Mum's accusing eyes glared at me through my confession, through the victory of pragmatism over optimism. My heart broke for Mum, sitting there holding Gran's hand, waiting in vain for the flicker of eyelids closed forever; she was living a fool's dream. I refused to deceive myself, to give in to the fantasy that Gran would wake up any moment and be her beloved cantankerous old self again. I'd *seen* the veiled truth in doctors' eyes as they discussed Gran's case with Mum. I'd *heard* the charity in their voices as they kept her hope alive with best-case scenarios. No mention was made of the worst-case scenario; Mum didn't ask, and they didn't offer it. But I knew.

We'd lost Gran. I felt it in my in the pit of my stomach, in the marrow of my bones. We might still have her body; it would lie there frail and still, kept alive by and hope and prayer, by medicines and daily nourishment and care, but *she* was gone. As the past few hours ticked away I'd convinced myself that Gran, even if she should awake, would never be the same again. While Mum sat there grasping her hand, stroking her bony fingers, hanging on to straws of hope, I had fought for sense and reason. I refused to be blinded by hope. I had to be rational and strong – for Mum.

Neville's voice cut through my musings.

'It wasn't there, I suppose.'

'What? Oh ... the stamp. No.'

'Inky, you do realise, don't you, that this is no time for sentimentality. You know as well as I do that Mummy isn't capable of any kind of rational action concerning that stamp. Even before this happened she was in danger of losing it through sheer bloody-mindedness. Now, Rika isn't much better, but you, Inky, you know better. We've got to find that stamp and keep it in a safe place. Do you agree?'

To my credit, I paused for the longest time before I gave my answer.

'Yes.'

'Then come home, and let's look for it.'

❄ ❄ ❄

Neville's Beamer, parked outside our house, was empty. Maybe he'd walked down to Streatham High Street to get a bite to eat. I entered the garden gate, walked down the path, turned the key. The moment I entered the house I knew something was wrong, and two steps later, standing in Gran's threshold, I knew.

Neville and Norbert were both there, demolishing Gran's room, inch by inch. They had moved all the furniture over to one corner and had pulled up the carpet in another. All enmity put aside, they now worked in brotherly unity; right now they were searching her photo album trunk. Neville sat on the floor beside the open trunk. He had an album in his hand, the one with the Quint family photos. He had taken out half the photos; they lay in a heap beside him. I caught him in the act of removing the next photo, turning it over to check its backside. Norbert was doing the same with a newer album.

They obviously hadn't heard my key in the lock, so intent were they on snooping. Incongruously, they were both dressed as if for the office, in suits and ties and – horror of horrors – laced-up shoes. It was the shoes that did it. They summoned Mum's spirit, and lent me her words. I yelled into the silence:

'What in the name of ten million suns are you two doing?'

They looked up, guilt written all over their faces.

'Ahhh ... hello Inky,' said Norbert. He jumped to his feet and put on the loving long-lost uncle act. 'Great to see you again! We just decided to continue the search ... we see that you'd already started, at least that's the conclusion we'd jumped to, seeing as how you'd emptied the closet, and ...'

'How'd you get in the house?'

'I happen to have a key,' said Norbert. 'When I came earlier this year I had a copy made; after all, you never know.'

Rage welled up in me, all the frustration and helplessness accumulated over the long empty hours of waiting suddenly finding a new form, a new energy in which to exit my body. I wanted to lash out at them both, scream and pummel them. It lasted less than a second. My knees buckled under me and I almost fell. Instead, I grasped for the door jamb for support, swayed a little and then steadied myself. I said nothing. What could I say? It was wrong for them to enter the house, wrong to start searching Gran's room, but who was I to talk? I had led the search party.

'Are you all right, Inky? You look exhausted.' That was Neville. Big bad Neville, who'd never spoken a friendly word to me in his life, all of a sudden solicitous.

I nodded, suddenly aware of my exhaustion. 'I hardly slept at all last night. I just want to ...'

'You need some sleep. Why don't you run off to bed.'

I waved my hand towards the mess in Gran's room.'

'We can't leave it like this. Put everything back the way it was. Mum'll be furious. And Gran ... Gran ...'

'What about her? Has she woken up?'

And that was what woke *me* up. Neville's question sharpened my groggy mind. I looked up, met his eye, and I saw not the arrogant bully I'd always known but a frightened child, a naughty little boy who had done something wrong behind Mummy's back, and feared the consequences. Coward!

I'd had enough of these two idiots. They'd both raced here, not out of concern for Gran but because of that damn stamp. That was all they cared about. They hadn't even asked how she was. They *wanted* Gran not to wake up, because then they could take control of the stamp – if they found it. They'd bully Mum into handing it over, and knowing Mum's complete indifference she would, without a whimper. But first they had to find it. How could I have even *dreamt* of collaborating with them, even for a second? How could I have succumbed to Neville's coaxing, his silky lecture about being practical and realistic? I was as bad as them, the only difference being that I felt guilty about it. And all I really wanted was for Gran to wake up and be her cantankerous old self again. I'd have given anything in the world for her to trundle in on her rollator right now and give me the tongue lashing I deserved, to flay me alive with her fury. That was the Gran I knew and loved.

'Get out,' I said, and my rage finally found its outlet. 'Just get out. Both of you. Out of my house. Right now.'

'But …'

They actually cowered before me, these two uncles of mine. They quaked before my fury, Norbert in his crisp Wall Street pin-stripes and Neville in his immaculate white shirt and Gucci tie. I took a step forward, fearless, threatening.

'Didn't you hear me? I said *get out.'*

They edged around the room, heading for the door, their eyes fixed on me. If I hadn't been so furious I'd have found it funny, laughed out loud. Now I was just sick to my stomach.

I glanced around and saw one of Gran's walking sticks leaning against the wall. I grabbed it, waved it at them. They edged backwards through the doorway.

'Inky, listen ...'

'How dare you! How dare you come in here and mess around in Gran's room. How dare you! You haven't even asked how she is. What kind of monsters are you? What kind of – of – of ...' I searched for the perfect word but all I could come up with was my old staple. 'What kind of bloody *wankers?*'

They were in the hall now, edging backwards towards the front door, me herding them out with the stick raised aloft.

'At least tell us where she is, which hospital!'

That was Norbert. His hand was on the door handle, though he still faced forward. He opened the door. Neville slipped through it like the slick little worm he was, but Norbert braved my wrath a second longer. He stood in the open doorway, eyes pleading for that last piece of information.

'What hospital, Inky? Where is she?'

'St George's!' I yelled, brandishing my stick like a club. Norbert flitted through the door. I slammed it behind him and collapsed against it, sinking to the floor.

After a while I got up and went to the kitchen. I was hungry.

The fridge was empty. We had not done our usual Saturday shop. I opened the freezer, pulled out a ready-meal, and stuck it into the oven.

Then I returned to Gran's room and began the long over-due clean up.

❋ ❋ ❋

An hour later I returned to the hospital. As soon as Mum, sitting at Gran's side, saw me, her eyes lit up. 'Save me,' they said, 'from these two morons!' Neville and Norbert didn't even look at me; whether from shame or anger I couldn't tell. Surely they wouldn't have told Mum what they'd done to Gran's room? Neville was ambling up and down the ward muttering and looking at his watch every now and then. Norbert was reading the *Financial Times* at Gran's other side. Neither spoke. The man in the bed across from Gran was as motionless and silent as ever. He had no visitors.

I pushed a chair up next to Mum and she leant towards me. 'No change,' she whispered, but I could see that already. Gran lay as silent as ever, a frail and crumpled ghost of her old self. It was amazing how, without the fire of her personality to activate it, weak and insubstantial her body looked, as if the fragile remnant of life still in it would slip away at any time. And even if it didn't, if life continued but without the force of a healthy mind – would it still be Gran? Would Gran want to live as a vegetable? I knew the answer to that. So did Mum. And I remembered the eerie prediction she had made on her very first day with us: six months to live, she had given herself. We were nearing the deadline.

The ward door swung open and a team of doctors and nurses marched up to Gran's bed. They all smiled and nodded at Mum and me before turning their attention to Gran. Immediately, the mood among us all perked up. Neville stopped his strutting and shot up to Gran's bedside, pushing his way into the now closed circle. Norbert slowly folded away his *Financial Times* and put on his most self-important expression. We all left the room.

The news, after the consultation, was not good. Gran could remain in this state for the rest of her life, which would, with luck, be short. She could wake up in a moment with severe brain damage, unable to function as a human being, unable to speak or even recognise us. Or she might be as good as gold.

'What's the probability of brain damage?' that was Neville.

'High, I'd say, considering her age.' Neville and Norbert looked at each other, dismay written all over their faces. Their concern was so transparent. Gran, it seemed, would either stay in a coma until she died, or, if she did wake up, would have brain damage. Next to those two options the possibility of her being normal again, normal enough to recover the Quint and hand it over to them, were slim. And that, presumably, was all they cared about.

❄ ❄ ❄

Once the medical team had left, Neville and Norbert turned fidgety and talkative.

'I really have to get back to New York,' Norbert said. 'I've an important meeting on Monday and I don't want to be too jet-lagged. I guess I'll go back to the hotel and book a flight. I left the return flight open as I didn't know what would happen with Mummy but as it is ….'

He shook his head, an expression of deep gravitas written across his face.

'Yes, I've got to get back too,' said Neville. 'There's really not much I can do here. When – if – she wakes up, or, or anything, you'll call me, won't you, Rika.'

And then they both turned their greedy eyes on me. And I knew what they were thinking. And I knew I'd won. There was no way they could get their hot little hands on Gran's stamp, without my help. But my triumph was short-lived. I looked at Gran, lying there oblivious to us all and to her own life. And more than anything, more than I wanted the stamp, I wanted her back. Neville spoke.

'Aaaah, Inky, um, what happened earlier, you see, we have to be realistic. We have to be prepared. You heard what the doctor said …'

'Go,' I said. 'Just go. Both of you.' And so, for the second time that day, I threw my uncles out.

Chapter Thirty-seven

Rika: The Sixties

She ought to be exhausted, after the hours spent at Mummy's bedside, but sleep just would not come. The Beast was scratching at the edge of her consciousness, demanding entrance. Could she? Could she possibly?

What choice had she?

'Rajan!' she whimpered into the night, into the darkness of her room. 'Rajan! Help me!'

He had never failed to come, to help. But tonight he was silent.

It had been tough, so tough, but she had found him again. She had found him in the depths of her soul: the real Rajan, the beautiful being who had led her through the tangled weeds, the thorns of adolescence, who had shown her the way out of her confusion and insecurity and heartbreak. He had shown her a different path, one of strength and courage, one that lifted her out of herself and held her straight and true: he had connected her to the earth and to the heavens and to a sense of self that was solid and sure.

And then he had died.

But there was no death.

In their final months she and Rajan had often discussed death. Rajan had been sure, so sure, that it did not exist. 'The body dies,' Rajan had said, 'and falls away. But consciousness, the life that inhabits the body, lives on.' He had no fear of death, Rajan had said.

There was the story of the sparrow, flying through a lit hall which was life on earth. Rajan had disagreed. His words had always stayed with her:

What if life on earth is actually a dark hall, he had said. What if we came from light, and return to light? What if this is the night, and real daytime comes afterwards? 'I think we long for light, for God, for joy, because we remember it. I think the memory is slumbering deep inside us. I think it is all inside us, Rika, and all our stumbling through life is to find that light. I think we return there after we die.'

She clung to whose last words; and so Rajan was not dead. He had returned to the light, and in that light he was alive for her, and pure, and strong, and, most of all, he was with her. *Always.* And so Rika had reached out to him – and found him.

All these years Rajan had been a living presence in her soul. There he was, always. She had only to turn, turn away from her own weaknesses and problems and dilemmas; turn within, to an outstretched hand. He was an anchor, holding her steady through all the ups and downs of life.

So Rajan had lived on, whole and perfect. Love incarnate.

Rajan was an outstretched hand within her, an invisible hand she could always grasp. A silent inner hand that gave her courage when she felt fear, light when she felt dark, strength when she felt weak. Rajan lived within her. He was her silent mentor, her spiritual guide, her Guru. She clung to that hand, and it had sustained her all the years: through the ups and downs of marriage, through Eddy's illness and his death, through the trials he had left behind. Helped her to raise Inky. She could speak to him, in silence, just as she had spoken to him when he was alive, and he had given her answers, clear, solid answers, just as he had when he was alive. *Have no fear, Rika. All is well, Rika. You are whole, and good, Rika.* She could conjure up his face, smiling, beautiful, his eyes melting with love, the way he had been that last evening before – the evening before her life had crashed in upon her.

Rajan was her anchor. He had kept her calm through every storm.

❋ ❋ ❋

Except for one memory; that one night of the accident. The fall. The horror. She would never, ever go there, not even with a thought. It was the one horror she could not bear.

She had packaged that horror into a neat little bundle and called it 'the Beast', and pushed it into the darkest corner of her soul, never to think about again. Pushed it behind a thick wall, slammed the reinforced iron door shut, locked it and thrown away the key. She had sworn never to see those terrible pictures again, never relive the horror of the night her life fell apart. Rajan's face, blood-covered – no. Never; the horror was too great. The moment a memory, a thought, slipped into the light of consciousness she pushed it away, back into its prison.

In India she had learnt the techniques; a way to master the mind, to never be in thrall to unwanted moods and thoughts, to master the darkness. *She* was in charge, in control, not the Beast. That was true independence, true freedom. She had used her techniques to keep it there. To force it back; used all her power to keep it locked away, to never again enter the light of day, the light of consciousness. Perhaps, she had thought, she had hoped, it would wither away and die.

But the Beast, the one thing she was unable to face, had lingered there in the depths. Behind the wall it lurked, in darkness. She had kept it imprisoned for thirty years. But it had brought no satisfaction. No relief. No freedom. Through all the years, all the ups and downs of married life, the joy of motherhood, the struggle for survival, it had loitered, that

Beast, reminding her of its presence. *One day*, it said, *one day you must release me.*

Tonight it writhed within her, rumbled and prowled, scratched at the door of her awareness, demanding entry.

She had always known that one day, she would have to face the Beast.

That's why she'd kept the letter.

When it first arrived, soon after Inky's birth, it had let loose a small earthquake within her. She had told them, warned them, in that very first letter! *No mention of the past, please.* And no letters from Mummy. No contact with Mummy. Not yet. She couldn't talk to Mummy, or write to her. Not yet. Mummy was too close to the Beast. She couldn't deal with Mummy.

And, now here was a letter from Mummy and obviously, it would be about the Beast: Mummy would be asking for forgiveness, or some such thing. She couldn't deal with that. Or could she? She had turned to Rajan, and he had smiled back from within and said, silently, *One day you have to go there, Rika, back to that night. Why not now?*

Rajan had wanted her to open it, she'd thought at the time. She had left the letter on the mantelpiece for a week unopened. Inky had been just a baby; her marriage had been intact.

'Why don't you open it?' Eddy had asked, and Rika had been tempted: one day, she would have to face the Beast; she knew it. When she was strong enough.

But not just then. There was the baby, and the marriage, and the start of a wonderful new life. *No Beast for now*, she'd thought. Rajan was right there too, a strong presence within her, a zone of comfort and safety. It was not the time for unpleasantness. So she had shoved the letter into that Ikea storage box and left it to brew. For years. Eighteen years, while she gathered the strength she would need to one day release the

Beast, to face it with courage. Let it out of that mental dungeon and into the light.

She had thought the way to do that was to put the past firmly in the past and forgive Mummy. To melt the ice between them, break the silence. Forgiveness was the first step. So when Marion had tentatively mentioned that she had to go to Canada and Mummy needed care, Rika had taken the plunge.

'Send her to me,' she had said to Marion.

But it hadn't worked out. The moment Mummy stepped into that Arrivals Hall at Gatwick the whole plan fell apart. It was as if she and Mummy had stepped back in time: back to that bickering, mutual resentful state. Needy teenager, bossy mother; that's what they were, all over again. Would they never break out of it? She had pushed the Beast back into its dungeon.

And now Mummy lay on a hospital bed and she might die or stay in a coma for the rest of her life, and it was *all her fault*. Just as it was all Mummy's fault, back then.

Rajan! Help me! What should I do? What can I do?

Nothing. No answer. She was helpless, and all alone. Rajan stayed silent, as if he had nothing more to say.

She could read the letter now. Could she?

What a time to release the Beast! It was a bad time, the worst! Mummy in hospital with her head all bandaged up! Mummy's head shattered, just like Rajan's, back then! She couldn't!

Do it, Rajan said. *Read the letter.* She could hear him as clearly as if he were in the room with her, speaking out loud.

Read the letter.

Yes. It might be a bad time, but it was the right time.

Dawn was just breaking when Rika got up, had breakfast, and prepared herself for the day. She opened the cabinet door, slid out the Ikea box. The letter lay on the top. She picked it up, pushed it into her handbag, and slid out of the house without waking Inky.

Chapter Thirty-eight

Inky: The Noughties

I woke up late on Sunday morning. No sign of Mum. She must have left early to return to the hospital. Still in my PJs, I made myself breakfast. A bowl of cereal in my hand, I walked over to the phone. The answering machine light was blinking. I pressed the button: ten new messages. I went through them; a couple were from Neville and Norbert, but most were from Marion. Marion! Neither Mum nor I had spoken to her since the accident; we'd been too caught up in events. But it was too early to call her now. I'd do it later. Instead, I now speed-dialled Sal.

Apart from the hasty handing over of the house key so he could feed Samba, I hadn't seen Sal for a couple of weeks. In fact, not since the day we watched *Charade*. He was as tied up with his studies and his job, as I was with Gran's life and her care.

With a start I realised something: I missed Sal dreadfully. I went over to the couch with my cereal bowl and the telephone, cuddled into a heap of cushions, and settled down for a nice leisurely Sunday morning chat. I told him all about Gran, and what I had gone through in the last two days. No, not even two days, though it felt like six. A day and a half. Sal, the doctor-to-be, was both empathetic and knowledgeable. He told me a bit about more about shear injury, and how unpredictable the outcome was at this stage.

'If she's got brain damage it would have been better for her to have been killed,' I said.

'Don't say that. It's not true. Not necessarily.' Sal replied.

There was a gap in the conversation. I took a few more spoons of cereal.

'So,' said Sal after a while, 'did you hear from George Cloo-ney? Or did you contact him.'

I realised with a start that I hadn't even had time to call George Clooney; in fact, I had completely forgotten about George Clooney, just as he, apparently, had forgotten about me.

'It's been three weeks,' I said to Sal. 'I think I'll write him a note. Nothing like taking fate into my own hands. No sitting around for this girl. And I need a distraction from all this Gran drama. What do you think?'

'Go for it!' said Sal. That's what I loved about Sal: he was always totally supportive.

'I mean, I don't think much of the *Daily Mail*, but it's just a beginning. He could easily move up to the *Guardian* or the *Independent*. What with the scoop on Gran – in fact, that's probably why he didn't call. I bet he got a promotion with that story! He's a good writer.'

Sal chuckled, but it seemed cold.

'What's the matter?'

'Oh, nothing.'

'And how are you? What've you been up to?'

'Oh, nothing much. The usual. Uni and work, work and Uni.'

'Can you make it over this afternoon? We can go and see Gran together.'

'Inky, I can't come this afternoon, I'm working. In fact, I've got to go now to start getting ready. I'll see you around. Say hi to your Mum and I hope Nan'll be all right.'

And suddenly he was gone, and the house was hollow and empty. So I went to the hospital.

❊ ❊ ❊

Mum was sitting next to Gran, and I saw it at once: the letter, in her hand, still unopened.

'Hi, Mum!' I said. She started, and looked up; she had been lost in thought, or in some other place, and had not heard my approach. I smiled, and pointed to the letter.

'Aren't you going to read it?'

She shook her head, and said nothing.

'Mum!' I said. 'Go on!'

She looked around, and shook her head again.

'It's so – so busy here,' she said. 'So chaotic! Nurses rushing in and out, taking blood pressure, adjusting Mummy's infusion – it's just the wrong – atmosphere. I need peace and quiet.'

'Oh, *Mum!*' I said, exasperated. 'Just read the damn thing and be done with it!'

And to my surprise, she did. As if she'd been waiting for a final push. She let out a huge sigh, slid her finger under the closed flap of the envelope and tore it open. She began to read, silently, but couldn't have read more than a sentence or two before dashing the letter aside.

'I can't,' she blubbered. 'I just can't!' Mum, crying! That was a new one.

'Shall I read it to you?'

'Yes. Do that.'

So I took the letter gently from her hand and began to read. The handwriting was somewhat spidery, but somehow, reading slowly, I managed to decipher the words:

'My dearest darling Rika,

Yes, I know you aren't used to such language from me. But this is how I've been addressing you, in my mind, for the last twelve years. Over and over again: dearest Rika, please write, please call, please come home!

My dearest Rika, I wanted to say all these years, aloud, to you: forgive me. Forgive me the years I spent neglecting *you, not loving you enough, rejecting you, even. It wasn't because of you. It was because of me; because I was so wounded, after <u>my</u> worst night. Instead of seeking healing I nursed the pain of losing Freddy. I let it kill the natural love I bore for you and all my children. Love is dangerous, I had learned; love brings the risk of pain and I was afraid to love again.'*

I paused, and looked up, to see how Mum was taking it. The words were so untypical of Gran, so serious, so sentimental, even, that I was astonished. And a little bit scared. Mum was too, I could tell; she had buried her face in her hands, but briefly removed them to nod at me.

'Go on.'

'And now we have heard from you! At last! You cannot imagine the joy your letter has brought to all of us! To Granny, Daddy, Marion, even the twins! Your aunts and uncles, and cousins! Rika has written, and she has a baby! A little Inka!

'I know you said we should never ever mention that terrible night again. You said you didn't want to hear from me, ever again. This tells me that however well you have pulled your life together, you have not forgiven me. And I can't blame you, knowing what you know. The thing is, Rika: you don't know the whole story. You ran away too quickly.

'Rajan is alive!'

✻ ✻ ✻

Mum cried out. 'What? What did you say?'

'Rajan is alive,' I repeated. She grabbed the letter from me, and read on in silence, her hands shaking, blubbering as she read.

Once again, I was left out in the cold. Would I ever learn the whole story? When Mum had finished the letter she flung it away and threw herself on to Gran's bed, almost tangling herself up in the infusion tubes, and cried – cried and cried as if she would never stop. I picked up the letter and finished reading it, in silence.

Chapter Thirty-nine

Dorothea: The Sixties

Dorothea stood rooted in the doorway, but only for a second. Rika, screaming at the window, then swung around to face her mother, shrieking wildly:

'You bitch! You killed him! He'd dead! Rajan's dead and it's all your fault!'

She dropped the torch and ran to the bed, where she buried her head in her pillow and pummelled the mattress with her fists.

'Oh Christ!' cried Dorothea, and ran to the window, picking up the torch on her way. She shone it down to see what Rika had seen. The circle of light searched the bushes below and finally found Rajan, his head stuck on the fence, his half-turned face blood-streaked, the stave poking out from the top of his skull.

'Oh shit!' Dorothea ran, taking the torch with her, out the door, along the passage joining the Annex to the house. She flew up the stairs to the bedrooms and pummelled on Matt's door.

'Matt! Matt! Wake up! Wake up!'

But she couldn't wait; she opened the door and barged in, lunged towards the bed and shook Matt until he was wide awake and sitting up.

'What's the matter?'

'Quick, get up, it's an emergency! Rajan fell on the fence. It went through his head.'

'Good God.'

Matt shot out of bed in a trice, grabbed his medical bag and ran out the door in his pyjamas.

Dorothea ran to Humphrey's door and Ma Quint's. She shook them both out of slumber, gave a breathless account of what had happened. They ran downstairs; Dorothea stayed behind and rang the hospital for an ambulance. She replaced the receiver and took a moment to catch her breath; for it seemed she had not been breathing.

Her heart was pounding like a jackhammer. Her brain red hot, burning; mind black but for the one thought: *No. No. No. Not again. Don't let this happen again. Oh no, God, not again. Please not again.* Over and over and over, the jackhammer: *No. No. No. Not again.*

She joined the others downstairs. She could not look. She had seen, already. There was Matt, doing something, shouting something. She could not hear what he was shouting, because of the scream in her own head. *No. No. No.*

Basmati was already there, and she was screaming, the shrill panicked scream of a mother for her lost child. Dorothea laid her hands over her head and shook it as if to banish reality, shake the nightmare out of her brain. But the nightmare was real, and the horror, and she could not shake it away.

But then the real Dorothea, the practical head-on-her-shoulders Dorothea, slipped through the cracks of shock and heard Matt calling:

'Have you called the ambulance? And we need the fire brigade too! They need to cut through the damn pole!'

Dorothea ran back upstairs, dialled 999 again, this time demanding a fire engine. She deliberately refrained from adding that there wasn't actually a fire. Cutting a man down from a fence spiked through his head might not be considered an emergency—who could possibly survive?

Back down to the yard.

Humphrey had his arms around Rajan's body and was holding him up, preventing his head from slipping further down the stave. Dorothea looked away. She could not bear the sight. Rajan's head! His beautiful face, bathed in blood, his body limp and lifeless. Not again. She had seen. She knew. The stave had pierced right through the top of his head. He was gone. Gone. Gone already.

Still: there was Matt, doing his best as a doctor should. Perhaps he had a few breaths left in him. A few. He must have, otherwise Matt would not be working on him, would he? Dorothea had no hope; what could a doctor do, with a brain speared through? Yet still that scream: *No No No.*

From the open window of Rika's window, just above the scene, came an agonised keening, loud, primeval, almost a howl. Rika's bedroom light was off; Rika was crying to herself, in the dark, all alone. Dorothea longed to go there, place her arms around her daughter, but she couldn't. Rika's last words resonated in her heart. *I hate you! You bitch! You killed him!* She would have to deal with that, but later. First this nightmare had to end. *Rajan had to be saved! He had to be saved! Oh Lord! Please! I'm sorry! I'm so sorry! Forgive me!*

Visions came to her of a similar nightmare: seventeen years ago, in a Kitty front yard. Freddy lying on the ground with a garden fork stuck out of his abdomen. Her cries for help, and no help coming; the blood, the blood! Freddy's life force ebbing from him as the blood oozed from the four wounds in his belly. Dorothea pulling off her blouse, and then her skirt, pressing it against the wounds, and seeing them turn slowly red. The crowd, standing around and gawping and nobody doing a thing. The ambulance, arriving over an hour later, when it was too late and Freddy had bled to death. Her hope and her faith sinking into the darkness as Freddy's blood sank into the earth. The blackness of despair left behind.

Not again. Oh, dear God, not again!

The wail of an emergency vehicle. Thank God, the ambulance. But what could anyone do?

It wasn't the ambulance. It was a fire-engine. In a city of wood like Georgetown, fire was taken seriously; there was always the fear of it spreading, growing out of control. Many times, Georgetown had been inundated by fire. Medical emergencies, on the other hand, were private. Not urgent. The ambulance was taking its good time.

Ma Quint had taken Basmati aside and was holding her, comforting her. Basmati was struggling to get to her son, screaming for him, but Ma Quint held her back.

Marion and the twins came down the front stairs, drunken with sleep, their hair dishevelled. Dorothea had to keep them away. She couldn't let them see Rajan.

'Come,' she said sternly, turning Marion around. She grabbed the boys' hands, one in each of hers, and led them up the stairs.

'Where's that bloody ambulance?' she heard Matt cry. It seemed Rajan had already been cut down from the fence. Everyone was talking, chattering. Cars were stopping on the street, people getting out to come and watch. She felt like screaming at them all. Instead, she took the children upstairs and called the hospital once again. A sleepy voice answered.

'Is the ambulance on its way? I called you twenty minutes ago!'

The voice on the other end was so disinterested Dorothea wanted to scream and tear its owner apart.

'We still tryin' to find the duty doctor, Ma'am,' he said, and yawned into the phone as if to deliberately mock her.

'What! You mean you haven't sent anyone yet?'

'No, Ma'am. We doin' we best.'

Dorothea knew very well what their best would be. Only last week there had been an article in the papers about a woman with a breech baby who had died because the ambulance had never arrived. She knew, because she was the one to write a Letter to the Editor complaining about the lackadaisical emergency services of the Georgetown Hospital.

'You stay sitting there!' she commanded the three children, who, not yet quite awake, were sitting around the dining table waiting for further instructions, rubbing their eyes and yawning. The twins were as tame as lambs at this time of the night; thank goodness for that.

Dorothea called Dr Ray Wong, their own general practitioner and a personal friend of the family. This was an emergency.

'I'll come,' said Ray, and Dorothea breathed out. *Forgive me! Heal me! Save me!*

But, said a stern voice within her, *what's the point? The boy is dead. You saw him. Nobody could survive that. No ambulance and not a hundred doctors.*

But a tiny spark of hope glimmered within her. Matt was there, and Ray was on his way.

❊ ❊ ❊

Rika had stopped her howling. Dorothea debated whether to go to her, but knowing Rika, remembering her last words and the fact that she, Dorothea, was responsible for this present catastrophe, it was better to stay away. Stay far away. Rika was a loner; she dealt with every drama in solitude. It had always been that way. Rika rejected her; how much more would be that rejection now! No: better to leave Rika alone. They would deal with her the next day. Right now, the emergency was Rajan, not Rika. Perhaps Ma should go to Rika; but Ma was busy tending to Basmati, who was still in hysterics. Later she'd send Ma to Rika. But hopefully, Rika had cried herself to sleep. She would be calmer in the morning. Or not, as the case might be. But everyone else would be calmer, at least.

She had to do something about those children! This was no place for them; but now they were awake and too excited to go back to bed. Already the twins were at the window now, thrilled at the sight of the fire-engine, wanting to see the fire. Dealing with them would also keep her busy.

Dorothea picked up the phone again and dialled Leo's number, her brother-in-law. After a while, Leo's wife picked up the phone.

'Belinda, we have an emergency here. Can you take the children for the rest of the night? I'll drive them over. Marion and the twins. I'll explain when I get there.'

'Of course!' said Belinda. 'Bring them over.'

So Dorothea herded the children back down the stairs and into her car, under great protest: the boys because they would miss all the fun (Where's the fire? Anybody dead?) and Marion because she thought she could somehow help. 'I could serve drinks and snacks,' she offered.

She drove them the five minutes to Leo's house in Kingston, where Belinda and Leo were up and full of concern. Belinda gave her a cup of tea 'to help her relax', and Leo insisted on coming back home with her, because maybe he could help in some way. When she returned the crowd had grown yet more; several cars had followed the fire engine and were now parked all along Lamaha St, as well as those passing by who had stopped out of curiosity. Their occupants had gathered round to watch the goings on, rather disappointed that there wasn't an actual fire. Dorothea, enraged, shooed them away and stood guard to keep them from returning;

otherwise they'd have possibly pushed away the doctors in their eagerness to ogle.

There was still no ambulance; but she hadn't expected one anyway. Rajan lay on the ground, the tip of the wooden spike still sticking out of his head. Matt and Ray were working on

the wound; they had stopped the bleeding, it seemed. Dorothea swayed; she was going to faint. No, she wasn't. She had
to know.

'Is he …?'

Humphrey looked up. 'He's still alive,' he said.

'Oh thank – thank God!'

*Thank you! Oh, thank you! You saved him! Now save me! Give
me peace!*

'By a miracle,' added Matt. His face was glum.

'But, Dorothea – we can't do much,' said Ray, also looking
up. 'He can't survive this. Not possible.'

That's when Dorothea finally burst into tears. She had not
cried for seventeen years, not since the night when Freddy
died, when the ambulance had finally come and the paramedics had declared him dead and covered him with a white
sheet and packed him into the back of the vehicle like a
slab of meat. She had howled in despair then, just as Rika
had howled this night, but never again. Back then, it was
Humphrey who had comforted her. And now, again, it was
Humphrey. He rose to his feet and put his arms around her.
She cried into his chest.

'My fault! All my fault!' she blubbered, and in her heart she
wailed: *I'm sorry! So sorry! Forgive me, save me! Heal me! Make
me whole!*

Humphrey did not contradict her. He only held her, strong
and silent. Dorothea let herself cry. Gave herself permission.
She disintegrated. Dorothea Quint was not real. She was a
mirage, an image. Hard as steel on the outside, only to protect
this inner core, this softness, this vulnerable truth. Hardness
was not strength. She had played a loser's game. And now she
was nothing, just a withered vine in Humphrey's arms.

Finally she stopped crying. The fire engine had provided
a stretcher and they had manoeuvred Rajan onto it and were

transporting him to Ray's car, which was a station-wagon whose back seats could be lowered to create an almost flat space at the back. They shoved the stretcher in. It was a little too long; the flap at the back had to remain open. Matt climbed into the back with Ray; he crawled into the space between the lifeless body and the side of the car, to hold on to Rajan and make sure he didn't fall out. Humphrey climbed into the passenger seat, Ray into the driver's seat. He leaned out of the window.

'Call the Medical Arts Centre,' he said to Dorothea. 'There'll be a duty nurse – tell her what happened, and to prepare the emergency room for us. Tell her to call Dr Ali – the surgeon. We'll be there in ten minutes.'

'I will,' promised Dorothea, and she did. And after she had done so she got into her own car and drove to the MAC in Thomas road. Basmati came with her, and, because Basmati clung to her and would not let go, Ma Quint. The Medical Arts Centre was a private hospital where several doctors, Ray included, had their surgeries: the best hospital in the country, as up-to-date as possible. Damn the Georgetown Hospital! Damn the non-existent emergency services! Damn them all!

But, a little voice argued, *they probably couldn't have helped anyway.*

Rajan is going to die. You saw him. He is half-dead already. Dorothea, this is a second man's blood on your hands. First Freddy, and now Rajan. All because of your interfering, ferocious temper. All because, as Rika said, you're a bitch. Oh Lord, have mercy!

❄ ❄ ❄

In the morning Rajan was still alive, by some miracle. Matt, Ray, and Dr Ali had worked on him for hours. Humphrey and Dorothea, Ma and Basmati, had waited in the waiting room, taking turns to nap, leaning against one another, or lying across the chairs and resting a head on the other's lap. At one stage they had needed blood; all four had been tested. Dorothea was found to be a universal donor. She had given blood, and returned to the waiting room. To wait, and nap, and worry, and cry.

They had stabilised Rajan and put him into an artificial coma. There was nothing more to do. Everyone was exhausted.

Dorothea drove them all back home. Matt was saying that in spite of the best they had done, Rajan would probably die the next day. They had not been able to remove the piece of metal still stuck in his head. His own skills were not up to it; he was not a brain surgeon, after all. And though Dr Ali *was* a surgeon, he too was not trained for such a sensitive operation.

'Removing that pole needs an expert,' said Matt. 'We can't do it; to do so would risk opening a major artery. And there's only one expert I know of who can do it. My friend, Professor Cohen. But he's in Chicago. I'll call him first thing tomorrow.'

A chill went through Dorothea. She could not say a word. Rajan would die. Tomorrow. How could she ever face Rika again?

Rika. Where was she? The Annex was still dark and silent; was she asleep? Hopefully. Dorothea tentatively tried the handle on the door. It moved, but the door would not open. Rika had locked herself in. In a way, Dorothea was glad. She could not face Rika. She could not tell Rika that Rajan would die. Not tonight, at any rate.

Rika would have fallen asleep from exhaustion. Just as she, Dorothea, was about to do. She went up to her room and got into bed. Humphrey's arms were waiting for her. She cried herself to sleep, and vowed to turn over a new leaf.

She slept until midmorning. Matt had been up much earlier; he had tried and failed to get hold of his friend Professor Cohen, who, it turned out, was vacationing in Florida. A few more calls, and Matt had managed to speak to Professor Cohen

– whom he called Josh – at his hotel, and describe the case to him in detail. At breakfast he was smiling.

'The Prof's the best!' he said. 'He's sending a medical plane for Rajan! He's going to operate on him himself!' He looked at his watch. 'The plane'll be on its way right now.'

As if on cue, the telephone rang. Humphrey answered it, called Matt, who listened for a while, spoke a few words, and returned beaming to the table.

'I told you: he's the best! Pulled a few strings, and hey, presto! The plane should be landing at Ogle just after midday. There's some red tape to cut through regarding landing permits, visas and the like, but he's done this before and knows the ropes.'

Dorothea let out a whoop of delight. 'What do you think, Matt? Can Dr Cohen do it?'

'If anyone can, it's him!'

'But,' said Humphrey slowly. 'I can't afford this, Matt! A plane, all the way from America! That'll cost a fortune!'

'Don't worry about it,' said Matt. 'I'll pay for it.'

'But …'

'Not another word,' said Matt. 'What are friends for? I've got the money. We'll do it.'

'I can't thank you …'

'Where's Rika?' asked Ma Quint suddenly.

'Still asleep, probably,' said Dorothea. 'She'd locked her door last night. She must have been in shock.'

'Did nobody attend to her?'

'Well – no. We were all too busy with Rajan,' said Dorothea. 'And I had to get the children away. But you know Rika – she likes to be alone.'

'But I'm sure she would have appreciated a little comfort,' said Ma Quint. 'Oh dear. I suppose that was my job. She wouldn't have accepted it from you, Dorothea.'

'Exactly!' said Dorothea. 'She must hate me more than ever now.'

Ma Quint scraped back her chair. 'That's true. This is my job. I'll go to her now. Let's hope sleep has calmed her down. And at least we have some good news for her.'

She hurried from the room. A few minutes later she was back.

'I've been calling and knocking but she won't answer the door!' she said. 'I need the spare key.'

She ran upstairs, returned with a key, and ran over to the Annex. Again she was back.

'Rika's gone!' she cried.

Chapter Forty

Rika

She had taken Mummy's hand in her own and held it, crying and speaking at the same time.

'Mummy!' she cried. 'Oh Mummy! I'm sorry! I'm so sorry!'

And then she was still, quite still, crying silently, Mummy's hand in hers. Mummy lay as ghostly still as ever. A living corpse, her mouth caved in, hollow-cheeked as she was not wearing her dentures. And then …

A slight flutter, as of a baby bird awakening to life.

Rika sat up straight.

'Inky!'

Inky looked up. 'Mmmm?'

'She moved! Her fingers, they moved!'

Rika loosened the fingers of her hand clasped around Mummy's, whose own hand now lay still on her palm, as if the baby bird had died.

'No!' Inky stared at her grandmother, corpselike as before. Rika held her breath. Had she imagined it? Was it wishful thinking? But then it happened again. The fingers twitched in Rika's hand. They both leaned in, called out together:

'Mummy!'

'Gran!'

'We're here!'

'Can you hear us?'

'It's me, it's Rika! Come back! Come on back! I love you!'

Nothing. Rika and Inky fell into silence, watching. And then … Mummy's eyes twitched, just a little. And her fingers, again. Inky took her other hand, and that twitched too. Rika beamed at Inky.

'She's waking up!' she whispered. The tiny bird trembled ever so slightly in her hand, fleshless and silky. She shuddered at the joy of it.

Mummy's eyes opened a slit. Inky pressed the bell for a nurse. People came, people in white, doctors and nurses. They hustled and bustled around Mummy, all white efficiency and care, and partitions went up, the lights went on. They shooed Inky and Rika from the bedside, out of the ward. Out in the corridor they clasped each other in joy and comfort and hope.

❀ ❀ ❀

Later, much later, all was quiet again. Mummy lay there, still as a stone except for the gentle rise and fall of the bed-sheet over her breast. Her eyes were open just a slit. Sometimes she blinked. Rika and Inky gazed at her face, holding their breath, waiting for a miracle. Life had returned to this fragile body; but what quality of life?

Then, Mummy turned her head towards Rika. She seemed to be straining to lift it. Inky reached over and held it up, plumped up cushions beneath it, and then Mummy opened her eyes fully. Her lips parted. She croaked, trying to speak. Her tongue slid gently over her bottom lip. She made a little chewing motion with her toothless mouth. Hands twitched, little birds fluttering again. And then the moment came where she seemed to pull all her faculties together in one great grasp at life. Her eyes flew wide open, her gaze found Rika, and it was as full of fire as ever.

'Now we is quit!' she said, lisped. Her eyelids fell shut, she shuddered, and her head fell back against the pillow.

Rika gasped in horror. 'Is she …?'

But then the whole little body shuddered from toe to tip as it took one deep breath, and relaxed again into sleep.

When Mummy woke up completely Rika was right there, waiting.

'Mummy,' she said. 'I'm sorry. So sorry!' She could hardly see for the tears welling in her eyes. She sniffled and blew her nose and leaned in to hug her mother. Mummy raised an arm, thinner than ever before and almost weightless, and placed it around Rika's shoulder. She patted Rika on the back.

'Is what you got fuh be sorry?' she muttered.

'For being the biggest asshole on earth,' Rika blubbered.

'So,' said Dorothea. 'You an' me gon' be friends at last?'

Chapter Forty-one

Inky

Gran's complete awakening was slow but steady. Mum took a few days leave and I took a few days off from work, and we took turns at her side. She seemed not to appreciate our company at all. It was the same bossy Gran of old who returned to us, much worse for wear; her voice with half the volume and lacking the increased authority of a rollator to barge her way through life. She was crotchety about being tied to a hospital bed, and having a man across the way from her – the same man – who really did nothing more than lie there all alone.

Mum, meanwhile, was in a delirium of joy, almost euphoric. Gran's awakening plus the news of this fellow Rajan being alive – well, it was like thirty years of Christmas all rolled into one for Mum. In the following days, bit by bit, she told me the rest of the story, no longer reluctantly and hesitantly, but in her own true voice: about Rajan and her friendship with him and the first date with him. And then, just as she was about to fall in love, he fell, and died.

Or so she had thought.

'Oh, Mum!' I sighed. 'What a waste of time! Of everything! If only you had read that letter when it first came! Why didn't you?'

'I couldn't,' she said sheepishly. 'I was a coward.'

'What a lot of will power, though, to keep it for so long! Eighteen years!'

'Oh, *that* was nothing,' said Mum. 'No will power at all. I didn't *want* to open it! I feared it! There was a huge thick scab over a deep aching wound and I knew very well that reading

Mummy's letter would crack open that scab and I'd be right back there in the wound and bleeding to death, like Rajan.'

'But – how could you keep that pain so well out of sight, all those years? That must have been will power?'

But Mum only shook her head.

'Because I had a different memory of Rajan, and I kept that one alive. I could conjure up his face, smiling and strong. I clung to that image. I could talk to him, and he would talk back. He became so real to me, Inky! So real, that he pushed the painful memories away.'

'Then why didn't you just throw it away?'

'I couldn't do that either. Because I knew, I just *knew,* that one day I had to find closure. That I couldn't run away for ever. That the letter would be the key to facing the pain, forgiving Mum, finally confronting the Beast in me. I knew it, Inky, but I kept saying, one day. Not now. You know I'm a first class procrastinator!'

I nodded. Mum had that tendency – to delay unpleasant matters until they could no longer be avoided. She did it with her bills, and she'd done it with this letter. Typical! Me, I like to get things over with as soon as possible. Mum was still speaking.

'Somewhere inside me, was a little voice. I thought it was Rajan's voice; I used to talk to him, you know! A voice telling me that in the end, I had to return to love. Reconcile with Mummy, accept her plea for forgiveness. It had to come, one day, and the letter represented that day. I used to have whole conversations with Rajan: a sort of angel Rajan, advising me what to do. *Open it,* Rajan would say. *Later,* I'd reply. *Later. I promise.*

'But I kept pushing that day into the future delaying it. Because I was so afraid. Afraid of the pain. Of dragging up the memory of Rajan's death. Terrified. Mummy said she locked *her* pain away, turned hard and cold; well, I locked my pain away too, but in a different way. I banished it, refused to let it dominate my mind, my life. And yet it was always there, in the background. Even if I refused to look, it was there.'

She shuddered. 'His face – with that – that rod sticking out of his head …'

She wiped away a tear.

'And yet. The letter. It told me the story was not over. That one day there had to be closure, and reconciliation. But now, that's easy too. Because Rajan is alive.'

She was still for a moment, her face one huge smile.

'Inky! He's alive! *Alive!* I can't believe it! It's like, like, a resurrection!'

And she fell into my arms, crying for joy. I wanted to caution her, tell her not to be too euphoric; after all, Rajan wasn't the same Rajan she had known. Brain-damaged! That could very well be worse than death. In my eyes, at least, it was. I'd rather be dead than brain-damaged. But I couldn't tell that to Mum. Not now. Of course not.

'I wonder how he could possibly have survived,' I said.

'Well, I guess Gran will tell us the details, once she's home.'

'Mum,' I said, 'This is an amazing story. You should turn it into a novel!'

She burst out laughing. 'Maybe I will, Inky, Maybe I will, one day!'

And she opened her arms and squeezed me so tightly I yelled for release.

'Inky,' she said then. 'It's time to go home. And you're coming too.'

And she didn't mean Streatham Hill.

❊ ❊ ❊

Of course, it wasn't all song and dance. As soon as he heard that Gran had spoken, Neville was down in a flash and doing his best to take charge. We wouldn't let him. But Gran was nice to him, and I suppose that's what gave him the courage to ask.

'Mummy, should I bring the Quint for you?'

Mum was in the loo. I don't think he'd have dared to ask in her presence. Mum had turned quite cranky over the last few days, and belligerent; quite unlike herself. Lack of sleep, probably.

'The Quint?'

'Yes. You know, the stamp. The postage stamp.'

Gran's forehead wrinkled. 'Yeh … yeh … I remember now. The Quint, they call it. I been on TV with it. I hide it good an' proper.'

'You always liked looking at it. Shall I bring it for you?'

'Yeh, bring it over. Go on. Is nice to look at. Bring back memories.'

'Er … good. I'll bring it. But, um, could you tell me where to find it?'

'Find it? Yeh, of course, mus' be in my handbag. Probably. Where me handbag?'

'It's at home, Gran. We took it home. You think it's in there?' I frowned. I knew it wasn't. But I couldn't tell her that without admitting I'd searched for it. But then Gran frowned too.

'No, I remember now, is not in de handbag. I decide is too dangerous. I put it somewhere. Somewhere real, real safe, where nobody can get it.'

Neville's eyes literally gleamed with excitement.

'Good, good, you're remembering. Now just tell me where, and I'll get it.'

Gran's frown deepened as she thought about it. She scratched her temple, just below the bandage, as if trying to release a secret buried in her brain.

'"I can't remember right now,"' she said at last. '"But it gon' come to me soon. Don't worry, I know is a safe place. A safe, safe place."'

But Gran's super safe place remained out of reach of her memory. Neville had to return home unfulfilled.

They sent Gran home after a week, and still she could not remember.

'Once I is in me room, I gon' remember,' she said. But she didn't. She sat on her bed giving me orders as to where to search, but each potential hiding place turned up a blank. After two weeks of ever more frantic searches Gran had to admit it: she had lost the Quint.

'I always said you should put it in a bank safe,' was all Mum had to say on the matter. She seemed almost relieved that the stamp was gone. She was just too happy to care.

I was pretty distressed, but tried not to show it. All that drama, all those hopes, and all for nothing. Life couldn't get much bleaker. There had to be an upturn. Somewhere. I tried to think positive: at least Gran had survived, more or less intact.

Chapter Forty-two

Inky

Gran eventually told us the whole story of how Uncle Matt saved Rajan, and about the touch-and-go night at the hospital, and how Gran had given blood – Mum was amazed at that and fell all over Gran in gratitude – and how this hotshot brain surgeon from America had sent a plane over from America for Rajan and all kinds of stuff.

'Basmati flew over the next day,' said Gran. I noticed how her speech pattern had changed dramatically; she had dropped her heavy Creole accent, just as she had during the Old Girls' Reunion. I realised now how much of all that had gone before was play-acting on her part. I wondered why; I'd have to ask her some time. Later.

'We hired someone else to look after my parents, so she could be with him. And then she came back and I went over. We wanted one of us to be always with him, so Basmati and I alternated all the time he was in treatment and rehab. Uncle Matt paid for everything, Rika! Everything! He was so generous! And he got other doctors to work for free as well. Everyone was so wonderful, so generous with their time and their skills. They all did their best.'

'But he's brain-damaged,' I interjected. 'Was it worth the trouble? The expense? Wouldn't it have been better to let him die?'

After all, one has to be reasonable, rational. Sometimes it's better to let a person die, if the only alternative is a life not worth living. But obviously, I was alone with this opinion.

They both glared at me. The both exclaimed, in unison: 'Inky!'

'Life is precious,' said Gran firmly. 'And in his own way, he's happy.'

Whatever, I said to myself. I had my doubts, but it wasn't my place to speak out.

❊ ❊ ❊

The next two weeks flew by. Of course, I had to see Sal before I left. We had not met for several weeks, and I feared the friendship was crumbling amid the stress of his studies and, in my case, the on-going drama of the Quint, and then Granny's accident. Sal, who at first had been just as wrapped up in the mystery of the stamp, seemed to have withdrawn himself from my life completely. Looking back; that withdrawal had started just around the time of the *Daily Mail* article. And I missed him. Sal was the girlfriend I didn't have, and I needed him so much as a sounding block.

But all this time – nothing. No more Sunday visits, no more meals at Wong's. I hadn't noticed his absence in my life at first, wrapped up as I was in caring for Gran and keeping up with the rollercoaster of events. We'd had a short chat after Gran's recovery, but since then—nothing. Now I noticed his absence as a yawning hole in my life. I speed-dialled his number.

'Sal … can you come down here? Or shall I come up to you? I've got to see you,'

'Why? What's happening? More drama with Gran?' He sounded distant, cold even.

'Yes, it never ends!' I told him that we were going to Guyana for Christmas. It's then that I had my brainwave. The words just spilled out.

'Sal, why don't you come too? It would be brilliant to have you there! We could discover Guyana together! I'm so excited about going but with you there too it would be so much better! Go on, say yes!'

And I knew he would. Sal loved travel and discovering new places, especially off-the-beaten-track places. This trip would be just the thing for him, for us both; it would be a hundred times more exciting with him at my side.

'You'll come, won't you? You have to come!' I finished off.

The silence held so long I thought he had hung up on me.

'Sal?'

"Inky, I'd love to come. But sorry, I can't.'

'Why? Why not? Is it the money? Don't worry about that. We'll get it together somehow. Maybe your dad could lend you some. It's just the flight you have to pay for; we can live for free at our old family home. Go on, say yes!'

'I said, I can't, Inky. I really can't. You see ....'

The pause was so long that again I thought he'd hung up. But finally, he broke it.

'Cat's coming back,' he said. 'The week before Christmas. She doesn't like Australia, and she misses me. Didn't she tell you she was coming?'

Chapter Forty-three

Inky

It was pouring with rain and the middle of the night when we arrived at Cheddi Jagan International Airport. It took ages to inch ourselves through Immigration and Baggage Claim, but at last we emerged into the hot wet night, all around us, the hustle and bustle of people pushing overladen trolleys into the arms of overexcited relatives. Among the waiting throng stood a sodden man under a sodden umbrella holding up a sodden sign saying 'QINT'. Gran grumbled about a certain Evelyn who was 'too lazy to drive to the airport she-self' and contin-ued to grumble the whole drive down, as was her wont. Mum, meanwhile, had grown progressively more silent through the entire trip, as was *her* wont. Now, sitting next to me in the back seat of the taxi staring out the window, half-turned away from me, she retreated into complete silence. I don't know what she was staring at, since there was nothing to see but rain.

Rain! I'd never known a tropical rain, and this was the best of it. Water sluiced down in a virtual waterfall from above, gush-ing onto the taxi as if it were a rock it would sweep away in a mighty torrent. It was as if some giant in the sky had decided to open the heavenly floodgates. It hammered on the roof of the car and fell in sheets into the darkness outside, swallowing up the countryside. Through the window I could see not a thing but water, could hear not a thing but the roar on the rooftop and, drowned but unrestrained by the rainfall, the whine of Gran's perma-gripe, directed at the taxi driver.

The car moved slowly, its headlamps cutting a vague white funnel through the rain. The road appeared more as a river, and I wondered at one point if the car would simply sink into a torrent of water, never to be seen again. After a while Gran's nattering petered out; she had fallen asleep. And so had Mum, leaned against the far door of the back seat. Only I was wide awake, and, of course, hopefully, the driver. The driver turned up the radio; it was Bob Marley, 'No Woman No Cry'. The car bounced through the rain to the rhythm.

After a while the rain diminished and finally stopped, and we picked up speed. A penetrating, sickly sweet, nauseating smell attacked my nostrils. I thought the driver had let out an enormous fart, and he must have read my mind because I saw his twinkling eyes meet mine in the rear-view mirror. Seeing that I was awake he half-turned to me and said, 'Diamond Sugar Estate, ma'am. We very near Georgetown now.'

At those words Mum awoke with a jump and pressed her nose against her window, but of course there was nothing to be seen; outside the car it was all still black, though there now seemed a certain greyness to the night signifying that dawn was just over the horizon. Up to this point excitement had kept me wide awake, but now drowsiness crept through me, and I nodded off. Mum spoke her first words to me since we'd left the plane:

'Inky, why not lie down, put your head on my lap. It's not far now.'

I was tempted; but if Georgetown was 'not far now' and if the rain had stopped and it was going to be lighter there was no way I'd sleep away my arrival. I assumed there'd be a bed waiting for me at 'home'; until then I wanted to stay awake.

Slowly the darkness began to lift and I could see the outlines of a village, a quaint gathering of frail wooden houses on stilts so thin they looked about to buckle at the knees under their burdens. The houses were completed with rickety staircases, rusty tin roofs, louvre windows with half the lathes missing, and they sat in yards and gardens teeming with growth, all bathed in the unearthly grey light of pre-dawn. The rain had left great expanses of water so that some of the houses seemed to be standing in shallow lakes, while others, built lower and close to the road, huddled in sodden clumps behind overflowing gutters.

A sense of complete alienation washed through me, chilling and somewhat frightening. What was I doing here? This was not my country, not my home. Homesickness flooded me, a deep longing for the familiar colours and smells and noises of Streatham High Street; a longing for Sal. Where was he, what was he doing? Was he back with that bitch Cat, happy at last, all memory of me erased? A deep, ugly, surge of jealousy gripped me. *He's mine!* I yelled silently at Cat. *You dumped him and I caught him! How dare you claim him back!*

Ever since Sal told me about Cat's return it had been there, coiling around my heart like a vine of thorns: jealousy. And behind that jealousy, deep down, something else. Something I didn't want to admit. Not even to myself. But I had to.

Love. I loved Sal. Maybe, I always had. And the moment I realised it I wanted to tell him. I wanted to call him and shout it down the phone. So many times, in the days before our departure, I'd stared at his name in my mobile, thumb poised above the dial button. But I couldn't. I was too proud, or, maybe, too scared. What if he rejected me? He was Cat's. I'd had my chance and messed it up. Even on the drive to the airport I'd toyed with the temptation; sitting on the plane, waiting to leave. And then I'd taken the plunge. Not called him – I was too much of a coward for that. I'd tapped a message into my phone. Three words. Three words that said it all. And pressed *send.* And switched off my phone.

I loved him and wanted him. I wanted him right here with me, holding my hand, gazing out the window with me as village and countryside gradually morphed into the wider streets and great white buildings of Georgetown.

❀ ❀ ❀

I recognised Central Georgetown from photos I had seen; the Town Hall, the Parliament Building, the Bank of Guyana. I recognised the tree-lined avenue of Main Street, seen up to now only in photos on the Internet. But how familiar!

A few minutes later the taxi drew up outside the huge wooden house I'd seen in Gran's photos. It was enormous; the photos had not conveyed the sheer bulk of the place, overpowering and commanding, nor the sense of eccentricity captured by its quirky architecture, bits sticking up and bits sticking out. It looked top-heavy, too weighty for the thick columns on which it rested; it perched like a giant bird between folded wings, ready to fly away. A dog barked, and lurched towards the closed gate where it leaped and snarled in welcome.

I fell in love with that house at first sight.

The taxi driver gave three short blasts of the horn as we drove up. Gran opened her car door and just sat there in the front seat waiting to be helped out, apparently still too tired to speak. Mum crawled out of the back seat and helped her out. I got out myself and looked up at the house again and saw a face at a top window. A few seconds later the front floor at the top of the outside staircase opened and a plump woman in a flimsy nightdress, her hair bobbing on her shoulders in two fat plaits, hurried down the stairs, huffing with excitement. She hauled the dog away (his name, I gathered, was Turtle) and tethered him to a leash under the house, and then bustled out of the gate.

'Granny! Granny! Welcome home!' she cried, as she ran to the taxi. This must be the notoriously lazy Evelyn who had sent the taxi instead of driving up to meet us: Aunt Marion's daughter, Gran's granddaughter, Mum's niece, my first cousin,

though several years older than me. She flung open the taxi
door, bent down, and hugged Gran. She was at least three
times Gran's size, and I thought she'd smother the poor thing.
Gran let out a little yelp that sounded like 'help' but could just
as well have been 'hello'.

By this time I was round the car and standing next to them,
and so it was my turn to be folded into that voluminous embrace. As Evelyn, a virtual stranger to me, closed me in her
arms with another whoop of delight I found my initial distaste,
and the inclination to push her away, shift away in favour of a
kind of shy pleasure. This kind of familial affection was totally
foreign to me, but it seemed to have a disarming power; there
was something so warm, so genuine, and so innocent about it I
couldn't help but be touched. I smiled back at Evelyn.

'You gon' to love Guyana!' she said to me, still holding me.
'I so *happy* you came! Families belong together! I gon' to show
you around Georgetown as soon as I can!'

Chapter Forty-four

Inky

Evelyn showed me a bed and I fell onto it and didn't awake until – well, I had no idea. The room was dark, the wooden shutters closed, but the louvres were open and through the slots slashes of bright sunlight fell into the room, leaving a striped pattern on the wooden floorboards. I remembered. In the foggy minutes before I fell asleep, Evelyn had unfurled a mosquito net from above and tucked it into the sides of the bed; now, it had been untucked and was curled into a bulky knot hanging above my head. My watch was no help; it said 4.23 but that was English time and I wasn't sure of the time difference. Four hours? Five? Six?

I rolled to the edge of the bed to grab my handbag from the bedside table. Still groggy with sleep, I fumbled in it until my fingers found the flat metal of my mobile phone. I had a missed call, from Sal. My heart leaped. Ignoring the expense I immediately tried to call back but there was no reception. It must have arrived in the seconds before I switched off the phone at Gatwick.

I needed a pee. I stumbled to my feet and headed for the door; I vaguely remembered the bathroom was on the other side of the hallway. Sunlight streamed into the white tiled room from an open window, and a fresh breeze against my skin made me realise how hot and clammy I was from the journey and from sleep. I peeled off the T-shirt I'd slept in and stepped into the shower. A delicious cascade of cool water sloshed away the skin of sloth and dried sweat and fatigue clinging to my body. I washed my hair with the remains of a bottle of shampoo, rinsed away the foam, and dried myself with a huge fluffy towel. Wrapped in the towel, I returned to my room.

Behind the open sash window was the slanting top-hung shutter known here as a Demerara window. I pushed it open with its pole. A panorama of green treetops and red roofs and blue sky dotted with two or three small, fleecy clouds greeted me. The pert call of a bird: *kiss-kiss-kiskadee* over and over again, gave an unexpected lift to my heart, a clean, joyful refrain that filled me with hope. It was a kiskadee, I later learned: a little yellow bird calling, according to the French, *'Qu'est qu'il dit?'* The call filled me with delight – I felt a sense of home unlike any I had had before.

And, I realised now, I was hungry, and surely that was coffee in the air?

I turned away from the window, got dressed, and went downstairs. Seated around the dining table were several women, a few children, and a man.

Evelyn sprang to her feet as I walked into the dining room, a corner of the huge open-plan ground floor. She rushed over to me with a cry of joy, took my hand and led me over to the one empty chair. Only after I'd taken a seat did the identity of my table companions register.

'Hello Inky!' Mum said breezily. 'Slept well?'

'You not going to say hello, Inky?' said a familiar alto voice. I looked up.

'Marion!' I cried, jumping to my feet and running to her chair to hug her. 'What are *you* doing here?'

'Last minute decision,' Marion said. 'I've been fighting the urge to come back ever since I heard you all were coming. Yesterday I gave in and jumped on a plane. I arrived a couple of hours ago. I haven't even gone to my room yet – see?'

She gestured to a corner of the drawing room, to a cluster of luggage.

'I gotta go!' said Gran, speaking for the first time. 'T'ings to do.' She was speaking Creolese again. She pushed her wheel-chair away from the table and rolled off, disappearing into the hallway. The rooms here were huge; plenty of room for a wheelchair, plenty of turning circles. Evelyn and Marion were chattering away, telling me of all the plans they had to show me around.

'May I interrupt to introduce myself – David, Evelyn's hus-band,' said the one man at the table. I had hardly glanced at him until now, as he half rose to offer me his hand from across the table.

I took his hand. We smiled at each other; he was a good-looking man of some kind of obscure racial mixture; brown skin, tight black curly hair, a pleasant white-toothed grin. He waved in the general direction of the children.

'And these are Alison and Nicholas!' I smiled down at the two of them, shook their hands.

'Ally,' and 'Nick,' they said simultaneously, correcting their father. With that, breakfast conversation turned to the general chit-chat of family reunions after long separations.

After breakfast Mum said to me,

'Would you like me to show you the house, Inky?' and of course I said yes. And so she took me around, up and down stairs.

I noticed she omitted the Annex.

❊ ❊ ❊

'And this,' Mum said, 'is my very favourite place in the whole house. Follow me.'

She began to climb a narrow spiral staircase, which lead into a dome of light. It was a round, window-lined room, with wooden floorboards and a peaked roof. The view was spectacular; a canopy of green from the trees, interspersed with red and silver roofs. In the distance, the Atlantic sparkled silver and grey up to the horizon. The sky was in touching distance. A kiskadee chirruped. It was breathtaking.

'The Cupola!' Mum announced. 'I used to spend hours up here, writing in my diary, writing short stories, dreaming of goodness knows what. I loved this place.'

She bent down, fiddled a bit with a floorboard, lifted it up, and laughed. She lifted what seemed like a bug-eaten ancient child's exercise book aloft.

'The novels I used to write!'

She replaced the book with a chuckle and stood up. She closed her eyes and turned in a slow circle, arms spread wide, as if recalling the past. When she stopped rotating she was facing inland, away from the sea. She opened her eyes, and the light fled from her face. She was staring at a house half-hidden in the foliage; there seemed to be a cleft among the trees between our house and that one, giving us an open view.

Mum gazed at the house, almost as if she were in a trance. And then she took a deep, audible breath.

'Inky, this is it. I need to be alone for a while. I'm going into the Annex. It's time.'

She turned away and walked back down the stairs. At the bottom, she turned into the corridor that led to the Annex, a room separate from the house but joined to it by a sort of covered bridge.

Chapter Forty-five

Rika

Rajan was alive!

Rika threw herself onto her bed, just as she had so many years ago, and wept, just as she had so many years ago. But now she wept for joy, relief and gratitude.

If only she had known! If only she had not been such a coward, if only she had stayed: she would have spared herself so much heartache, so much pain! It would have been she who had gone with Rajan to America, she who would have held his hand through all the medical procedures. Well, Basmati too, of course, but she would have been there, at his side, helping him through.

But.

Had she not run away she would not have travelled South America. She would not have gone to India, stayed in that wonderful Ashram, learned all the things she had, turned her life around. She would not have married Eddy, not have had Inky.

She went to the window, and looked down. She saw it all, just as it had been that night; Rajan, the spike through his head, the blood. She saw it in her mind's eye, without fear, without horror. Within her there was only calm.

She laughed to herself. What a fool, what a bloody fool she had been! Rajan had been alive, all the time, and she had conjured up some spirit-Rajan, some placebo Rajan; an imaginary voice, an imaginary anchor.

Rajan, an angel! A saint, up in heaven! What nonsense! Those voices she had heard, thinking they came from him!

They came from her! They were the voices of her own strength, her own true self, her own guiding spirit! She had been listening to herself! Everything she had sought in that fake Rajan, had been right here, inside her! What a travesty! Yet, maybe, it had been necessary. Maybe she had needed that spirit-Rajan, a familiar image, a face, a form, to cling to, to keep her steady? But what did it matter. Here she was, and all was well. No fear, no horror, no Beast.

Everything was right, just the way it was. Everything had fallen into place. And Rajan was alive!

She turned away from the window and returned to the dining room.

'When can we go and see Rajan?' she said.

Chapter Forty-six

Inky

Marion, Gran, and I were sitting in the gallery drinking coffee and chatting when Mum returned. Ever since she had found out about Rajan's survival something about her was different. I couldn't put my finger on it. It was as if some hidden darkness had vanished from her spirit, and I suppose that's exactly what had happened. The shadow of Rajan's supposed death had left her. But now, as she returned from the Annex, she was different again. This time, it was not that something had left her. She had gained something: a sense of complete peace emanated from her. Peace, and a highly contagious exultation.

'When can we go and see Rajan?' she said.

'Don't you want to rest for a day?' Evelyn asked. 'Settle in? Get rid of your jet lag?'

'No,' said Mum. 'I want to go today. Inky can stay if she wants to. I'm going.'

'I'm coming too!' I cried. What jet lag? I was energized as never before, longing for movement and adventure and discovery.

We had already learned that Rajan no longer lived in the old house in Waterloo Street; that had been rented out for several years. Rajan and Basmati had gone up to the County of Essequibo after his return from the USA, and were living on his grandparents' farm on the Pomeroon River. So it was there we had to go, Mum, Marion, and I.

Of course I would go to the Essequibo!

❊ ❊ ❊

It was a long trip, and I discovered on the way just how Guyana got its name: the word 'Guiana' means Land of Many Waters, as apt a name as could be.

First we had to drive back up the East Bank of the Demerara River, the way we had travelled last night from the airport. As Georgetown straggled out, the car turned to the right and we found ourselves at the dock of a floating bridge, a pontoon bridge, as Marion explained, across the river. On the other side we drove for about an hour, up to a small town called Parika on the next big river, bigger even than the Demerara: the Essequibo.

At Parika's wharf we climbed down some rickety stairs and into a small boat that slowly filled with other passengers; we were handed life jackets and a moment later we were speeding across the river, the boat almost upended as it tore across the water. It took a long while, as the Essequibo is twenty kilometres across at its mouth, and by the time we reached Supenaam on the far bank we were all soaked through, but laughing.

Then it was into another car, and a drive along the coast to Charity; up a little further, and we had arrived at Rajan's home.

❊ ❊ ❊

The farm was a place of exceeding beauty, on the east bank of the Pomeroon River. We stepped from the taxi into a wide-open space covered with white sand and dotted with flowering bushes, hibiscus and oleander. At the centre was a large wooden two-story house, surrounded by banana trees. To the left, at the edge of the sandy area, was the rainforest, and before us, stretching off beyond the cleared space, coconut trees, tall palms reaching out into the distance. To the right was the river.

Beyond the main house was a cottage, painted a fresh cobalt blue with mango-yellow shutters and door, and mango-yellow railings on the wraparound veranda. Unlike the main house, which was on high stilts as tradition demanded, the cottage was built just a little above ground level. A short flight of stairs as well as a ramp led up to the veranda. A concrete path led up to the cottage.

'Rajan's brother lives in the big house with his family,' explained Marion, 'and Basmati. Rajan has a personal carer who looks after him, an Amerindian from a nearby village. He's in the best hands he could possibly be.'

As we walked past the big house a couple of half-naked children ran out to greet us, laughing and grabbing hold of our hands. A woman's voice called them back; I looked up to see her, in the window, smiling and waving to us and reprimanding the children to leave us alone. We continued on to the cottage.

Another woman a few years older than me, a baby on her hips, came hurrying down the stairs of the big house. She was an Amerindian, her long black hair falling in a silky sheet over her shoulders. She trotted up to us, smiling.

'Come with me!' she said, and led the way to the cottage. We walked up the stairs to the veranda.

'He usually sits at the back,' said the woman, whose name, we learned, was Rosa, and she led the way around.

Mum's arms were folded over her chest and her face was a mask, unreadable. She seemed to have withdrawn into herself, like a turtle; her elation gone, to be replaced by trepidation. She said nothing as we followed Rosa around the corner of the cottage. Here, the veranda expanded, forming a little open-air room.

Three people were in the room. An Amerindian man sat on the floor cleaning a fish. A thin grey-haired man sat in an armchair, and a plump, much older, white-haired Indian woman sat next to him, leaning into him, an open book in her hand.

She closed it, and a glance at the cover told me it was a book about birds.

The man looked up when we approached.

I had never seen a face like his. Was he a child or a man, or both? Indeed, all the beauty and purity and total guilelessness of childhood seemed to shine through the outer veneer of middle age. He was beautiful. No other word for it. His face shone with that subtle beauty that shines from within rather than from the symmetry of external features. For, while his features were indeed well balanced, they were marred by an ugly scar, a puckering of flesh on his right temple. And yet the overall impression was beauty, and that beauty turned to perfection when his eyes fell on Mum, and that shine turned to radiance, as if the form that enclosed him was but an effigy, and the real life lay beyond.

He spoke, or tried to speak, but those emerging sounds spoiled the first impression of perfect beauty, for they were guttural, ugly sounds, grunts rather than words. He held out both arms to her.

Mum simply cried out something indistinct, and fell to her knees before him. He leaned forward, she leaned up, and their arms encircled each other and pulled each other close. Mum buried her face in his neck, and she sobbed, great, heaving sobs that shook her body from top to bottom.

I wanted to cry too. Marion wiped tears from her eyes with the back of her hand, and turned away, as if it was all too much for her.

When they drew apart I saw the man's face again, and his eyes were the only dry ones in the room, his smile the only one. Everyone else looked miserable. Especially Mum, when at last she turned around. Holding the man's hand in both her own, she murmured:

'Rajan, oh Rajan. All these years … I thought you were dead … I'm sorry. So sorry.' she buried her face in his shoulder, drew back, and said again: 'I thought you were dead, Rajan, I thought you were gone: Oh I wish, I wish – I'd have come back long ago. I'm so sorry.'

She looked now at the old woman.

'Basmati? You! *You* could have written me, said something. Why didn't anyone *say?*'

That last word, *say,* was a cry of despair, an accusation aimed at all of us, at God, at the entire universe; a wail of utter desolation.

'Now, Rika, don't start blaming Basmati! It's all your fault for not reading Gran's letter! How could we know you hadn't read it? When you didn't reply we thought you couldn't bear it, couldn't bear the thought of him being – you know. Like this.'

She gestured towards Rajan, and Mum just hugged him again, and he hugged her back.

Marion continued. 'You were married, with a young child. We assumed you had decided to put Rajan, the accident, behind you. Not forgive Gran, as we had all hoped you would.'

Mum looked down. 'I know. It was my fault from running away in the first place. That was so ... cowardly.'

'Cowardly! I can't imagine making my way *alone* through South America! At sixteen! And then to India!' said Marion. She reached out to stroke Rika's back. 'You're not a coward ... that was terribly brave, in a different way.'

'It was pure flight, Marion. It wasn't bravery at all. I ran away.'

'Why didn't you stay, to check if Rajan was alive?' I asked. Mum glared at me.

'Inky! I was sixteen! Of course I assumed he was dead! He had a pole sticking out of his bloody head!'

'But, Mum, there was a doctor in the house! You could have ...'

'Uncle Matt wasn't a doctor to me. I was sixteen! Uncle Matt was just my beloved uncle, my Godfather, who came in his holidays bearing gifts and being nice to me. I never knew him as a doctor, not at all. Why would I think of him as a doctor at a time like this?'

'But you could have waited for the ambulance?'

'Ambulance? What ambulance? One of Mummy's pet peeves was the unreliability of emergency services. People died every week because of ambulances never turning up. This wasn't modern day UK, Inky. This was brain-drained Guyana of the late sixties. Nothing worked.'

She sighed.

'To me, he was just dead. And there was only one thing to do: flee from that house of horror.'

'Your parents must have been worried sick!'

Marion nodded. 'Mummy was frantic, Rika. We were all frantic!'

Chapter Forty-seven

Rika

And at last she was alone with him. Inside the cottage his room was large, light and airy, with windows on three sides. A glass door led onto the west veranda, overlooking the river and the small dock leading out on to the water. Two boats were moored to the dock. Rika imagined Rajan as a boy, living here, going to school by boat. Growing up, falling in love with Fatima. Learning the skills of gardening and farming, learning to scale coconut trees barehanded and barefoot.

Inside, the wooden walls were painted a paler shade of yellow; pretty landscape paintings, Guyanese art, hung here and there on the walls, with now and then a portrait. Her own portrait hung in place of honour, above the bed.

He sat on a Morris chair across the room from the bed. She walked across and pulled up a pouffe so to sit right next to his knees, placed her hands on his thigh. He turned to smile at her.

'Oh, Rajan!' she sighed, overwhelmed with sadness. He laid a hand on hers, then looked up to point at her portrait. Then he pointed to her.

'You!' he said. 'Rika.' His smile widened.

'Yes. That's me.' She bowed her head and laid her forehead against his hand. And then it came. In a rush. All the mourning and the grief and the horror of the years gone by, mixed in with all the relief and the joy and the gladness and the gratitude of the now; it all passed through her in waves that swelled and surged, rose and sank. Her body heaved to the outpouring of all that she had pushed beneath the earth of her being; it shook as that earth quaked and gashed wide and all the pain found freedom and all the joy release.

Rajan placed a hand on her head. On and on rolled the waves, like the tide of an ocean coming from the dark, waxing and crashing on the shore of her awareness. It seemed to never end. She gave herself into it, let it happen. For too long, she had controlled this underground torrent. Too long she had held it back, and now there was no reason to do so. The Beast was free, and it was not ugly after all, not bloody and fearsome, but benign and transforming, taking with it the burden of the years as it escaped into the light.

Gradually, finally, the waves subsided until all that was left was an occasional shudder. Her face was still buried on Rajan's thigh, his hand still on her head, like a blessing.

He spoke, a whisper.

'Rika!'

She looked up, and met his gaze. She sat up then, straightened her back, still holding his gaze. Her hands on his thigh opened and his slid into them.

He was still smiling, but differently. It was a serious kind of smile, and it was centred not on his lips but in his eyes. They held hers.

She could not look away. In those eyes there was so much – so much – what? What was it in those eyes? Something simple and straight and so very eloquent. There was only one word for it: love. Love, unfiltered and uncontaminated.

Not the kind of romantic love she had seen in his eyes that last night they were together. No; this was a different kind of love; that of a brother for a sister, perhaps, or of the dearest kind of friend, a simple love that is complete in itself.

Within her something else heaved, and it was her own love, coming from a source deep inside herself and rising up to meet his own. And her love, too, was no more the love of a woman for a man. There was no desire in it, no wanting. Her love, too, was that of a sister for a brother, or for the dearest kind of friend. There was no passion in this love, rather a deep calmness and a sense of *coming home.*

She was content.

And then the spell was broken, for Rajan's smile widened and he let go of her hands and placed his on either side of her cheeks.

'Oh, Rajan!' she cried, this time in joy, and leaned into him and his arms pulled her close and then encircled her. She buried her face in his shoulder in an embrace that said all that need to be said, more clearly than the words they would never speak to each other.

❊ ❊ ❊

Later, she helped him into his wheelchair and pushed him down the ramp and into the garden. The concrete path led across the hot white sand between the houses and into the cultivated area of the garden. Rajan pointed and grunted to show Rika where to wheel him. He wanted to be taken among the rose bushes, and when they were there, he signalled for her to help him out of the chair. He stood on his feet, wavering a bit, and bent over to remove a pair of secateurs from a pocket in the chair; with that in his hand, he tottered forward towards a particularly flourishing rose bush. His legs seemed to be made of rubber; his knees gave but always he caught himself and though his movements were jerky, uncoordinated, he made it.

Rika was right beside him; she wanted to reach out to support him, but some instinct held her back. Rajan could do this. She watched, holding her breath, as he opened the secateurs. His right hand shook and jerked as he brought them up to the stem of a half-open rose, placed its stem in the V of the blade. Snip! His fingers closed over the handles and the rose bowed down towards him; he took it in his left hand.

Rose in the left hand, secateurs in the right hand, he waddled back to the chair, Rika at his side, longing to reach out to hold him steady, but holding back. With jerky, uncoordinated movements he replaced the secateurs in its pocket, took the rose in his right. He held it out to Rika, and the smile on his lips and in his eyes was brighter than the daylight.

Chapter Forty-eight

Inky

We stayed the night in the big house and Marion and I returned to Georgetown the next day. Mummy stayed behind; for a few days, she said, to get to know Rajan again.

She returned after three days, and that very evening, at supper, Gran delivered the Grand Finale. She reached into her bra and pulled out a tiny plastic zip-lock bag. I knew that little bag. I knew its contents.

Gran handed it to Mum.

'Here you are, Rika,' she said. 'It's yours.'

Mum's jaw dropped. 'You're giving it to me?' Her expression changed, softened. 'Mum – you don't have to. I know you're sorry and so am I. You don't have to somehow pay me back. We both made mistakes. It's all behind us now. The stamp is yours; I know how much you value it.'

She pushed Gran's hand away. Gran waved it at her in annoyance.

'Take the damned t'ing! Is yours!'

'Leave it to me in your Will, if you insist,' said Mum. I personally thought she was being stubborn all over again. If Gran was giving it, why refuse? There was the answer to all her problems, and she was turning it away! I shook my head in disgust.

'Rika! You din' hear me? The t'ing belong to you! Is yours already!'

Marion laughed out loud.

'You better tell her, Mummy, or else she never going to take it. Put it down and tell her.'

Gran obeyed. She laid the plastic zip-lock bag on the middle of the table and finished off the story.

'I told you Uncle Matt arranged for Rajan's treatment, right? It was damned expensive. But that Professor Cohen, he led the team and he wouldn't take any money. And other doctors too, donated their work, and Matt led a fund-raising drive – and anyway, it was done, thanks to Matt. He picked up all the expenses that weren't covered. We couldn't thank him enough. So – Daddy gave him the stamp.'

'Daddy gave Uncle Matt the stamp? His precious stamp?'

'Yes. Matt had always coveted the stamp. He had been offering to buy it for years, for decades. He kept raising the offer, but Humphrey wouldn't sell. Now, he just gave it. As a thank you for all that Matt had done.'

Marion chuckled. 'Uncle Matt didn't even want to take it! It was so funny! But Daddy just sent it, with FedEx. He insisted.'

Mum gave a little gasp of amazement. 'He did that, for Rajan? Gave away his most precious possession?'

'For Rajan, and for you. You were gone; we hadn't heard from you in weeks by that time, but we kept hoping, hoping. And when you turned up, or when you contacted us, we wanted to tell you that Rajan was alive; we thought that would lure you back. Rajan's life was precious, but so were you. What was a little stamp in comparison? As you keep saying, Rika: it was only a little scrap of paper. Humphrey saw that now.'

'Wow!' was all Mum could say. Her eyes were moist. 'But then – if it's Uncle Matt's, why do you say it's mine?'

'He gave it back,' said Gran. 'When he finally accepted it, it was under a gentleman's agreement – no paperwork involved. He wanted it to come back to Daddy, to the Quint family, eventually. He knew how much Humphrey loved that stamp, and he wanted it to return to our family, rather than become an object of auctions and greed and escalating prices. It was in

Matt's Will; that the stamp should come to Humphrey. But then Humphrey died. Before him.'

She looked at Mum. 'After Humphrey died, the stamp didn't have anyone to love it any more. But there was you, Rika. You're Matt's Godchild. He was always close to you; he doesn't have any daughters of his own, just the three sons. So he put you in his Will instead of Humphrey. That's the thing I was supposed to tell you.'

'So Uncle Matt died too? So many people died and I never said goodbye …'

Mum's buried her face in her hands. She seemed more bothered by Uncle Matt's death than delighted by the fact that the stamp was hers.

Gran seemed overcome with emotion, a thing I'd never seen before. On the verge of tears. Gran, my stalwart, heart-of-steel Gran! So Marion took over the story.

'No. Rika. Uncle Matt was diagnosed with pancreatic cancer a few months ago. No chance of survival. So he sent the stamp back to us to pass on to you. He knew you had moved home in the UK and didn't have your new address. So he sent it to Gran – via FedEx, insured to the hilt – explaining that it was for you in lieu of an inheritance; it was cheaper and less hassle that way, less complicated. There wasn't any paperwork about a sale or a gift to him anyway. You could sell it or keep it or do with it what you wanted.'

Gran had by now collected herself and took up the story again. 'I was supposed to tell you and pass it on. I wanted to give you the stamp and tell you the story and make everything right again.'

'So Uncle Matt – he's still alive?'

'Yes. So it seems,' said Marion. 'I'm in touch with his family – they promised to let me know as soon as – well, when he goes.'

'I need to see him,' said Mum. 'I need to go – to thank him. Before it's too late.'

I had to put in a word here.

'But why didn't you tell us right away, Gran? About the stamp, I mean. That it belongs to Mum? Why this whole theatre about finding an heir and all that?'

'Rika's fault.' Gran looked at Mum, almost accusingly. 'You seemed so indifferent; to me, to the stamp – hostile, even. I tried to get you interested but the more I talked about the stamp the more you rejected it. My lovely surprise: all spoilt! I couldn't get through to you. So I tried, I tried so hard, to make you realise how valuable it was. What it meant to your Daddy. I even tried to make you jealous, by pretending to look for an heir.'

Gran suddenly switched moods. She gave me a sly look.

'And Inky. So excited! An ol' lady got to have she fun!' she said. 'You t'ink I didn't see how much you wanted it? Coveted it? The greed shinin' in you eyes? I had to tease you a lil bit. Cat an' mouse.'

But then she turned serious again, dropped the game and the accent.

'Nothing worked. Rika was indifferent to everything.'

'Mummy! If you'd told me then what you have just told me now, about Rajan and how it paid for his surgery instead of playing stupid games I might not have been indifferent. How Daddy gave up his most precious possession for the surgery.' Mum, eyes more moist than ever, was looking at Gran with a strange expression, as if she were seeing her for the first time.

'But – but, I couldn't tell you that either! You hadn't replied to my letter. You hadn't forgiven me, I thought. You'd said you didn't want to hear *one word more* about that night. There's so much history attached to that stamp. It played such a role in Rajan's recovery … I didn't want to just hand it over without you knowing the whole story … you had to know! But I couldn't find the words. I couldn't break the ice. In the end we all thought, that is, Marion and I and everyone, that you had to *see* Rajan for yourself first. That brain damage doesn't mean a person is worthless. Then you'd understand. We wanted to bring you here. But you wouldn't come, you refused.'

'Still – you should have told me! Right away!'

'Rika, stop complaining; stop blaming Mummy,' said Marion firmly. 'You have *no idea!* I mean, I was just a child at the time but Mummy was beside herself with desperation. Frantic about Rajan's survival, frantic about your disappearance, longing to hear from you, worried about you, alone in Brazil, a teenager with no experience of life. And then you didn't write to us – not properly – again for over a decade. We didn't even have a return address for you till Inky was born; that seemed to calm you down a little.

'You just *vanished* out of our lives. We couldn't tell you about Granny's death and Daddy's death. And Gran van Dam's too, of course. And all the family things like births and marriages. It's as if you didn't care a damn about us; you'd withdrawn from all of us, abandoned us. And then when you did write us you insisted on not speaking a word about 'what happened'. No mention of it, you said. So we thought very well, that's probably for the best. You were married with a new baby; maybe it was better to put the past behind us. Like Granny always said.'

Mum, by now thoroughly put in her place, bowed her head. She said nothing. It seemed to me that Marion was right. Mum had wallowed in a lake of self-pity all these years, never asking after the lives of those she had left behind – those who had loved and cared for her.

'In the end, the mountain had to go to Mohammed,' Marion said. 'Mummy moved to London, with the sole aim of giving you the stamp. But she couldn't.'

'The wall!' Gran said. 'The wall was too high! I had to break down the wall but I couldn't! Because the wall was in you, Rika. You couldn't forgive. Yes, you tried to do your duty on the surface. But I knew you hadn't forgiven me.'

'She's a lot like you in that, Mummy. You can't forgive either.'

Gran gave Marion a nod of acknowledgement and continued.

'In you, Rika, I saw history repeating itself. We both lost the love of our life, violently and suddenly; and we both stewed in our own private broths of misery for decades; and I knew we had to climb out, but how? I couldn't find the words. I found myself in a stupid charade, trying to provoke you into some kind of – I don't know. Some kind of direct accusation. But you just wouldn't let it happen.

'After my accident I realised how short life was. It can be snuffed out in a moment. We *had* to get this done. I knew there was no way around it, and talking wasn't the answer. You had to come back and face everything and meet Rajan. By force if necessary.'

She cackled then, the familiar old Gran-cackle. I saw a smile play on Mum's lips.

She turned to Gran. Her eyes were big and soft, and her whole face seemed to glow from within with warmth and contentment. She rose from her chair, and, just as she'd done with Rajan earlier in the day, she knelt on the floor before Gran and took her hands in hers. Gran leaned forward; Mum rose up to meet her and the two of them simply melted into each other. I couldn't bear it. Too much lovey-dovey for me. I got up and left the room. It was the only way to keep my eyes dry.

Chapter Forty-nine

Dorothea

It was over. Her work was done, and she was weary. Weary, but satisfied.

Dorothea was a woman of action. She was not given to introspection. She had no time for dreamers and navel-gazers, which, perhaps, had been the whole problem with Rika, who was her very opposite.

But now, alone in her old room, she lay on her bed and closed her eyes. It was time to recapitulate it all. And her whole life, it seemed, had, in fact, been driven by feelings. Actions had their roots in feelings.

The suppressed anger of her youth.

The bliss of first love.

The anxiety of the war years; the anguish at Freddy's disappearance, the joy of his return.

Her utter devastation at his death, turning into yet more fear.

The fear of loving too much, for love inevitably means loss.

Dorothea had built an armour around her heart, and with that in place she had battled the world, and repaired it.

She had not repaired herself. She had thought herself strong, but she was only hard, and hardness can hurt. *Had* hurt. Hurt Rika, the child she had feared to love too much. She had pushed Rika away, failed to understand her. Failed her.

And then there was Rajan's accident. The utter turmoil of that night of horror: worse, even, than the night of Freddy's death. The agony of fear; the spark of hope; her heart cracking open to release the pent up fear, and love, and anguish. The fervour of prayer, the agonised cry of her soul; *make me whole!*

After that everything had changed; her actions no longer driven by anger and fear, but by something else, deep and real and thoroughly fulfilling.

Just one thing missing: Rika's forgiveness.

Now, she had that too.

She smiled to herself, and opened her eyes. They fell upon a framed photo on the wall opposite. In the picture were two slim young men, bright eyed and smiling, their arms around each other, one dark, one fair; one in uniform, one in civilians. Smiling at the camera, the day before the ship set sail taking Freddy off to war.

Dorothea stood up and, without using her cane, limped over to the wall, took down the photo, returned to the bed. There, she gazed at the photo, kissed it twice. Smiled, and lay down again, her hand clasping the photo to her breast. She took a deep breath. Then let out the longest sigh of her life.

Chapter Fifty

Inky

There was that bird again, chirruping outside my bedroom window: *Kiskadee! Kiskadee! Kiss-kiss-kisskadee!* Joyful, fresh and carefree, which was exactly how I felt on this, my second morning in Lamaha Street. I lay enclosed in my mosquito net tent, last night's drama playing over and over again in my mind. Relaxed, at ease, at home in myself; smiling into the half-light, I hugged my pillow in glee as I looked forward to what the new day might bring, now that we'd all walked out of yesterday's shadows.

Marion had promised me all sorts of delights; a trip to Kaietuer Falls, in the Interior; a visit to a rainforest resort on a creek in the Essequibo District; wild animals in the Nature Reserve and a dash up to Diane McTurk's otter refuge in the Rupununi. And then, of course, there was Christmas coming up – a grand Quint family Christmas, my first! All that to be squeezed into the three weeks before my flight back to England.

At that thought my smile faded and a dark fist grabbed hold of my belly. At home, there'd be Sal and Cat, revelling in their reunion and reawakened love, wanting to share it all with me. How was I to deal with that? *Sal, Sal, why didn't I realise? Why didn't I speak my mind, my heart?* It was a dull sickness inside me, an inner ache that not even the unalloyed joy of the kiskadee's song could dispel. I reached under the mosquito net for my mobile on the bedside table, switched it on: again no signal. I reckoned there'd never be a signal out here and switched it off. I clambered out of the net and perhaps a little too violently pulled it from the mattress. Maybe there was an Internet Café somewhere I could use. I'd email him and see what was up. No. I wouldn't. I couldn't. It was over and I had to accept that.

There was a soft tap at the door and it opened gently. Marion poked in her head.

'Ah, you're up! Morning, Inky. Sleep well?'

'Like a baby!' I said, and pushed my heartache away. 'I'll be down in a sec. What are we doing today?'

Marion didn't reply at first, so I looked up. Her face seemed drained, empty, yet her eyes so full it made me stop and take a second look.

'Marion? Are you OK? Is something the matter?'

'Yes, actually, there is.' She came into the room then and took hold of my two hands. 'Inky – Gran died last night, in her sleep. It's all a bit – sudden.'

In spite of the morning warmth I went all cold, and my knees gave way. I sprang out of bed.

'No – I don't believe it – she can't be! She wasn't ill or anything! Last night she …'

And then I knew it was true and a great gulf opened in my being and I fell into it. I sank back down to the bed and began to sob, sob and sob for everything I had lost and now could never recover. I cried for Gran and her lost love, I cried for the burden she had carried so many years and finally laid down last night. I cried for the young girl who still lived in an old woman's body, the young girl who should have been my friend but who I rejected because I only saw the old woman.

Marion came and sat down next to me. She put an arm around me and said,

'Don't be sad, Inky; she was ready to go and she's in a good place. Come and have a look at her.'

I resisted. I could not bear to look at Gran as a corpse, the life and energy of her gone forever. I shook my head and pressed the heels of my hands into my eyes as if to stop the tears. But Marion wasn't having it. Her voice became brisk and no-nonsense; she got up and pulled me to my feet.

'Girl, you coming down with me if I got to carry you there meself.' And so she led me down the stairs to Gran's room, a small one just off the stairwell. Mum was there already, sitting on a chair next to the bed. She got up when I entered, and we fell into each other's arms. I broke out in sobs again, but Mum was quiet and calm and only rubbed my back.

'She's all right, Inky. She's at peace,' she whispered into my ear.

'But she's gone!' I wailed. 'I never got to know her properly!'

'Well, look at her now and you'll see all you need to know.'

Until now I had refused to even glance at the body laid out on the bed, afraid of that awful spectre, death, hanging there above it. Now, I looked.

'We haven't moved her at all. This is how we found her,' Marion said.

Gran lay on the bed straight out as if already in her coffin. Her hands were folded over a photograph, only the edges visible. No; two photographs. The edges of a second photo peeked out from behind the first. Next to her on a bedside table were the separated parts of an empty picture frame. On the wall above her was another picture frame, also empty.

I knew whose photos she chosen to die with. Knowing Gran, she'd gone on to be with those two husbands. Freddy and Humphrey. Would they form a blissful threesome in heaven? Or would they, as Mum believed, merge into some great blissful Oneness? One day, I too would know.

On Gran's face lay an expression of unutterable peace. Her lips were slightly raised at their corners, as if she had died smiling. I could not but gaze at that face, and as I did so I too felt that peace, and my tears dried and I knew Mum and Marion were right. She was in a good place, and at peace; this corpse was but the husk that had once enclosed her. She had left it behind, and moved on.

❀ ❀ ❀

In spite of the preparations for Gran's funeral, and, a week later, the funeral itself, to which half Georgetown came, Marion kept her promise and we went to all the places she'd planned, and by the time my holiday came to an end I had fallen in love, and more. It was as if my feet had walked a swamp all my life, but now I'd found my footing. Maybe it was the exuberance of nature, the majesty of that waterfall plunging eight hundred feet into a jungle gorge; maybe it was the warmth and openness and simple lovingness of the people I met; maybe it was Christmas, and the good food and the celebration and the wonderful people who came in and out of the house all day; maybe it was Quints who flew in from America and Canada and even the UK – imagine! I had Quint cousins in London! – and who folded me into the family like a long-lost daughter.

Or maybe it was the food. Christmas! Pepperpot! That legendary dish Marian had enticed me with back in Streatham; prepared days in advance by Marion and Evelyn, because it tastes better over time: beef stewed with cinnamon, orange peel, cloves, hot pepper, preserved with an Amerindian preservative called cassareep that colours it black, and served with plait bread! Or the traditional Christmas Black Cake, made weeks, months ahead of time by marinating fruit in rum; moist, juicy, out-of-this-world delicious! That Christmas I died and went to heaven.

Maybe it was the stories. The love-story of Granny Quint, now a legend in the family; Mum, telling for the first time of her travels in South America and India; the stories of other members of Quints spread across the world. My family. Stories of wounds opened and healed that cured me of the sickness

I'd carried with me, it seemed, all my life. I could not bear the thought of returning home. Mum, who spent half her time up on the Pomeroon river and the other half with us, was staying for at least another two months; why not me too?

'No,' said Mum, quite adamant. 'Back you go. You need to take care of ... matters. And Sal. And your life, waiting for you.'

'But I don't want that life anymore!' I wailed. 'It was just all so – empty.'

'If your life was empty then it was because *you* were empty. Now go back to it with the fullness you feel now and put that fullness into your life there. You can do it, Inky!'

'But Mum – Sal ...' And I told her then. I told her I loved him, but had lost him, to Cat. I thought she'd sympathise, but she only laughed.

'Just go back and meet him and see. It's not over until the fat lady sings,' was all she said to that, which I found most unhelpful. I told her so.

'See, Inky,' she said then, 'One thing I learned through all this, is not to live in fear. Face your fears, and see what happens. I think you want to stay here not because you really want to, but because you're afraid of a life without Sal. Go back, and face that fear. Take it one day at a time. You'll be fine.'

'*You* can talk!' I said, somewhat bitchily, remembering the huge pile of unpaid bills in unopened envelopes in her room. That one unopened envelope stuck to the back of her wardrobe. 'It took you thirty long years to face your fears. And that letter! If you'd faced it back then, how much hassle it would have spared us!'

Mum laughed, a relaxed, open laugh. 'You're right,' she said, 'but that's why I can talk! Learn from my mistakes. Go home, Inky. Don't be afraid.'

And then Mum gave me the stamp, the precious Quint.

'Put it to auction,' she said, 'and pay off all my debts.'

❀   ❀   ❀

And so I returned, reluctantly, to my private little hell. While waiting for my luggage at Gatwick I reached into my handbag for my mobile, which was lying right at the bottom with some other unused stuff. My fingers closed around a packet of pre-rolled cigarettes. I drew it out and stared at it, bemused. I had not smoked a single one since boarding the plane on my way out, three weeks ago, and what's more, had not even *thought* of smoking since arriving in Guyana. I chucked it in a bin, took out my mobile and switched it on. Five missed calls, all from Sal.

So I called him back, heart rattling like a jackhammer.

And when I arrived home there he was, sitting on the wall outside, waiting. I dropped the suitcase I'd been lugging up from Streatham Hill Station and just ran to him and flung myself at him and I didn't even have to say *I love you* because he knew, and I knew it when his arms closed around me and his lips found mine. And the word 'Cat' didn't even get an honourable mention.

Chapter Fifty-one

Inky

I did all that Mum had said. There was a heap of post for her and countless phone messages. I checked her email but there was nothing in particular, except from some woman called Nora Docherty who said she'd call, and she did, no less than five times, each time leaving a voice mail saying she'd try again. When next I rang Mum I casually mentioned it. Mum let out a shriek that rendered my left ear deaf, or almost so.

'Nora Docherty, she's only just about the top agent at the top agency in London!' she cried when she finally found her tongue. 'Inky, phone her at once and give her my number over here.'

So I did that and next thing we knew, Mum had a literary agent who thought her book was 'marvellous, fantastic, unputdownable, and yet so full of insight and wisdom', with 'characters who crawl into your soul and take possession of your heart'. (That's what she said in an email to Mum, who forwarded it to me.) In other words; mega-wicked.

And next thing we knew, four big London publishers were hungry for Mum's last novel and Nora Docherty was holding an auction for it, and *next* thing we knew, Mum accepted what is known as a 'major deal' which I learned in publishing terms means a six-figure advance, but Mum wouldn't tell me the exact amount; and she came back to England to meet with agents and publishers and various business people.

I haven't read it yet, Mum won't let me, but will do so as soon as we get the ARCs – that's Advance Review Copies, as I now proudly know.

With that deal in her pocket, Mum made another decision. The Quint was set to bring us a small fortune at auction; we'd set some of that money aside for ourselves, for boring things like investments and pensions and getting my career started, and we'd give some to Marion to renovate the Lamaha Street house; we no longer needed to sell it. Renovated, it could be rented out, and stay in the family. If there was anything left over we'd found a charity, which was to be named 'The Dorothea Quint Trust for Women in Need' which Marion was to run in Guyana, and which would be a financial fund for Guyanese women who needed help, 'WIN' for short. Mum breathed a deep sigh of relief. Yes, that's what we'd do.

❊ ❊ ❊

Finances all sorted, Mum returned to Guyana again, and that's when she told me her decision, over Skype. She would move back to Guyana, live on the Pomeroon River with Rajan. She had already spoken to his brother, who lived in the big house; she would add an extension to the blue cottage, or maybe add another storey, a room at the top, in the canopy; a little blue room, with windows all around.

'A room of my own,' she said.

I was shocked.

'Mum! You can't just throw your life away like that! I mean, it's all very noble and self-sacrificing and everything but why should you take on such a burden? Think of yourself! Why should you give up your life for him? I mean, with all due respect, he's just a …'

'Stop it, Inky. Just stop it!' interrupted Mum. 'Not another word!'

'But, Mum. What kind of a life will it be? I just don't believe in women sacrificing themselves for men. I mean, you're a feminist too, aren't you?'

Mum's eyes were fierce now. 'No, Inky, just no. Just leave it.'
I couldn't leave it.

'But, Mum ...'

'Listen: don't come with *you have to think of yourself first*
nonsense, because that's not my philosophy. And it's not a sacrifice or a burden. I'm not giving up my life for him. This *is* my
life. This is what life is calling me to do now, and that means it's
exactly the right thing. I won't lose myself. I'll find myself. Do
you think that life in London is particularly fulfilling? It's not
the circumstances that define who we are; it's how we handle
them. And this is it, for me.'

She took a deep breath, then said:

'I never told you this, but I've always been a fish out of water in London. I guess I'm one of those back-to-nature freaks
at heart. I've been thinking for a long time about where I'd go
on retirement, which isn't so far away. The only problem was
that huge debt – I couldn't have left you with that. But I've
longed for somewhere tropical, somewhere without a winter,
a garden, overflowing with bougainvillea and hibiscus, mango
and coconut trees – oh, for years! I've always missed that sense
of Home. What could be more perfect than this?'

'But – what will you do all day? Read stories to Rajan?'

Mum looked annoyed for a moment, but she caught herself, and answered calmly.

'Finish my novel. Write new novels. Learn to paddle a ca-
noe, drive a motor-boat. Get into gardening, my hands in the
earth. Grow flowers. Learn to play the guitar. Perfect my Spanish and Portuguese, read novels in those languages. Read *lots*
of novels, in fact. Practice Yoga. Meditate. Teach Amerindian
children, read them stories. Be with Rajan, learn his language.
Just Be.'

She grinned. 'I always had the makings of a hermit. An
ascetic. But with that list ...'

But I wasn't giving up that easily. As romantic as it all sounded, I hated the thought of her throwing away her life like that. I'd always thought Mum would find some nice middle-aged man to settle with, to grow old with. I had to say something.

'But, Mum – it'll mean looking after him for the rest of your life!'

'I won't be looking after him. He's got a personal carer for the hard bits of looking after him; the physical bits.'

Still. I had other plans for Mum. Once, back in Guyana, a nice middle-aged man had come to visit, an old friend of Mum's, apparently. An old boyfriend? He'd taken us out to dinner at the Pegasus, which is Guyana's best hotel, and it turned out he was divorced. His name was Don, and he must have been good-looking in his day, though now he was balding and had a paunch, and he kept gazing at Mum, in a flirty sort of way, but admiring rather than lusting. I don't blame him; Mum was positively luminous

The thing is: it seemed to me her radiance came not because of Don, and not even because of Rajan. She was glowing because she'd dropped that huge heavy burden she'd been schlepping around for decades, and now she was light and free, the way she was supposed to be. And at the Pegasus she just glowed and sparkled and looked so special, and Don looked so old and tired. Still. Why not? At least he was a man, presumably healthy.

'What about that guy Don? I bet he's interested. I bet you could catch him like that.'

I snapped my fingers.

Mum just laughed mysteriously and shook her head. But I still wasn't giving up.

'But, Mum! Rajan! I mean, in all respect … what kind of a marriage will that be? What about communication? You can't even talk to him!'

'Who said anything about marriage?' A wave of relief swept through me.

'So – it's more of a platonic thing?'

She nodded. 'I suppose you could call it that. Inky, when I was young, Rajan practically saved my life. He pulled me out of a deep hole of insecurity and self-doubt. I owe everything I am now to him – truly. I feel such gratitude – I just want to be able to give back. I'll be happy here, believe me.'

Silence descended between us, and then she grinned cheekily.

'I guess you could call this dropping out, like people did in the Sixties, like I did. Just with a bit more financial security! One of the perks of middle age is that you don't feel the pressure to be normal and live normal lives. The bane of my teenage years! Oh yes! Thank goodness that's over. Who cares what people say!'

Another silence as I tried to digest all this. My voice broke when I spoke again.

'But, Mum! You can't just – just *disappear* like that! It's like – like – running away again! I mean, what about, about – *me?* Won't you miss me?'

She laughed, and even through the Skype screen her eyes twinkled. 'Inky, why don't you be honest and say what exactly you want to say? That *you'll* miss *me?*'

I hung my head. It was true. That was the core of the problem.

'I'm too *young!*' I finally wailed.

'Inky! You're nineteen, adult, about to start University. That's the age young people move out anyway. Just about all of my cousins were sent by their parents to the UK or USA or Canada to study, and they were younger than you, going to a foreign country, where they knew no one! It was an adventure! You're in your hometown, and you've got Sal. And you've always insisted on how independent and reliable and responsible you are.'

That, too, was true. How often I had teased her in the past, after I had taken care of something she'd forgotten: joked that I was the parent and she the child. How condescending I'd been. How arrogant, even.

'I suppose we can visit each other,' I said, reluctantly, after a while. 'Often. But I'll still miss you.'

She chuckled. 'Inky, I think you're suffering from Empty Nest Syndrome! Who would have thought it! But you'll get over it. You'll see. And you'll end up loving it.'

Epilogue

The Quint was eventually acquired at auction by a mysterious anonymous bidder, by proxy, over the phone. The price was good; enough to change our lives forever.

About a week later I was in the kitchen cooking pepperpot when Sal called out from the front room, his voice urgent. I walked over and stood in the doorway; he was watching the news on TV.

'What's up?'

'Amazing,' said Sal. 'Unbelievable!'

'Well, tell me! What happened? Some new celebrity death?'

'Well, I suppose you could call it that. The Quint is dead.'

'What on earth do you mean?'

'It just came on the news. You know the anonymous purchaser? It happened to be the owners of the original British Guiana One-Cent Magenta – the Du Pont stamp. They bought it – and burnt it. Officially, with witnesses.'

My jaw dropped to the floor. 'You're kidding! Why on earth – oh! I get it.'

'Now there's still only one British Guiana One Cent in the world. The moment the second one turned up, the first one lost value. So they bought it, only in order to destroy it.'

'Wow,' I said. 'That's just – Granddad would turn in his grave. He loved that stamp.'

'No. I think he'd be OK with it. In the end, he chose to give it up for a greater good: for Rajan. For Rajan's life. A sort of – freedom, maybe.'

I thought about this. And yes, it was true. As Mum would say: freedom and happiness come with letting go. It's clinging that makes us miserable: clinging to things, and ideas, and our own little selves.

I nodded. 'Yes. You're right. Granddad would approve. And so would Gran.'

An Afterword.

The story you have just read is, of course, fiction. And yet it was inspired by fact: by the true story of the rarest stamp in the world, the British Guiana One Cent Magenta, sometimes described as the Mona Lisa of philately.

For collectors, the value of the One Cent Magenta lies in both its uniqueness and its history. After a shipment of stamps from the UK failed to arrive in British Guiana, a new batch of stamps was printed locally. But the quality was poor, and so the Postmaster General of British Guiana ordered that each stamp be hand-signed in order to prevent forgeries. Of the one cent stamps printed, only one survives, bearing the initials of postal clerk Edmund Dalziel Wight. This is the One Cent Magenta. But that's not all.

Just like in *The Small Fortune of Dorothea Q*, the One Cent Magenta has quite a bit of personal family history attached to it. Edmund Dalziel Wight happens to be an ancestor of mine, my mother's great-grandfather. Often she told me the story of the stamp's genesis, pointed out to me the post office where E.D.Wight used to work. "The stamp is now worth a small fortune," she'd say, and there we have it: the spark of a story.

As I grew older, the tale of the innocent signing of a stamp that would go on to earn a fortune fuelled my imagination. *What if* another one of those stamps survived within the family, I asked myself; *what if* it turned up in one of those drawers of junk I used to burrow through as a child?

Those 'what ifs' never left me and, after the publication of my first three novels, it became the inspiration for a novel in which just such a stamp turns up – a family heirloom worth millions. *The Small Fortune of Dorothea Q* is the result.

LETTER FROM SHARON

First of all, I want to say a huge thank you for choosing *The Small Fortune of Dorothea Q*. I hope you enjoyed reading Dorothea's, Rika's and Inky's story just as much as I loved writing it – and I hope it took you on a voyage into another world, just as writing it took me back to days gone by!

If you did enjoy it, I would be forever grateful if you'd write a review. I'd love to hear what you think, and it can also help other readers discover one of my books for the first time. Or maybe you can recommend it to your friends and family…

A story is a wonderful thing to share with others—it connects us in so many ways, makes us all part of the same world, unites us in spirit. I know I'm with YOU in spirit with every story I write; I feel I'm right there behind the words, between the lines, holding out a hand to you, hoping to cast a spell to draw you in. If the spell worked, well, I'd love to hear from you—drop me a line on my Facebook or Goodreads page, or through my website.

And if you'd like to keep up-to-date with all my latest releases, just sign up at the website link below.

Thank you so much for your support – until next time.

Sharon Maas

sharonmaasauthor

www.bookouture.com/sharonmaas

Of Marriageable Age

A spellbinding story of forbidden love. Three continents, three decades, three very disparate lives

Savitri, intuitive and charismatic, grows up among the servants of a pre-war English household in Madras. But the traditional customs of her Brahmin family clash against English upper-class prejudice, threatening her love for the privileged son of the house.

Nataraj, raised as the son of an idealistic doctor in rural South India, finds life in London heady, with girls and grass easily available... until he is summoned back home to face raw reality.

Saroj, her fire hidden by outward reserve, comes of age in Guyana, South America. When her strict, orthodox Hindu father goes one step too far she finally rebels against him... and even against her gentle, apparently docile Ma.

But Ma harbours a deep secret... one that binds these three so disparate lives and hurtles them towards a truth that could destroy their world.

❅ ❅ ❅

'A big book, big themes, an exotic background and characters that will live with you forever.' Katie Fforde

'Beautifully and cleverly written. A wondrous, spellbinding story which grips you from the first to the last page... I can't recall when I last enjoyed a book so much.' Lesley Pearse

It's a wonderful panoramic story and conveys such vivid pictures of the countries it portrays. I was immediately transported and completely captivated. A terrific writer.' Barbara Erskine

'A vast canvas of memorable characters across a kaleidoscope of cultures... her epic story feels like an authentic reflection of a world full of sadness, joy and surprise.' *The Observer*

AVAILABLE NOW IN PAPERBACK AND eBOOK